AF281547

ALCHEMICAL
HEARTS

Hollow is Thy Name

ALCHEMICAL HEARTS

HEARTS

Hollow is Thy Name

JAEL JARMILA LIVAS

FSC
www.fsc.org

MIX

Papier aus ver-
antwortungsvollen
Quellen
Paper from
responsible sources

FSC® C105338

For my mother.
Because you deserve a soft epilogue.

"You taste like heaven, but God knows you're built for sin."
— Framing Hanley, Built for Sin

"Paint me a heaven of love with your bloodied mouth,"
— Federico Garcia Lorca, from Summer Madrigal; Collected Poems (ed. y
Christopher Maurer)

"Lovely-eyed. Death-touched. Witch."
— Odysseus Elytis, tr. By Olga Broumas & T. Begley, from The Dream

II

CONTENT & TRIGGER WARNINGS

This story is a dark, contemporary romantasy novel and contains mature content that is not suitable for all audiences. Such as: abusive relationships, blood, bones, cults, death, demons, emotional abuse, explicit sexual and suggestive contents, misogyny, occult, profanity, racism, religion, sexism, Satan/The devil and self-harm.

Reader discretion advised.

Chapter 1

The Confessional

"And it was Death itself who stood behind me, with his arms wrapped around me as tight as iron bands, and his lipless mouth kissing my neck as if in love. But as well as the horror, I felt a strange longing."
– Margaret Atwood, Alias Grace, 1996

The Bone Church stood in perfect silence between the bleak and black branches of the ancient birch trees surrounding the area, as twilight began to drown the world in its half-light. April loved the clear and crisp air of October nights, the rich dark blue of nightfall as the last hours of afternoon evaporated between the trees that rose bare from the earth. There was a certain kind of excitement in the atmosphere, one, that kept little children awake the night before the first day of the new school year and seemed to be now coursing through April's veins too. It was the evening of the eleventh new moon of the year and after tonight's opening ceremony, another year began for all the apprentices that studied the secret art of alchemy at the monastery school in Prague, the very city of alchemy. After sunset, the young scholars gathered at the Bone Church, a little outside the city, waiting in anticipation, brimming with excitement.

April and Will stood quietly side by side, watching their parent's car disappear from their view, its headlights feeling their way through the darkness of the driveway, crossing the other lights of the still-arriving limousines. Will sighed deeply and April looked at her brother from the side. The light streaming towards them from the Bone Church and the small spots the lanterns made on the ground, illuminated Will's features just enough for April to see them in the twilight, reflecting her own emotions. But even if the world had been pitch-black around them and all lights would have been lost in the void, April would have always known what her brother was feeling, just as he always knew what was going on inside her. Will met her gaze, smiled at his twin sister and took her hand. He lifted it, his lips brushing over her knuckles, lightly kissing her skin, then squeezed her hand and April returned the touch with a smile of her own.

The twins let go of each other and reached for their suitcases. They turned round and walked at a leisurely pace towards the portal of the Bone Church. At the entrance stood a group of girls who scrutinised the twins and then continued talking without greeting them. None of them were friends with either Will or April, and none of them was nearly as gifted as the twins. They kept a straight face and entered the old building.

Inside, the thick walls protected the apprentices from the cold and kept out the biting autumn wind. The lit candles in the candelabras and the heat of the bodies of the gathered alchemists, warmed up the room even further. If it hadn't been for all the bones and skulls, one could have deemed the Bone Church to be cosy place. If one was inclined towards such morbid things at all – the twins surely were.

"Well, well, look who arrived here! I almost thought you weren't coming!" April and Will were greeted by Sergei, who broke away from one of the groups standing around.

"Nice to see you again," Will replied with a grin and smacked Sergei's hand.

"Everything all right, April?" she was asked and shook Sergei's hand as well.

"Everything's fine," April replied and allowed the other to kiss her on both cheeks. April wasn't close friends with Sergei, unlike Will, but his manners were always impeccable and that was something April appreciated.

"Where did you leave your Valkyrie?" Sergei then continued to ask, as he put his arm around Will's shoulders and pulled him towards the small group.

"Ginger's *Scottish*," April said and raised an eyebrow disapprovingly, which Sergei only acknowledged with a wink.

"Probably late, as usual," Will replied, giving April a meaningful look. *Don't start a fight*, his eyes said, and she averted her eyes ever so slightly, but nodded. Will hated discussions about culture appropriation and the importance of heritage, that would most likely end in nasty arguments with the simple explanation that people should just be *nice* to each other and keep their shit to themselves. April agreed, but she was of the opinion, that certain things needed to be discussed. Especially if they ended in arguments. They reached Sergei's group of friends and April nodded to them in greeting.

"Hey, Vadik, take the suitcases of the two Blackwells and put them with our luggage," Sergei said, glancing at April, "a lady should never have to bother carrying her own bags. That's what men are for."

April smiled lightly at Sergei, knowing that this was his attempt at appeasement and his excuse for having called her best friend a Valkyrie, and with another nod, April accepted his apology. A soft smile tugged on Sergei's lips while his eyes still skimmed Aprils face. Only when she lifted her eyebrows, did he turn his head with a grin.

While the young men engaged Will in their conversation, April broke away from the small group and began to wander around the Bone Church. Here and there she greeted classmates or girls from her dormitory, but her gaze was always directed towards the door, looking for a head of red hair and that beloved face of her dearest friend Ginger, who was indeed late, as usual. April had very quickly lost track of who was standing where, or in which part of the church her brother was, and thus she strolled towards the side doors, her hands gently brushing the pillars. April loved the Bone Church in its spaciousness and familiarity. But what she loved even more, was the sensation of being surrounded by the spirits of the past, which had been stored in the bones and skulls for centuries and allowed those who recognised them, to share in their powers. Her skin touched old stone and bone, and a tremble of excitement rushed through her. For a moment, April allowed herself to close her eyes in pleasure, as she felt that hidden power of each alchemical substance in the material surrounding her surge through her body. Sighing satisfied, April let her breath flow warm over her lips. They were so dry from the cold that April could easily peel off the fine skin on them with her teeth, until she tasted her own blood, then sucked the lower lip even further, tasting the red liquid on her tongue.

"April!"

Expecting to see her best friend, April turned around and realised too late that it was a young male who had spoken. Her initial excitement turned into the opposite when her eyes fell on one of her classmates she couldn't stand. Luke Harris was making his way through a group of girls towards April, who tried to flee at the sight of him, but was blocked by another group and tripped over their suitcases. She cursed under her breath.

"April, it's so good to see you! I was hoping to meet you here before the ceremony!" Luke was now standing in front of her, his American accent drooling into her ears, his voice as annoying as the sound of a fly that was trying to find its way out of a locked room. He stood so close that April could see the blue sparkle in his grey eyes, his hair as always perfectly blow-dried, and his too white teeth smiling at her. April turned her nose up, registering that Luke was blocking her only other way out of the small space in which he had manoeuvred her, while a row of skulls stared at her from the left side, with their hollow and empty eyes. April wanted to believe she could read pity in the dark sockets, but the shadows on the bone skin turned the non-existent faces into mocking masks. Piss-holes.

Those skulls had certainly belonged to a bunch of old men, who had delighted in keeping a harem of pretty housemaids, while they gorged on their privilege of being a male, while cooking up all sorts of liquids in their underground kitchens, hoping to create gold, far away from the prying eyes of those who did not believe in the wonders of their science. And to hide from the authorities of course.

"I wanted to pick up on our conversation we had before summer break, since you obviously didn't get my letters!" Luke smiled winningly. April grimaced.

"I did get your letters and *deliberately* didn't reply to them," April answered dryly.

"Oh, that doesn't matter," Luke said and took a step closer. April moved to the side.

"I know you're such a hard-working student and always have a lot to do! It doesn't matter if you haven't found the time to answer me, I understand that!" April opened her mouth to respond, but Luke cut her off.

"I'll get straight to the point: as I wrote in my letters and hinted at before the holidays," Luke continued, "I wanted to ask you when you have time to go out with me. My little cousin's christening is next month, and I really want you to meet my parents! So, what do you think? How about next weekend?" April blinked. Then she cleared her throat and stretched up to her size. Unfortunately, it wasn't very impressive due to the many missing inches. Fuck that.

"I don't know how I'm supposed to have been unclear before the holidays, or all the times before that when you've got on my nerves with this question, but in case you've somehow missed it, my answer has always been *no* for over a year. *No*, I don't want to go out with you or even spend time with you. I have *no* interest in you, you've only ever annoyed me, so... Until now I thought you just weren't the brightest, but I'm starting to think you're doing this on purpose! Now, if you could just leave me alone...?" April tried to push past Luke, but he held her by the arm.

"April, wait a minute! I just want..." With a hiss, April tore herself away and began to hurry in the opposite direction. "April, just a moment!" She heard him shout behind her and made to get away as quickly as possible.

"April!"

She cursed again. Glancing back, she realised that the idiot was following her. She hurriedly went round a few people and tried to orientate herself in the church. Where was her brother or his friends when they were needed? By now, the last of the apprentices had arrived and the nave of the Bone Church was full, brimming with the heat of excitement, conversations and laughter.

"April, wait!"

She didn't turn around but dodged into one of the side aisles and ducked behind some pews. With her back arched, she kept walking, looking for her brother or Sergei, but couldn't identify them in the sea of dark cloaks or the outlines of faces in the twilight of the candlelight. April glanced back and saw Luke shouting at three girls to get out of the way, so April almost ran along the rows of pews towards the other side of the church. She could feel the dead looking at her, whether with amusement or disapproval she could not say.

There! The confessionals!

Nobody was in this part of the church. Presumably everyone was now slowly making their way to the sacristy, which would open shortly and reveal the passage to the catacombs. April rounded the last bench standing in her way, hurried to the right-hand box, tore aside the velvet curtain, stepped inside and pulled the fabric back again. It was almost completely dark in the confessional. April took a step away from the curtain, panting, and bumped the back of her knee against the wooden bench.

"Damn it," she mouthed, but then dropped onto the seat. She listened carefully to hear if Luke had been able to follow her and tried to get her breathing under control. She exhaled slowly. An unexpected clearing of the throat to her right elicited a small gasp of shock and April flinched.

"Bloody Hell! Oh my God, I didn't know anyone was in here, I'm so, so sorry," April stammered and rose from the bench. The fright and the tension made her legs tremble and to be on the safe side, April leant a hand against the back of the confessional.

"No problem," came the reply from the other side. "If I'm not mistaken, you were in quite a hurry to get in here!"

The voice that spoke from the other side was clearly male and completely foreign to her, with a light Russian accent. April could hear that the other person was young. He had a deep, beautiful and somewhat raspy voice that sent a shiver down April's spine.

"Yeah, um, I... Well, there's this guy who's bothering me and can't leave me alone. For some incomprehensible reason, he doesn't understand what *no* means and won't leave me alone! If it's okay, I'd hide here for a few minutes, then I'd leave you again to your...um, whatever," April said and listened for an answer. But all April heard from the other side was a soft laugh. Then, an intake of breath to say something, when Luke's voice rang out from not too far away.

"Have you seen April Blackwell? She must have passed this way! No? Then get out of the way!"

April winced and cursed quietly again. She noticed a movement through that wooden-carved window that divided the confessional. The stranger had stood up and for a brief moment a strip of light fell into the darkness of the confessional and April could make out the outline of the young man.

"Is that the guy who's bothering you?" the stranger asked, peeking past the fabric of the curtain. "The blond one who's shouting and making a pissed face?"

"Yes," April said quietly and clenched her hands into fists. Luke's voice sounded again, a little closer now, and the stranger dropped the curtain again.

"That's him."

"If you want, I can help you get rid of him," the stranger said and April felt his gaze on her, even though she couldn't see his face.

"I have an idea of how you could get rid of him for good, but... I'd need your permission for that. I don't want to cross any lines," the stranger continued. April swallowed and nodded hesitantly. Then she realised that the other person couldn't see her in the darkness of the confessional and cleared her throat slightly.

"Okay," she said and nodded again. She could need some help.

"Well then," answered the stranger. He pulled the curtain aside again, stepped out of his part of the confessional and the next moment he pushed away the curtain on April's side and joined her in the booth. In the brief moments that light streamed into the confessional, she saw a young man, tall and slender. His hair was dark, and his skin shone brightly in the twilight. The curtain closed again, but a small gap remained open. The stranger stood now very close to April and scrutinised her with an unreadable gaze. Suddenly, the booth seemed too small: the atmosphere around the young man seemed to crackle and April felt as if all oxygen was sucked from and around her and into that whirring aura of his. And there was something...dark and dangerous emanating from him. April couldn't describe it differently, just...the pure essence of nightfall. That kind of darkness you found only in your scariest nightmares, combined with that eerie feeling that befell her whenever she wandered through the graveyards on a sleepless night. That kind of thrill and pleasure she got from it, always accompanied by a breath of fear.

No one said anything for a few seconds as the two looked on, simply taking each other in, while April felt a tremble in her very bones. The stranger was devastatingly handsome, and the shadows of the confessional cloaked him almost tenderly – a prince born from darkness. Or was he an apparition? An angel? A messenger from death itself? Bloody *hell*, who was he? She had never seen anyone like him, and April had seen many men up close. They heard Luke's voice calling April's name again.

"My method will be a little drastic, but effective," the young man said quietly and then pushed past April to sit down on the wooden bench. "But I'd have to touch you for that. Would that be all right with you?" he asked and then looked at April questioningly. She swallowed hard. April didn't know this young man and apart from the fact that she had been able to judge him by his looks so far, she knew nothing about him – except that he made her feel things no other man had ever evoked in her, with that deep and raspy voice of his. He spoke with the voice of a secret lover, deeply buried inside her, softly murmuring, while his lips and tongue drew circles on the skin of her neck, his hands wrapped around her waist, pushing her down on him, while she tried to keep quiet, afraid to be heard, knowing there were people next door – and that she was doing something forbidden. Something sinful.

April's cheeks heated and her skin flushed. She blinked the images away, slowly beginning to understand the simple laws of attraction, and how a voice could turn someone on with just a few words, now that she was facing someone as handsome as this man. But it didn't change the simple fact that he was a stranger, and she didn't know him. Her only real clue was his scent, for they said that a person's smell indicated if one got on with someone else. April leaned forward and breathed in silently. *Pine forests and freshly fallen snow. The cold breeze by the sea, waves crashing and falling, sea gulls soaring overhead and…*

"April! Where are you? Let's talk!" Luke's voice was very close now and April heard a series of curse words, then a couple of girls snapping even less pleasant things in return, and then Luke barking something unintelligible back to them.

"Okay," April said, brushing her hair behind her ear. As long as it worked, she was willing to do whatever it needed to get rid of that bastard. And if she was honest with herself, she didn't mind this young man touching her, on the contrary. He would make a nice change from all the others.

The stranger stretched out his arms, taking April's hand ever so gently, then pulled her onto his lap with a swift and decisive movement. Startled, April sucked in her breath.

"What the hell are you doing?" she hissed, not having expected...*this*. Goddamn, he was suddenly so close.

"Something that will keep that guy away from you forever," the stranger answered softly, a subtle smile twitching around his lips. "Trust me." The young man lifted his hand and stroked the hair of the girl sitting on his legs over her shoulder in a flowing motion, exposing her slender neck.

"Trust me," he whispered again into her ear, taking in her heavy breathing, her face, her lips... Then, very slowly, he leaned closer. She opened her mouth to say something – and looked directly into his eyes for the first time. Her perfume mingled with his scent. Pine forest met pomegranate and lilies.

Her breath turned shallow and they interlocked eyes, neither releasing the other. The young man lifted his other hand and placed it carefully on her shoulder. And at the same moment as the curtain of the confessional was torn open from the outside, he leaned forward and pressed his lips onto that sensitive spot in the crook of her neck.

April stifled a gasp. Blood shot through her body and an electrifying sensation travelled down her spine, as the young man's breath caressed her skin, kissing her neck again. She bit her lips to supress a moan.

"Oh, sorry!" Luke's voice rang out and the light from the church spilled into the twilight of the confessional. The young man broke away from April's neck and looked at the intruder with a fixed gaze, face unmoving. Not a single muscle twitched. April took advantage of the moment and scrutinised the face of the person on whose lap she was sitting. The stranger had high cheekbones, fine lips and a defined jawline. His face was even, and his eyes were dark. Or were they actually bright and had only caught the shadows around them? Whatever. He was beautiful.

"What is it?" the young man asked in a cold voice, without blinking once, his eyes still fixed firmly on Luke.

"April?" Luke asked instead, looking at the young woman sitting on the stranger's legs with her back turned to him. She instinctively and not without satisfaction raised her arms and put them around the stranger's neck. April continued staring at his face and shifted her weight ever so gently. She felt the young man tense up underneath her thighs. He blinked and his eyes shot to her for a brief second, an unreadable expression in them, then he looked back at Luke. April held her breath.

"Can I help you in any way?" the young man asked Luke again, this time more forcefully and cuttingly.

"Erm, well... no, I'm... just looking for someone, but... April? Is that you?"

April didn't answer, but only saw the stranger raise his eyebrows as he cleared his throat. She felt his hand slide from her shoulder and down her back, feeling his way down her spine, while the other hand traced the outline of her thigh. The soft fabric of her dress scraped over her naked skin beneath and April noticed how her body reacted instantly. She shifted her weight again, moving her hips ever so slightly, adjusting her position in his lap, feeling him tense up even more, while she caressed the stranger's neck with her fingertips, letting her other hand trace his jawline and leaned in even closer. The scent of the forest and sea beguiled her, and she wanted more. God, what was she doing? Luke's eyes slid from the girl back to the strange guy and nodded slowly.

"Sorry to interrupt," April heard Luke say, then he stepped back, and the shadows fell over them again. April froze. She and the stranger listened and waited.

"What the fuck," they heard Luke's voice mumble, then the sound of footsteps walking away.

Suddenly realising the overall situation and now also acutely aware of the heat that had begun to gather in her middle, April pulled away and stood up hastily on shaky legs. She took a step back and smoothed out her clothes. What the hell just happened?

"So, um… I…" April breathed out deeply, not knowing what to say, trying to regain control. Should she apologise? Saying that she got carried away the moment she had felt him under her thighs, or should she just walk away and… Damn it. *Focus, April.*

She felt the blood rush to her cheeks and thanked the darkness that it didn't show. Her heart raced, while a subtle sort of shame rippled through her at the memory of how his skin had felt beneath her fingers and how she had wanted to keep exploring. There was not only shame, but also desire.

"I'm Jack Rosier. I'm new to the school," the stranger interrupted her thoughts and stammering words, and April exhaled in relief. Jack stood up and held out his hand to April, who gratefully took it.

"April Blackwell," she said quietly. Jack looked at the young woman again. Now visibly embarrassed, she avoided his gaze and brushed her hair behind her ear again, even though none of the strands fell into her face. A smile tucked at the corners of Jack's lips.

"Thank you," murmured April and looked at him again. "Really! I hope that…taught him a lesson." Jack grinned lightly. "That's for sure. You should have seen his face! That expression was worth its weight in gold! He looked pretty stupid, especially when he recognised you," he added and laughed. It sounded raspy and he cleared his throat again. April's heart fluttered. *Dear Lord…* She looked around, trying the get that tremble in her gut under control.

"Well then… I should go and look for my brother and my girlfriend. I mean, my friend, who is a girl…I mean, um… Sorry…" April shook her head and started again. "My brother and she are standing around somewhere. Probably. Waiting for me. The passageway must be open by now." She cursed her voice. Why couldn't she talk smoothly to him, the way she had always observed the other girls do it, whenever they were talking to their latest prey? With voices soft as silk, so that even April had felt drawn to them, drowning in their alluring siren song, framed by beautiful hair, soft eyes, soft gaze, soft lips.

April's eyes dropped to Jacks lips. She took another deep breath. *Focus.*

This man in front of her did no good to her logical thinking. In any kind of way. She forced her gaze up again, staring into his eyes. That wasn't much better, but April continued talking, ignoring the pulsating between her legs.

"If you want, you can come with me. Then we can accompany you through the catacombs and you won't get lost or anything. I'm sure my brother won't mind and..." Her voice trailed off. Embarrassment was a nasty feeling. She never felt like this with the others. Usually, she kept her cool.

"I'm happy to stay here a little longer," Jack then said, and April nodded. Relieved. Disappointed. She took the chance to look at the young man once again, his face, half drowned in shadows – he was blessed with the beauty of a fallen angel.

"See you... around then?" April replied hoarsely, feeling the heat on her cheeks, hoping he hadn't noticed that she was staring at him and took a step back. Jack nodded, April gave him one last fleeting smile, then pushed the curtain aside and stepped out of the confessional. For a moment she simply stood there, the Bone Church and its pillars once again omnipresent around her. She shook her head, turned round and disappeared in the direction of the sacristy.

And while April joined the small group of Sergei's friends at the altar, amongst which April could see her friend Ginger, and stepped through the entrance to the tunnel system that led from the church to the school, Jack Rosier slowly sat back down on the wooden bench. He leant his head against the wall behind him and closed his eyes.

He heard the distant voices of the young alchemists as they walked to the sacristy, talking to each other, about holidays, books, dates, laughing and exchanging news. With his eyes closed, Jack listened to the sounds echoing around the church until they became less and less frequent and quieter. And when he was sure that he was the last one in the church, he stepped out of the confessional and walked down the centre aisle towards the altar. In the sacristy, Jack could see the glow of candles marking the passageway: the entrance to the catacombs that stretched from this area to the city and underneath it, in branching tunnel systems in all directions. A spider's cobweb in which they all were mere flies, lost in a maze of secrets and watching eyes; hidden, ancient, undisturbed, waiting, whispering, murmuring, flickering spectres of stone and bone.

As Jack placed his hands on the altar and sank to his knees, he saw in his mind's eye the maps he had studied and memorised for months. He saw the paths and shafts of the catacombs, recalled all the branches in his mind and then closed his eyes again. His lips moved slightly as he spoke silent words, his hands folded. He thought he could hear the laughter of that young woman in the distance, the scent of lilies and pomegranate still surrounding him, the taste of her skin still on his lips. So soft. So fragile. He had wanted to taste it, when his lips had met her neck. He had wanted to taste her with his tongue, that skin, inhaling that smell, letting his teeth grace over it. With his eyes closed, Jack imagined he could see her with her friends, following the torches through the tunnels. The shadows of those passing by cast in jagged shapes on the walls, the echo of voices thrown back and forth from the cold and damp stone walls. Jack saw her in front of him, as April Blackwell walked through the corridors, turning to him again and again, her dark eyes brushing his, and her face... *Her face.*

The shock Jack had experienced, when he had recognised her face in the semi-darkness of the confessional still lingered in his bones, even though he had heard that American guy shouting her name through the church. After Jack had kissed that beautiful swan neck of hers, he felt that from now on, he was the only one allowed to shout her name – deeply buried inside her. For hell's sake, the desire for that young woman was still pumping through his veins, and all it had taken were mere seconds, a touch, a glance – and he had been undone. Jack had known that she would be here, but he hadn't expected any of this. Running into her on the very first evening had been a little too much of a coincidence, even for his taste, although it was rather her, who ran into him. Yet actually seeing April Blackwell for the first time in person, so unexpectedly, so predestined by fate... And the way she had looked at him: enquiring, suspicious, but not without curiosity. Her body had melted so perfectly into his, and the way her eyes had taken him in; deep, devouring. And her face... Her face.

It had been so easy to read it. The features that were so familiar to him. A face he had seen often enough in photographs: for the first time on the black and white one, that stood on the desk in his grandfather's study. A face that mirrored April's and yet... Of course, he had ran a background check on her himself without any difficulty. Although the spies worked for his grandfather and thus for the order, it was Jack they were loyal to. Having his own network within the shadows of the order, had proven to be of immense value to his mission and far from the order's headquarters, Jack had earned their trust. It was pitiful that in the end, love was still stronger than fear, for fear was so much easier a force to wield. Jack had experienced it first-hand.

As he stood up again and crossed himself, he felt relief rush through his body. No matter what, the two women were not the same. No matter how similar they looked, the young woman he had recently touched and the spirit of the one who had long since departed this earth; they were not the same. Doppelgangers, nothing more. Jack had known that April was different. He had known it the moment he had looked into her eyes. The moment she had grinded her hips against him. Oh, that girl knew exactly what she had been doing and Jack was musing over their brief encounter, letting his mind wander farther, delighting in thoughts that sure were blasphemous to have, especially in a church. What a beautiful, terrible temptation the devil had sent his way, her face dancing still in front of Jack's mind's eye.

He raised his eyes to the hanging cross in front of him. He looked disdainfully at the figure nailed to it and bowed to it with a mocking smile. The smile still half on his lips, he entered the sacristy and allowed himself to be swallowed up by the tunnels and shadows of the catacombs.

☽ ☆ ☾

The laughter of the young alchemists echoed through the long corridors of the old monastery. Nobody knew exactly what kind of convent it had once been and whether nuns or monks had lived here. In the meantime, however, the old building had been converted into a school. According to the legends and stories surrounding him, the founder of the school had appeared at the gates of the city on a dark, foggy night. A man on a black horse, wearing an equally black cloak, his face covered by a hood and pockets filled with scrolls, flasks, vials and liquids that no one had ever seen before. The mysterious man never revealed where he had come from or why he had chosen this exact city to preach his knowledge about alchemy. Historians tried to retrace his steps, but it was as if he had appeared out of nowhere. What the young apprentices of alchemy were taught, was that the old master, the first alchemist, brought light into the darkness of the materials from which the cosmos was knitted. Teachings and knowledge about how new insights could be gained were then passed on from generation to generation in no other place than the old monastery, with its cloister, gardens, neighbouring cemetery and small church, where the tunnel ended, that the apprentices took from the Bone Church and then emerged from the catacombs back into the open.

The tunnel system was widely ramified and all alchemists, whether still in training or not, used it to move around the city and its surroundings undetected, underground and far away from the public. Even if the majority of the world no longer wanted to know anything about the alchemical teachings, except some shrewd yoga teachers and spiritualists, there were still enough people, especially those in positions of power, who made use of that ancient knowledge. These deals between the alchemy guild and politicians, business sharks and other bigwigs in various sectors of industry, were done in secret. Nobody wanted to publicly admit to profiting from a pseudo-science, a view that the alchemists ridiculed, for they knew their knowledge and skills were invaluable and made sure to be well paid for. With their methods, they were able to overcome every limit of science and advance into areas that no human soul had ever been able to grasp before. However, the most important credo of the alchemy guild was that they set themselves apart from all charlatans, witches, sorcerers and druids, for their practices were heathen and of pagan origin – and thus blasphemous.

Some years ago, before the twins had started school – April and Will were still children at the time – there had been a serious scandal at the monastery school: a group of girls had secretly formed a coven and in addition to studying alchemy, had also dedicated themselves to the teachings of witchcraft. When one wave of flu after another struck the school and the girls' classmates fell ill, suffering from terrible delusions and dreams, the teachers got to the bottom of the matter. It didn't take a moon for the girls to be discovered. That very night they were taken from the monastery by guild knights and one by one they disappeared in the black carriage that stood outside the convent gates, the horses as black as the steed of the first alchemist and grand master of the guild. No one had ever seen or heard of the girls again. Some said they had been locked up in the city dungeons and others reported recognising the girls in a court trial. Sentenced to death, they were said to be waiting for their day of execution, or to be taken out of the city and burned at the stake in the grey, icy wasteland further north, as was fitting for witches. Others said that the girls had been dead for a long time.

The story of the girls who had sold their souls to witchcraft, had always held an immense fascination for April, truly fuelled by the fear and terror which the girls must have experienced when they were accused of witchcraft and taken away – a nightmare that haunted April since early childhood. She knew that she had no reason to worry and that her fascination was similar to that of people who loved horror films and yet... Something about the girls' story and their decision to take up black magic, the desire for more, that alchemy hadn't been enough for them, or simply a crazy idea born from the whim of a moment; something about it had captured April's interest. She was a good student and a promising alchemist, she didn't want anything come into her way, and thus she kept those thoughts to herself, knowing that even showing interest in such things could arouse mistrust. But it was difficult not letting the mind wander and dive deeper into things that were marked as forbidden, for their allure was hard to resist. Perhaps this was precisely the reason why the alchemical teachings went hand in hand with faith: to keep the mind of every alchemist untainted, clean and pure, because alchemy was a science that required concentration and precision, and only when the substance was pure and unsullied could the experiments and the production of elixirs and tonics be successful. Although April tried to pushed thoughts about the witches and the coven they had formed at this school to the back of her mind, she couldn't help but imagine the girls' faces in front of her, whenever she stepped through the passageway from the catacombs into the school's small church. For over the doorway the admonishing words were written in old fashioned letters: *maleficae malae*, evil witches. In the half-light of the church, April thought she could see the witches' large eyes fixed directly on her, staring straight into her soul. She imagined that she could hear their whispering in her head, their laughter mingling in the wind with the rustling of the leaves and then getting lost among the graves of the cemetery, blending with the white petals of the apple trees in early spring, or the winding green of the ivy...

"April?" Will touched his sister gently on the shoulder, bringing her back to reality. The young men around them laughed, Sergei spun round in front of the altar and April realised that she had obviously lost the thread of the conversation some time ago.

"Come on, Blackwells! What are you waiting for!" Sergei clapped his hands and then pulled Will with him towards the exit of the monastery church. April followed a little more slowly and let the young men run past her and out into the open. The cold night air hit them sharply and April breathed deeply in and out. Apprentices bustled around the square in front of the church. The monastery loomed large, majestic, commanding respect, and at the same time wonderfully familiar in the darkness. The windows were all brightly lit, and voices and laughter echoed out to them from the cloister. A content smile graced April's lips as she followed her brother, Ginger, Sergei and the others across the square and through the welcoming gates of the school.

From the refectory, the clatter of tableware being spread across the many tables could be heard from afar and April was glad not being part of the kitchen group the very first night of the school year. Normally they all sat together with the people of their choice, except on the first evening of the new school year and opening ceremony; the evening of the eleventh new moon of the calendar year, the night on which the veil between the worlds became particularly thin. Therefore, the school's apprentices sat in their respective classes that evening: the oldest ones at the window side, while the younger ones were seated on the opposite wall of the room. The teachers took their seats, where the abbess or abbot of the monastery once had sat.

With Ginger in tow, April pushed her way past a group of girls who were whispering excitedly, looking around curiously and were no doubt among those who had just started their training.

"There's the table with the candles for the ceremony!" said Ginger, pointing to the entrance of the cloister.

"Shouldn't we take our suitcases to the room first?" asked April, but let her friend drag her along anyway.

"Oh, let the boys do it for us. That's what they're there for after all. Sergei himself told us so!" Ginger replied, her eyes twinkling with amusement. April laughed softly.

"All right, but only because you're making sense for once," she returned, stepping up next to Ginger at the candle table.

"Anyone who hasn't washed and changed for the ceremony has no business at this table!" The voice of their teacher sounded behind the two girls, who immediately turned around.

"Madame! Nice to see you again!" said Ginger, beaming all over her face. Madame Tarkovsky returned the smile and held out her hand, which Ginger then took and curtseyed. April did the same.

"Has your luggage been taken to your room yet?" asked Madame and the two girls looked at each other.

"Presumably yes," April answered for them both and Ginger nodded in confirmation. "At least Sergei's friends brought them here for us."

"If Mr Ivanov has taken matters into his own hands, your suitcases are probably already in your bedroom," Madame then said and winked at the two girls with a smile. All three giggled until Madame clapped her hands and sent the girls upstairs to wash and change into their ceremonial dresses.

The opening ceremony began at eight o'clock. By that time, night had fallen, and the monastery was surrounded by shadows, no moonlight brightening the darkness. The eleventh new moon night of the year seemed to be charged with an extraordinary energy. April sometimes thought that she could actually feel the atmosphere of this special night prickling on her skin, like a thousand butterflies brushing her arms and settling in her hair. April had often wondered what it would be like to spend the night alone instead of performing the ceremony with the other apprentices. She would retreat somewhere quiet and perform her own rituals, similar to the ones her mother used to perform when they were little children, but which April remembered only vaguely. She would go out of the city, under the open sky. April would become one with the night and the stars, slowly opening herself to the whispering in the wind and speak to her ancestresses, murmuring through the veils of the worlds. She would invite the spirits of the otherworld to join her, welcome them into her circle and read oracles. She would let them tell her secrets of the past, hundreds of candles around her, making sure no one would see her, for it would look a lot like witchcraft although conversing with your ancestors was no witchcraft but simply becoming very quiet and listening to the voices within. And there was no harm in that, right?

Her twin's face appeared in April's mind's eye. Perhaps she would let her brother join in. No, she thought as she spotted Will at the bottom of the stairs, leaning against one of the walls, his eyes wandering over the apprentices already gathered there. No, Will would *definitely* be there, whether he wanted to or not. Nothing and nobody could come between them, no new moon night, no prophecies from the otherworld, and nothing else either. The threads of their lives were tightly knotted and interwoven with one another, and she belonged to him and he belonged to her. They were one.

As if Will had heard April's thoughts, he lifted his head and looked at her as she came down the stairs, Ginger by her side. As instructed by their mistress, the two girls had washed, combed and styled their hair and changed into ceremonial clothes. Will pushed himself off the wall and held out his hand to his sister, who took it on the last step and smiled at him. Will lifted his hand and briefly touched April's cheek.

"My love," he whispered softly. She was so beautiful in her black dress. The sparkling stones in her dark hair shone silver like the stars and Will gently pressed a kiss to her temple. April looked at him lovingly. He touched her neck and put his hand on her shoulder and in an instant, images of earlier that evening flashed through April's mind. She saw Jack Rosier's pale face before her for a moment, his eyes fixed intently on her. April blinked the memory away. Will raised his eyebrows questioningly and looked his sister in the eye.

"Are you all right?" he asked, and April nodded.

"I was just thinking about something," she said and smiled. She squeezed Will's hand to let him know that everything was fine and then nodded towards the other end of the corridor.

The teachers had appeared at the entrance, all dressed in their black robes, holding a candle. The conversations died down and the young apprentices began to line up on either side of the corridor. Three boys, who were one class below April and Will, walked past the rows and pressed a white candle into each of their hands. Then three girls followed and lit the candles. When they reached the last student, the three girls stood opposite the teachers on the wall, facing them. Silence reigned for a few moments. Only the breathing of those gathered and the crackling of the flames, the wind outside and the rustling of the trees could be heard. Then a girl in a night-blue dress stepped out of the row, where April and Will were standing. Kenna was in April and Will's class, but not friends with either of them. April knew her well enough to know that Kenna couldn't stand oranges, preferred to get up earlier than everyone else and that her mum had published a book about new methods of distillation.

Kenna positioned herself in the centre of the aisle and turned towards the exit. Then she began to sing in a clear voice. After the first passage, two other girls who had stepped behind Kenna, followed her lead and after the first verse, everyone else present began to join in. Kenna led the procession as the precentor and walked down the corridor singing solemnly. Imitating her example, the other apprentices followed. April's voice blended with a hundred others and the sounds rose high to the vaulted ceilings. And as they passed through the archway, they entered the cloister in an almost majestic procession. Singing like this, the flame of her candle before her eyes, April felt goosebumps spread all over her body. She smiled instinctively and looked first at her brother, then at Ginger. They both returned her smile as they followed the procession. Towards the end of the song, Kenna had walked through the cloister once and met the end of the procession formed by the teachers. All the apprentices now stood in the cloister and then approached the window arches. In the centre of the cloister was the small herb garden, with lilac trees and roses growing between the beds. Hardly anything was still in bloom, just a few rose petals that reflected the candlelight in the darkness. They sang and sang, and the longer their voices echoed in unison from the walls of the cloister, soaring up to the night sky and the stars, to the dark moon, out into the night, sending them forward in time and back into the past, the more April felt how they all became one. How the alchemy of voices, the exchange of their energies, refined and then took on new forms. April felt the presence of her brother next to her very clearly, felt how Ginger's body heat increased and she herself began to warm like the sun and then she took her eyes off her candle, lifted her gaze and looked across the garden to the opposite side of the cloister – straight into the face of Jack Rosier.

He too had his eyes fixed on her, his face a bright spot in the shadows, like the withered roses in the garden, a white petal in a sea of darkness. A wave of heat shot through April's body like a flash flood and she tried to control her breathing but couldn't take her eyes off the young man. It was as if she could see a thousand other faces in his face. Another wave of energy surged through April, hot and cold at the same time. Overwhelmed, April closed her eyes.

She saw a clearing in the forest, a fire, surrounded by figures wearing animal skulls on their heads and staring into the flames through empty eye sockets. She saw marble-white corridors of a house, a rose garden in the snow and then – a light so dazzlingly bright that it made April dizzy. She had the feeling of being pushed under water. A cathedral with statues of angels, in the place of the cross a squat figure with bat wings, horns and a tail. April struggled for breath; her eyes twitched under the closed lids – she heard voices from far away. The flood of images would not stop, but April could no longer recognise anything, they were a blur of colours and sounds and smells and… She wanted to scream, but her throat was knotted tight and she felt like she was going to fall or faint. A jolt ran through her and April ripped open her eyes.

She was still standing between Will and Ginger in the cloister. The assembled alchemists were still singing, the candles were still burning and, as if April were waking from a bad dream, she looked around with wide eyes and a pounding heart. She felt her entire body trembling. She looked forwards again, straight ahead, through the rose bushes and bare lilacs to where Jack Rosier had been standing – but his place was empty. Only his candle remained on the windowsill, the flame flickering in the wind.

The singing died down. And after minutes of silence, the conversations resumed. The candles were placed on the wall, torches were lit in the cloister. The first ones laughed again and set off towards the refectory. April was pulled along, saw Ginger's lips moving as she spoke to Will. She saw Will laughing, Sergei's face, Kenna brushing her hair out of her face and looking at April.

"Come on, April! Let's pick the best seats!" Ginger called to April. Her friend's hand slipped from April's grasp and the red head disappeared in a sea of dark robes, glittering hair clips and sparks of light.

"I'll be right behind you," April said half aloud, seeing Will turn to her, his eyes fixed on her questioningly. But April just shook her head, let herself fall back as the stream of other students flowed past her.

The cloister was deserted, and April leaned against one of the walls and took a deep breath. Her pulse returned to normal and April's mind slowly began to clear up. She looked around her. The candles were lined up, one next to the other, on the wall ledges. The image conveyed something so peaceful that April felt calmness begin to spread through her body. No racing heart, no crazy flood of images. There was only her breath flowing through her body, filling her lungs and oxygenating her organs. Her hands stopped shaking and she placed them flat against the stone wall behind her. April closed her eyes and concentrated fully on the feeling of the cold stone under her fingers. She felt a little further, feeling the bumps and tiny protrusions, and then she heard someone step in front of her. April blinked in surprise as she looked into her brother's eyes instead of Jack Rosier' because for some reason she had expected to see the strange young man in front of her.

"What's wrong?" Will asked April and then took her in his arms. She sank against him and closed her eyes. His scent calmed her more than anything else, and if she had felt a residue of excitement and confusion in her body seconds ago, Will's touch took that away too, leaving peace and calm.

"I had a vision," April whispered softly close to Will's ear. He tightened his arms around her and hugged his sister closer to him. He felt her heartbeat against his chest and then a sudden fear spread through his stomach. In a low voice, April told him about what she had seen, but never mentioned that it had been Jack Rosier's gaze that had stirred the flood of images or what had happened between them in the Bone Church. Her cheeks still flushed remembering their encounter in the confessional. April stopped talking and only now did she realise the tears running down her cheeks.

"Don't worry, my love," Will whispered, pulling her even closer to him and burying his face in her hair. "It's going to be all right," he murmured, gently cradling his sister in his arms. And while he stroked his sister's back, comforting, holding her close, he inhaled her scent deeply. The smell that reminded him of tender nights, cuddles and his sister's face in the pale moonlight that fell through the curtains of his bedroom; her regular breathing and the beating of her heart so close next to him, while his fingers played with the dark strands of her hair.

Chapter 2

Calcinatio

"I continued in oblivion lost,
My head was resting on my love;
Lost to all things and myself,
And, amid the lilies forgotten,
Threw all my cares away."
– St. John of the Cross, The Dark Night of the Soul

The dusty light of the morning sun fell through a narrow gap in the velvet curtains. April blinked into the whitish light and turned onto her side. She had only just woken up and was still half asleep. Nevertheless, she fumbled on her bedside table for her wristwatch – it was just after seven. April stifled a groan and buried her face in the quilt. She yawned and closed her eyes, only to open them again as the memories of the previous night slowly seeped back into her consciousness. Sleep had washed away the intensity and now in the sober light of the new day, April could look at the images she had seen in her vision with calmer thoughts. Until now, April didn't know how and where to place the images, nor did anything about them seem familiar. Either the images were simply the product of her wild imagination and an excess of sensory impressions and overload, or April would simply have to be patient and wait to see if the images would materialize, in one way or another.

April sat up in her bed and let her eyes wander round the room. A total of 21 girls slept in the dormitory, divided into three classes. The school's teaching staff preferred to teach the apprentices in smaller groups, especially as the teaching of alchemy demanded a great deal of precision and attention, and nothing made a situation more confusing than too many people in one room, especially young people. This, and the fact that alchemy required a lot of prior training, was the reason why girls were only accepted at the school at the age of 18 and boys at the age of 20, by which time they had completed the first two cycles of their lives and first part of their third. Most of them used the rest of the third cycle and the fourth to devote themselves to an in-depth study of alchemy. April was one of the older students and, together with the others who were her age or even slightly older, she looked after the younger ones, especially those who were new to the school. Although you were no longer a child at 18, you were still a long way from being a woman and the support of other young women was worth a lot at that age.

Most of the girls in the dormitory were still asleep, but others were already getting dressed. April smiled, knowing that the nuns or monks who had once slept here would turn over in their graves if they saw what the dormitory looked like today. Things were scattered everywhere: extravagant dresses, tights and garters, elaborately embroidered underwear, hair clips, combs, satin bows and frilly blouses hung over the backs of chairs. Underdresses decorated with lace, silky dressing gowns over the back of the bed, mirrors on the walls, small tables in front of them full of creams, tinctures, and other make-up. Glitter poured into small bottles, nail polish in various shades of red and a pile of books, perfume or jewellery from the night before on every bedside table. Cassettes, magazines and records were piled up in boxes on the walls, which were occasionally played on the old record player by the window. The girls had hung photographs, magazine clippings, icons and tarot cards on the walls. There were a pair of slippers here, wool socks there and high-heeled boots peeping out of chests that had been pushed halfway under the beds. It was a marvellous mess that had its very own order and was bursting with femininity.

Humming contentedly, April made her way to the bathroom, greeted the already awake girls in a whisper on her way there, registered that Kenna's bed had already been made as usual whenever April got up, and walked down the cool corridor to the washrooms. Most of the girls, especially the early risers, were the kind of girls who liked to make the most of the morning hours but were not particularly talkative and carried out their morning routines in silence. The ice-cold water running from the tap into April's hands, which she then used to wash her face, woke up the last sleeping part of April that had got used to going to bed in the early hours of the morning and getting up again at midday during the summer break. It would take April a while to get used to the school schedule again, but it was also good to get back into the old routines and follow a more regular daily life. On the way back to the dormitory, April crossed Kenna's path, who was carrying a bunch of roses in her arms, which she then distributed around the room, one rose for each girl, and put the rest in a vase that stood on the dresser in front of the large mirror right next to the entrance to the dormitory. April and Kenna smiled briefly at each other but said nothing. It wasn't that they had anything against each other, it was just that they had nothing in common apart from their love of singing. However, as there was only ever one lead singer and this was never April, the two girls had come to a silent agreement that it was best to leave things as they were, and they stuck to it.

They always had breakfast in the refectory. April got up earlier than her brother and Ginger, so she usually sat alone at the breakfast table, either reading the newspaper or one of her books.

"Good morning! How are we today?" April was greeted and Sergei dropped into the seat next to her.

"Good morning," she said without looking up from her book, which elicited a snort from Sergei. April raised her head and looked at him apologetically.

"Sorry, my manners leave something to be desired," she then said and closed her book.

"Don't worry," said Sergei and began to spread his pancakes with elderberry jelly. "I'm used to being stubbornly ignored by beautiful girls like you. I wonder if you do it on purpose to make yourself seem even more mysterious and unapproachable," Sergei added and winked.

Now it was April's turn to snort, which drew out a laugh from Sergei. April's gaze fell on Sergei's plate.

"Say, isn't the jelly meant as a *topping*?" Sergei followed April's gaze and then looked at her again, unconcerned.

"Says who?" he replied and then began to eat his pancakes bathed in elderberry jelly. April just shook her head when Sergei offered her a piece.

"Thanks, but I've already had my overdose of sugar for the day," she said, smiling and pouring fresh tea into her and Sergei's cups.

"Thank you," murmured the young man next to April, placing his hands around the warm china. "Did you see, we've got a new student! Arrived yesterday with the little ones, but he's our age. Well, actually a little older but he'll be in our class."

"Really?" April said unconcernedly, but felt her heart begin to pound harder and her stomach tighten uncomfortably.

"Yes. He used to go to a school in Wallachia. Seems to have learnt all sorts of things there. Really, the guy can seem a bit scary. He's very pale and awfully quiet."

"Or you've just read too many vampire stories," April said and now it was her turn to wink at him.

"Very funny," came Sergei's reply. Not a second later, Sergei raised his head and then nodded towards the entrance to the refectory.

"That's him," he said quietly, and April turned round. As she had expected, Jack Rosier was standing in the doorway. He was fully dressed: his black shirt tucked neatly into his trousers and he was wearing a thick jumper and jacket over his arm. A little lost, he looked around the refectory. His gaze fell on April and Sergei, who immediately raised his hand and beckoned Jack to him. April clenched her jaw. Her eyes met Jack's. She turned to Sergei.

"Since you're about to have company, I can let you eat your drowned pancakes on your own. I want to go to the library before class."

With these words, April swung her legs over the bench and stood up. In the meantime, Jack had arrived at her seat and looked hesitantly back and forth between April and Sergei.

"This is April Blackwell. Usually, she isn't that rude but since it is a library case and April's a bookworm, she has good reason to leave two men to their breakfast and withdraw her wonderful, feminine presence!" Sergei introduced April with a wink, and Jack nodded slowly, a half-hearted smile tugging on his lips.

"We're already acquainted," Jack then said, and Sergei raised his eyebrows in surprise.

"Really?"

"Fleetingly," April interjected and reached for her books. "See you later," she then said to Sergei, nodded curtly to Jack and set off out of the refectory, feeling the gaze of the two young men on her back.

The pupils spent the first part of the day in their respective half-classes. At the beginning of each week, an introduction to the new topic or sub-area of alchemy took place on the first day. The input was always of a theoretical nature and took up the entire morning. After lunch, the practical learning and development of the new subject matter began. This year, the twins were divided into separate half-classes and April was glad that at least Ginger was in her introductory group, at least for the first trimester. After the long summer break that had stretched into autumn, sitting still and listening, was a lot harder than April remembered. It wasn't that April didn't appreciate the theoretical input, as she was one of the few people who liked to spend their free time in the library reading specialised literature to deepen their acquired knowledge, a love that April and Will shared. But with all the fresh and unprocessed impressions of the previous evening and the stick figures that Ginger had scribbled in her notebook, apparently dancing something like a ringlet, April had been distracted all morning. She was glad when they were finally released and sent on their lunch break.

While April and Ginger ate their meal, Ginger told April everything she had left out in the letters they used to send back and forth during the summer break. As always, Ginger had spent the summer with her family in the Scottish Highlands, in the small village where she had grown up and where her family had lived for generations. April, in turn, talked about her summer spent with her father's family in the south of England. April and Will had spent their early childhood years in Wiltshire, where her father's parents owned an old manor with extensive gardens and grounds. As the children grew older, however, Mrs Blackwell longed for her home in the East and so they all moved to an old house a few hours from Prague, where April and Will now attended alchemy school and where their mother had been a student herself. The move was not difficult for the twins, as they now lived in the neighbourhood of the stronghold of alchemy, and for the inquisitive twins, weekend trips to the city's most wonderful libraries were the greatest gift their parents could give them. Once, when April and Will must have been about ten years old, the little family visited their mother's cousin further north. The town where the cousin and her family lived was similar to the towns where April had always imagined the princesses from fairy tales must live. The snow transformed the town and the surrounding landscape into a candyfloss world. The finest powder snow, glittering lights, frozen ice rinks in the middle of the city, where people went ice skating, ate sweet pastries that were not as good as the ones her mum could bake, but still a treat for all the senses. April had made friends with her mum's cousin's little daughter at the time and the two girls still kept in touch by letter.

"Well, in any case, Dad said that our great-grandmother won't be alive much longer and that it would be better if we visited her again during the Christmas holidays," April said, concluding her remarks from the past summer months.

"And what about Christmas with your mum's family?" Ginger then asked and April raised her shoulders.

"I guess that will be cause for discussion. At least as far as Will and I are concerned," April replied, sighing softly. April and Will agreed on almost everything, but when it came to deciding where to spend Christmas, April always voted for her mother's family and Will for her father's, for the simple reason that April liked her grandmother Ludmila's pastries better, while Will preferred the library at Blackwell Manor.

"We'll see," April then added, pouring herself another cup of black tea.

After lunch, Ginger and April made their way to their timetabled lab. The two girls crossed the convent courtyard, entered the church and then made their way through the tunnels in mutually agreed silence. Further ahead, they heard a group of girls laughing, the sounds reverberating off the walls a thousand times louder.

Ginger held out her hand to April, who took it. When they had first entered the catacombs, Will and April had instinctively held hands and made a rule that neither of them would ever wander through the catacombs alone. At least in pairs. And after a few weeks, Ginger also began to belong to the pair. April waved her clasped hands forwards and backwards and Ginger laughed. Her sparkling eyes were so familiar to April and the redhead's laughter always filled April with peace. She loved looking at her friend. Her beautiful red hair, those shimmering eyes and freckles. Ginger reminded April of soft October mornings. The ones you go out for a stroll in the countryside, colourful leaves brushing your boots and the rich, heavy scent of harvest lingering in the air. Ripe blackberries and the soft earth saturated from last night's rain. Oh, April loved her friend. April squeezed Ginger's hand lightly and the girls looked at each other, smiling.

They had to turn a few times before they emerged from the last tunnel, which led into a small hall at the end of which was the gate to the lab. Other students were standing together in groups in front of the still closed door, waiting for their teacher. April let her eyes wander over the crowd, then spotted Will waving to his sister and her friend. The two girls made their way through the others that were standing around until they were next to Will. Only now did April realise that Will was not alone and that someone else was standing next to him. This someone was slightly taller than Will and his eyes immediately sought April's as she stepped up next to her brother.

"April, Ginger! This is Jack Rosier! Jack, this is my sister April, and this is Ginger!" Will immediately introduced them to each other, pointing first to Jack, then to April and finally to Ginger.

"Nice to meet you," Ginger said immediately and held out her hand to Jack. He shook it.

"The pleasure is all mine." Jack's eyes flicked to April, but she made no move to shake his hand. She didn't want to touch him. Not after last night. Not after what had happened between them. She was sure he as well remembered all of it. And although it was spineless behaviour and because she was ashamed of what had happened in the confessional, she had decided to keep her distance in order to preserve at least a small remnant of her pride.

"We've already met at breakfast," April said curtly when Will gave her a warning look.

"Really?" he then said, looking at Jack in surprise.

"I didn't realise you were brother and sister," Jack then said to Will, but continued to look at April.

April narrowed her eyes but returned the look. Why did her brother have to choose Jack Rosier of all people to talk to? Weren't there enough other students to befriend standing around and if not, couldn't he have just waited until April and Ginger arrived so that Will could talk to his sister, who definitely had more right to talk to him than some run-of-the-mill alchemist apprentice who had trained somewhere in Romania and who April just didn't quite like in the light of day? Maybe it was just the dim lighting in the catacombs, the wind howling through tunnels far away, the presence of death that could be felt so clearly in these halls underneath the city that put her in a mood, and it had nothing to do with Jack, but April couldn't have said for sure.

"Come in, ladies and gentlemen!" The door behind them was pushed open from the inside and their teacher, Mr Zagajewski, beckoned the students waiting outside to come in. April let herself be pulled along by Ginger and they sat down at a table of four with Will and Jack, having already decided that they would certainly have to work together in this lesson. Once everyone had sat down and had their writing materials ready, Mr Zagajewski began the lesson.

"Welcome to the new school year from me too! This year will bring a lot of new things and will certainly push you to your mental and physical limits! As you heard in the introduction this morning and you are now in your fifth year, we are mainly dealing with the fifth alchemical transformation stage: *fermentatio*. Who of you can explain me the basic principles of this stage to me? If you've been paying attention this morning, this shouldn't be a problem for you." The corner of Mr Zagajewski's mouth twitched and his bright eyes scanned the room.

"Mister Ivanov!" Zagajewski then said happily and nodded encouragingly at Sergei. The heads of everyone in the class turned to Sergei. He cleared his throat and began to speak in a firm voice.

"In this process, fermentatio, also known as *putrefactio*, a large amount of a substance is transformed into a substrate by adding a small amount, or a process that has already been initiated is accelerated. In the second case, the substance functions as a catalyst, meaning, a ferment or enzyme."

"Very good, Ivanov," said Zagajewski and stepped up to the blackboard. April saw Sergei's friend Cynlaef pat him on the shoulder and Sergei playfully wiped the sweat from his forehead. Two girls sitting at the neighbouring table giggled softly. April turned away, inwardly rolling her eyes. Pathetic. They were no longer teenagers and yet some of the girls in her class acted like it. Somehow today was not her day.

While April was transferring what Zagajewski had written on the blackboard into her notebook, she sensed that someone was watching her. As unobtrusively as possible, she turned her head to look round, but no one was looking at her. She frowned, continued writing and after a few seconds felt like she was being watched again. She shivered.

"Please note that the putrefactive gases that are produced during fermentation in the absence of air, can be reused or even have to be reused in some cases!" Zagajewski's voice filtered back into April's consciousness and she tried to shake off the obnoxious feeling of being watched.

"Yes, Mr Rosier?" At the mention of Jack's name, April lifted her head again and looked at the person called. The young man had put down his pen and folded his hands on the table in front of him, his eyes fixed straight on the teacher.

"What about these processes on the spiritual level?" Jack asked, leaning back in his chair. The class fell silent. April raised an eyebrow in surprise. No one had ever asked such a question before.

"Spiritual level?" asked Zagajewski, putting the chalk aside. "What do you mean by *spiritual level*?"

"Well," Jack sat up straight again and then nodded his head at the writing on the board. "You can apply the seven alchemical transformation stages to any substance you want to transform, can't you? If the human body is also made up of substances, which is true, then shouldn't the spirit or soul also represent a substance? One that perhaps cannot be measured in the same way, but a substance nonetheless."

"Perhaps," replied Zagajewski. "What are you getting at, Mr Rosier?"

"Fermentation is a two-stage process: first the putrefaction, then the fermentation phase. First, something is left to die, from which something new then arises; on an alchemical level, that would be a ferment. In the writings of George Ripley, this process is directly linked to body and mind. So, what happens on a spiritual level when an alchemist, male or female," he glanced sideways at April, who was staring at him just like everyone else, "carries out this process?"

The class fell completely silent. And at that moment, April realised that there were things she hadn't been told about. That there were other alchemical teachings that they didn't teach *here*. And still looking at Jack, April suddenly felt terribly stupid. Yes, she had read books, lots of books. She had read herself into all the subsections and side arms of the subject matter at school and had done so with great dedication. But she had never thought to go through the first standard works and read them in their original version, the way they had been handed down. They had been taught the meaning of the things written in the old texts, but they had never seen or actually read them. The knowledge had always been presented to them by one of their teachers, pre-digested. But what if April would read something else from these texts? What if there were several ways of interpreting the well-known traditions? April looked at Will and Will looked at her.

The two knew many things, had read through many libraries, but in school they had never questioned the material itself, because the focus had always been on the practical. The school trained them as potion masters, poison mixers and healers. But what if there was more? More to know, more to discover, more to *be*?

Zagajewski began to formulate an answer to Jack's question. From the corner of her eye, April saw her brother looking at the teacher with a concentrated expression on his face, while she looked back at Jack. He exchanged a quick glance with Will and then looked at Zagajewski again. And while April's eyes rested on Jack, she sensed that something dangerous was emanating from him. Something strange, something dark – something that attracted her and for which a deeply buried part of her hungered. Jack Rosier meant change and for the first time April understood what her mother had always whispered to the twins and then winked at her husband, who then took her in his arms and had kissed her.

"Alchemy is so much more than substances and their reactions or their creations. It is not just a natural philosophy, science or medicine. Alchemy is in all things."

And while Zagajewski instructed the class on how to make a reddish-brown mixture of ammonia and hydrogen sulphide, which they would then use to make Liquor Hepatis, the base for the Balm for the Soul, the thoughts in April's head began to wander towards new levels and a horizon yet to be discovered.

April, Ginger, Will and Jack worked together during this class, not without Ginger glancing uncertainly at the other groups, comparing and contrasting, careful not to fall off or slow down. As Jack poured one liquid into the other, he murmured quietly: "I'm curious to see how the others will react when they realise that this alchemical process will not pass them by without a trace."

"What does *that* mean?" asked Ginger, helping Will to prepare the next four vials.

"Not much, except that such a process demands more of you than you think. To put it in Dylan Thomas' words: *'Do not go gentle into that good night'*." April snorted. Jack looked at her.

"What?" he then asked, tilting his head. "Not much," she replied, accepting the glass vial Ginger held out to her, echoing his own words. "But it seems there's more to you than I expected," she said, and the corner of Jack's mouth twitched.

"A poet's soul, for example," Will interjected and grinned at Jack. He smiled back, then put all the vials on the wooden tray. And while he went to the teacher to have their work checked and the other three began to clean the table, April's eyes fell on Jack's handwritten notes.

The old self must die, so that the true self can be born (rebirth). Now that the old, inauthentic self has been dismantled/discarded and the authentic parts have been brought together (first four stages) must be killed, you will never again be able to be the person you once were and return to what was (life and version of yourself), is forever impossible. Like a butterfly in a cocoon, in the chrysalis stage, the new and unknown merges with the core of a being's nature and the true self (note so self: compare Ripley and Flamel), the true nature of everyone is revealed (find more old texts on that). Putrefactio – the rebirth of the phoenix from its own ashes; the union of the soul with the spirit, through fire, passion; hunger for…

A soft clearing of the throat interrupted April's reading and made her flinch ever so slightly. Feeling caught and embarrassed she turned around. Jack stood beside her again and then looked from her to his notes, the empty wooden tray in his hands.

"Sorry," April said simply, taking a step back.

"It's alright," Jack said, setting the tray down. Ginger and Will were on the other side of the room, getting fresh rags to wipe the table, so April took the opportunity to turn round to face Jack.

"My brother doesn't know anything about what happened in the confessional, and neither does Ginger, so I'd be glad if it stayed between us," she said quietly, so hastily that she almost fumbled with her words.

"Who do you take me for? I am not the sort of man who kisses and tells, you know. But of course, I do understand you and will do as you wish," Jack answered slowly and then looked from her to Will.

"You're twins, aren't you?" Jack asked, and April nodded.

"Yes."

They were silent for a moment while Jack's gaze was lost in space.

"What you wrote there," April then began cautiously, "is that your personal opinion and ideas or did you learn that where you went to school before?" Her curiosity had won out and from the subtle smile that now graced Jack's lips, April knew that he had noticed her reluctance while asking.

"Both," he replied. He was just taking another breath to continue talking, when Zagajewski clapped his hands.

"Listen up, everyone! Over the coming months, we will devote each week to a different exercise and experiment, meaning that each week you will learn to perform a different form of fermentation, so that by the end of the year you will have mastered the most important ones and be able to perform them in your sleep! You will be able to produce the most vital potions, poisons and antidotes that you will need in life."

"That depends on what kind of life we choose," Jack said so quietly that only April heard him. She glanced at him, silently agreeing.

"But since I want you to master the other processes and transformations you've learnt so far as well, I'll have you repeat them in small groups. I'll divide you."

A sigh went through the class and Zagajewski smiled with satisfaction.

"Ivanov, Robinson and Mr Blackwell, group one. Kuznetsov, Novak and Svensson, group two. Seymour, Thurkell and Kingsley, group three. Miss Blackwell, Kaneko and Kostov, group four. Who's left? Ah yes! Miss Fergusson, you can go to group one, and Mr Rosier, you belong to the last group. I think that was four. Any questions?"

Everyone in the class shook their heads while some made a note of who they were in the group with. April scanned the room with her eyes for Ren and Ivaylo, the latter nodding to her as he caught her gaze.

"I want you to work through all the levels you've learnt so far in your groups, one to five. Who would like to remind us of the five stages? Yes, Miss Kingsley?"

"*Calcinatio, solutio, separatio, conjunctio* and now also *fermentatio*," said Aisling and Zagajewski nodded contentedly.

"Exactly. Well, today's class is over! I'll be expecting you on time tomorrow, as usual and recommend that you already start reviewing the material today. It will be easier to perform the experiments tomorrow if you fully understood what you learnt today. And don't forget, there will be more and more to revise as the weeks go by and you will be tested at the end of the school year!"

April and Will exchanged a look and Will rolled his eyes slightly. The twins were firmly against exams.

"Hey, April!" The girl turned round and saw Ren making his way through the other students packing up. She smiled back at him.

"What's up?" she asked, stuffing her notebook into her bag.

"I thought we could quickly agree as a group on how we want to handle the assignment. Ivaylo, come over here!" Jack, who was also in their group, leaned against the table and crossed his arms. His face wore no expression, neutral at best, and April wondered what he was thinking, since seconds before while they were talking his face seemed to be so full of life, animated and his eyes glinting. Maybe he just hated assignments. Or group projects. Or both.

"Well, there are four of us, which is an advantage, compared to the other groups," Ren continued talking after Ivaylo had joined them. At the back of the room, April watched as Mr Zagajewski also packed his things and she signalled to Will and Ginger that they shouldn't wait for her. Then she turned her attention back to her group.

"We could split up," Ivaylo suggested and looked round questioningly.

"Everyone does a topic, and we work on the new one together."

"Isn't the point of this thing that we work through the material thoroughly? Wouldn't it make more sense if we went through it together? That way we have several opinions and minds thinking and can work on a wide range of topics," April answered, looking at the others.

"Fine by me," Ren said and nodded. Then he pocked Ivaylo in the side. "We can work in pairs. I'll work with this loser here and you two can work together," Ren said and then pointed to April and Jack.

The two looked at each other, April less than enthusiastic. It would have been easier for her to study with someone she already knew. Last year she had written a very good term paper with Ren. And besides, it would also facilitate things if April hadn't to work with the guy with whom she basically had made out in the Bone Church, which for one was certainly blasphemous, and secondly, only thinking about it, made her blood flow into body areas, that made it very hard to concentrate.

"Perfect," Ren said without waiting for an answer from either Jack or April. "Ivaylo and I will do stages one and two, and you guys do three and four. And then we can sit down together for fermentatio. It makes more sense to work on the fifth stage later in the trimester anyway, when we've learnt more and know more. See you then!"

Ren grinned contentedly and set off to leave the lab. April sighed. Fine, she could be decent. She could force her body to be calm, whenever Jack's eyes wandered over her. She could behave, for God's sake, she had known this guy only for a couple hours really. She wouldn't allow some handsome Russian-Romanian dude, or wherever he came from, influence her academic career! He was really just an arrogant prick. Exactly! Jack was an arrogant know-it-all. April breathed out, now smiling. She shouldered her bag and walked towards the exit. Ivaylo pushed past her with a quick "See you later!" to catch up with Ren. They were the last ones. April stepped out of the lab and looked into the long tunnels ahead of her.

"No one wanders the catacombs alone," April heard her brother's imploring voice say, and then Jack's words, echoing in her mind.

Do not go gentle into that good night.

So, she turned and looked back into the lab. Jack had packed up and then stepped over to the teacher's desk. Zagajewski raised his head and Jack said something that April couldn't understand from a distance. Zagajewski replied and Jack nodded slowly as he listened to the teacher. Aprils sat down on a ledge that jutted out at the corner and stared into the tunnels. Waiting for Jack. *No one wanders the catacombs alone...*

The torches shook ever so slightly in the wind that always seemed to blow through the catacombs. The tunnels stretched for kilometres underground and no one really knew how many there were or where they all led. April stood up again and stepped to the bend where the tunnel branched off in two directions. April had only walked it once before, when she and her second-year class had gone on an excursion into the nearby woods. Now she looked along the stone walls and sent her thoughts through the tunnel. She felt the wind and imagined she could smell the odour of decaying leaves, the earthy scent of a forest. April let her consciousness feel its way along, gliding over stones, always following the subterranean wind and then... She heard a laugh.

April opened her eyes, but she was alone in the tunnel.

Someone was laughing again.

It was a girl, no doubt, but the laughter sounded hollow and as if from far away. Cautiously, April took a step into the tunnel.

"Someone's there?" she whispered and felt her heart begin to pound harder. The wind picked up a little and April shivered. She listened intently, but all she heard was the rumbling of the wind and then – footsteps

"April?"

She flinched and turned round. Behind her stood Jack, an old-looking book tucked under his arm, the other hand in his pocket, scrutinising her.

"Are you alright? You look like you've seen a ghost," he said, stepping into the tunnel next to her.

April swallowed. Her heart was racing. He had startled her. The laughter in the wind had startled her. She had probably just imagined it. Because she had wanted there to be something. Something more than what she could see and observe.

"All good," she said curtly, then nodded to the book under his arm.

"Some extra reading on *how-I-annoy-my-teacher-during-lessons-by-asking-prentious-questions?*"

Jack laughed. It sounded raucous and the sound of the laughter rippled through her like warm summer rain, dripping down the skin on her arms, her hands, her waist, lower... No. *Focus.*

She breathed.

"Unfortunately, no, but that sure sounds like a book I'd like to read! Are you still waiting for someone? For...something?" he then asked, bringing April back into the present moment, his eyes darting to the tunnel behind April, from where she thought to have heard the laughter.

"In all honesty, I was waiting for you," April replied, clearing her throat as Jack's eyebrows rose.

"My brother and I agreed that none of us would go through the tunnels alone, the catacombs are too dangerous," she said quickly. "And since everyone has already left, I waited for you."

"So that I can walk you to school?"

"Maybe it is the other way around. I'll walk you, because after all, you're the one who's new here, aren't you?"

"True."

Jack smiled at April and the two of them set off. They were silent for the first part of their way back to the monastery. April was lost in thought.

"Can I ask you something?" Jack said at some point in the silence, which was only disturbed by the echo of their footsteps in the tunnel and the crackling of the torches.

"What do you want to know?" April said, looking at him from the side.

Everything, Jack thought, but silenced the quiet voice inside of him.

"I don't want to seem rude with my question," Jack said. "I know we've only known each other since yesterday, but… Somehow, I cannot figure you out," he continued, looking briefly at April.

"So, what's the question?" said April, frowning.

"I guess my question is whether you're okay with us having to work together," Jack then said slowly.

Lie, whispered the voice inside of him.

I want to know whether you liked it when I kissed you, or not.

"Normally I have no trouble reading people and recognising their, I don't want to say weaknesses, but rather…behaviour patterns, within a few seconds," he added. "But I'm not sure about you."

Did you like my lips brushing over your skin?

Is that why you grinded against me?

Did you feel what that it did to me?

Can you read it in my eyes, that I want more, now that I had a brief taste of you?

"I guess," April began slowly, brushing her hair behind her ear, "that I don't know what to make of you myself," she then said. "I know that Will likes you, I saw that right away, and I can see that Ginger has nothing against you either. You worked well with us today and you seem pretty intelligent, which I like. But…" April's gaze was lost in the emptiness in front of her as she searched for the right words.

"I guess I'm not unbiased as they are, partly because of what happened last night. Honestly, I'm kind of embarrassed and if there's something in my life that I find unpleasant, I try to avoid it in the future. But since I can't avoid you because we work together, I have no choice but to deal with my uncomfortable feelings."

"I didn't mean to make you uncomfortable or to put you in an awkward situation yesterday, or make you do anything that you would regret later. Forgive me," said Jack, looking at her uncertainly. Had he jeopardised and ruined everything in his ignorance?

She regrets it.

She hated it.

She hadn't liked it.

"You asked, I gave you my permission, it worked. It's all right, don't worry, it has nothing to do with you," April brushed his last sentence aside.

"How about we start over?" Jack said abruptly and stopped walking. April did the same. "What do you mean?" Jack smiled and held out his hand.

"Hi, I'm Jack Rosier, pleased to meet you and to be your lab partner!" he said.

"April Blackwell, the pleasure is all mine," she said with a smirk, grabbing Jack's hand.

"*Enchanté,*" he murmured and lifted her hand it up to his mouth. His lips brushed over April's knuckles, as he breathed a kiss onto her skin, then let go of her hand. He smiled at her too. April's heart was pounding in her chest, but the feeling of relief prevailed, and as they seemed to have sorted things out between them, they walked the last bit of the way back and chatted easily, talking about what they had learnt in class today and glancing at each other from the side every now and then.

April was at peace with herself and the world again, when she went to her room after dinner to grab her books to study in the library, as they always did. But when April stepped into the library, walking towards the corner Ginger, Will and she always occupied, she saw Jack sitting next to her brother, talking to him, and she stopped abruptly. An unpleasant feeling spread inside of her and April clenched her hands into fists. What was wrong with her? She had been content until just now. Satisfied that Jack and she had remained neutral, almost friendly and had even enjoyed talking to him on their way back to the monastery. But was there no place in this building left where Rosier wasn't around to mess with April's mind?

Will lifted his head and spotted his sister standing halfway behind a bookshelf. He quickly stood up and pulled her behind the nearest corner after a single glance at her face.

"What's he doing here?" April asked as soon as her brother let go of her. Will peered around the corner. Jack had lifted his head and looked at Will for a moment, then continued working.

"He's studying with us," Will replied to his sister, scrutinising her. He sensed that she was upset again, for the second time that day.

"Did you adopt him or what?" April hissed, looking angrily at her brother. "Just because he works with us in the lab and I have to do group work with him, doesn't mean he's one of us!"

"April!" Will interrupted her quietly. "Please! You of all people should understand! Jack's new here, he doesn't know anyone and he's alone. I think it's only fair if we make his start here a little easier! I don't understand what you have against him per se anyway. He's been nice and friendly so far. He's polite, works well with us and that's saying something! I like you to remind of Sergei and how it was working with him or one of his friends and, as far as I can tell, Jack's also intelligent!

There's nothing wrong with him being here! I thought you'd come back from the lab together and you'd hit it off! At least that's what it looked like to me…"

April felt the anger that had flared up so suddenly sinking back into her. She didn't even know what kind of problem she had with Jack Rosier. Was it only her embarrassment from last night's events or was there something else? She listened inside of her, the curdling in her blood, the quickening of her heart. There was just this feeling…this foreboding and the certainty that Jack and she would never be able to be friends, not in the same way as with Will or Ginger. So far, Jack had done nothing but help her get rid of Luke and ask some unconventional questions in class. He had communicated and talked quite openly, at least, more open than she had. So, it had to her, didn't it?

"What's wrong, April?" her brother asked worriedly, taking her face between his hands. His thumbs rubbed softly over her cheeks and he leaned his forehead to hers. April thought of the voices she had heard in the catacombs. The laughter in the wind in the tunnels. She thought of the pictures she had seen the night before, those haunting visions before her inner eye. Something was wrong with her. Her thoughts kept slipping away and something had changed since April had entered the Bone Church last night. She couldn't say what, but it was as if April no longer had complete control over herself.

"I'm scared, Will," April whispered, feeling tears well up in her eyes. Will swallowed, seeing April's distraught face from the night before. And his own visions he had seen so clearly in front of him again, as if he were looking at paintings in a gallery.

"I think there's something wrong with me," April said, then looked into her brother's eyes. She could see the pain she felt in them, as the twins always felt what was going on in each other's minds. "Something changed last night," April continued. "There's something *inside* me that…scares me. It's like… I'm beginning to understand something I don't want to know, but I can't stop it either."

"Have you noticed any of this at home?" asked Will, stroking his sister's hair away from her tear-stained cheeks. April lifted her shoulders.

"Bad dreams, but that's nothing new."

"No," Will replied, knowing that his sister had been crawling into bed with him at night for as long as he could remember when the dreams got too bad. Even when the twins got older and they barely had room next to each other in the same bed. Will had bought a bigger one a year ago for this reason and April slept with her brother in the same bed half of the nights.

"You know what," Will then said and brushed the last of April's tears away. He smiled at her encouragingly. "What do you say we find a way to shed some light on the whole thing together. We'll find out what's going on and you'll see, in the end it's something quite harmless and we'll find a very simple explanation for it. Agreed?"

April sniffled and nodded.

"That's a good girl," Will murmured and pulled his sister into a hug. When April had calmed down completely, the twins went to the table where Ginger and Jack had been working all the while. The two of them registered April's teary eyes without a comment and Will pushed her into the seat between him and Jack. The small group worked together for the rest of the evening until it was time to return to the dormitories. Ginger and April didn't talk about what had made April cry. Ginger knew that her friend would talk to her when she was ready and Ginger had always accepted and respected that fact, for which April was eternally grateful.

While the lights were turned off one by one in the monastery and the last of those who had been out in the corridors until a moment ago went to bed as well, Jack Rosier lay awake in his bed. He listened to the last whispered conversations of the boys in his dormitory, some spoken in a language he recognised but did not understand, others a mixture of languages; but there was something strangely reassuring about it. Jack knew that Will had his bed almost at the other end of the dormitory, just next to Sergei Ivanov. Jack turned his head towards the window. The night was dark, no moon was shining, of course, it had only been a new moon yesterday. It all fell into place: the eleventh new moon of the year, the beginning of a new cycle, his transition to this school and the fact that they were going through the fifth transformation stage in class, which, if successful, would open the ninth gate after the dark night of the soul had been survived. With the last light of the moon, the old one had died and the new was born after the conjunction of moon and sun. It had only been a partial solar eclipse, but it had been enough. The transformation that this natural spectacle, which had taken place in the sign of Scorpio, had unleashed, would shake this world. Jack had seen it in April's eyes as she had looked over at him through the herb garden under the cloister's arched window. He had read it in her eyes, tonight, when he could still see the fine traces of tears on her cheeks. She could feel it happening too. Not consciously, but soon she would. What Jack's mother had predicted was finally coming true and even though Jack knew he was playing a dangerous game, he had made a promise to his mother and nothing and no one in this world would be able to stop him from keeping it.

Jack turned on his side and his eyes fell on the letter he had received from his grandfather today. Jack would not fail. He would do what he had been sent here to do, and in the process, he would fulfil his mother's last wish and give her what she deserved. He would avenge her, so that she could rest in peace.

Chapter 3

Made of Bone

"Childhood dotted with bodies.
Let them go, let them be ghosts.
"No," I said,
"make them stay, make them stone."
– Gregory Orr, from 'Origin of the Marble'

What was new at first became part of everyday life. The lessons progressed and with each passing day the students learnt to understand the material better and applied it in newer and newer ways. After the day's lessons and dinner, April, Will, Ginger and Jack sat down at one of the desks in the library and worked on their learning material. Some days it was homework or revision of previous years' material, and other days they didn't work at all, but left the books on the table and talked to each other. It was strange to see how quickly Jack had fitted into their little group, and although it always gave April a pang of jealousy, she could see that her brother had a best friend for the first time in his life, just as April had Ginger as her best friend. The days were getting colder and the nights longer. The experiment they had begun on the first day of the school year was now coming to fruition. A yellow ferment began to flow from the blackness of decay, a kind of golden wax, heralded by a brilliant spectacle of colour.

"This, ladies and gentlemen," Zagajewski commented proudly, while the apprentices stood around his table and looked at the glass bowl in the centre, "this is the so-called tail of the peacock or peacock's tail, whatever way around. The smell of the *Liquor Hepatis* is unique!" Ondine and Kenna, who were standing next to April, looked at each other with wrinkled noses.

"You don't believe me?" the teacher exclaimed with amusement and then laughed. April and Will exchanged an amused glance.

"I implore you! Come closer and smell it. Don't be shy!"

The apprentices looked at each other suspiciously. Then Jack cleared his throat and stepped closer, the others made space for him. Jack leant over the glass bowl and audibly sucked in the air. His surprised face was reason enough for everyone else to smell it too.

"Balm for the soul," said Zagajewski, looking round with satisfaction.

"That's what we're going to get out of this today. A perfume."

April raised her eyebrows, catching Jack's gaze. She lifted the corners of her mouth and he did the same, but the thoughtful expression on his face remained.

At the end of the lesson, each student left the lab with a bottle of fragrant of Balm for the Soul and they were all sent back to the monastery. April was tired from the day and when she sat down briefly on her bed in the dormitory after placing the books on the floor next to it, she slumped back, exhausted. April breathed in and out deeply and looked at the ceiling. It was remarkably plain compared to the rest of the convent, but all the girls' things scattered around the room more than made up for it. With November coming to an end, most of the girls had brought out their warm clothes and so, long coats were now hanging over the backs of the beds and matching fur hats on the bedposts. April yawned and closed her eyes for a moment, sighing softly. Just for a moment, she thought. Then she would go down to the others and then...

April was standing in a church that was flooded up to her knees. She smelled the foul odour of canal water and, looking around, she saw small Venetian gondolas criss-crossing the nave. The gondoliers were clothed in the black cloaks of the alchemists' guild, but they wore beak masks on their faces. The setting sun shone through the stained-glass windows of the church and the longer April looked at it, the redder it became, until the sun was crimson in the sky. Red light poured through the windows and made the water around April glisten like liquid blood.

April slowly turned to the altar, but instead of it, there was a kind of throne. And the longer April looked at it, the more the shadows around it seemed to come to life. The darkness formed itself into shapes of animals; she spotted a deer, a panther and a bear, slowly circling the throne. April blinked and as she wiped her eyes with her hand to see more clearly, a figure emerged from the shadows. The figure wore the traditional robes of the alchemy guild, but on its head was an animal skull. April felt herself being watched through the empty eye sockets where the animal's eyes had once sat.

"Come here," said the figure with the animal skull and held out his hand to April. The voice that sounded from under the skull seemed unpleasantly familiar. Without really meaning to, April stepped forward and grabbed the figure's hand. It was cold and strangely stiff and, as if in slow motion, April allowed herself to be led to the throne and sat down on it. Other figures emerged from the shadows, also with animal skulls on their heads and over their faces, carrying strange gifts in their hands. The figures placed these gifts on the floor in front of April's throne and then made way for one of them, who carried a crown made of bone in his hands. This was also placed at April's feet and then they all backed away from the throne. April raised her head. A pyre had been erected in the centre of the church. April saw transparent figures throwing bundles of brushwood onto the woodpile and then retreating.

"What will it be," Jack's voice suddenly murmured close to April's ear. She wheeled round, but only looked into the empty eye sockets beneath two horns.

"What will it be, the crown or the pyre?" the voice whispered again, and April took a step back, away from the figure with Jack's voice, away from the throne.

"Choose!" the figure hissed again and took another step towards April. She shook her head, trying to back away further, but only stepped into the void. She cried out.

April heard the bear roar, and as she fell into the darkness, colourful playing cards flashed before her eyes. She tried to reach for them, but only grasped at nothing.

April gasped and pressed her hand over her racing heart. She breathed heavily and choked. She coughed. Then, very slowly, she began to regain her composure.

She must have fallen asleep. She finished rubbing her eyes in an attempt to banish the images, but they remained stubbornly behind April's eyes. One of the images, however, had burned itself into her memory more than others: a tarot card, colourfully and artistically painted. And suddenly April realised what she had to do.

When April entered the refectory, she immediately looked out for Ginger. She let her eyes wander round the room. At the back table sat Kenna and her two friends, Aisling and Ondine, and next to them a few girls from the younger years. April turned her head to the left and saw Sergei sitting at the end of the table with Vadik, Ivaylo, Ren, Neil and three boys who were in another class. Will was nowhere to be seen and there was no sign of Jack. Ginger wasn't there either, so April turned on her heel and headed towards the library. The corridors were deserted, most people were either eating or on their way back from the laboratories, some of which were a good distance from the monastery. Some alchemical kitchens were located directly below the city or were connected to the buildings above via cellars and floor hatches, and to get to some of them, one had to walk for 15 minutes. April slowly began to relax after that disturbing dream. She felt herself breathing more deeply again and so, humming softly, she made her way through the corridors. April climbed the stairs to the next floor and as she turned the corner at the centre landing, she bumped into someone.

"Jack!" she exclaimed in surprise and he, too, had his eyes wide open.

"April," came out of him after he had stared at her for a moment. He was unusually pale by his standards and looked overtired, his eyes dark-rimmed.

"Where do you come from," April then said, scrutinising him more closely. "You kind of just disappeared after class. I wanted to ask you if we wanted to work on our essays together after dinner tonight."

"Been busy, sorry," Jack mumbled, but avoided April's gaze. "Where are you going?" he then asked her, running a hand over his face.

"Dinner, actually, but none of you were there," April replied, not mentioning the fact that she had actually been looking specifically for Ginger. Jack nodded slowly.

"Well, then. I'll be right behind you, I've got a few things to take care of," he said and without another word he pushed past April and hurriedly descended the stairs. April looked after him, a little taken aback.

Ginger wasn't in the library either, so April went back to the refectory without having achieved anything. She entered and immediately caught sight of Ginger's flaming head of curls. Her friend had lifted her head at the same moment and beckoned to April when she saw her standing in the doorway. Relieved, April walked through the dining room and sat down next to Ginger.

"Hey, I was looking for you," April said immediately and took a plate from the pile.

"We were doing some group work and then I went to pray, I'm sorry, I forgot to tell you," Ginger replied and pushed the bowl of bean salad over to April.

"Never mind," said April, accepting the bowl gratefully.

"There's something I wanted to talk to you about," April continued in a lowered voice and looked around the room briefly. April noticed that Jack had just entered the refectory, but he was immediately called over by the boys from her class and Sergei, who was filling up the tea pot at the samovar for his table, pulled Jack along with him.

"Uh, you're making me curious," grinned Ginger, who had followed April's gaze. "Is it about a boy?" the redhead asked hopefully, earning a withering look from April.

"No. It's *not*. Why would it be?"

"Right, I hadn't really noticed. But…Luke has stopped bugging you. Why is that? Have you got any ideas?"

"No," April said, feeling the lie rushing through her veins and burning in her face.

"What I'm actually getting at," April said, gruffly taking the bowl of sauerkraut from Ginger's hands and putting some on her plate, "I had a dream earlier. I know it might sound crazy, but I fell asleep for a minute and I had a dream and I feel like, no, I know I really need someone to read my cards."

Ginger raised her eyebrows.

"Cards as in *tarot cards*?" April's friend then asked also in a lowered voice and April nodded. Tarot cards weren't specifically forbidden at school but reading them wasn't exactly a favourite either. Too many witches used this craft, was always the answer and so card reading belonged behind the closed door of the dormitory, where the young women, dressed in their silk nightdresses and dressing gowns on their beds, read the fate of the other girls from the cards in the light of the candles with a meaningful expression. A game that they all took seriously enough.

"I need someone who's really good at it. A professional. Do you know anyone?" Ginger looked at April thoughtfully.

"No one off the top of my head. But I can ask around if you want," Ginger then said, and April gratefully squeezed her friend's hand.

"Can we sit down?"

Juniper's voice snapped April and Ginger out of their conversation. On the other side of their table were Juniper and Morrigan, girls from their dormitory who were no closer friends of either Ginger or April. Juniper didn't wait for an answer, but put her plate and cup on the table, climbed over the bench and sat down. Morrigan did the same. April sighed inwardly.

"So, how's it going?" Juniper started the conversation and smiled at the two friends.

"Well enough," said Ginger, pouring herself another cup of tea.

"I'm surprised to see you here," Juniper said, turning to April, who raised her eyebrows.

"Why is that?"

"Well, I thought you were sitting with your new boyfriend!"

"Boyfriend?" asked April uncomprehendingly, exchanging a look with Ginger, who had at least as big a question mark on her face as April.

"Why yes, it's been doing the rounds for weeks. After all, you turned Luke down at the beginning of the year and then made out all the more brazenly with someone else in the church confessionals!"

Ginger choked on her tea and April patted her on the back.

"I think you should learn how to drink, you're getting old enough," April said amusedly to Ginger, who coughed gratefully while April helped her to take a sip of water, whereupon Ginger calmed down again.

"Whatever you're saying," April then said to Juniper, leaning forward a little. "But since it's rumours, it must be true," April added, dripping with irony, and Ginger snorted softly. Now it was Morrigan who spoke.

"There's always truth in rumours!"

"And since I'm sure it was Luke you heard it from, it's guaranteed to be true," Ginger sneered mockingly, earning a scowl from Juniper.

"Believe what you want, Ginger," Juniper said and then pointed her fork accusingly in April's direction. "But you'll see, April's not who she says she is!"

With these words, Juniper signalled to Morrigan and the two of them got up at the same time and left the table without clearing the plates behind them.

"Creepy," muttered Ginger, making a choking noise that April could only agree with.

While these talks were taking place at the girls' table, Jack had been listening to the ongoing table conversations of the young men a few tables away.

"What do you think, Jack?"

"What?" Jack was startled out of his thoughts and noticed the other boys all looking at him expectantly.

"What have I missed?" he then asked, earning a laugh from Sergei, who put a friendly hand on his shoulder.

"You seem a bit confused as of lately," Neil then said. Jack made a dismissive motion with his hand.

"Oh well, I'm always like that," he said, putting some more dinner on his plate. After taking a few bites, he addressed the others at the table after a moment's hesitation.

"Are any of you close friends with Luke Harris?" he asked as casually as possible.

"Nah." Cynlaef snorted. "He'd rather hang out with the other Americans than us or the Brits. We're too foreign to be part of his crowd. Why do you ask? Did he do something stupid?"

"If so, all you have to do is say so and we'll take care of it," said Sergei, looking at Jack seriously.

"It's well known that he and his friends always get away with a lot," Vadik added, and Andrei murmured in agreement. "Also, they hate our guts for being of Eastern European origin, which is ridiculous."

"And racist," added Cynlaef. "So, did he do something?"

"Nothing serious," Jack said and then looked over to the table where April and Ginger were putting their heads together. "He just made me...uncomfortable, that's all," he then said.

"You can say that again," Sergei said. "The guy really has a few screws loose! I intercepted him with Will last year because he was getting on April's nerves all the time. Really, that guy knows no bounds! And especially with April! He needs to be taught a proper lesson! We could accidentally pour a bucket of acid over his hands, which he always wants to use to take what doesn't belong to him!" Cynlaef next to him laughed.

"What?" said Sergei indignantly, shrugging his shoulders. "I'm right!"

"Of course, you're right," said Vadik, nodding over to April. "But why don't you make it easy for yourself and just try your luck with her? I heard that Harris had finally given up."

"Really?" Sergei muttered and looked over to the other table. Two girls Jack only knew by sight joined Ginger and April at the table at that moment.

"Yes," said Neil. "They tell each other a lot of things anyway."

"What do you mean?" said Sergei, looking at his friend. He shrugged his shoulders.

"Only yesterday I heard a couple of girls saying that April had a boyfriend and that Mr monkey brain alias Luke Harris had finally given up."

"April has a boyfriend?" Sergei said in surprise, horror clearly visible on his face, disappointment in his eyes.

"It's just a rumour," Jack then said, remembering Luke's stupid face when he had discovered Jack in the confessional with April.

"But there's always truth in rumours," Sergei pointed out and continued eating.

The boys dropped the subject, but Jack unobtrusively scrutinised the young Ivanov. Jack looked from him to April and couldn't help but notice that the young man next to him was a good match for April. Her quiet but brash manner would complement Sergei's openness and generosity perfectly. In the few weeks that Jack had known April, he had quickly realised that she was the kind of person with whom trust and openness, had to be earned. She was extremely selective in her choice of friends and very possessive of Will. She was quiet and could come across as aloof. But Jack had already experienced and observed her in many different situations: when they studied together in the library or talked to each other, it seemed as if a fine layer of ice melted and then the words just flooded out of her. She could be enthusiastic about so many things and when she caught herself talking for several minutes at a time, she would look at the other person in shock, press her hand over her mouth with a caught smile, and those were the moments when Jack's heart sank to his knees. Those moments when her eyes were so open that he thought he could see to the bottom of her soul. Jack drained his cup in one go and then stared at the bottom of the china. No matter how much he desired her and wanted to make her his, it was better for his mission if he kept his thoughts and jealousy to himself. And as they all left the dining room and Jack caught April's gaze as the group of boys passed their table, he vowed to himself to stare less at April in future and banish his desire for her into the depths of his heart; out of sight, out of mind.

Hours later, Jack looked into the eyes of his reflection. The only sound to be heard was the dripping of water as it fell to the bottom of the sink. He had a job to do and if he wasn't careful, April's eyes, which always seemed to see through him, would be his downfall. Nothing escaped those eyes. Jack stared at his reflection. The only sound that could be heard was the steady drip of water as it fell into the sink. His face was rigid, an emotionless mask. You could read the anger and despair only in his eyes. He breathed heavily, crumpling a letter in his right hand. Then Jack closed his eyes and opened them again as he pulled a lighter from his pocket. The flames devoured the paper greedily and an acrid odour spread through the room as the fire licked at the letter. Jack dropped it on the floor, where it disintegrated into ashes. And then, with each successive stabbing pain that came over him in waves, he knew there was no escape from the darkness. It was not the night that haunted him, but that bottomless darkness that knew no end and that consumed everything else that possessed even a spark of life. When he left the washroom, he left behind the smell of fire and metal. Drop after drop of water fell into the sink, occasionally shattering the icy silence.

☽ ☆ ☾

For the rest of the week, all the students had been assigned to work in the monastery's greenhouses and gardens, to prepare them for winter. Will had always liked working with plants and flowers, even though he definitely didn't have a green thumb. Quite unlike his sister or father's grandmother. Old Lady Blackwell was the guardian and creator of a sprawling rose garden that would make any gardener of Versailles fall over with jealousy. Today was a cold day and Will was glad, that he could work in one of the greenhouses, unlike others who had to dig in the cold earth outside in the herb garden.

"Lunch break!" shouted Madame Tarkovsky after she had pulled open the door to the greenhouse and let in an icy cold wave of air.

"At last," murmured Ren, who was repotting plants next to Will at the table. The two looked at each other and Will shook his head with a grin.

"Come on, it's still better than scraping soil off the pavement in the cold," said Will, letting Ren pull him along.

"I'm just more into things that light up and can be heated with fire," Ren said, and Will laughed. Outside, it was still as cold as it had been that morning when Will and his group had taken refuge in the damp but warm greenhouse.

"Go on ahead, I'll wait for my sister," Will said to Ren, who gave him a thumbs up as he walked and then headed towards the refectory. Will took the other path to the herb gardens that lay outside the monastery walls. The school had several gardens, and they were all used to grow every kind of plant they needed for their alchemical experiments and everything else they made in the farm building.

Will turned the corner and immediately spotted April standing some distance away, talking to Sergei. She laughed and Will couldn't help but smile too. How pretty his sister was. Will would give anything to hear her laugh so freely all the time. April looked up, as if she had felt her brother's gaze, and interrupted the conversation with Sergei. He said something to her briefly, then nodded to Will and moved away before he could reach them.

"What did he want?" Will asked as soon as he stepped next to his sister, who was still smiling contentedly at him.

"Oh, nothing special. He invited us to his family's Christmas party. Apparently, half the school is supposed to come, but I can't say for sure. At least a lot of people have been invited!"

"I'm hardly surprised at this," said Will, looking in the direction in which Sergei had disappeared. "His family is very large and wealthy. Half of Petersburg's high society will probably be present at the party."

"Probably," April agreed and then looked at him questioningly.

"What?" Will replied, shrugging his shoulders. "It's clear what I think and it's also clear that you really want to go." He sighed. "We can go there for all I care, but only if mum and dad are invited too," he said, and April gave him a big hug in response. Then she pulled him inside the building with her, where they warmed up after the cold outside with a cup of tea and a freshly cooked lunch.

Humming contentedly, April spent the rest of the afternoon digging in the hard earth and letting her mind wander. Sergei's family was indeed among the better-off people in St Petersburg. April and Will had once spent a weekend with the Ivanov family when their parents had attended a conference in the same city. Sergei's mother was a lovely woman, widowed with five children. Sergei had a younger and older brother, who was in the military, and three younger sisters. The youngest was just old enough to start convent school in a year's time.

That weekend, it had been during the Christmas holidays, Will and April had been taken by Sergei and his sisters to a small frozen lake where they had spent the day ice-skating. When Sergei had approached April earlier, she had been loading a box of small potted plants that had to be taken to one of the greenhouses along with all the other boxes. They had chatted casually for a while and at some point, Sergei had cautiously asked April if they had any plans for the holidays. And so, April had told him that Will wanted to spend the holidays in England, while she wanted to stay here and spend Christmas with her mother's family. Sergei had then told her about the big party that his mother and aunts and uncles and grandparents and cousins and everyone else in the family were organising and that he wanted to invite April and Will there. Sergei quickly added that others from the class he was friends with, had also been invited and that he would be very happy if April and Will came too. It would be a party like no other, with cake baking, winter walks and ice skating, a ball and a big feast.

"Take your time, you don't have to make a commitment straight away or any-thing," he had said at the end. "But, as I said, it would be an honour and my greatest pleasure if you, April, I mean, if you two would come. Oh yes, and if you do come, don't forget to bring extra warm clothing and a ball gown! But you'll look pretty in anything anyway, no matter what you wear," he had added, and April had laughed.

Now April let her imagination run wild. She imagined the most beautiful dresses she could think of to wear to the party and in her mind, she was already on a phone call with her parents, convincing them to go to Petersburg, now that Will had agreed. And since Russian Christmas wouldn't begin until January anyway, the Blackwell family would have enough time before then to visit their relatives and travel to St Petersburg towards the end of their winter break.

It was beginning to get dark and April, like everyone else working in the herb garden, started to pack up the tools and put the last of the plants in the crates.

"Good work, Miss Blackwell," said Mrs Hawthorne, who was her Professor of Herbology, and sent April to the greenhouse on the west side of the convent. "If you hurry, you'll be able to make your way back without any extra light," said Mrs

Hawthorne and then went over to the other students, who were responsible for collecting all the tools and putting them away in the outbuildings. April sighed softly, as she had no desire to make her way behind the monastery to the west side in the semi-darkness of nightfall. April had a total of six crates to carry and grudgingly realised, that she could only carry two at a time. She cursed quietly.

"We'll walk three times then," muttered April and set off. The terrain behind the monastery was uneven and led past the orchards along the monastery wall, following a foot-trail down the slope and then through a small group of trees that stood around an old well. From there she could already see the first greenhouses. On her way, April passed a couple of girls who were on their way back to the monastery from the greenhouses, where they had spent the afternoon working. It was warm in the greenhouse and April placed the two crates next to the entrance, closed the door and then made her way back to the herb garden to fetch the next two boxes. The mist was already descending between the trees and the last light of the day made the November sky glow pink and lilac. The fallen leaves rustled under her feet and April ducked under the hanging branches. Her gaze fell on the well that lay to her right. For some unknown reason, out of a curious feeling, April stopped and then stepped towards the well. It was overgrown with ivy and there was no rope hanging from the winch. The well had not been used for many years, but it still carried water. It lay in complete darkness and obscurity and could not be seen when April bent over the edge of the well. April picked up a stone from the ground and threw it into the well. She counted the seconds to see how deep it had to go. One, two, three, four – the stone splashed into the water. April picked up another stone to verify her result – then she heard a whisper.

A murmur.

A laugh in the wind.

April raised her head. The well and the stone were forgotten.

There, she heard it again! It was coming from between the trees!

April stepped away from the well, took a few steps into the thicket, always following the whisper – it died away again. April stopped. Then the delicate laughter sounded directly behind her. April whirled around, but there was nothing to be seen except the black trees. April's heart was pounding, and she was scared. There was *something* that was not attached to a physical body that was trying to confuse her, or she was slowly going mad! The wind picked up and the dry leaves rustled as they were stirred up. And then the wind carried the sound of voices towards her. April followed them, stepping out of the grove, always following the sounds, until she realised that she actually knew them.

"Out of my way, Harris!"

That was Jack's voice! April stood still. She pressed herself against the monastery wall and crept to the next ledge. She peered round the corner and saw Jack and Luke standing next to the fence of the orchard. Jack had his arms crossed, Luke his back to April.

"Why should I?" Luke said now, jutting his chin out. April pressed herself into the shadows.

"What are you doing?" Jack sighed annoyed and tried to walk past Luke. But he stepped into Jack's path again and blocked his passage.

"I won't let you through until you tell me how."

"How *what*?" April heard Jack's voice saying. He clenched his jaw, clearly making an effort to keep his voice calm. April peeked out from behind the wall again and at the same moment Jack looked in her direction. April quickly retreated, hoping the shadows concealed her enough, not wanting Jack to feel like she was spying on him, which she was clearly doing at the moment. She definitely didn't care what Luke thought.

"How did you get April to spread her legs for you? Did you force her?" Luke asked, and April felt the blood rush to her face. Jack laughed.

"What makes you think I had to make her?" Jack said mockingly and leaves rustled under his feet as he took a step towards Luke. "Is it so inconceivable that she was in the confessional with me voluntarily?" Jack continued, his voice becoming more menacing with each word he spoke.

"You think the world of yourself, don't you?" Luke spat out and Jack laughed hoarsely again.

"And what are you going to do now, Harris? Your friends aren't here like last time. This time it's just you and me and the darkness." A shiver ran down April's spine as she heard Jack's reply.

"It was cheap of April to get involved with scum like you," Luke replied, and April felt the anger flare up like fire inside her. "Did you really think I didn't know what shithole of a family you crawled out of, Rosier? Do you think I don't know what kind of business your family is involved in? That I don't know what backward cultural circles you come from, where good Christian people are staked in their graves and disturbed in their final resting place?"

"*Shut up*," Jack hissed, but now it was Luke who laughed.

"You and your clan of devil worshippers and promenade mongrels will be wiped from this earth!" Luke said quietly and grabbed Jack by the collar. April clenched her hands into fists and was about to intervene when she saw the look in Jack's eyes. His eyes stared unforgivingly into Luke's face. There was no shred of kindness or warmth left. Just coldness.

"You have no idea what you're talking about, Luke Harris," Jack said in a voice that scared the shit out of April. Her fingernails dug into her palms. "You talk like you heard it from your father or your uncles or whoever. You think you can wash your hands in innocence, preferably in holy water, and that you can trample on people like us as you please! But you forget that we are made of different stuff than you are. We are made of bone and with the powers of darkness we shall destroy you!"

"Are you threatening me?" Luke asked, laughing derisively. He took a breath to say something else when April stepped out of the shadows.

"What's going on here?" she asked, and Luke sprang round to her, letting go of Jack's collar.

"April!" Luke said, smiling broadly. "How nice to see you here at such a late hour! Not cosy and warm with the others yet?" Wordlessly, April approached the two of them and stood next to Jack.

"But what am I talking about," Luke laughed again and ran his fingers through his hair. Then he straightened his jacket and tie and looked at the other two.

"Of course, you're out here! Probably looking for our dear Jack! The devil's bride to his son's freak! There's nothing more tempting than using the cover of darkness for your nefarious deeds, is there? Bet you like to be taken in the dirt, don't you, April?" Luke stepped towards April, and Jack immediately pushed himself in front of her protectively. "You'll see what you get for refusing me," Luke said, staring into April's eyes, taking no notice of Jack. "You're a half-breed, just like him. Your beauty could have saved you, but now you're doomed, witch." The blood in April's veins froze.

Something that had been hidden deep inside her lolled and sucked in the rage that coursed through April's whole body. April reached out, but Jack's hand was quicker and grabbed her wrist in mid-air. Luke laughed.

"Fuck off," Jack growled, and finally Luke did as he was told. He was still laughing, mocking, looked back at them, shook his head and then disappeared from their sight. Time seemed to stand still.

April was shaking with rage, staring at Jack's hand, which still held her wrist in an iron grip.

"Let go," she hissed when Luke was out of earshot, staring into Jacks face. His eyes were on her, April read anger and worry in them, but then Jack nodded and let her go. Snarling softy, April took a step back and bumped her back against the wall of the monastery. Suddenly, all the tension fell from her body and thus weakened and shaky on her feet, April sank to her knees. Jack was beside her in an instant.

"Are you all right?" he asked, helping her to sit down.

"Does it look like it?" April said gruffly, but let Jack help her, nevertheless. As soon as she was seated, April leant her head against the wall and closed her eyes. The anger was still trembling in her limbs and made April incredibly tired. Suppressing it wasn't easy. She wanted to let it out. Let it roar. Leash out. Strike. Hit. Hard. She wanted blood.

"He wanted you to snap," Jack said quietly, as if he had read April's mind. "Because then he could have told everyone what a crazy bitch you are. And just how right he is about…everything."

April didn't answer him and just concentrated on getting her breathing under control again.

"I know," April said eventually and opened her eyes. Jack had sat down next to her, his feet up, hands flat on his thighs, staring into space.

"I'm sorry about what he said to you," April said quietly, and Jack looked at her for a long time.

"Ah, that's right, you overheard everything," he said, tilting his head. There was no accusation in his statement, just an observation. "He said things to both of us that should have had his teeth and tongue ripped out and fed to the crows," Jack continued, and April nodded.

"Yes."

Neither of them said anything for a while. Night had fallen around them by now and with it the icy cold. April's teeth began to clatter, and Jack looked at her worriedly.

"We should get you into the warmth," he said and stood up. He held out his hands to April, who grabbed them and let him pull her to her feet. For a second they were so close. They looked each other straight in the eye and everything April felt, the anger, confusion, worry and fear, she read it all in Jack's eyes and for that one moment she felt completely understood. She even forgot to notice the rush of heat cursing through her body, swirling through her insides and pulsing in her stomach.

"I have a few more crates to take to the greenhouse," April then said, letting go of Jack's hands. April missed the lack of warmth in the same moment. "They're still in the herb garden," she then added, and Jack nodded.

"I'll help you."

"Thanks."

They walked the rest of the way to the herb garden in silence. There, April headed for the four boxes still standing around. Jack bent down and picked up three and April lifted up the last crate.

"I can easily carry two," April said, nodding at the three crates in Jack's arms.

"It's not a woman's job to carry around heavy things," was the only answer April got and so, with a subtle smile, she followed Jack out of the herb garden and back to the greenhouses.

The humid warmth immediately hit them as April opened the door and let Jack through first. Inside, April and Jack placed the boxes with the other two that were already there, and April switched on the light.

"Here we are," she sighed softly, looking around the greenhouse.

"Where do the pots need to go?" Jack asked, taking off his cloak. April did the same and rolled up the sleeves of her jumper.

"Mrs Hawthorne wants them at the back with the other baby plants," April replied and bent down to get the first plants out of the box. So, Jack and April walked back and forth, carrying the pots from the crates to the back of the greenhouse. When they had transported them all there, April began to sort them and put them in their right places.

"Can I help you?" Jack asked, but April shook her head.

"No, thank you. You've already helped me enough," she said, smiling weakly at him. Jack nodded slowly and leaned against the table next to her.

"On several things," April added, but without looking at Jack. "Thanks to you, I got rid of Luke and..." Her voice trailed off as she thought about the previous encounter. "Are you all right?" April then asked abruptly, and Jack looked at her in surprise.

"What?"

"I heard what he said to you about your family and stuff and... I wanted to ask you if you were...okay?"

Jack just looked at April for a few moments, so she lowered her eyes in embarrassment and turned her gaze to the plants in front of her.

"What he said is meaningless," Jack said, turning to April. "Don't worry about me, really," he said quietly, looking at the young woman with his head tilted. Her hands stroked the leaves of the plant in the pot and her eyes looked here and there. Then April nodded. She bent down and lifted the last cabbage plants from the ground and placed them with the others. April turned to the other side, where there was a small sea of fire lilies, and leaned to smell one of the flowers. She closed her eyes and a soft smile played around her lips, the scent of the flower calming her troubled thoughts and tense nerves.

Jack watched her and as she began to smile and his eyes travelled to her lips, he felt an irrepressible desire to take her face in his hands and kiss those beautiful lips. He would then lay her onto the table, push her into this sea of flowers, her hair intertwined with the lily blossoms, crowning her like a saint. He wanted to feel the breath flowing from those lips into his mouth, onto his skin. He wanted to feel her body wrapped around his, feel the heat between her legs, touch her, feel just how wet he could make her. And with his tongue he would feast on her, her juices sweeter than nectar and ambrosia. She would taste like fucking paradise. She looked like heaven, but dear Lord, she was made for sin. And no God nor devil would keep him from having his unholy ways with her. Maybe not now, but someday.

Fucking hell, he wanted her so desperately.

When he realised what he was thinking, he quickly averted his eyes and stared at the roses behind April, afraid that she could read his thoughts on his face.

"Why do you like lilies so much?" he then asked, looking at the plant next to him with apparent interest, his full attention focussed on the feathery petals of the blue iris. April turned to him in surprise. He tried to push out the images his imagination had placed inside his mind, April's swollen lips, dilated pupils, an ecstatic gasp, a sweet moan – her body so warm and soft, the taste of her blood in his mouth… *Enough.* He could have slapped himself. Jack breathed hard.

"What makes you think I like lilies?"

Jack shrugged his shoulders and looked at her briefly. "You draw them in your notes when you're bored in class and you often wear jewellery shaped like lily cups," he said. *And you smell like lilies. And pomegranates and cherries*, he thought, but was careful not to say it. If she also tasted like those red fruits if he kissed those beautiful lips? April looked at him, still puzzled.

"You've noticed that? Well, lilies are indeed my favourite flowers, along with roses of course," she added with a smile, which Jack returned slightly. April gently touched a petal of the lily next to her with her finger. "Lilies symbolise beauty, dignity and femininity. For me, they symbolise everything that a woman is," April then said, gently tracing the contours of the calyx. Jack bit hard on his lower lips, stifling a moan.

Dear lord, she was cruel. Touching the fucking petal like *this*? Jack had to keep himself from begging her to stop. Or to kiss him. Lick him. Whatever.

"This one stands for passion, love and strength," April smiled, not noticing anything of Jack's internal battle for control. "The fire lily is said to attract lightning, so you shouldn't take it indoors." She chuckled softly and then nodded to the white lilies on the other side of Jack. For hell's sake, even her laugh made him so fucking hard.

"The white lilies represent purity. They're part of almost every wedding bouquet and are given when you're at a loss for words in times grief. Madonna lily, death flower," April said quietly and stepped next to Jack. He tried not to tense up. Tried not to breathe in her scent. April looked closely at the white flowers and he couldn't take his eyes off her.

"There's an old German folk song," she murmured, brushing the flowers gently with her fingertips, and then began to sing with a low and hushed voice.

"Drei Lilien, drei Lilien, die pflanzt ich auf mein Grab. Da kam ein stolzer Reiter und brach sie ab." April raised her eyes and looked at Jack again. *"Ach Reitersmann, ach Reitersmann, lass doch die Lilien steh'n. Die soll ja mein Liebster doch noch einmal sehen. Und sterbe ich noch heute, so bin ich morgen tot, dann begraben mich die Leute ums Morgenrot."*

"What does it mean?" Jack asked hoarsely, still staring at her lips. That woman was a miracle. Hell sent, heaven blessed.

"It translates to as much as: *three lilies, three lilies, I'll planted them on my grave, then a proud horseman came and broke them off. Oh horseman, oh horseman, leave the lilies standing. So that my beloved shall see them once more. And if I die today, I'll be dead tomorrow, then the people come and bury me at dawn.*"

"I didn't know you could speak German," Jack then said, taking in April's face. Her cheeks had gained a rosy blush, and Jack wasn't sure if from embarrassment or the simple joy of singing.

"There are many things you don't know about me, Jack Rosier," April answered and smiled at him.

Do it again, he wanted to say. *Say my name and smile like this again and I'll be yours forever, my beautiful, cruel saint.* He swallowed and gripped the edge of the table with his hands so tightly, that his knuckles turned white.

"It's a pretty dark song," Jack then said, his voice rough from all the unspoken words. "Aren't you a little too young to be thinking about death though?"

"As if you haven't thought about it," April said with a subtle sneer.

Jack just smiled, finally tearing his eyes away from this beautiful woman, who was torturing him, without her even knowing what her presence did to him. How she made him forget what he was supposed to be doing. How she made him dizzy, lightheaded and risking his composure, he had worked so hard on for many years. To not give anything away. And here she was, tempting him with every word that came over those lips, making him hard and horny as fuck. He would definitely have to take a cold shower. Jack turned away from her, putting on his cloak and then helping her into hers. Then they switched off the lights, leaving the greenhouse dark and seemingly deserted. Only humid heat and the lingering scent of lilies remained.

Arriving at the bottom of the stairs leading up to the girls' dormitories, Jack and April stopped. It was completely silent in the monastery and for a few moments it seemed to April that they were the only living beings on this earth.

"Thank you," April then said into the silence. She searched the twilight for Jack's eyes.

"For what?"

"For everything," April said, and Jack frowned.

"And I'm really sorry," April added more quietly and looked to the side. She could only see her own reflection in the windowpane, and behind it the black night.

"What could you be sorry for?" Jack asked, looking at her, slightly confused.

"Because... Because I didn't trust you like Will did from the beginning on."

"But you didn't have to," Jack interrupted her and took a step towards April. "Trust is earned," he added quietly.

"It's not just that I couldn't give you the benefit of the doubt Will gave you, it's that I *distrusted* you." Her voice broke off. April felt guilty and pretty bad, she didn't dare look at Jack.

"Why?" April heard Jack say. She exhaled shakily.

"Because I have the feeling that you're hiding something, keeping something from us. Something that's been there from the beginning and I... The first night, when we were standing in the cloister, during the new moon ritual, you looked at me and then... I saw things. Images. Visions. And since that night, they keep coming back and they're terrible. They frighten me. And they only started when *you* appeared." April knotted her fingers and stared at her hands.

"There's a dark power emanating from you that I've never felt before in my life. And I know I'm talking about a feeling, a hunch, nothing more. And I wish I could risk it, so that we could be friends, like you are with Will and Ginger, but I..." April couldn't go on. She broke off and her eyes were lost somewhere on the floor in front of her. April knew in her heart of hearts that they would never be friends. Not when she kept fantasizing about his hands on her body, as they travelled over her naked skin, touching her waist, her hips, the insides of her thighs...

"You don't trust me," Jack determined and tilted his head. April pressed her lips together and shook her head.

"But if you could guarantee me that I have no reason to harbour this feeling against you..." she said, searching his eyes for anything that revealed that she was being delusional. That this sense of danger that emanated from him, was nothing to worry about. She cleared her throat, staring again at her hands. They were full of soil. She would have to scrub them.

"I mean, I've seen and heard you stand up for me today and I wish I didn't feel and think the way I do. If you could tell me that I'm wrong about my hunch, that I can trust you completely, then I will do so." Cautiously, April raised her head and searched Jack's gaze with her eyes. He, however, only looked down the hall, his eyes fixed on where the corridor was lost in darkness.

"I won't let it hurt you. Not if I can prevent it. Good night, April," Jack said, and with those words he turned and walked down the corridor. April watched until the shadows of the convent walls swallowed him up completely, leaving her alone with the turmoil inside her.

"Witch!" The voice echoed accusingly through the church. April knelt before the bone throne, on which a figure sat, bathed in bright light, looking down upon her.

"Ordeal by water," said the figure and stood up.

"If she swims, she's a witch. If she drowns in the river, we know that she was a good, Christian soul.

"No," April groaned as she was pulled to her feet. Invisible hands dragged her out of the church, she stumbled into bright sunlight, heard the cries of the people, so inhuman – they made sounds of such primal nature that it made April feel sick. Then the glistening waters of the Vlatva river before her. On the other side, the golden roofs of the city rose from the firmament in all their splendour. Statues of angels, gargoyles and saints gazed from the balustrades of the towers at the spectacle below and the sun burned. The air shimmered above the tarmac. April was pulled up again, yanked by her hair and she cried out. She was lifted into the air and a second later she hit the surface of

the river hard, the dirty waters crashing over her head as she was pulled into the dark
realm of nightmares.

Jack swayed with fatigue as he staggered into the washroom well past midnight. He felt like shit. Every muscle ached, and he felt nauseous. He fumbled for the light switch. The neon light flared up and bit into his tired eyes.

"What the –" Jack exclaimed, instantly wide awake. Will sat with his face buried in his hands, huddled on the floor next to the washbasin, his body trembling. Jack slithered towards him and shook his friend.

"Will? Will! Can you hear me?" Jack's voice became panicked when Will didn't respond, and just as Jack reached out to slap Will hard across the face, Will raised his head slowly and looked at Jack with dark eyes. There was infinite sadness in his gaze and a fear that Jack had only seen once before in the eyes of a wounded deer he had discovered on one of his forays through the woods of his homeland.

"Jack." Will's voice broke away and he slumped powerlessly into Jack's arms, where he began to sob uncontrollably.

Chapter 4

Solutio

"When I met myself on sharp peaks of ice, and tasted myself dissolved in the lulling heavy sea, in the talking night, in the spiraling stars, what did I know?"
– Kenneth Rexroth, from Sacramental Acts: The Love Poems; The Reflecting Trees of Being and Not Being

On the day of the Velvet Revolution, which was celebrated extensively every year, the students of the monastery were busy decorating the school all morning so that the festivities could begin after lunch. As every year, the monastery school welcomed a number of professors, scientists and others working in the field of alchemy. The afternoon was filled with lectures and panel discussions, then as usual there would be a dinner, a tea ceremony and then the students were free to pursue their own celebrations. The student association of one of the city's universities organised a gigantic firework display every year and many young alchemists took the opportunity to mingle with the normal mortals and witness the fire spectacle.

The girls' washroom had been constantly occupied since the early afternoon. The young women went in and out of there as they got ready for dinner. The group of girls who had been assigned to the convent kitchen for the day came cursing into the dormitory just before dinner, complaining about the incompetence of certain boys who also had to help in the kitchen, and then shooed the last of the girls out of the bathroom, saying that they now had full right to spend the remaining time before dinner getting ready without being disturbed.

April and Ginger were among the first group of girls to slowly made their way to the dining hall, both of them relieved not being on kitchen-duty that day. From a distance, they could already hear the members of the chamber orchestra tuning their instruments and the chatter of those who had already gathered in the refectory echoing through the corridors. April and Ginger arrived outside the dining hall and immediately looked for Will and Jack. They found them standing in the nearby corridor, Jack leaning against the open door to the herb garden, while April could hear the voices of Sergei, Andrei and Neil outside.

"There you are!" Will greeted his sister and Ginger with a smile and waved the two girls over. Jack nodded to them, but avoided April's gaze and looked out again, where the evening sky spread pink over the monastery. April did the same and avoided looking in his direction. They both remembered their last conversation of the other day very well and now neither of them really knew how to deal with the other.

"Sergei wants to go down to the city to watch the fireworks later," said Will, who had noticed the subdued mood between his best friend and April but decided not to go into it any further.

"Shall we go?" asked Ginger, pushing past April into the fresh evening air. April shrugged her shoulders and looked questioningly at her brother.

"I don't care," he said and then nudged Jack with his leg. "Jack?"

"We can go for all I care, even though I don't like large gatherings and crowds."

"There are plenty of spots where there will be hardly any people," Ginger said, wiping Jack's statement away with a wave of her hand.

"Well then," Jack muttered, giving April a quick sideways glance. "I guess we're not going until after the ceremony, though, are we?"

"The ceremony actually is part of our visit to the city," Ginger corrected him. "Usually, those of us who come along, go into town with candles. There we light more candles, which we let float on the river, and from there everyone goes their separate ways. The basic rule is simply that all students are back at the monastery before midnight. There will be a check, but we can stay awake as long as we want afterwards. Usually there is a big party in the common room which lasts way past midnight. Especially if the Russians are the ones in charge of organising it. After all, we don't have lessons tomorrow. If you guys want, we can go to the party as well after the fireworks," Ginger added, humming contentedly. The bell rang, announcing that the food was ready. And so, all the rest of the students, teachers and masters poured into the refectory for dinner. April, Will, Jack and Ginger followed them.

The procession of candle-bearing apprentices began the walk down to the city at around ten o'clock. If anyone had seen them from afar, it would have given the image of a line of fireflies moving through the darkness, or moths attracted by the light of the Golden City, which seemed to shimmer with excitement and energy on this November night. The young people from the monastery school arrived in town and were looked at with some irritation by passers-by, but they were allowed to be as they were, as a few of the townspeople knew the young people in their dark clothes and cloaks by sight. New candles were lit on the riverbank and then lowered into the water.

Music was playing somewhere, and the reverent silence was broken by the whistling of the first firework being shot into the night. The students suddenly alert, started to move and within minutes the small crowd dispersed. They all immersed themselves in the play of colours of the people around them and the fireworks that turned the night into day above their heads. Colourful iridescent sparks of fire rained down on the city, pink, blue, green and golden birds and dragons spread their wings of fire. Golden rain, swirling circles, spirals and stars popped into the sky. People exclaimed enthusiastically, clapped or pointed out into the night with amazed eyes, where fantasy became reality. In the midst of this spectacle of colour, Jack stood next to Will, Ginger and April on a balustrade a little higher up, further away from the river, where they had a very good view of the fireworks. A hundred other people were also standing at the viewing point, watching the jubilant fire colours with the happy eyes of children. Jack looked around and for a brief, sweet moment he forgot everything else and let himself fall into the warmth, the colours and the sparks of fire.

April saw Jack's features relax, and an almost happy smile played around his lips, and she felt something inside her loosen up and she breathed a deep sigh of relief. Jack must have sensed that April was looking at him, for when he turned his head in her direction, she quickly turned away and looked back at the fireworks, feeling his gaze on her. April squinted cautiously to the side. Jack was still looking at her, but this time thoughtfully and with a sad line around his mouth. Then he looked at the ground until he raised his eyes to the sky again and looked out into the night, which was ablaze. And as the four of them watched the fireworks, each lost in thought, none of them noticed the figures moving purposefully through the crowd in their long cloaks and hoods.

While the fireworks still exploded above the Vlatva river, the sounds of amazement and exclamations of joy suddenly started to sound distorted. And from one second to the next, cries of pain and fright resounded through the crowd. April, Will, Jack and Ginger lifted their head, alarmed they looked at each other, as the cries seemed to ripple through the people coming closer. Then something exploded not too far away. People shouted and the heavy scent of gasoline hang in the air. As if on command the world erupted into chaos.

"That's a Molotov cocktail!" Jack shouted at the others and within seconds he pulled them away from where the second bottle exploded, just a heartbeat later. "Let's get out of here!"

While panic and disorder took over around them, April, Ginger and Will followed Jack's lead, the sounds of explosions ringing in their ears. The air became dense, it was difficult to breathe. April focused on Jack's back, holding her brother's hand, while she tried not to stumble, afraid to be trampled on by people but someone pushed her from behind, and April fell onto the floor. Although her hands prevented the worst of the fall, she cut her fingers on broken glass. She cried out in pain, and the next moment she was being pulled up by Jack, his eyes widened in horror. He looked at her bleeding hands briefly, then held her wrist and dragged her through the crowd. They had lost Ginger and Will. April tried not to cry, her sliced skin burned like hell.

"Come on we have to move!" Jack shouted at her. April nodded, every inch of her body trembling.

"Will," she managed to say and saw that Jack nodded.

"I know!"

They continued their way through the crowd, getting elbows in the side, legs kicking at them. More explosions cut through the air, followed by even more cries of pain. When Jack turned his head towards April, she saw that his lips were bleeding, and someone had hit him on the temple with something sharp. He staggered slightly but didn't let go of April.

"We shouldn't have come in the first place," she heard him say as he swayed lightly but still, he continued pushing his way through and finally out of the crowd. April felt like a drowning woman breaking through the surface of the water. Air. She could finally breathe. With a jerk, she was yanked forwards and she cried out again.

"Run!" Jack pulled her along and thus April couldn't do anything else but to follow him. They ran away from the viewing platform and into one of the neighbouring alleyways. Jack didn't let go of April's hand as they continued running until April's lungs ached.

"Stop," she managed to say. Jack slowed down. He looked up and down the alley, then pushed her into the shade of the houses.

"What's wrong?" he asked, his voice slightly panicked and looked her up and down. "You hurt?"

"Can't…run anymore." April coughed.

"Okay, then let's take a short breather. But then we have to keep moving!"

April nodded and let the stone wall catch her.

"What do you think is going on there?" she asked out of breath and nodded into the direction where they had come from. Jack pressed his lips together.

"Seemed to me like a bunch of troublemakers."

"That was more than just making trouble," April replied. Jack's lip was still bleeding and the blood at his temple began to dry. Although there was blood all over his face, he still managed to look beautiful and April hated herself for thinking that but wondered how it would taste like to kiss him right now. What his blood would taste like in her mouth. Maybe it was the fumes in the air, making her unable to think straight. God, how was it possible for someone to look this hot with blood on their face? Or was it exactly this beaten and bloody look that made him even more attractive?

"What?" Jack suddenly said, having felt her staring at him.

"You're injured," April said with a raspy voice, casting her eyes onto the ground, afraid that he would be able to read her thoughts. Her desire.

It was different with him. All the other guys she had been with had never stirred this kind of lust within her. Sure, she had been able to explore some darker parts of her when she had been with them, wondering where this need of feeling pain and pleasure intertwined had come from – and whenever April now looked at Jack, it felt like he was the answer to that question. Holy Mother Mary, those fumes *truly* were getting to her head.

"I know. We should get going," he said, and April nodded. She pushed herself from the wall and the two of them started moving again.

"Where are we going?" April said. "Back to the school?"

"No," Jack said. "Not yet. I told Will and Ginger to meet us at Apollinaire should we get separated. It's better to get off the streets as soon as possible. It's not safe out here. At least not as of now."

"Okay," April nodded slowly, her head started to spin, and her hands were still burning. Jack led them unerringly through the alleyways and a few minutes later they opened the doors of the Church of St Apollinaire. Inside it wasn't much colder then outside, but it wasn't warmer either. Jack made his way through the nave to the altar and when April hesitated, he just waved her over.

"We need to clean those cuts, otherwise you'll get an infection. And that would be an ugly sight."

"Are you saying my hands are unpleasant to look at," April said jokingly, but her voice trembled from exhaustion and thus her words came out rather serious. Jack stood next to the basin with the holy water, stretching out his hands towards April, who then showed him her bloody palms and fingers full of cuts.

"Oh shit," Jack said beneath his breath as he took in the wounds. He then gently took April's hands and pulled her over to the altar, where the communion chalice stood, beautifully arranged with a handful of white lilies and a laced tablecloth.

"I would never say that any part of you, April, is unpleasant to look at, on the contrary. And for what's worth, these hands of yours better heal quickly for I can imagine many ways I want you to use them," Jack talked lightly, but the brief look he gave her, sent shivers down her spine and her insides purred.

"Try to push out as much blood as possible into the cup – that way we can make sure any bacteria are flushed out. Then we'll get these cuts cleaned up." April obeyed silently. She hissed slightly as she clenched her hands into fists, watching the blood spill out in between her finger, dropping into the chalice.

"Isn't this desecration?" April murmured at some point and watched as Jack pulled out a handful of gauze bandages from somewhere in his cloak. "How come you have bandages with you?" She added, looking at Jack irritated.

"I'm an alchemist. It's not an unusual thing that some experiments can go horribly wrong, thus I rather be prepared," he said and laid the bandages out on the tablecloth, then he motioned her over to the basin with the holy water. Carefully he took April's hands into his and laid them into the water.

"Now that's desecration," April said with a low moan. "We cannot do this!"

"Yes, we can," Jack replied and started to wash out any dirt from the wounds and brushed gently over the cuts on April's hands. "I wouldn't mind desecrating everything the church considers sacred just to make sure you're okay. I would burn down the heavens and raise hell if only to ensure you're being taken care of. Besides, there's actually nothing as healing as holy water," he continued. "Did you know that the water's structured in a certain way depending on what it is exposed to? Well, holy water, specifically, is exposed to prayers, meaning when shock-frozen and looked at under a microscope, this water here would freeze into the most beautiful ice crystals, reflecting the vibrations of the prayers, chants and hopeful thoughts it was exposed to. Water has a memory. Thus, water that has been sanctified in such a way is disinfecting and healing. So, no, this is not desecration." April had listened in silence, but her heart was pounding in her chest, watching Jack's hands washing her own, gently stroking over her skin, and now, his fingers went still as he looked at her. She lifted her head and as she looked into his eyes, she saw the candles reflected in them.

Yes, his eyes were blue. The blue of the Northern sea, daring her to dive in, to lose herself. A gentle tug at her hands made April realise she had been staring at Jack, but he just wordlessly pulled her over to the altar, where he bandaged her hands.

"You might not be able to work in the lab for a while," he then gently said as he was done. April stared at her hands, now covered in white gauze. Then her eyes fell upon the chalice.

"Jack!" she exclaimed and pointed to the bowl. They both stood now next to it and stared at April's blood that had gathered in the middle of the cup. Instead of a small pool though, the blood had formed itself into a symbol.

"That's...neither a Christian nor alchemical symbol, is it?" April whispered now and looked from the blood up into Jacks face. He was staring at the red liquid and as it had happened in the confessional, April had the impression that all air around her was sucked in by his gaze, that fire in his eyes. The shadows from the faraway walls crept closer and April shuddered.

"No," Jack then finally said, his voice so grave and dark it seemed to vibrate from the stone walls, echoing through April's bones. With an abrupt motion, Jack turned away from April, away from the bowl, facing the pews, looking towards the church portal, his gaze was lost somewhere in space. An unpleasant cold spread through April's body.

"There is an ancient prophecy," Jack began to talk, slowly turning round to April. "It says that those who are demon-born will bring down the Holy Church if not kept in check." His eyes were still filled with that fire, his features smooth, but somehow estranged. He looked at her in a way he never had before – as if he was seeing her, but not actually seeing *her*. Something brushed at the edges of her consciousness, uncoiling itself from the depths of her chest, like a snake that had smelled the scent of her next prey.

"What does that have to do with anything?" April hated how fragile her voice suddenly sounded. Hated that she felt as if she was losing the ground beneath her feet. Hated that the Jack she had thought to know had disappeared from on second to the other and had now been replaced by a stranger. Or had he been a stranger all along?

"It means that the Holy Church can be brought to its knees."

"But why should it be brought to its knees?" With a pang April realised that she was trembling. That Jack's voice sounded exactly like it had in that dream. In that horrible, nightmarish dream.

"Because the Church condemns too many, and in its name too many horrific things have been done and are still being executed. It has…"

The portal was pushed open and Ginger and Will rushed into the church.

"April! Jack!" Within seconds, Will had ran up to them and pulled his twin into a tight embrace. April could feel his body trembling, felt his racing heartbeat and with the same intensity, the same firmness, she held onto her brother, a silent sob rushing through her.

"It's hell out there! Are you hurt?" April heard Ginger say and then Jack answering.

"April fell into broken glass, her hands are cut open, but…" The same moment Will pushed his sister a couple of inches away from him and inspected her hands.

"You took care of it," Will noticed and then kissed the bandaged hands of his sister. "I was so afraid," he whispered so quietly, only April could hear it. He then leaned his forehead against hers, and the twins breathed each other in. It was okay. They were reunited and everything was alright.

"What the fuck is that!" Ginger's voice let them all turn towards her. She stood next to the communion chalice as April and Jack had minutes before, staring into it. Will let go of his sister and stepped next to Ginger.

"Holy shit! Now that's something!" Will said and looked over to Jack. "That's a rune!"

"You know what it is?" Jack's eyes lit up as he passed April to look at the chalice again.

"Sure! I came across it a couple months ago, when I was reading that book about ancient runes, you remember April?" She nodded and looked from her brother, to Jack, to Ginger.

"Yes," Will continued, pointing into the bowl. "If I am not mistaken this run signifies as much as key or gate."

"*Key,*" Jack echoed silently, his eyes not leaving Will's face. "*Gate,*" he then murmured and turned around himself, taking the whole church in. "Of course," he said and then began to laugh.

The other three looked at him dismayed. But Jack didn't notice. He laughed louder now, and then, before any of the other could react, Jack lifted the chalice, wiped away the tablecloth and the lilies, that landed on the floor, and poured the cup's content onto the altar. Ginger gasped, Will froze and April cried out. The blood began pouring from the chalice onto and over the stone surface. But there seemed to be an endless flow of blood now, as if the bowl had multiplied whatever amount April had let drop into it and now... The blood flowed over the altar, the steps and between the floorboards and where it touched stone, strange signs began to form and within seconds the four were standing in a mosaic of bloody symbols that spread around them in elaborate helixes and then, slowly began to seep into the ground, not leaving any trace.

"Dear Lord," Ginger whispered into the sudden silence, trembling. "That was..." They never learnt what Ginger had wanted to say, because not another word escaped her lips. She just stared at where the blood had been seconds before. After what seemed to have been hours, Jack began to speak.

"I must make a confession." April's eyes darted to his face, but Jack's gaze was trained on the floor, then he took a small step back. "When I was told that I would change schools and come here, I made it my mission to find out as much about this city as possible. As *the* city of alchemy, I knew I would only have to dig long enough, until I would find *something* interesting. Truth is, I did. In some old reports I found a mentioning of an old archive that was supposed to be located in these catacombs, under this city. It further said that ancient knowledge was stored there, the kind of knowledge the authority was not to know about and... the guild neither. I tracked down that archive, and once I had managed to get access to it I... I found this." Jack pulled out a folded piece of parchment from his pocket and held it out for the other three to see.

"What's that?" Ginger asked, inching closer.

"It's a map," Will answered in Jack's stead as April stepped to his side. Indeed, it was a map. It was, in fact, a map of Prague. April recognised the outlines, some streets and buildings but...couldn't make out what the notes on the side or the markings on it said.

"I didn't understand it until now," Jack continued and tapped onto several points on the map. "There are so many churches in this city, monasteries, holy buildings. Someone had marked these five churches, aligned them and..."

"It's a cross," Will said and Jack nodded. "Do you think they were built that way on purpose?"

"Yes, for the king who had let these churches built, was very religious, obviously, and when you look at them it's a perfect cross."

"A cross as in the Holy Cross?" Ginger interrupted, looking at Jack.

"I think so," he answered. "But now...What else does a cross signify?" With these words Jack looked at April who had kept quiet the entire time.

"The kind of cross they use in treasure maps," April offered her suggestion reluctantly and was gifted with one of those smiles, the real smiles Jack only showed to them, his friends.

"Exactly," he said and motioned around them. "Apparently, this church," he pointed again to the map, where the two lines of the cross met, "this church is the cross point. This church is the X."

For a while no one said anything.

"But...what does it have to do with us?" Ginger asked and looked into the round.

"I believe there is *something* beneath this church. Blood that forms itself into runes and symbols doesn't just seep away like that. There must be another purpose.

There must be something beneath us," Jack answered, his eyes taking in the walls of the church.

"What on earth could be under this church?" April said and crossed her arms.

"I think whatever it is, most certainly is not *of* this earth."

"Are you talking about an entrance to hell?" Will asked, looking at Jack. "Because there are ancient stories about this city and why it was chosen by the alchemist as their base. Some say it's because some doors and tunnels of this city lead directly to hell and thus to the eternal flame."

"Why should the alchemists care about that?" Ginger countered. "The guild is part of the Holy Church of Rome!"

"And isn't the Church that one institution that has the greatest interest in things related to hell and all that has crept out of there?" Jack argued.

"Or fallen into it," April added drily, feeling Jack's eyes on her.

"And why again should that be of any interest to *us*?" Ginger's voice snapped April out of her thoughts.

"Because we can all feel it," Jack said, stepping away from the altar, raising his hands and holding his arms out as if he wanted to take in all of the stone-cold beauty surrounding them. "The old order is about to fall. It is not just the church or the guilds. The world is dying, and I have little interest being sucked into the destruction that comes with it. If anything, I want to wield it like a sword."

"That's blasphemous," Ginger hissed.

"It is indeed a dangerous thing to say," Will softened Ginger's words, but looked at Jack in a thoughtful way.

"Maybe. I don't care. I don't care if you will continue on this path with me, or not, but I will find out where this is leading me. And I would be honoured to have you by my side, so... Take some time to think about it and when you've decided, meet me under the portrait of Mary in the cloister after evening mass. I will wait for you."

☽ ☆ ☾

April rolled from one side to the other, turned the pillow over, then the blanket. She lay down with her head at the foot of the bed, but that didn't help either. What seemed like hours passed before April decided to get up, as sleeping was out of question. She was tired and staggered, but the buzzing thoughts in her head wouldn't let her rest and she hoped the cold air would help her think better. As April tiptoed past Ginger's bed, she heard a delicate snoring coming from under the pillow, scattered strands of red hair spread out on the sheets like a halo.

It was indeed fresh outside; the air was cold but clear and it smelled of snow. Bundled up tightly in her warm coat and fur hat, April made her way across the courtyard to the monastery church. The door was heavy and not particularly quiet as it fell back into the lock after April had stepped through the church portal. Her thoughts were still a stormy sea and April longed for the absolute peace and quiet that could always be found in churches so that she could sort out her thoughts. As the day had not yet dawned, April thought she was completely alone until, after a few steps, she spotted someone sitting in one of the pews at the front of the nave. She stopped and as the sound of her footsteps died away, the other person turned round.

Of course, it was Jack's eyes that found April's gaze. He lifted the corners of his mouth slightly and April moved to sit next to him. The bench creaked softly, and April let out a barely audible sigh as she took off the hat and leaned back.

"I see I'm not the only one who frequents this place for some quiet contemplation," Jack said at a normal volume, but due to the eerie and reverent silence that captured any church when there was no mass or service, Jack's words echoed incredibly loud through the room.

"No," April said quietly, and they looked at each other for a moment. Then April turned her head away and looked forwards to the altar. Her eyes travelled slowly along the details of the pulpit.

They had returned to the school minutes before midnight. Everyone was talking about the riot that had taken place in the streets of Prague a couple hours before.

The riot had made national news and the buzzing of phones had accompanied them for the rest of the evening; worried parents that were callings, friends that had lost each other in the crowd and the news ticker broadcasted updates every other minute. The teachers had been worried and when they had made sure that even the last apprentice had returned safely to the school, the massive gates of the monastery were closed, locked and blocked. Surprisingly though, the riots in the city had not diminished the apprentice's festive mood and for hours April had heard them in the common room: Japanese karaoke, some sort of roulette, smoking, drinking- and card games. But maybe they did it all just to forget their fear, the panic that had rushed through them and the echoes of screams and explosions, still ringing in their ears. Even April could hear them still and if it were not for the flashbacks she saw whenever she closed her eyes, then the subdued pain of the cuts on her hands and bandages itching ever so slightly reminded her of what had happened. After all the disquiet of the evening and first part of night, April cherished the solemn quiet of the church, letting her gaze wander over the pews, the altar and the ever-burning candles.

"Do you believe in a god?" Jack's question came out of the blue and broke the silence between them once again. April looked at him in surprise. Jack's eyes looked clearly and calmly into hers. It was a serious question.

"Why do you ask?" April then replied and Jack shrugged his shoulders slightly, reviewing in her mind what he had said earlier that evening, about bringing the church to its knees. Saw the symbols on the stone floor again. Oh, what a bloody mess she was in…

"Just because," Jack answered, though they both knew that there was more to his question. April was silent for a few moments while she thought about an answer.

The preaching of a god or a divine trinity had somehow always been present in her life. The tradition of alchemy and the church had always been closely intertwined in this country, but April had never found an explicit answer to why that had been so. When April and Will had been small children, they had accompanied their parents on their short journeys, visits to various monasteries scattered all over the continent, and partaking in various masses and attending lectures about religious teachings had not been an unusual thing for them to do. But it had never been about faith, but more about the knowledge that was carefully guarded and protected behind those thick monastery walls and libraries. There had never been table prayers or anything like that but attending liturgical services or lighting candles on memorial days had been an integral part of it.

And then there were also memories that April had kept secret like the burial place of a treasure; memories of her mother kneeling on the floor in a circle of candles, swaying back and forth and with a trembling voice, tears in her eyes, begging her ancestors to stand by her side and help her, while April watched her through the keyhole. All this and whispered conversations behind half-closed doors, the wink of her father's eye when he hid certain books behind others on the shelves so that the 'book-eaters' wouldn't find them. April quickly realised that the book-eaters were the people who knocked on the front door of the old house, where April and Will had spent most of their childhood, on certain evenings. They were scholars, alchemists and guild members who paid a visit to the Blackwell family. April and Will had always been sent to bed hours too early and their mum had told them not to show their faces and not to leave their rooms if possible. April had never liked these people and at breakfast the morning after, her mum always said wearily: *"These people eat your heart alive and tear you apart like an old book just to find out what language you were written in."* That was when April had begun to realise that there were book-eaters who didn't really eat books but sucked the knowledge out of other people and used it for their own gain. Even as she grew older and, in time, accompanied her parents to certain events with Will, April gave these people a wide berth. They were members of the guild of alchemists who were far too fond of taking things apart without putting them back together again when they were done. Will and April had soon learnt that their parents didn't agree with the guild on everything and that it was better not to talk about it in public. As far as God was concerned, April had formed her own opinion.

"I was taught alchemists should believe in a god. To walk the path of light," April answered Jack's question, but didn't look at him. "I do not find comfort in the regular Christian teachings, but rather in the Orthodox rituals and practices surrounding it. The architecture, the liturgy, chants and community. But I don't like the idea that it's an old man or his son telling us what we can and can't do. A God, who encourages people to suffer, to long for death and to regard this life as inferior. A God who wants you to tolerate abuse and even encourages you to be quiet and turn the other cheek. I think there are few things more contemptuous of women than the teaching of an all-powerful God, a heavenly father, to whom we should submit. But I cannot tell for certain, if there is a God or not. No one can. But I do believe there is something greater out there." It was only when April had finished, that she realised what she had just said out loud. She didn't look at Jack and hid the sudden surge of fear and anxiety behind a motionless mask. April clasped her hands together so that they stopped shaking.

Had she gone too far out on a limb with her statement? And why had she said what she was truly thinking? She had never done that to anyone other than Will before. Maybe because of what had happened earlier tonight. Maybe because of the way Jack had said, *I don't care.* Maybe because of that look in his eyes and soft tremble in his voice when he spoke about the dark sides of the Holy Church and how the world they knew, had begun to collapse around them.

"I see," Jack said quietly, and April felt him looking at her from the side. She raised her eyes cautiously. Jack smiled slightly. Then he looked up at the ceiling paintings above them.

"And what about you?" April then asked, unable to bear the silence. "After all, Luke called your family a clan of devil-worshippers!" Jack looked at April for a long time and she returned his gaze without blinking.

"And you think I'm a devil worshipper too?" Jack then asked slowly, tilting his head.

"I'll believe whatever you tell me," she replied, and Jack raised his eyebrows in surprise.

"That sounded very different the other day," he said softly, his eyes travelling over April's face.

"Maybe I've changed my mind," April replied even more quietly than Jack had spoken.

"At the risk of being struck by lightning, now that I'm going to say another blasphemous thing and thus pushing my luck today," Jack continued, "I agree with your heretical opinion." Jack averted his eyes and looked back towards the altar. "Why should there only be one God? One Lord? Or why any form of deity at all? What if this something is completely beyond our comprehension and we never have a chance to understand it as the humans that we are? What if it is beyond the limits of mundane understanding?" Jack broke off and looked at April again. "My life has taught me that there must indeed be things greater than us. Fates that know how to elude our horizon of knowledge, but that doesn't make them non-existent. I am not a fatalist, but I believe that we all have a destiny to fulfil. To walk a path that is predestined for us, with the power to decide for or against it."

"A free will," April concluded quietly, and Jack nodded slowly.

"Yes, maybe that's it." He smiled slightly. "I'm convinced there's a lot more out there than we're being led to believe. Things that don't bend to any natural law and are therefore perhaps a natural law themselves. Things like magic."

"Magic?"

"Magic, sorcery, miracles... Whatever you want to call it. Things that the Old Testament knew, by the way. But yes, something that sees more and knows more than the naked eye can see."

"That sounds a lot like witchcraft," whispered April. Suddenly she felt a tingling sensation in her back and had the uneasy feeling that she was being watched. Jack was still looking at her, but it wasn't his eyes that triggered this uneasy sensation in April.

"You can feel it too, can't you?" Jack breathed softly, his eyes darting towards the altar. April held her breath. "Someone or something doesn't want us to talk about it," he whispered. He looked at her again. His eyes pierced April and again she had the same feeling she'd had the first night of the school year when Jack had looked at her through the cloister, staring at the bottom of her soul. Right before her mind was swept away in a flood of visions.

"Whatever we will find beneath that church," Jack said quietly, "I'm prepared to go all the way."

"It could be dangerous," April whispered, fear spreading through her body. "We could die in the process."

"We'll do that one day anyway," Jack replied gently. "So why not for this?" Slowly, he lifted his hand and with the gentlest of touches, he wiped a tear from April's cheek with his thumb, which had stolen unnoticed from the corner of her eye.

"The question now is what do *you* want to do," Jack continued, his hand still cupping April's face tenderly. "What do you *really* want to do? Because I think you've known the answer to that question for a long time. You just don't want to admit it." Jack's eyes didn't falter, continued staring into April's and her heart was pounding hard. She thought she could hear the blood rushing in her ears. She breathed faster, her body trembling. For another second, April remained motionless, then she stood up abruptly and without saying another word, she turned and left the church, Jack's gaze at her back.

☽ ☆ ☾

The cold water now lay still in the sink. With his hands resting on the edge, Will leaned slightly over it, his eyes fixed on the clear surface, his body tense. Will no longer knew whether he had been staring into the water for hours or just a few minutes, maintaining his concentration.

"A relaxed mind that resonates with the vibrations around it is an agile mind and has the ability to overcome the limits of consciousness", Will heard his mother's voice and he had to stop himself from turning round or looking for her face in the mirror above him. He knew she wasn't really there, but he felt her presence so strongly around him that it wouldn't have surprised him if she had been. Will exhaled

deeply and let the tension flow through his arms into his hands and from there, through his skin, to the solid ceramic of the sink. Will's thoughts became calmer and the surface of the water seemed to come towards him. It came a little closer and a little further. And as Will gazed into the water, almost in a trance, it seemed to him that the surface darkened and he could see deeper than the bottom.

Will didn't know whether he really heard the voices or just thought he heard them. The shadowy figures whizzing through the water drew him deeper and then an acrid odour rose to his nose. He heard the crackling of fire, heard screams. Distorted, filled with fear. Screams of death.

Will wanted to pull away, out of this trance, but his hands would not let him go and bound him in these depths. He could already feel himself beginning to lose the connection to his body and he scolded himself, playing with such things, but he knew he needed to know more.

He had seen it coming in his dreams; had seen April lying on a stone floor, her eyes closed and a pool of blood spreading around her head like a red flower. The fires around Will were burning and he heard the screams. People were running around in panic, ducking away under explosions and there at the end of the square the pyres were burning. Will stumbled towards them, saw the women and girls tied to stakes and the fire eating away at them. None of them cried or screamed. Their eyes were fixed on the sky, their spirits had long since crossed over into another realm. Will heard someone call his name. He turned round. A rider, cloaked in a darkness, was coming towards him on a night-black horse. Someone pulled Will out of the way, his grip ironclad around his elbow.

"Will!"

He tried to turn towards the person, but the smoke from the fires stung his eyes. He could feel the tears gathering. He wanted to help the others, untie them and free them from the fires, but the grip on his arm was merciless, holding him tight.

"Will! Damn you! Can you hear me?"

He lifted his head slowly, his vision blurred by tears. The sky above him was grey, blackened with soot, no sign of the sun. And as if rain was falling, Will's eyes overflowed with the accumulated tears and he closed his eyes.

"Will! You idiot, look at me!"

Someone shook him and slowly Will felt his body again. He blinked and lifted his head. He saw Jack's distressed face, the whitewashed walls of the washroom, the neon light above them, flickering.

"Jack?" croaked Will, and Jack breathed a sigh of relief.

"I..." Will began to speak and then collapsed in Jack's arms.

☽ ☆ ☾

Ginger was the last person to leave the church after the evening mass. She had her hands buried deep in her pockets. The Hail Mary was still echoing inside her. She had looked upwards, trying to find an answer in the paintings above her. She had looked at April, who was standing next to her in the pew, her face closed, her attention turned inwards. Jack and Will had been standing on the other side, Jack facing forwards, Will leaning slightly forward bent on the pew in front of them. He looked pale but determined. Ginger knew that the other two had already made their decision. The priest's voice had echoed through the church vault and Ginger had looked up at the saints. Beautiful, gentle and merciless, they had stared down at Ginger, the way they have looked at her since she could remember.

She was standing again in the pew next to her mother, brothers, sisters, her cousins, listening to the sermon, her father's voice, the priest of their little community, echoing from all around, all the while Ginger could feel her heart beating in her chest, a wild animal, caged and angry, that wanted to break free. Her mother had always told Ginger that she had a wild heart, like she did, her grandmother and the women that came before her. Ginger had never understood what her mother wanted to tell her. What did it meant to have a wild heart? Ginger had asked her once and then her mother had told her a story, about how her great-

great-grandmother had been saved from a dark and gruesome destiny, because one of the elders had pitied her. He took her in, married her and she was then taught the ways of God and that had saved her soul from eternal damnation and fires of hell.

"What kind of dark destiny?" Ginger had asked, and her mother had sighed.

"The one that comes with having a wild heart. It's not safe to have a heart like this, thus we must keep going to church, keep the Lord's name in our prayers and ask for forgiveness for all our sins."

"What sins did I commit?" little Ginger had asked.

"Nothing, my darling, not yet. Therefore, you must pray to not be led into temptation. Speak your prayer now, darling Ginger. Let's pray together and all will be well..." Her mother's voice still echoed in Ginger's thoughts and her mind automatically recited the Lord's prayer.

Our Father, who art in heaven, hallowed be Thy Name, Thy kingdom come...

During today's mass Ginger's gaze had been lost in the colours and the golden reflections of the candlelight, the sounds of the singing had merged with them and Ginger had looked ahead, her eyes full of tears.

Thy Will be done, on earth as it is in Heaven.

But she had seen no altar, only the flickering light of the candles. Their light had made the stained-glass windows blink open, letting Ginger know that a night filled with life awaited her outside, and just as suddenly, Ginger had felt a longing in her chest for the vastness of the highlands of her homeland. For the smell of the wilderness, the wind in her hair. Ginger had seen some of the girls in her class kneeling with their heads bowed in prayer, their hair covered by shawls and veils, just like hers, and in that same moment Ginger had known that she never wanted to bow to another again. Her freedom and the freedom of all people would always come first for her. And as Ginger walked to the portrait of Mary, she knew that the other three would already be waiting there for her.

And forgive us our trespasses, as we forgive those who trespass against us. And lead us not into temptation but deliver us from the evil one.

Jack was leaning with one shoulder against the wall, April with her back next to him. Will had sat down on the stone floor of the cloister and only lifted his eyes from the flagstones when Ginger stopped in front of them. April smiled and exchanged a quick glance with Jack. Ginger held out her hand to Will and pulled him to his feet, not without noticing that although April's attention was back on Ginger, Jack's eyes were still on April. He smiled contentedly and it was only when he noticed Ginger looking at him and saw her raised eyebrows, that he narrowed his eyes and turned his gaze to the herb garden. Jack slowly crossed the corridor and stepped between two pillars that separated the cloister from the garden. The night above them was dark and hung heavy over the monastery. And as Jack looked up at the sky, the first snowflakes began to fall.

For thine is the kingdom, power and glory.

Fucking Amen.

Chapter 5

The Price of Blood

"Is it burning? or is it my life which must begin again?"
– Marina Tsvetaeva, from Bride of Ice: New Selected Poems; Poem of the End

The sun had already disappeared behind the cityscape although their lesson had only just ended. For a week now did the four met up after classes to continue their research on the phenomena they had witnessed in the church. After they had agreed to embark on this journey together, Jack had led Ginger, Will and April to the underground archive he had spoken of. It had taken them an hour to get there. Not only was it rather far away from the school but also deep below the usual tunnels the alchemists used to navigate through the catacombs. April had noticed that Ginger breathed more heavily with every tunnel and shaft, every ladder they took that led them deeper and lower, until even April had the impression of the earth pressing in on her from all sides.

"I don't know what you expected," Jack had sighed when he saw the faces of the other three. "The archive was meant to stay hidden." And indeed, what the archive contained better remained hidden: there had been hundreds of books about old alchemical teachings, books about wild herbs, grimoires and other rather witchy things. But there had also been stacks of bibles, old Slavic church books, musical scores for organ and philosophical scriptures in Hindi. There had been so many more things, hidden in the shadows and April would have liked to take more time to explore everything, but they had agreed on taking only as many books as they were able to carry and get back to the monastery as quick as possible.

That night they were lucky and didn't ran into any of the teachers who were patrolling the corridors since that incident in the city on the day of the Velvet Revolution. There were rumours about who the rebels were, but none of them were caught and the authorities were still searching for them. The apprentices who had experienced the riot first-hand had been questioned not only by their peers but also their teachers who then forwarded that information to the elders of the guild and the police. April, Will, Ginger and Jack had also been interviewed but none of them mentioned anything about the bloody letters on the church floor. But ever since then, the four had been extra careful. They hid the books they had taken from the archive in a room just under the roof in the west wing of the monastery. No one ever went up there and thus the four had installed themselves rather cosily in a corner. They had brought up a small heater, notebooks and biscuits. After class they went to the kitchen to make some tea that they would take upstairs with them in flasks that kept the tea warm. Then they would usually work until curfew, or rather a couple minutes before that, so that they would reach their dormitories just in time.

April enjoyed those long evenings, researching and reading, letting her gaze wander over to her brother, dark brown hair falling into his eyes, the brows slightly knitted, or over to Ginger, who moved her lips when she read silently about archaic blood rituals. And then there was of course also Jack, and though April tried not to look at him too often, she couldn't help it. She had so many questions that she wanted to ask him. But whenever Jack looked at her, when he had caught her staring, his eyes asking *what?* April simply lowered her head, eyes trained on the pages in front of her.

This evening was no different, except for Will, who was missing, since he had felt unwell since lunch and had gone to bed early. Even Ginger looked paler then usual and April was worried her friend might get sick as well. And so, while April was brooding over the question of how Jack had actually found the archive without them noticing it until he had told them about it, her attention slid over to Ginger, who leaned her head against the wall, eyes closed.

"Ginger? You alright?"

"Just tired," the redhead murmured and opened her eyes again. April and Jack exchanged a quick glance.

"Maybe it's better if we all go to bed," Jack suggested, and April agreed. They passed by the kitchen, where they brewed tea for Will and Ginger. April and

Ginger agreed to meet in the dormitory, since April wanted to check on her brother, before going to sleep, and so she followed Jack through the corridors to where the boys had their quarters. Most of the young men were still hanging out in the common room and thus the dormitory was fairly empty, with the exception of Cynlaef who laid on his bead with headphones, eyes closed and not taking any notice of them.

April knelt next to Wills bed. She gently touched her brother's forehead, which was indeed rather warm and a fine layer of sweat graced his skin. April looked at Jack worriedly.

"I think he has a fever," she murmured and watched as Jack stepped next to her. He bent over Will, touching his forehead, then his neck and nodded.

"Seems like it."

"Do you think we should call the nurse?"

"Maybe just let him sleep. It usually helps. If it gets worse over night, I shall take him over to the infirmary first thing in the morning."

"Thank you." April nodded in agreement. She caressed her brother's cheek so gently, Jack had to turn away, too intimate was it to watch them. He heard how April kissed Will, then stood up.

"I am worried about him," she whispered and as Jack turned towards her, he saw fear in her eyes.

"He'll be fine. Don't worry," Jack said quietly. After a moment of hesitation, he stepped closer and brushed a strand of hair behind her ear. "You really must love him so much," Jack then said, his hand lingering one moment too long on April's cheek to be casual.

"I love him more than I could ever put into words," she answered softly, her eyes interlocked with Jacks, who felt his heart speeding up. Those eyes. Those terrible, wonderful, dark eyes. And this girl… This *woman*… She consumed his every thought, and he feared the consequences. The impact it had on his mission, let alone April herself. And yet – he could not look away. Didn't want to.

"The bond between twins is unique," April continued, finally breaking eye contact. Her gaze came to rest on Will's face. There was so much love in her eyes and Jack wished she would look at him like that. Just for a brief moment. Just for a second. He would give everything for her to look at him like that.

"I don't think many people understand the kind of relationship twins share," she murmured. "You know, if I had to kill myself so that Will could live, I would do it without hesitation, without any second thought. I don't care about my own life if it comes to him. *Gladly*, I would kill myself if it meant that he would live on."

"Those are rather sombre thought for such a late hour, don't you think?" Jack interrupted her softly. He then touched April's shoulder and let his hand slid down her arm, to her wrist. He tucked gently and April understood. They left the tea on Will's nightstand and Jack led April out of the dormitory.

"I'll look after him," Jack reassured her after another look into April's worried face.

"I know you will," she said with a faint smile. "Thank you, Jack and…sleep well. I'll see you tomorrow in class."

"Yeah, good night." And while April made her way back to her own dormitory, Jack turned round and made his way to the washrooms.

When did he start to care about her? Catching feelings was worse than catching a cold, and if Jack didn't tread carefully, he would be knee-deep in shit far too soon. Unless he willed his heart to become cold as ice, the moment he betrayed that little trust she had in him, he wasn't sure if he was willing to pay the price of a bleeding heart.

While April and Jack had checked up on Will, Ginger made her way back to the girl's dormitory. On her way there she bumped into Sergei. She was on kitchen duty tomorrow morning, and she was tired, and her head was spinning, and she wasn't really in the mood to deal with anyone. But because she was raised with manners, she swallowed her annoyance and bad mood.

"Oh, hello, Ginger! I'm glad to find you here!"

"Sergei, what's up?" Ginger said courtly, trying to smile. She wasn't sure if she looked convincing.

"Not much. I haven't seen you guys at dinner," Sergei answered, pushing his hands into his pockets. Dear Lord, he looked nervous, much in contrast to his usual collected demeanour.

"We were studying," Ginger answered, tilting her head. Sergei nodded and began chewing on his underlip.

"Is there...anything else?" Ginger asked slowly, feeling a headache blooming at her temples. She felt like shit.

"Ehm, yes, honestly, I was looking for you and hoped that... Look, I... You know April pretty well, right?"

Ginger's lips curled into a grin. "Well enough," she answered, trying to hide the smile.

"Yeah, so...I was worr...I mean, *wondering*, if by any chance, you would know if she... You know, like... Do you know if April...?"

"Has a boyfriend?" Ginger interrupted him, taking in Sergei's wide eyes with satisfaction. She snorted. "Oh, come on," she said and shook her head. "Everyone knows you're into her. You have been pining after her for years now!"

"Everyone? I thought I had been subtle about it."

"No, it was pretty obvious. Except for April. But you know her. She's in her own little world in which she has only eyes and ears for her brother and my gorgeous self of course."

"Then...she doesn't have a boyfriend?"

"No. Did you hear it from Luke?" Ginger sneered, as she saw Sergei's face. "You know Luke, he was probably just pissed because she rejected him and thought he would spread some nasty rumours about her."

"So, you did hear them as well?"

"Sure, I did. Even April knows about them, but guess what, she doesn't really bother. Why should she? If you want my personal opinion: just ask her out. Be upfront. That way she won't miss it, alright?"

"Okay," Sergei nodded, and Ginger heard him breathe out. "Thank you, for…telling me. That was very kind of you."

"Anytime." Ginger already turned to leave as Sergei's voice held her back.

"Oh, and Ginger? I am sorry about calling you a Valkyrie. Really. Cynlaef called me out on it the other day. Said it was awfully impolite not only towards you, since you're Scottish and all, but also in regards of those who have Norse ancestry. As you may know, he's grandparents came from Iceland and apparently, he has some Viking blood or something. Therefore, I am really sorry."

"Don't worry," Ginger waved it away. "I mean, there are many Scottish people with Norse ancestry, it's not as unusual since Danes had invaded and occupied the Isles for decades."

"Oh, I didn't know that. So…do you have Viking ancestry?"

"Me?" Ginger laughed. "Oh, no. You don't get it more Scottish than my clan. We are real Scots. We are the worst among our kind. Although, I wouldn't mind having Norse ancestors. Did you know, that if a Viking woman was pissed off by her husband, she was allowed to cut off is balls and pin them to a wall? And if he treated her badly, she could get a divorce anytime and the shame was on him. They were rather progressive! Especially compared to how women are treated by the law nowadays in regards of marriage, childbirth, abortion and what not." Sergei laughed now too.

"No, I certainly didn't know that. I guess, I have to ask Cynlaef about it. Thank you, you truly made my day with this information! And of course, also for helping me in regards of April. Really."

"My pleasure."

And with that the two bid each other good night, and Ginger took the stairs that led up to the girl's dormitory. She had a proper headache now. She was tired and her limbs felt awfully heavy. She would be sick, she could feel it, and she was sure as hell that it was in that bloody underground archive that she and Will had picked up something nasty, that now was flowing through her system. She made a mental note to cuss Jack out for it later. But now, she *really* needed some sleep.

☽ ☆ ☾

The next day it was just April and Jack meeting at their usual spot in the cloister after classes. Both Ginger and Will had been confined to the infirmary, and after a quick check up, Jack and April headed to the greenhouse for today's classes. April was put into a group with Sergei, who first asked about Will and Ginger and when April told him they were ill, he said he would check up on Will before going to bed and April thanked him for it.

"That's very kind of you," she murmured and began to fill a pot with fresh earth.

"Don't mention it," Sergei said grabbing the seedlings and waited until April had filled up the pot. While he then gently pushed in some of the seeds, April felt his gaze on her.

"What?" She asked and raised her eyebrows.

"Nothing. Am I not allowed to look at you? You're pretty, that's all."

April snorted. "You better focus on what you're doing instead of talking nonsense."

"You don't think you're pretty?" Sergei only asked and put down the bag of seedlings, while grabbing another pot.

"I don't think that it is of any importance. Besides, beauty fades, there's nothing eternal in that."

"My mother usually says that it is person's soul that makes them look pretty."

"So, you want to say I have a pretty soul?" April pursed her lips.

"I think you have a beautiful soul and a good heart," Sergei answered, without responding to her sarcastic tone.

"You don't even know me well enough to say something like this," April sighed and refilled another empty pot. "You think I have a good heart when in reality I might be full of bad surprises."

"I do love a challenge," Sergei said with a smile and his eyes blinked. April chuckled lightly, shaking her head.

"What's that even supposed to mean…"

"Five minutes till the end of the lesson!" Mrs Hawthorn's voice rang over to them and cut Sergei short who had opened his mouth to reply something. April turned her back on him and began to tidy up their workspace. Once she returned to the table where Sergei had cleaned up, he handed April her books which she then grabbed, but he held onto them, forcing April to look at him.

"I wanted to say that I am sure those sides of you that you don't like are as loveable as the rest of you and I would love to get to know you better. That's all. And maybe, along the way, I shall prove you that you *do* have a good heart, even though you do not seem to believe it yourself!" Sergei let go of April's books and turned round, stepping next to Cynlaef who was already waiting for him in the entrance. April just stared at them as they left the greenhouse, her books strangely heavy in her hands as she made her way back to the monastery.

April groaned and buried her face in her hands, breathing deeply in an out, the scent of hundreds of books surrounding her. One of the main reasons she liked to work in the library. Maybe the main reason.

Jack looked up from his homework.

"You all right?" he asked, lowering his pen.

"I don't know," April grumbled against her hands. Jack raised his eyebrows and closed the book he had been leafing through.

"I can listen to you if you want," he said. "I'm a poor substitute for Will and an even poorer substitute for Ginger when it comes to problems that demand the wisdom of a woman, but...I've got time and I'm here for you."

April stilled, then lifted her head and slid all the way back against the back of the chair and drew her legs up. Jack had also leant back and was looking at her expectantly.

"I don't even know where to start," April mumbled and sighed.

"Somewhere is always good. No matter where," said Jack.

April cleared her throat.

"Hm... so, what do you think of Sergei Ivanov?" she asked, squinting at Jack, who was sitting opposite her. He looked at her in surprise. Why was April asking about Sergei? Was she interested in him?

"What I think about him in general?" Jack asked and April nodded. He was silent for a few moments.

"Well, he's perfectly alright," Jack then said. "As far as I can tell, he's a decent guy, performs well in class and his friends only have good things to say about him. His family is well off and he's respected and recognised in the society of Petersburg. I consider him a friend."

April frowned at these words.

"Why do you ask?"

"Not much," she answered. "He spoke to me today. In class."

"Which is nothing special, since he often talks to you, right?" Jack asked. April shrugged her shoulders.

"I thought so too, but he just said that he wouldn't mind getting to know me better. And I don't get it. He went on about how he thinks I have a good heart and pretty soul or whatever."

Jack chuckled. "Really? He said that?"

April looked angrily at Jack. "Yeah, what the hell is so funny about it?" Jack was still grinning.

"Oh, nothing in particular, just that you didn't understand anything Sergei was actually trying to tell you."

"Are you saying that I'm too stupid to understand what some guy was saying to me?"

"No," Jack sighed deeply. "That's not what I wanted to say. Of course not. I meant, that you didn't understand what Sergei said to you *indirectly*."

"And what was that?"

"He wants to go out with you! He fancies you! Whatever. Something like that." Jack looked directly at April and watched her facial expressions, not without amusement. At first her eyes widened, surprised, then shocked. She opened her mouth to say something, then shut it again. Then she looked at Jack uncertainly.

"I don't believe that. Not Sergei."

"And why not?"

"Because it's *Sergei*! That's not possible! It's absurd! We've been classmates for years!"

Jack raised his shoulders. "Nothing is impossible," he said.

April was still looking at him doubtfully.

"And you surely know that he fancies me?" April followed up. Jack pulled up the right corner of his mouth.

"It's obvious. Everyone who's friends with him thinks you're great, by the way."

April raised her eyebrows. "*All* his friends?" she asked, now looking Jack straight in the eye. Slightly amused, slightly provoking and slightly tense.

"I don't know," Jack then replied and tilted his head, making sure to avoid the question as skilfully as possible. "But Sergei for sure! Andrei, Vadik and Neil too. But they'll let Sergei go first."

"That sounds awfully weird and certainly isn't what I wanted to know," said April, raising her hands in defence. Then she groaned slightly and buried her face in her hands.

"That's totally stupid," April murmured and stared at her still empty paper.

"Does it surprise you that much that guys find you attractive?" Jack then asked, leaning forward. "That you're likable? Loveable?"

"Fuckable?"

"I didn't say that."

"But that's what all guys think," April said dryly and crossed her arms.

"Maybe. But would that be so bad? To be *desired*?" Jack replied, raising an eyebrow.

"I don't want a random men's unasked attention. I like to have some say in that."

"Then someone's attention in particular?"

April didn't answer. She bit her lip and stared out of the window. Only the slight arch of her brows revealed that she was upset, maybe even a little pissed. Oh, she was indeed beautiful when she was angry. Jack hid his smile yet did not take his eyes of her. He didn't tell her that he had overheard the whole conversation in the greenhouse. How Sergei had smoothly paved his way with words towards April's unbreachable walls that she held up ever so carefully, not letting anyone in. But by the way he had seen her react to his question, Jack dwelled in the thought that maybe, just maybe he himself had gotten under her skin with his own words.

"Come on, April, Sergei likes you and the only reason he's being cautions is because you blew off Luke Harris."

"Yeah, another guy who thinks I am just some pretty girl."

"But you are pretty," Jack replied. "Although I'd rather describe you as beautiful. And you're sure no longer a girl."

April's eyes snapped back to him, but Jack did not avert his eyes. For the brink of a moment, he let her see all the desire she evoke in him, all the sinful thoughts he had about her about all the ways he wanted her. Just for a second.

"I think you should date him," Jack then said into the electric silence that had built up between the two of them. April squinted her eyes in surprise.

"What? Why should I?"

"Because he likes you and he's a good man. I think he's good for you."

April snorted disdainfully. "Good. Why is it always *good*? What if I don't want *good*?"

"What is it then that you want?" He looked at her, challenging her to say what he wanted to hear. To admit to the things he knew about her, the things she hid so well even from her brother. And he wanted her to say the words that would give voice to his very own thoughts too. Words that would awake all those fantasies and dreams he had about her, ever since his lips had touched that pretty neck of hers.

They stared at each other in silence.

"I didn't ask for any of this," April murmured, finally averting her eyes.

"We rarely ask for what life throws at us yet still we have to deal with it."

They were silent for a while, Jack not taking his eyes off April.

"I guess you're right. With everything," April said slowly, her fingers drew invisible circles on the blank paper in front of her. "Maybe I should go out with Sergei. Let him treat me like a princess, be real nice and sweet to me." She lifted her eyes, staring right into his. A soft smile tugging at the corner of her mouth. She bit her lower lip to keep herself from grinning. "I bet he knows exactly how to make me feel really good."

"If that's your idea of fun," Jack answered, a wicked smile curling his lips, which did not escape April's notice. *Two can play at this game, princess*, he thought and let his gaze wander over her appearance. The dark hair, the faint blush on her cheeks, her collar bones – and lower. For a brief second, he closed his eyes, licked his dry lips while he imagined tracing his teeth over the soft skin of her abdomen. A second later he stood up abruptly and looked directly into April's face, who had raised her eyebrows.

"What about doing something that's actually fun?" Jack asked and closed the button of his jacket.

"Like what?" April stared at him and Jack wasn't sure if he read curiosity or hunger in her eyes.

Without a word, Jack scooped up all their papers and books, then he put a finger to his lips, motioning her to be quiet. With a quick glance around the library to make sure all the other students were busy, and no one was paying any attention to them, he waved April to follow him.

April didn't know exactly why she had followed Jack without thinking. It was probably his demanding demeanour and dominant character that shut down those parts of her brain that usually functioned properly. They just didn't seem to work around him. April wasn't sure if she was angry, upset or thrilled when she followed Jack through the catacombs and a handful of shafts that led them directly to Apollinaire, that one church that had revealed such bloody miracles that have been the subject of their research ever since.

"We shouldn't be here," she mumbled.

"You've said that for the twentieth time now," Jack sighed as he made his way to the altar.

"It doesn't make it less true," April grumbled and followed him reluctantly. "What are we doing here anyways?"

"I thought it would be nice to get some more material to work on," Jack answered as he rounded the last bench and stepped next to the basin with the holy water.

"Material? What do you mean?"

"Unless you had been able to memorise all the symbols on the floor last time, I thought it would be a good idea to make them appear a second time and take some pictures. We could then use those to translate the symbols, and then figure out what they mean."

"And how do you want to do that?" April crossed her arms in front of her chest and watched as Jack walked up and down, scrutinising the floor, looking for whatever he was looking for, while April thought he was acting unnecessarily mysterious, with that serene look on his face, his black cloak billowing around him.

God, she hated that he looked this handsome.

She still observed his every move while he walked over to a small, wooden door near the altar, which he then locked with a chain that he pulled out of a pocket, whilst April looked on with wide eyes.

"Where did you get that chain from? Is that another one of your precautionary measures you carry around like the bandages last time?" April sneered, concealing her surprise. Jack walked back to the portal of the church where he installed another chain, locking the doors so that no one would be able to enter the church. While Jack made his way back to where April was standing, he let his gaze wander across her face and down her body. April's face flushed lightly.

"You might be surprised in how many ways chains can be used, although I do prefer other precautionary measures while using them."

"I have no idea whether you're joking or actually mean what you're implying," April said and clenched her teeth. Oh, boy, that man wasn't good for her nerves. And her body was an evil traitor.

"What am I implying, April?" Jack murmured, halting in front of her, his eyes bored into hers. April felt all air being sucked from her lungs, as Jack stood so closely and all of his body seemed to vibrate, his aura electrifying and she, drawn to it like a moth to flame. One day she would burn herself.

April turned round and brought some physical distance between them.

"And how did you plan on getting those pictures?" April asked, without answering Jacks dangerous question.

"Oh, I thought we would simply recreate what happened last time."

"You want me to draw blood?" April asked with a frown.

"I could do it for you, if you want," Jack offered and pulled out a knife. April stared at it. What else did he had hidden within the folds of his clothes? More weapons? Poison? Red roses? It could be anything.

"You want to hurt me?" April asked with a slight tremble in her voice, while she lifted her eyes from the blade and looked into Jack's eyes, and somehow, she wasn't entirely sure, if he wouldn't actually hurt her.

"I know how to inflict pain on someone in ways that it is pleasurable. And I'm pretty sure you'd be into knife play." Jack's dark voice washed over and through April and she willed herself not to look away from those all-consuming eyes of his. Didn't want to.

And for the second time that day, she thought to see some kind of hunger reflected in them. An appetite for something, that April wasn't sure she was willing to give in while all her body screamed to do so.

"Give me the knife," April said hoarsely and stretched out her hand. Jack immediately placed the blade gently on her palm, his fingers brushing her skin. With steady hands, April lifted the blade and drew it across her palm, the biting pain a welcomed relief, as it distracted her from the heat that was gathering in her middle and the wetness between her leg.

I'm pretty sure you'd be into knife play.

She watched, mesmerised, as the blood flowed from the cut in her skin and the red liquid collected in her palm. She felt that Jack guided her to the communion chalice that stood on the altar, watched the blood drop into it and then the symbol emerging at the bottom of the cup.

A second later Jack clasped April around her waist and lifted her onto the altar. A small gasp escaped her lips. What the…? She was now seated right next to the cup, staring at Jack breathlessly, heat waves flooding her veins, as he stepped between her knees. Suddenly, she felt exposed. And she was so fucking wet. Holy shit. Her thoughts were anything *but* holy. April didn't know if she would ever recover from how Jack had grabbed her waist and lifted her up onto that altar so effortlessly.

"We need to get that cut fixed," Jack murmured, a blink of an eye later, he had a gauze bandage in his hands. He gently wrapped the fabric around April's hand, tugging the ends neatly in and planted a soft kiss on the bandaged back of her hand. Jack was still standing between April's thighs and as he looked up at her, she noticed that she could now look directly into his eyes, their faces on the same level. Was he that tall? April had never realised it.

"Ready?" Jack breathed softly but before she could ask ready for what, he grabbed the chalice and then emptied it all over the stone surface. Blood spread around Jacks feet, licking its way across the floor, down the steps, forming into loops, lines and symbols. It was only now that April realised that Jack had lifted her onto the altar, to keep her own shoes clean. Within seconds, Jack snapped a few of pictures of the bloody letters and symbols that covered the stone floor with a camera. Wherever this thing had come from…

April looked around her: she sat in the middle of a mosaic of blood, consisting of symbols and signs, bursting with archaic energy, in the same way the skulls did in the Bone Church. April thought she could hear them whisper; the signs murmured something into her ear, that she did not understand yet felt she had known for a very long time. A tugging at her memory, words of a language never learned yet so familiar. April stared and stared and only when she heard another snap of

Jack's camera, did she lift her head. The lens was pointed at her. He slowly lowered his hands.

"Did you just take a picture of me?" April asked, the whispers gone the same moment.

"Yes," Jack answered simply, still looking at her.

"Why?" April managed to say.

"Because you look beautiful sitting on that altar. You look like an angel of death or the queen of night with that face and all that blood around you." And the same moment Jack had spoken those words, images, that April had seen in dreams, flashed before her mind. She once again saw the church, a sea of blood all over the floor, sitting on that throne made of bone, Jacks voice purring softly in her ears, while she stared into his eyes, his face hidden behind an animal's skull, its horns looming over April's head.

"What will it be, the crown or the pyre?" the voice whispered again, and April took a step back, away from the figure with Jack's voice, away from the throne, shaking her head, trying to back away further, stepping into nothingness.

With a panicked gasp, April slipped from the altar, stumbling, but before she could hit the floor, Jack grabbed her by the arms, making sure she didn't fall. April's heart pounded wildly in her chest and with horror in her eyes she looked at Jack.

"What...?" Did he begin, but April tore herself away, faintly realising that the blood had vanished between the cracks of the floor, leaving the stone surface as clean and cool as before.

"Whatever is happening here, I want it to stop!" She hissed, backing away. Her back met the wall, her legs trembling. "Whatever kind of shit you're trying to get access to, I don't want it," April rasped, shaking her head.

"It's okay," Jack said slowly, taking a step into her direction. "What did you see? What did you hear?"

April's eyes darted into all directions, that creeping sense of being watched, observed, elicited a tingle in her neck that she wanted to shake off. She wanted to scream, shout, let all those feelings escape from her lungs. Let those horrors vanish from her mind… She felt Jack's hands on her shoulders as he slowly wrapped his arms around her, pulling her into a gentle embrace.

"It's okay," he murmured again, one hand cradling the back of her head. She took a sharp breath – then allowed herself to lean in, nestling her cheek on his chest, listening for a heartbeat, inhaling his scent – sea air, pine forests and first snow. She took another deep breath.

"You're going to think I am crazy," April finally whispered in response. "That I am some sort of *freak*."

Jack pushed her a little away from him, so that he could look her in the face.

"No, April, I would never think that. If anything, I believe you're *gifted*."

April lifted her gaze, looking into his clear eyes. It was unusual for someone from Romania to have blue eyes like this, April thought, realising at the same time, that although she knew that Jack had visited a school in Walachia previously, she had no idea about his actual origins. He had a Russian accent but his name… *Rosier*. Wasn't that originally a French surname even though Jack pronounced it in an English way? Maybe he was a mixture of many countries across Europe, with his Eastern European features dominating his face, just like Will and April's.

"It's a dream I had," she said quietly, her voice trembling lightly, not taking her eyes from Jacks face. The face of an angel, kissed by death. A marble king, knight of darkness, alchemist prince. A beautiful man with a vicious sparkle in his eyes, whenever he curled his lips in that devious way of his. But right now, his lips weren't drawn into one of those wicked smiles, that made him look like the devil himself. Especially with that challenging gleam in his eyes, daring April to give in to the darkness that radiated all around him and had drawn her in from the very first moment. Right now, those two pools of Northern seas looked at her with such sincerity and openness, so much honesty, that April could feel the tears prickling in her eyes.

"What kind of dream?" Jack asked softly, lifting his hand, touching her cheek ever so lightly. A shiver ran down April's spine and for a brief second, she closed her eyes.

"A dream I had before. I saw it again. Just now. The church submerged in red water or...blood. And then there is this throne were usually the altar sits. And there are pyres being erected in the nave of the church. I am led to the throne and am offered...a crown." April's voice trailed off, as she once again saw the images that had flashed through her mind. "And then there is someone," April whispered, now looking away from Jack, no longer able to meet his gaze, not when she could still hear his voice in her ear. That voice that came from the person hidden beneath the animal skull. "He tells me to choose between the crown and the pyres. But I can't. For it is either death or selling my soul to the devil and thus eternal damnation."

"How do you know you would be selling your soul to the devil?"

"I can feel him," April said, her voice not even a whisper.

"But believing in a devil means to believe in a god," Jack said quietly, taking in April's face once more. "And you said to me that you don't believe in a heavenly father."

"Does there need to be a god to make sense of the devil?" April asked, drawing her gaze back at Jack.

"Could it be a demon then?" Jack asked, tilting his head.

"A demon? As in *angels and demons?*"

Jack nodded. April bit her bottom lip thoughtfully.

"Maybe. But if it is a demon, what does it want?"

"What all demons do."

"And that is?"

"Didn't the bible teach you that?" Jack asked and then there was that smile again. Mocking, cryptic, deflecting. "*And lead us not into temptation, but deliver us from evil,*" he murmured, while tugging a strand of April's dark hair back behind her ear.

"What about angels then?" April asked, her breath hitching as his fingers touched the skin of her neck, searing like fire.

"They usually are here to help and guide us. They are part of our path to salvation. But remember, demons were once angels too. And so was Lucifer."

The tension between them seemed to magnify with each breath April took, heat radiating from her flushed skin, soaking in all the electricity emanating from Jack. She wanted to devour him.

"We should go back," April said instead, stepping away from him, her heart racing.

Almost. She had almost given in, knowing well enough that she shouldn't. She may have told Jack about the visions she had seen, but she was smart enough not to tell him that she knew, that they were a warning too. The demon behind the skull had spoken with Jack's voice.

No. She wouldn't give into him.

And though she wanted to know what it would taste like to kiss him, what it would feel like to drown in his darkness and that magnetic energy of his, that seared through her like lava, she was still clear enough in her head to keep that distance between them. She was known to be a rational person and she wouldn't overthrow all of her logical thinking and instincts, only to get a taste of what would probably consume her in the end. It didn't matter that Jack was the first that had been able to awaken those desires within her, that rushed through her veins. It didn't matter that he was the first one who seemed to see beneath the quiet surface, the calmness and innocence. It didn't matter how many implications he planted within his sentences, making the blood flow to April's middle in such a delicious way. No, she was a smart woman. She wouldn't give in. She may not have believed in a god, but that didn't mean she would give into temptation so easily. Sinners payed in one way or another. Even the angels had fallen from heaven.

Jack accompanied April back to the girl's dormitory, neither of them saying a word on their way back. It was long passed curfew and thus the two of them scurried as quietly as possible through the monastery, careful not to bump into any patrolling teachers.

"You will be okay?" Jack whispered nearly soundlessly as they halted in front of the door of the girl's dormitory.

"Yes, I'll be fine," April answered, trying a half-hearted smile. "I am used to bad dreams and weird visions like these by now."

Jack slightly shook his head, then taking April's bandaged hand into his and without any warning, he dropped to his knees.

"*What* are you doing?" April hissed in surprise, her eyes darting down the corridor. What if someone passed by? "Get up, Jack! What the…?"

"Thank you, April Blackwell," Jack interrupted her frantic whispering, his voice, subdued but loud enough that April was afraid someone would hear him. "I may not know enough about blood rituals to solve the riddle and mystery we're trying to decode at the moment, but…" He lifted his eyes to meet April's gaze and without averting his eyes, he pressed his lips onto the bandages, where it covered the cut that the blade had left in April's palm.

"I do know the price of blood," Jack continued, his eyes still locked on April's face. He slowly rose to his feet, cupping April's palm now with both his hands. "And I do not take this lightly. Thus, I thank you for sharing your blood. I will forever be indebted to you."

"You are no such thing!" April hated how meek her voice sounded, how much it trembled, confused about the things Jack had said, not sure how she was supposed to react. Jack once again lifted her hand up, but this time he kissed the back of it, then took it and laid it on his chest. His eyes interlocked with hers, April slowly spread her fingers and believed to feel Jack's racing heart through the fabrics of his clothes and bandages, knowing that *technically* it wasn't possible. Too many layers between them. Too far a distance that she longed to breach.

"You may not understand it now," Jack said softly, his gaze caressing her face ever so gently, and so much in contrast to how he usually looked at her, when he taunted her. So different to how he had looked at her when she had sat on the altar, his eyes basically piercing through her, not hiding the same insatiable hunger April felt in her own chest.

"But soon you will." And with that, he let go of her hand, turned round and left her in the moonlit corridor, the blueish shadows creeping at her from all sides. She still thought to feel Jacks heart beating beneath her fingertips and without wanting to, April lifted her hand to her lips, pressing her fingers onto the sensitive flesh and wished that Jack had kissed her lips instead.

Chapter 6

Separatio

"All people are driven to the point of eating their gods, after a time."
– Margaret Atwood, excerpt from Eating Snakes

Day was just dawning when April sat down at Will's bedside, the rosy colours of morning tinting the white walls of the infirmary, while she looked at her twin. As if he had sensed her presence, his eyes opened with a flutter and April couldn't help but smile as those beautiful dark eyes took her in. The same eyes that had looked at her with so much love all throughout her life. Her most favourite eyes in the world.

"How are you?" April whispered, gently touching Will's forehead. It was still hot, but cooler than the day before and she breathed an inaudible sigh of relief.

"Tired," Will murmured, reaching his own hands out and pulling his sister next to him into his bed. In an instant, April wrapped her arms around her brother and cuddled up to him. She rested her face on his chest, their breathes matching within a second and April was fairly sure that even their hearts were beating in sync.

"I've missed you," April heard her brother whisper into her ear, his breath caressing her cheek and as an answer she pressed herself even closer to him. April couldn't help the tears running down her cheeks.

"Hey," Will turned so that he could look into April's face. "What's going on? What happened? Talk to me." April nodded but the tears kept streaming down her face, and it took her a couple of minutes until she found her voice again.

"I think there is something terribly wrong with me, Will," April whispered, her breath jagged.

"What on earth could be wrong with you?"

"Do you remember the bad dreams I had all those years? And how I once told you there was someone else looking at me from the mirror?"

"I remember," Will said softly, stroking April's hair.

"It's the same kind of feeling again," she continued and sat up. She looked at Will, her eyes already rimmed red. "Whenever I look into the mirror it's like I am not seeing myself but someone else."

"And what if those two people are one and the same?" He asked cautiously, tilting his head.

"Then I fear I am a terrible person."

"Hush, you," Will said, pulling April back into his chest. "You are the most wonderful person I know," he murmured, planting kisses on her head. Then he looked into her face again, suddenly awfully serious. "You are my heart, April. Without you, I am nothing. All I ever was, is in you. You are forever part of the very fabric I am made of. You and I are the same. We are one and there is nothing and no one that could ever change that."

"You sure about that?" April sniffed again. Another tear escaped from the corner of her eye, which Will gently kissed away.

"Hundert percent sure. I promise."

She nodded slowly, kneading her fingers in her lap.

"I think I fell in love," April whispered. Weary she looked into her brother's face. But her fear was completely unfounded, for when she looked into Will's eyes, she saw that they had lit up and a broad smile graced his lips.

"This makes me happier than you could ever imagine," Will said, taking April's face between his hands, then kissed her forehead, her nose, her cheeks and her forehead again.

"You are not mad?"

"Why should I be mad?"

"Because…because…"

"Because you fear I will no longer love you? That I'll be jealous? April, for Christ's sake! All I wish for is for you to be happy! To be loved and love someone with all your heart!"

"It's not that easy," April tried to calm Will down. "I…am not completely sure about my feelings yet," she added when she saw the confusion on Will's face.

"I see," he murmured, but then grinned again. "I am happy for you nevertheless."

April smiled slightly, but in her heart, she felt a storm brewing as she tried to ignore the sinking feeling in her stomach as she realised what she had just confessed to her brother that she hadn't even been able to admit to herself.

"You are still the most important person in my life," April said, cuddling up to her brother who instantly wrapped his arms around her.

"I know," he murmured. "And you are still the most important person to me."

They didn't speak for a while and simply listened to each other's breathing, their hearts in unison, just as they had always done. At some point, April turned round and let her gaze wander around the infirmary.

"How's Ginger?" April asked quietly, as her eyes finally settled on a bush of red hair peeking from under a white duvet. A flowered quilt was spread over the blanket, apparently to keep the young woman warm underneath.

"She was feverish the whole night. Talked in her sleep, woke every hour, but never fully awake. Nightmares plaguing her. Around four in the morning the nurse gave her some potion. After that she fell asleep. She hasn't stirred since then."

"You think that potion was safe?"

"I hope so. Ginger went on and on about how Jack was responsible for us being sick, since she was sure we picked it up in the catacombs, whatever virus has us in a chokehold." Will chuckled and even April smiled.

"That sounds quite like her."

"Yeah. Did you two continued with our research?"

"Somewhat, yes," April answered reluctantly, still not having fully processed what had happened the night before.

"You want to elaborate or…"

"Rather not. Also, I need to get to get ready for classes," April sighed and got off the bed.

"Yeah, do that. I need someone with a brain to take notes for me since I am unable to attend class!" Will said with a wink and April snorted.

"You think you shall be well again for the weekend? Remember, it's the opera weekend and they are performing the Nutcracker!"

"I'll do my best," Will promised, knowing how much April loved those opera weekends they attended with their class and headteachers. April bent over her brother, kissed him on the forehead and left the infirmary with an air kiss, that Will captured playfully, eliciting a soft laugh from April.

☽ ☆ ☾

Ginger was haunted by nightmares. The fever didn't break until Friday evening and when she finally sat up, looking around the infirmary, she was chilled to the bone and felt as if all her organs had been shredded from the inside and someone had removed all muscles. She felt so weak. So tired. The nightmares still lingered behind her eyelids and in fear of them, she refused to fall asleep. Only when the nurse came, carrying a vial with some pretty strong sleeping potion, Ginger accepted and drank the bitter liquid. Carefully she lay back down, fearing that the whispers and screams of burning women on pyres would finally quiet. Ginger thought she could hear the voices of her friends from afar, April's laugh echoing from the walls while someone else was humming a soft tune. Was it her mother? Or was it the fever playing tricks on her mind? The instant Ginger laid down and was about to close her eyes, she saw a movement by the door. Ginger bolted up, knowing she should be the only one here and with horror she watched a barefooted girl, no, a young woman, hair flying lose, black dress with a white collar, slipping through the door, without even opening it. A sharp pain shot through Ginger's head and with a groan she fell back onto her pillow, feeling the pull of the potion and she once again slipped into sleep.

☽ ☆ ☾

Friday after mass, April sat in the pew for a while. Neither of the others had come, Ginger was still in the infirmary, while Will had gone to bed early, still weak from the illness. And Jack – Jack didn't show up at all. April had told the other girls to go ahead, as she wanted some time to think, and so she had been sitting on the hard wooden bench for over an hour, listening to the almost complete silence of the monastery church. April had closed her eyes, reviewing the past days and weeks.

They had made good progress with the subject matter and were also on schedule with the independent group work. The research for that took far less time than analysing the various signs and symbols, which they tried to translate with the help of the books from the underground archive. The difficulty was that there were several interpretations for each symbol and depending on the combination or context in which it was written, its meaning changed. In this respect, April was glad that she didn't have to grapple with the geometry and architecture of the buildings that bore these symbols like Will and Ginger did, or at least had been researching before they had fallen ill. She and Jack were both much better at translating and spotting the connections between things. April didn't know if what they were doing had any real bearing on their ability to begin to understand what they had found that November night and if they were truly onto finding a gate to hell, or whatever Jack hoped the symbols would reveal, but at least it gave her that sense of security that April always felt when she was lost down one rabbit hole of enquiry after another. And maybe at the bottom of one she would finally find her own Wonderland, or at least answers to some questions she had about life in general. And with a little luck – a small miracle itself.

In a fortnight' time, Will and April would be travelling home to their parents, where they would spend Christmas with her mother's family. Ginger would go back to Scotland, as she did every year, where her whole clan would gather to celebrate the birth of the Lord. And as April thought about the holidays, she wondered where Jack would be spending his winter break. April had no idea where his family resided, her mind once again weighing the possibilities of his heritage. She knew that he had previously attended a school in Romania, but she had no idea whether Jack had any family there. It was indeed a peculiar name for a Romanian family to have.

"Rosier," April whispered his name quietly into the church and let it roll off her tongue. She was just taking a breath to say the name again, a little louder, when the church door was opened, and an icy wave of winter air blew in. April turned round to see who had entered the building. Speaking of the devil.

Jack made his way to the front and sat down in the pew next to April, unbuttoning his coat with a soft sigh. April smelled the odours that filled the air in December: snow, wet earth clinging to boots, rotten leaves and smoke drifting from rooftop chimneys, as if the scents were attached to Jack himself.

December prince.

Jack glanced briefly at April from the side and April returned the look.

"Kenna says you're here to think," Jack said quietly, leaning back in the bench.

"Kenna?" April didn't like the soft stab of jealousy she felt, when he mentioned Kenna's name. Did the two of them spend time together? Had he been with Kenna while April had attended mass? April didn't recall having seen her among the other girls.

Jack nodded. His eyes wandered wearily over the altar and then back to April.

"I ran into her in the corridors, she told me where to find you."

"Where have you been?" April asked without responding to Jack's previous statement. He sighed softly and closed his eyes. He slowly let his head fall back until it came to rest on the edge. Jack stared at the brightly painted ceiling.

"Wasn't able to come," Jack replied evasively and closed his eyes.

"I see," April said, not meaning it in the slightest. But she also respected the fact that Jack didn't want to talk about it and so she changed the subject. She was not ready to dig into whatever was going on in Jack's head. Not after that weird incident the other night, as he had kneeled before her on the stone floor, his lips caressing her skin. Better she ignored what had happened all together, and as long as Jack didn't bring it up, neither would she.

"Are you going home for Christmas?" April asked, turning round on the pew so that she could lean sideways and look straight at Jack.

"No," came his reply and Jack opened his eyes again.

"May I ask why not?"

April's voice sounded hesitant and Jack heard how carefully and cautiously April said the words. He sat up again and then stared at his hands.

"Let's just say that I don't feel the need to see my father, grandfather or any of my other living relatives," he replied, looking at April with a faint smile.

"What about your mum?" April then asked quietly, trying to read in Jack's face what he wasn't saying.

"She's dead." Jack's jaw tightened.

"I'm sorry," April whispered, lowering her head. "I didn't know that."

"I never told you, did I?"

April looked at Jack. His eyes spoke of infinite sadness and she felt that the pain of losing his mother was still tearing him apart from within.

"How long ago?" April asked and then added hastily, "you don't have to tell me, of course, if you don't want to talk about her."

"No," Jack said hesitantly and looked briefly at April. "I mean, I don't mind talking about her. It's just that I never do, since I don't really have anyone, I want to talk to about her with. Don't worry though," Jack then said quickly when he saw April's face, "I don't mind with you." Jack smiled slightly and April returned the smile.

"She died five years ago. The doctors said she had consumption, which may be true, but I knew better. It wasn't the illness that killed her, but the environment she was in. It was poisoning her. Sucked all the life out of her over many years. So slowly and insidiously that by the time it was clear that she had been dying for years, it was too late."

Jack's hands trembled slightly, and April instinctively put her hands on them to stop the shaking. Surprised, he raised his eyes. His eyes met April's, she blushed and immediately pulled her hands away.

"What do you mean by her environment had poisoned her?" April asked quickly to cover the moment. Jack took note without comment and continued.

"My mother wasn't particularly happy in her marriage. She had married my father for financial reasons: her father, my other grandfather, had gone bankrupt and would have ended up on the street with the rest of his family if my mother hadn't agreed to the marriage. Because it was my father who proposed and who had fallen in love with her." Jack snorted briefly.

"I remember him saying to me after she died that he'd always known she wouldn't live long. He'd married her because she was so beautiful. His own father had advised him against it, but he hadn't listened. And then when they were both married, my mother would have started to show him her true face."

Jack felt the familiar anger flaring up inside him and he took a deep breath.

"He told me he should have listened to his father," Jack continued, his voice bitter and clenched. "He called her a *filthy witch*."

"That's cruel," April whispered.

"Yes. My father told me that my mother had cast a spell on him back then, so that he would marry her, and she could get his money. But you know what? Even if my mum only married him for that reason, it's his own fucking problem that he went for it. I knew my Mama. She never played games and she never fooled anyone. My father was just stupid and weak, and he still is to this day."

There was a crack and April looked down in horror at Jack's hands, fingers tangled together, causing the knuckles to crack again.

"Why did your father call your mother a witch?" April asked the question so quietly that Jack had trouble hearing her. He looked away, glanced at the altar, then at the paintings above them.

"It's almost curfew," Jack said instead of answering April's question and stood up. April sighed inwardly but nodded and stood up as well. Jack was already turning towards the church door when April's voice stopped him.

"Wait," April said and stepped forward.

Witch.

April still heard Luke's voice ringing in her head. Heard that one word in her nightmares and she wondered if Jack had thought of his mother that night Luke had called her that in the shadows of the convent walls. April looked at the altar for a few moments and then went to the table with the candles. Mindful and with

130

her thoughts on Jack's mother, she lit three of them. She remained there for a few seconds her gaze lost in the flames. Her heart ached for him. She felt sadness that Jack had lost his mother and that he harboured so much anger towards his father. A tear stole from the corner of April's eye and she wiped it away inconspicuously. Then she turned round and left the convent church at Jack's side.

It was freezing cold outside and the wind tore and tugged at their coats. April stopped briefly in the square and looked into the blackness above them. The sky was cloudy, and it smelled of snow. Jack had also stopped and looked at April, who was stretching her face towards the night sky above her. She breathed in and out deeply. Jack knew April well enough by now to know that she needed this moment to collect herself and surrender her thoughts to the night and wind, so that she could find peace and quiet again. And as Jack waited for April in the night, he wondered what April thought of him now that he had told her about his mother.

Well, April only knew what his father had said about Jack's mother and how she had withered away in that old mansion, but nothing about how she used to spend hours at Jack's bedside to chase away the bad dreams, or how she used to sing him the old songs of her homeland in a language that was not tolerated in the Rosier house. Or how Jack's mother had read to him from that old fairy tale book, with the eerie pictures of figures, the Bone King, the Midday Sun Witch and all those that put all the other scary stories he knew in the shade. And how his Mama then broke off mid-sentence, a coughing fit that shook her whole body and how she then pressed her hand over her lungs, smiling painfully at Jack and said:

"It's all right, don't worry, I'm fine, Jack."

He had known then that this was a lie, but for his Mama's sake he had nodded and kissed her on the cheek and then his mother had hugged him with tears in her eyes.

"Stay strong, my little Cossack," she had whispered gently to Jack, then put him back in bed and covered him up. And after all, April knew nothing about the horrific truth that his mother had confessed to him in the hours before her death. He turned his head and looked directly into April's face.

She stood next to him and looked at Jack expectantly. And as they stood there, just looking at each other for a few seconds, it began to snow. April raised her eyes to the sky and smiled.

"Let's go inside," she said, nodding towards the entrance. "It's getting really cold and we're far too late."

"Seems like it," Jack said, tearing himself away from the sight of April and how the snowflakes got caught in her dark hair and eye lashes.

They walked through the shadows to the entrance of the monastery, stepped inside and did their best to close the portal as quietly as possible. They walked silently through the corridor and then to the cloister. They didn't hurry, they were too late anyways. And as they walked along the arched windows, April suddenly stopped and listened. Jack did the same.

Footsteps echoed through a neighbouring corridor and alarmed, April looked at Jack. Soundlessly, Jack crossed the corridor and pulled April with him to a niche and pressed themselves into the shadow behind the statue of the Virgin Mary, which looked down benignly on anyone who passed by. It was completely dark in the corner, and a velvet curtain barely concealed the two of them. As April and Jack listened vigilantly to the approaching footsteps, they tried to breathe as shallowly and quietly as possible. And as they stood so close together, only a few centimetres separating them, their first encounter flashed through Jack's mind.

He remembered it clearly; hearing someone stumble into the confessional next to him, out of breath. He remembered the first time he had seen April in person and how her eyes had stared at him darkly. He had noticed her beauty straight away, but only now that he knew her better and she was even somewhat friends with him, did he realise that he really liked her and did not only desire her. April had quietly crept into his heart from that evening onwards and had found her way around all the closed doors that he had so carefully kept shut. It was her reserved and at the same time authoritative manner, the eyes that missed nothing and seemed to see deeper and deeper into his soul. Sometimes he even avoided looking at April directly, the fear that she could read what he was hiding from her was too great.

Everything she was not allowed to see.

With a painful pang in his chest, Jack thought of the letter he had received from his grandfather this morning. He urged Jack to hurry. Who knew how much time they had left. Jack also had to think about the photo that had been in one of the envelopes weeks ago, serving as a reminder. The picture of the woman who had haunted him since that day in his grandfather's office, the woman who had tortured and killed all kinds of people indiscriminately and with relish during her lifetime. A murderess who had sold her soul to evil. Agatha King.

Wicked, haunted, beautiful Agatha King.

Wasn't it an irony of fate that this girl standing next to him, pressed flat against the wall, was practically the spitting image of that madwoman? And that April was the one he had first met at this school? Jack didn't believe in coincidences, and yet sometimes he wished nothing more than that certain things were actually coincidences and not part of that noose that was tightening around his neck day by day. Jack had made a promise on his mother's deathbed and he would fulfil it, even if it cost him his life. He would somehow manage to fulfil everything that was asked of him and in the end everything would finally be alright. It was a reckless, stupid thought, because Jack knew exactly what he would have to face, no matter what. But his time here at the school, the time he spent together with his newfound friends, made him foolish and hoping, that he could keep this too. That for once in his life, he would get what he wanted.

Lie, whispered the evil voice inside Jack, and the weight of all his worries dissolved the desperate yet hopeful thoughts into thin air. No, there was no escape from his fate and sooner or later he would have to pay for what he had done. For what he was still doing.

Overwhelmed by all the thoughts, Jack closed his eyes and leant his head against the wall with a soft groan.

Startled, April flinched beside him and put a finger to her lips in warning.

"Damn it, be quiet!" whispered April almost silently and listened anxiously to the footsteps that passed them seconds later. Only after a while, when they were sure they were alone again, did they dare to come out from behind the statue of the Virgin Mary.

"That was close," April said quietly, looking down the corridor. Jack rubbed his eyes and face with his fingers. He could feel April looking at him with concern.

"Are you all right?" she asked quietly, tilting her head. Jack pulled his hands away and smiled miserably.

"Everything's fine! Let's go!" Without waiting for an answer, Jack started moving again and April followed him. Together they walked down the rest of the corridor to the stairs where they would part ways. Once there, they stopped. In the dim light of the candles that were lit in the cloister, Jack appeared in the semi-darkness like a ghost. Pale, almost transparent, eerie and unreal. His eyes were deep in their sockets and dark-rimmed.

"You look exhausted," April noticed and scrutinised him again. "Really shitty, in fact."

Jack laughed softly. "What a compliment!"

April had to smile now too. Following an impulse, Jack sat down on the bottom step of the stairs and leant his head against one of the crossbars of the banister. After a moment's hesitation, April took a seat next to him, drew up her knees and wrapped her arms around them. She put her head on the side so that she could look at Jack. He plucked at the sleeve of his coat, lost in thought, and then rubbed his forearm. A flare of pain was reflected in Jack's features for a fraction of a second, but so brief that April wasn't sure she had imagined it.

"Do you remember how we talked about death once? When you told me about the lilies?" Jack looked at April briefly. She nodded.

"I've thought a lot about death since my mother died. About how we only have a limited amount of time and we only get so much and no more. And that there are so many ways to shape our lives, but in the end, we are slaves to a fate that we have no chance of escaping."

"What are you getting at?" April asked cautiously, raising her head again so that she could see Jack better.

"Sometimes the weight of this destiny crushes me," Jack replied quietly. "Or at least the life that fate has planned for me." He didn't know why he was talking about it now. Maybe it was because he was tired or because of the way April was sitting there, looking at him like an angel. Or the cursed letter from the morning.

"Sometimes I wish this would all end. Sometimes I wish, *I* could just end it," he said quietly. April's eyes widened in shock.

"You can't say things like that!" Her voice had become louder and April tried to lower it again. "Whatever it is that's making you think like that, Jack, I'm sure we'll find a solution! I'm sure we will!" April put her hand on Jack's arm and looked him firmly in the eye.

Jack smiled tiredly. "I wish it was like that," he said.

Then, completely unexpectedly, he stood up and April raised her head in surprise. He scrutinised her for a few moments, pain in his eyes.

"Good night, April." And without another word, he turned around, leaving a confused April filled with a strange sense of sadness.

She was suddenly freezing cold. She shivered and stood up with trembling legs. What he had just confessed to her... Was that the reason why he so desperately wanted to find whatever the bloody symbols seemed to promise? Was that the reason he hoped to find a way to the underworld? One, that did not involve killing himself, but rather a door that opened up, and he only had to step through? Some kind of backdoor? A loophole?

April felt like falling. But was it her who was plummeting into the abyss, or Jack? What happened to an angel if it lost its wings?

☽ ☆ ☾

The mirror in front of Jack showed him a distorted version of himself. How much he had come to hate his reflection in recent years. This ugly something inside

135

him grew from day to day and gradually devoured all the good things around him. He let the cold water run down his forearms. The years in Romania had been years of loneliness. On days like these, he wished he had never had to come here. That would have made the pain, the burden he carried, more bearable. But now he always had the comparison in mind: how it could have been.

But the evil was there. It had burnt itself into him like a curse. And no matter how hard he tried to get rid of it, when the wounds healed, it still stared back at Jack.

Chapter 7

Stigma

"The rain fell; and, falling, it was rain, but, having fallen, it was blood."
– Edgar Allan Poe, from 'The Complete Works of E. A. Poe';
"Siope, A Fable"

It was freezing cold as the pupils made their way across the courtyard and out to the greenhouses. April had to work with Sergei again that day. Sergei, however, this time preferred to talk to Christian Nott in a whisper rather than help April repot the plants. When April overheard the name *Rosier* after a while, she moved closer and listened to the conversation between the two young men.

"I don't know," April heard Nott murmur doubtfully. "I know his father used to be a knight of the guild and was a little bit...let's say, *too invested*, but otherwise he seems quite normal to me. But his grandfather... he's out of his depth!"

"That's what I said," Sergei replied. "Just last summer, when we were invited to the Thompson's house, I met his grandfather. He spoke to some of the older people, including my stepfather. From what I gathered, there's something going on. Apparently, for years now!"

April raised an eyebrow. That sounded interesting.

"But doesn't his family belong to one of the more extreme groups? If the rumours are true, they've been excommunicated by the Pope himself! A huge scandal, as the family had been one of the most devout until then and had been labelled as extremely religious even in guild circles."

"That would fit: from one extreme to the other," Sergei added.

"True."

April frowned. It was difficult to pay equal attention to the plants and the conversation between the two young men, who were leaning against one of the desks, leafing through their books, pretending to read.

"Be that as it may," Nott murmured, craning his neck to locate Mrs Hawthorn. She was standing at the end of the other room, helping Ondine and Juniper with their plants.

"I think," Nott continued, "that good old Rosier somehow got our dear Jack involved." Nott lowered his voice even more and April struggled to understand what he was saying. But what she heard made her freeze.

"If the rumours are true, they abduct young girls and women for their rites, some sort of offering to their Dark Lord."

"Fucking Satanist," Sergei murmured.

"Oh yes, and that's not all. You know what they say about those who are in league with the devil... Have you ever noticed that Jack never washes himself with us like guys normally do? He's always got long sleeves on and," Nott paused and lowered his head, "he's always tugging at them. As if he wants to cover something up," Nott looked meaningfully at Sergei.

"You mean...?" he now said and faltered. Nott nodded.

"That's a bold statement," Sergei said and then suddenly turned to April. She quickly lowered her eyes and pretended to be completely absorbed in her work.

"Well, April, do you need help?" asked Sergei, stepping up next to her.

"With what?" April replied sullenly and looked at him disparagingly. "Standing around with my nose in a book is something I can do on my own. And unlike you, I would even be able to read it."

Sergei grinned.

"Cheeky as ever!" He turned to Nott and the two guys exchanged a grin.

April groaned. They were too stupid. Nott moved away and joined his work partner, who had suffered the same fate as April and had done all the work alone until now.

"Come on," Sergei then said conciliatory and gently pushed April aside. "You can rest now and watch me work." Sergei winked and April raised her eyebrows sceptically. But then she stepped aside and leant against the table. She watched Sergei's working hands in silence for a few minutes. How was it that his hands looked like they practised the piano for five hours a day? Well, maybe they used to. Sergei could certainly play the piano. The thought of Sergei sitting at the piano and practising hour after hour as a little boy, made April smile.

"What?" said Sergei, giving her a sidelong glance. "Don't you think I'm doing a great job?"

April snorted in amusement in response.

"I don't know," she replied, furrowing her eyebrows. "At least the plant is still alive."

Sergei just grinned and carried on working.

"You know, April," he suddenly said, "I think that in certain things you have a much worse image of me than I really am!"

April raised her head in surprise.

"Really?" she then said, suddenly unsure where this was going. April had known Sergei for years and had always assumed that they were friends, but April didn't really know much about him and they weren't that close. She knew his family reasonably well and knew who his friends were. She knew how he worked in class and that he was intelligent and courteous. But she didn't really know him as a person. Sergei tied the drooping stems and branches of the plant to a small stick and nodded.

"Yes, I guess it's in the nature of things. We're both descended from different peoples and the history of mankind can unfortunately prove in many ways that things didn't always run smoothly between these peoples. It seems to have been imprinted on our DNA."

"I don't believe that," April replied. "Maybe you've forgotten that my great-grandmother was from..."

"Maybe," Sergei interrupted her, knowing what she was getting at. "And yet you'd never get involved with a Russian man, would you?"

Sergei turned round to face her, the finished plant in his arms.

"Too bad," he said. "Because I'd really like to ask you out. If anything, I would love for us to go to the opera together this weekend And if you enjoyed yourself, I'll take you out on a proper date. But after what Harris has been through, I don't suppose you have the capacity for it. However, if you change your mind – let me know."

With that, he turned and went to Mrs Hawthorne, who examined the plant and nodded with satisfaction. She instructed Sergei to take the pot to the greenhouse next door and April could only stand there and watch him, not knowing what to make of this conversation. Which was never a good sign in her case. April hated being confused. Especially once she felt Jacks eyes looking at her from across the room, his brows slightly arched and that wicked smile on his lips – challenging her.

☽ ☆ ☾

After classes April went to the infirmary to check up on Ginger. April sat next to Ginger's bed on a hard chair, her boots off and her cold feet tucked under one of the many blankets under which Ginger was freezing.

"What's the news from the front?" Ginger asked hoarsely and let April help her sit up. She handed Ginger a cup of tea that April had made for her in the kitchen on the way.

"All quiet at the Western front," April replied with a wink and Ginger snorted.

"And what about the East?"

April's grin disappeared and she stroked the quilt thoughtfully.

"Not sure," April replied hesitantly, avoiding Ginger's probing gaze, who looked at April enquiringly despite her fever. "To be honest, I don't feel like talking about it," April added.

"If you put it so cryptically, I have to assume there's a male person involved," Ginger said, taking a sip from her cup. She grimaced. "That's disgusting! What's in it?"

"Our mum's secret recipe for a fever," April said, and Ginger rolled her eyes, but took another sip.

"Well, are you going to tell me about your boy problem or not? If not, I'm pouring the contents of this cup next to the bed!"

"You're impossible," April moaned and sighed deeply. And so, April told her friend about the events of the last few days yet leaving out all the flirty and seductive comments Jack had made while also not telling Ginger about the turmoil he created within her. Thus, she updated her best friend in detail about all Sergei had said to April, including the invitation for the weekend.

"If you ask me, it was obvious from the start. Only you are so dense and don't get it!"

"How nice you are," April replied dryly, nudging Ginger lightly with her foot under the blanket.

"Hey, watch out, I'm sick! And you can't do anything to sick people! They can say what they want unchallenged and are spared!" Ginger started to laugh, and April joined in, then Ginger started to cough, and the laughter stopped.

"No, but seriously now," said Ginger when she had calmed down again. "I think that's part of the reason why it was so important to Sergei that you go to his family's Christmas party."

"And you sure you won't be coming?" April asked, still disappointed that Ginger had politely declined Sergei's invitation because she wanted to return to her family in the Highlands for the holidays. Ginger shook her head.

"You should be with your family at Christmas."

April nodded slowly and her gaze wandered off into space again.

"I found a card reader, by the way," Ginger said abruptly, and April looked at her in surprise.

"Really? I thought you'd forgotten! And I wouldn't have minded, by the way."

"I almost did," Ginger admitted with a wry grin. "But then I overheard a conversation between Madame Tarkovsky and Miss Morrigan, and they mentioned a shop in the old town that the guild wants to close down. We'd have to go there on a weekend, it's quite a long walk. But on weekends we're usually, well, occupied with other...*stuff*."

Ginger lowered his voice a little more, even though there was no one around.

"Did you find out more? About the symbols and...stuff?"

April shook her head.

"Not really. We've been able to decipher more signs and a few runes, but hardly anything makes sense yet."

"Too bad," Ginger muttered. "I'm sure that if we somehow manage to find out its meaning, we could actually open some portal to hell or some shit. I can well imagine that if we were able to translate all the signs, we'll find an important message."

"And if not?" April replied. "What if it's just a boring sermon that some monk has carved into the stone and that is filled up by blood?"

"April," said Ginger, shaking her head. "Those signs aren't carved *into* the stone you know that as well as I do. No, these marks only *appear* when blood touches them!"

"And what do you think that means? Because if we assume that there is such a thing as magic," April broke off and hid her face in her hands. "Ginger," she whispered, looking at the redhead doubtfully. "Do you know what kind of danger we could be in?"

"But April, you were the first of us, along with Jack, to be excited about the idea and wanted to find out more! What happened to your no-consideration-of-loss-and-fuck-it attitude?"

"Maybe I *do* have something to lose," April said quietly.

"And that would be?" asked Ginger, placing her ice-cold hand on April's arm. The latter grabbed her sick friend's hands and tried to give her some warmth.

"You, for example! You, Will... Jack."

"We'll be fine," Ginger said, smiling at her friend. Her eyes had become feverish again and her gaze unclear and hazy. April brushed a red curl from Ginger's forehead.

"You should get some sleep," April then said slowly and got up.

She helped Ginger to cover herself up, who let her do so without resistance. Tiredness pulled at Ginger's limbs and it was so hard to keep her eyes open again. And as Ginger slipped slowly into the cruel land of fever dreams, she saw the figure of her friend glide out of the darkened room. And when the door opened and light from the corridor turned April's frame into a black silhouette against the brightness of daylight, April turned to Ginger one last time. And when April did, Ginger could have sworn she saw dark wings that seemed to envelop April in the bright rays of sunlight that blended with the contours of April's body. If anyone had asked her, Ginger would have said that an angel had visited her. But days later, when the fever was truly gone and her dreams were no longer filled with gruesome creatures crawling out of hell, Ginger wrote that memory down to her sick state, laughing at herself for having imagined for a second that April had angel wings, but deep inside a residual spark of doubt remained, not sure if perhaps the illness had only shown her what was already there, for she had witnessed too many weird things in the weeks leading up to this moment and she was sure a lot more crazy shit was about to happen still.

☽ ☆ ☾

Will stood at the bottom of the stairs, all dressed in his black suit, coat and scarf, Jack leaning next to him, as they waited for April. Other students of their class had gathered around the corridor, while some were chatting in front of the portal in the brisk winter air. It was already dark outside, and the alchemy apprentices were waiting for the cars to arrive, that would then bring them to the State Opera.

"Will! You made it!" He heard and turned round to face Sergei who had appeared next to them. Will lifted the corners of his mouth into a faint smile.

"I promised April I'd be well again by the weekend. She loves going to the opera more than anything."

"I know, she told me as much as she agreed on letting me accompany her as an escort," Sergei smirked and the moment Will wanted to reply something, taken aback by what he just heard, Jack straightened up, his gaze locked onto the staircase.

April stood at the top of it, a glittering dress of midnight-blue, her hair held back by a clip her mother had gifted her, which was an old heirloom of her mother's side of the family, the Košáks. With a face that didn't give away what she was thinking, April descended and took Sergei's outstretched arm. But then she walked directly over to Will and kissed him on the cheek.

"You're here," April said quietly and finally a smile broke from her lips and Will responded with an equally broad smile. He touched his sister's cheek and kissed her forehead.

"You look beautiful, my love," her murmured, letting his gaze wander over her dress, bathing in the happy sparkle of her eyes that his words have brought out. "And I hear Sergei is your escort for tonight?" Will tilted his head, biting down the question that burned on his lips.

"He is," April nodded, smiling at Sergei, then her eyes came to rest on Jack's face. He hadn't said anything until now, his hands buried in his pockets, but now he tilted his heads in her direction.

"You do look beautiful tonight," Jack said, ignoring the questioning look in Will's eyes.

"Stunning and breath-taking to be precise," Sergei added, and April shook her head.

"Thank you very much, but enough of the compliments. Unfortunately, Ginger won't be joining us tonight," April sighed and let Sergei help her into her coat.

"I only hope she will be well enough to travel home," Will murmured and April agreed.

"She seemed better, though," April said then, taking Sergei's arm who led her towards the heavy wooden door, which Jack opened and the four of them stepped outside.

The auditorium was brimming with chatting people and it seemed that all of Prague's wealthy families had agreed on attending the performance at the opera that night. Will felt slightly underdressed as two girls passed him, both wearing tiaras and dresses with ruffles. He turned round to check on April, but she seemed happy and content, her simple yet elegant dress hugged her slender frame gently, mimicking her every move, every breath. Only at a second glance and in the brightly lit auditorium did Will notice that her dress was elaborately embroidered with equally dark but shimmering threads. Beautiful. His sister was beautiful. She always was.

"I swapped tickets with Neil, now we can sit next to each other," Jack said holding a piece of paper under Will's nose.

"Huh?" He said, still looking at his sister who laughed at something Sergei just said.

"What's going on?" Jack knitted his eyebrows, following Will's gaze, then looking back at his best friend.

"Nothing's wrong," Will replied, making his way towards their seats.

"Are you jealous?" Jack asked, following Will on his heels.

"No, why would I be jealous?"

"Because maybe you wanted to spend the evening with your sister?"

Will sighed deeply, murmured an apology as they squeezed past an elderly couple, then sat down on their assigned seats.

"I'm not going to lie, I *was* looking forward spending the evening with April, but what rubs me the wrong way isn't that she's not with me, but that she's with *him!*"

"What's wrong with young Ivanov?" Jack asked, taking his seat next to Will.

"Nothing in particular. But...I don't know." He shut his mouth and opened the programme brochure.

Will knew exactly what rubbed him the wrong way. When April had visited him in the infirmary and she had told him that she had feelings for someone he hadn't thought that she was talking about Sergei, but, well, *Jack*.

Will looked at him from the side. His friend had opened his brochure as well, eyes skimming over the pages as he read whatever information the company provided that night about their production. Will couldn't care less about who was dancing that night. Had he been wrong? Had he misread the signs? The glances exchanged between Jack and April?

"I've never seen *The Nutcracker*," Jacks voice pulled Will from his thoughts.

"No? I think I have seen it nearly every single year," Will sighed.

"You don't like it?"

"No, no, I do. It's some kind of tradition, I think. They perform it every year and everyone goes to watch it around Christmas. It's just, I wouldn't mind watching something else for a change."

"Understandable," Jack said, closing the brochure and leaning back in his seat. Will was still looking at him, wondering, asking himself…

"What?" Jack groaned, turning his head again, brows raised in question.

"Nothing, nothing," Will murmured, shook his head again and forced himself to think about something else. "Have you ever been to the theatre?"

"Here?" Jack shook his head. "No. This is my first time. But I have seen Giselle in Petersburg with my mother, when I was five and a rather impressive reimagination of *Bolero* in Paris a couple years ago."

"Nice."

"Yeah. My mother loved going to the opera, you know," Jack continued, a shadow of sadness flitting across his face. "Unfortunately, she didn't get out of the house that much." Only when Jack had finished his sentence did Will realise that he rarely spoke of his mother, wondering, if he ever had before.

"She also loved concerts, going to ballets, getting all dressed up; she would wear her finest clothes and jewellery, and she looked…like a queen. She was the most beautiful woman I could imagine."

"You never talk about her though," Will said cautiously. A sad smile tugged at the corners of his mouth.

"I guess I never got over her death and that's why it's hard for me to talk about her." Jack and Will exchanged a glance.

But before Will could reply anything, the lights began to dim and the people around them began to quiet down. Once the lights were out and the conductor appeared in the orchestra pit, the auditorium broke into applause. After a quick bow, the conductor turned round, lifted his hands – and opened the performance with the overture.

☽ ☆ ☾

It was Saturday afternoon. Ginger would be released from the infirmary the next morning and had arranged with April to visit the card reader that same day. April was convinced that it had been her mother's secret recipe, that had brought this rapid recovery. Although Ginger was absent, Will, Jack and April wanted to get new books from the archive and bring back the ones they had already read. Will had left in the morning, as he had to run errands in town with Sergei and Pierre for the monastery. He had told April and Jack that he would wait for them outside the monastery church, from which they would enter the catacombs. April had arranged to meet Jack at the stairs, just outside the refectory and turned up on time, her books packed in a bag, her gloves and furry hat still in her hand. She waited five, ten, then twenty minutes. April grew impatient, then worried. It wasn't like Jack to have forgotten one of their agreements and decided to go in search of him. First, she went to the boys' dormitories. She hesitated, but then knocked on the door and waited. One of the younger students.

"Excuse me," April said, peeking past the boy into the dormitory. "Is Jack Rosier here?"

"No," the boy said, then nodded to the room behind him. "He left a while ago. Hung around here with Neil and the others before that. Talked about girls and other rubbish, were far too loud." The boy rolled his eyes and April hid a smile.

"Thank you," she said, and the boy nodded at her. The boy took a step back and closed the door. April sighed deeply. Then she would have to find Jack herself.

April looked in all the rooms all the way back to the refectory and the library. She looked in the farm buildings, even took a look in the chapel and then went back to the monastery. While April walked through the building she wondered, what exactly the boys had been talking about, since the boy had mentioned them having talked about girls. Had they also been talking about her? She didn't mind stupid rumours, but after the night at the opera she had agreed on going out with Sergei, simply because April wanted Jack to watch her going out with him. She wanted to see his reaction, wanted Jack to admit that he was as drawn to April as she was to him. She wanted him to be jealous.

On the second floor, her gaze happened to fall on the side corridor that led to the toilets, which no one used anymore because the pipes were leaking, and the convent had never seen fit to renovate the facilities since they had enough other washrooms available and the money was better invested elsewhere. Maybe Jack was there? That was the only place they had access to that April hadn't checked yet.

"Jack? Is that you in there? Jack?" April was standing in front of the old boys' loo with the *OUT OF ORDER* sign. She listened for a sound.

Nothing.

April hesitated and then went to the girls' bathroom. She waited outside the door for a few heartbeats.

Why did she suddenly have such a bad feeling? This queasy feeling in her stomach, a kind of premonition – and it was very, very unpleasant.

April pushed open the door to the deserted toilet and stepped inside. When she looked round the corner, her heart stopped for a moment in shock.

Jack was standing at the sink. A knife flashed in the dim light of the lamps in his right hand and he kept running it over his left forearm. Dark red blood was oozing from his arm and it didn't stop, covering his pale skin in elaborate lines and spirals. Why was there so much blood?

"What the hell are you doing?"

April's voice sounded far too shrill even to her ears, full of fear and dread.

Jack wheeled round and looked at the young woman with the dark hair and wide eyes with a deadpan expression. April's gaze lingered on his left arm. The entire lower half was a gaping wound, blood dripping onto the floor. Nobody said anything for a few seconds. Then April dropped the bag of books on the floor and rushed over to Jack. He stumbled back until his back hit the sink.

"Go away," he said hoarsely and tried to push April from him with his other arm. But she didn't let this put her off and grabbed the bleeding arm firmly but very carefully. April placed Jack's lower arm on the edge of the washbasin so that the blood now dripped into it; red splashed onto white ceramic and the smell of iron hung heavily in the air. April's breath came hard and a whistling sound buzzed in her ears. Then she took the knife, which Jack had used to inflict the wounds, realising it was the same one he had given her in the church to cut her palm, and put it out of his reach. April washed her hands and then examined the wound more closely.

"Oh," April's voice trembled, "that..." Her voice broke. She felt tears welling up in her eyes and something inside her wanted to break. What she saw paralysed her whole mind and she didn't know what to do. She stared at the wound, the slashed flesh, the blood still oozing out and already beginning to dry around the edges. April wished it would stop. Just stop. She didn't know what to say and, afraid of what she would find in Jack's eyes if she looked at him, she closed her eyes.

Please make it stop, she pleaded silently. *Let it be nothing but a bad dream.*

"Please," Jack heard April's voice whisper. He was out of it and only had eyes for the girl's murmuring lips. They were moving and he stared at a small crack from which a little blood oozed because they were too dry. So beautiful. So *fucking* beautiful. He wanted to lick it away.

His eyes travelled further over the face, up the cheeks to the closed eyes. He had never seen such thick eyelashes. He remembered the white snowflakes getting caught in them and imagined himself gently wiping them away. Jack could have looked at April like that forever. Then suddenly she opened the lids and two brown eyes looked straight into his. He felt as if she was looking right to the bottom of his soul.

The only thing you'll find, he thought, *is a pile of broken pieces. Fragments of a lost childhood, deep despair and the shards of long abandoned wishes and dreams.*

Overcome by inner pain, he closed his eyes. The stinging in his arm, which distracted him from the agony inside him, gave way to a softer pulsation within seconds. Confused, Jack opened his eyes and looked into April's shocked face. Her gaze lingered on Jack's arm, over which her hand hovered, only her fingertips touched his skin and where they met, a bright, warm light shone. This radiated out and intertwined with the veins that protruded from under Jack's skin and... healed the injured flesh. Jack and April watched in disbelief as his wound slowly closed and the skin healed within seconds.

Silently, April stared at Jack's arm, which she was still holding. She tried to form words for what she had just seen but couldn't say. Her breathing was intermittent and halting; April thought she might faint at any moment. And as she stared and stared at the healed wound, she suddenly realised what she was looking at. A dark mark shaped like a bird's claw, adorned Jack's forearm, with numerous fine silver scars criss-crossing it.

"What..." April started, and her voice cracked. She wanted to scream.

Surprisingly quickly, Jack pulled his arm out of April's hands and grabbed them instead. He clasped her hands, which were so much smaller, and kissed her knuckles, then pressed them to his chest. He looked at her.

"I won't say anything if you don't," he said hoarsely. April lifted her eyes. Then, very slowly, April nodded, and Jack let go of her hands. A wave of relief rushed through him and he closed his eyes. While he tried to understand what had just happened, what was happening right now, he felt a very delicate, almost tender touch as April's fingers gently stroked the mark. Her hands trembled as she touched the spot where an open wound had been a few moments ago. April felt Jack's gaze on her. The young man whose cut and scarred arm she held in her hands, who had lost all hope. And she now recognised what she was seeing with her own eyes, even though she still couldn't understand what had just happened. Once again, April stroked the scarred skin and realised that for some things there were no words. She carefully lifted Jack's arm and kissed the now closed wound, mark and its scars.

When April's lips touched the still sensitive skin, Jack held his breath and closed his eyes again, overcome with emotion. He felt tears gathering in his eyes. But this time they were not painful emotions, but feelings he had never thought he could feel. Jack carefully withdrew his arm as soon as he felt that April had also let go. He reached into his pocket with his right hand and, somewhat ashamed, pulled out a roll of gauze bandages. Knowingly, April took it from his hand and began to bandage his forearm. Now she understood, why he had bandages with him all the time. Now, many things suddenly made sense.

They didn't say a word and when April had finished, she reached for the knife and cradled it briefly in her hand. Then she looked at Jack for a long minute. There really were no words for such things.

Finally, she handed the knife back to Jack, who closed it and put it in one of his pockets.

"What you just did..." Jack began, and April knew that he wasn't referring to her kissing his skin, but to the other thing, that had healed it.

"How do you know it was me?" April's voice was thin. She looked at Jack and he just looked back. Then he lifted his hand and touched April's cheek. Gently, he wiped away the tears that even April hadn't noticed. His gaze slid from her cheeks to her eyes then to her lips and back to the last traces of tears. His hand was still on April's skin, but he didn't answer.

"What was that?" April whispered, her voice urgent, demanding. She put her hand on Jack's wrist by her face.

"I think you already know what that was yourself," Jack then said quietly, letting go of her.

"But how is that possible?"

"Guess it runs in the family," Jack said, turning away. "It usually does."

He turned to the sink and propped his hands on the edge. Jack looked in the mirror and saw April staring at her hands behind his back. He read wonder, fear and horror in her eyes. He knew these feelings only too well. At first it had fascinated him. But over the years, the fear began to settle in his heart, eating away at his soul.

"You should talk to Will about it," Jack said into the silence. April and Jack's eyes met in the mirror. She nodded slowly.

"What about you?" she then asked, and Jack turned back to her. He leant against the sink.

"I'll be fine," he said, and his gaze became as closed off as it had been when April had met him.

She raised her eyebrows. April highly doubted Jack would be okay, seeing the many scars around the mark that had already healed. Scars that were years old. But April just nodded. When Jack bent down and picked something up from the floor, April realised that she had dropped the bag of books and they were still scattered at her feet. April immediately got down on her knees and helped Jack pick up the books. They stood up almost simultaneously and Jack held the books out to April.

"Thank you," April said and put everything back in the bag. Jack then grabbed his cloak from over the cold radiator, took the bag with the books from her hands, and stepped towards the door. And while he held it open for April, she looked round once more and then followed Jack out of the washroom.

All that remained, was the dripping of water as it hit the bottom of the sink, the smell of iron and a shared secret.

Chapter 8

Conjunctio

"There was a star riding through clouds one night, & I said to the star, 'Consume me'."
– Virginia Woolf, The Waves

Lost in thought, April packed her bags, which she had placed next to her bed. Most of the other girls were still at breakfast and so April was glad that there were only two other girls in the dormitory with her, one of them asleep and the other with headphones in her ears and seemingly immersed in her own world. April had told Ginger that she would wait for her in the dormitory and as April could hardly bear to sit still and wait, she had started to pack her things. At the end of the week, most of the students would be going home to spend the holidays with their families. When Will had heard that Jack wanted to stay at the convent for winter break, he had written to their parents and asked if Jack could stay with them. Of course, her parents had agreed and until a few days ago April had been delighted, but now?

Yesterday, after finding Jack in the washroom and seeing the mark on his arm, she had thought she could handle it. She had thought she could accept what had happened, but later that evening, when Jack, Will and April were back at the convent from the archives and April was lying in bed, she couldn't bear it any longer.

The four of them had returned to their dormitories late at night in silence. As if everything was as usual, April had hugged her brother and wished the two boys a good night. She had tiptoed into the dormitory, changed silently and got into bed. And as she laid there, listening to the calm, even breaths of the other girls in the room, tears began to stream down April's cheeks. She had pulled the covers over her head and cried herself to sleep silently and shakily. April knew that she had to talk to Will, that it couldn't wait any longer, but Will had been assigned to kitchen duty today and April was going with Ginger to look for the card reader in the old part of the city.

While Ginger and April travelled by tram to the old town and the city with its nine hills passed them by, April had to resist the urge to tell Ginger everything. The exhausted redhead had laid her head on April's shoulder and closed her eyes. The illness had taken its toll on Ginger and she was still weak on her feet. Her lungs ached and after a few steps she was completely out of breath, but when April had looked at her worriedly and said that they could see the card reader after winter break, Ginger had shaken her head vehemently.

"No," the redhead had said, and had slipped into her coat. "When I was sick, I was delirious for a while, but when I woke up from it, I realised a lot of things." April had looked at Ginger questioningly, but she had just shaken her head and urged her to leave. They had begun to keep secrets from each other since the beginning of the school year. April kept things she shared with Jack from Ginger and her brother, and Ginger didn't share what she knew. And April was sure that Jack and Will also shared some secrets, that the two girls didn't know about. April wondered if this was the normal course of things and that in adulthood there were simply things you couldn't always share with the same people. But it gnawed bitterly at April's heart that there were things between her and Will. There was nothing April hated more than disagreeing with her brother, but what was worse was knowing that she was hiding something from him.

"We have to get out at the next stop," came the faint voice of Ginger and April was startled out of her thoughts. She nodded and helped her friend to her feet, supporting her as they staggered to the door of the still-moving tram, which opened moments later at their destination. The cold winter air immediately hit them unpleasantly, but the two girls had bundled up in warm coats and fur hats, put their hands in gloves and wrapped themselves in thick scarves.

It took a while for the two young women to find the shop they were looking for. It was in a side alley, the sign weathered. April looked up at the sky, which was already beginning to darken. It had been snowing since morning. In the light of the nearest streetlamp April stepped up to the shop window. The glass was dirty, whether from the rain and snow of the past months or because no one had cleaned it, was unclear, but clean enough for April to see a faint light behind the porcelain figurines, teapots, mirrors decorated with glass roses and all sorts of other junk that was on display.

Ginger stepped next to April, reached past her and pulled on a bell hanging next to the door. A melodic ringing sounded from inside the shop. The two young women waited a few moments, then saw a lamp in the front of the shop flicker and then switch on completely. The long figure of a middle-aged woman appeared behind the glass of the door, a long white candle in her hand, some kind of veil on her head. She looked mistrustfully at the two girls, but then opened the door.

"How can I help you?"

The woman's voice was in no way distinctive. It was neither particularly soft or deep, nor was it loud or quiet. No, it wasn't her voice that caught April's attention, but the piercing blue eyes and pointed nose.

"We're looking for someone who can read cards," April said and stepped forward. The woman's eyes settled on April and scrutinised her closely.

"And you can't do that yourself?" came the woman's reply and April and Ginger exchanged a quick glance.

"No," April then said hesitantly and frowned slightly.

"Hmph," the woman said and then stepped aside. Wordlessly, she waved the two girls inside and closed the door behind them. "I've actually stopped reading cards for young girls," the woman said as she led the two friends to the back of the shop.

"I wonder why," Ginger said, earning a withering look from the strange woman.

"Because girls like you always have the same stupid questions and don't want to listen to what the cards have to say anyway."

"I'm willing to listen to what the cards say," April said, looking around the back room. They were standing in some kind of parlour with velvet-covered sofas and armchairs, shimmering wallpaper adorning the walls, incense in the corner and candles and cushions with golden fringes everywhere. The woman went to a cupboard where she took out three cups, placed them on a tray and then went to the

155

samovar in the corner. She filled the cups with black tea while instructing the two girls to sit down.

As soon as they were all seated, a cup of steaming tea in their hands, Ginger and April on the sofa, the woman on the armchair, a rosewood table between them, the two friends let the woman scrutinise them closely. Nobody said anything for a while.

"You're from the convent school, aren't you?" the woman said after a while and the girls nodded.

"You're being taught alchemy, right?"

The girls nodded again.

"Then what the hell are you looking for in a place like this?"

Ginger looked at April and she lowered her eyes to the table. The woman also looked at April and waited patiently until she had collected herself and found the right words.

"I... had a dream," April began haltingly and looked at Ginger. She nodded encouragingly at her friend.

"In the dream, I... saw things. Things whose meaning I don't understand."

"Then don't you think it was the intention of the dream that you don't know the exact meaning of it?" the woman asked, her eyes flicking to Ginger. She had leaned back exhausted and rested her head against the back of the sofa, her eyes, still marked by the illness, resting on April, who looked at the woman uncertainly.

"Go on," the woman then simply said and stood up. She went back to the cupboard and took a sachet out of a drawer. She returned to the table and handed the sachet to Ginger.

"Drink this every morning to restore your strength," the woman said and then looked at April again.

"Speak, girl," the woman urged April and picked up her own cup.

"So..." April exhaled shakily and kneaded her fingers nervously in her lap, "I've always thought about my dreams that way. But in the last few weeks, I've been having them more often and not just when I'm asleep, but also when I'm awake." April avoided looking at Ginger for her next words.

"I've had...visions. And before you ask if I'm sure, yes, I'm sure they're visions, because I've had dreams like that since I was a child."

"I don't doubt it," said the woman, leaning back in her armchair. She sipped her tea and crossed her legs.

"My question is not whether your dreams and visions are real, but why you don't know how to interpret them yourself. You know witchcraft, so why don't you read cards yourself?"

April's throat tightened and she felt Ginger's uncertain gaze sliding back and forth between the woman and April.

"All I know about witchcraft is what I've read in books," April said, feeling her cheeks begin to burn. She knew from Will that even if it always felt to April as if her cheeks were flaming red, from the outside you could see nothing more than a healthy, rosy tinge. The woman raised her eyebrows, immediately recognising the lie, but with a glance at Ginger, she closed her mouth again.

"All right," the woman then said and sighed, "but only because you're desperate and still have a lot to learn."

Relieved, the two friends looked at each other while the woman pulled open a drawer on her side of the table and took out a stack of cards. The woman shuffled the cards for a while, then, mumbling quietly, she began to draw cards from the deck, placed them face down on the table, continued shuffling, picked up the cards that had been placed face up and shuffled them again. Then she looked at April and spread the cards out in a fan in front of them.

"Pick a card," the woman said, her voice suddenly soft and the sound of these words evoked some kind of déja-vu in April, but which she was unable to grasp. April stretched out her hand and let it glide over the cards. She felt the cool air against her palm and let it move on, her eyes fixed on the cards, before stopping abruptly and pointing to a card.

"Pull it out," the woman said. April did as she was told and turned the card over.

"The lovers," the woman murmured and let April hand her the card. The woman placed the card face up in front of her and looked at it while she collected the remaining cards and began to shuffle them again. As she did so, two cards peeked out, which the woman picked up again and placed next to the card that was already face up. And while the wondrous woman shuffled her cards again and again, pulling out new ones, putting them down or putting them back in the pile, the two young women watched the game of hands and cards with fascination, not daring to break the silence with a single word.

After a while, the woman put the cards down with a sigh and leant back in her armchair. She rubbed her eyes and took a sip of tea.

"What do the cards say?" Ginger's cautious voice sounded unusually loud in the salon and the woman looked at the two girls for a long time and sighed again.

"The cards told me things that concerned both of you and things that only concerned one of you."

"We have no secrets from each other," Ginger said quickly, grabbing April's hand. "Whatever you have to say, you can say to both of us."

"Is that so?" asked the woman, looking at the two girls, sighing deeply again.

"Very well," she continued and then nodded to Ginger first, "as for you, there is a secret hidden within your family that you are about to uncover. I think you have already begun doing so, that's why you feel the pull of home. I have seen an eagle, that will guide you, and you shall find many answers in the story of another. Someone who has been in your orbit for a while yet has not approached you yet. He will accompany you on your path for the medicine you are about to find for your very own family. The same medicine will also heal him and bonds that have been severed between ancient tribes. Yet you are also part of power imbalances and political schemes. The day will come when you will have to choose between what your heart tells you and what your mind tells you. You will have to make a sacrifice to set things right in the world. A great destiny awaits you, red-haired girl, which you can fulfil through courage and faith in yourself. There will be no deity, no saint and no devil to help you, only you alone can walk this path. And one day you shall be able to sing the song of death. But you are prey and have been marked as such. Tread carefully and learn whom you can trust. Betrayal is always present, but you will learn how to take revenge. And dear girl, God has nothing to do with it."

"And what if I..." Ginger doubted, but then immediately stopped when the card reader raised her eyebrows. Slightly ashamed and remembering the beginning of their conversation, Ginger lowered her eyes. Her sentence remained unfinished.

"Now for you," the woman said, pointing to April with the remaining cards in her hand.

"You keep secrets from your friends and even from the one who is most dear to you." The woman shuffled the cards until one fell out, which the stranger then picked up and looked at.

"The Lovers, again. Hmm, is it the one you love? A Gemini? Or maybe... You're a twin, aren't you? Yes, yes, of course, I see it now. There are two of you. You look both ways. Were you born in January?"

April nodded. Ginger looked at April from the side. She swallowed hard. Her heart rate had skyrocketed at these words and slowly April began to doubt whether it had been a good idea to visit the card reader. Who knew what she read in her cards, about Jack and her dark visions and everything that had happened between them? Everything April knew and had seen.

Everything April was capable of.

"But it's not for you to share this secret, so you're not to blame," the card reader said slowly, revealing various cards. "No, there's something else behind it. Strangely enough, your life seems to be closely interwoven with that of another young woman whom you don't know and have never met. A woman who is connected to you in some way. Not through fate, but through decisions that others have made for you." Another sigh followed these words. "You are playing games with things beyond your control. You are playing with the hearts of others. You are playing a very, very dangerous game, girl. But we all pay for our sins," the woman said softly and then looked April straight in the eye. "I see a bear hunting you down. Running after you through a thick, snowy forest... Who is he? An enemy?" April felt Ginger's gaze on her again. There was so much doubt in it and, for the first time, a hint of uncertainty. Perhaps even mistrust. A cold shiver ran down April's spine. The card reader meaningfully placed the entire deck face down and then drew the top card. She didn't show the picture to Ginger or April, but silently tucked it back into the deck, somewhere in between, so that April couldn't even remember where it was.

"Soon you'll be able to read the cards too," the woman said to April and leaned back in her chair. "Great forces are waiting for you. You still shy away from darkness, but deep inside you know that you have always been part of these dark energies. Your true nature has already begun to show itself and your blood is of great importance. And now go!"

The woman stood up and looked at the two young women with a steely gaze.

"Leave my shop and never return. Misfortune follows you like a dark veil, raven girl," she said, looking at April. "And if the henchmen of the Inquisition show up at my doorstep tomorrow, I know I was right with my reading, *witches.*"

April, who had already turned to leave, stood frozen. Slowly, she raised her eyes, but only met the woman's closed mask, a deadpan expression on her face.

"Come on, April," Ginger whispered next to April and pulled her friend by the sleeve.

For a few seconds, April couldn't move. The word stuck to her like a stain and she had to pull herself together not to wipe her forehead for fear the word would be written there for everyone to see. Only Jack had seen what she had done, April thought, still staring at the woman. Only Jack knew what she was capable of. No one else. Ginger tugged at April's coat again and then let herself be pulled out of the shop.

It was only after they had stood in the freezing cold for a few moments, with the two young women's hair covered in snow, that April realised where she was. Ginger began to put on her scarf and hat and April, still mighty disturbed, did the same. They made their way back to the monastery in complete silence.

☽ ✩ ☾

"Maybe that woman is just crazy," Ginger said, while the two friends had squeezed themselves into an alcove in the cloister, warm blankets over both of them and peeling tangerines with ice-cold fingers.

"I mean, if she's really right about what she says about us," Ginger continued, "then we'd both have to be weird birds. She wants to turn me into a heroine and you into what, my antagonist? So please!" Ginger's teeth chattered as she spoke. Quietly thanking her, April accepted one half of the tangerine.

"Maybe she just sensed what kind of books we're currently dealing with and then somehow turned it round on us. Don't you think?"

April didn't answer but continued to gaze into the snowy darkness that seeped between the arches of the cloister and the protective monastery walls.

"And what if she's right?" April then said, feeling the first tears gathering in the corners of her eyes. Whether from cold or fear, she couldn't tell.

"What, that we're *witches*? Well, listen!"

"Shh!" April looked around, startled. "What if someone hears you?"

"That person would be scratching their head at the absurdity of it and think nothing of it!"

"You say that now, but you never know what people really think!"

"And what are they supposed to think?"

April fell silent.

"April?" She showed no reaction.

"Is there something you've forgotten to tell me? Or deliberately left out?"

April bowed her head.

"I'm not angry with you, just so you know. But if it's something someone else has said to you or done to you, then you know I won't let it stand!"

"That's exactly why I didn't say anything," mumbled April, plucking the white lichen from a mandarin slice. Then she sighed. "To hell with it," April gave up and cleared her throat. "It was a couple of weeks ago or more, I don't remember that clearly," April began so quietly that Ginger had to tilt her head towards her friend to make out every word. "We were working in the herb gardens that day and there were plants I still had to take to the greenhouses and somehow I ran into Luke and Jack having some sort of confrontation."

"What do you mean by confrontation?"

"Well, nothing wild, just verbal, but no less nice for that. Luke, I mean, Harris, said some pretty nasty things to Jack and... me too. Mainly racist stuff and... he called me a witch." April only whispered the last word and had to stop herself from crushing the rest of her tangerine half in her hand.

"He did *what?*" Ginger's voice shook with anger.

"I wanted to punch Harris in the face, but Jack kindly stopped me, which was probably for the best. But... I haven't been able to get it out of my head since and I'm afraid there's some truth to it. Because sometimes there..." April broke off and looked upwards, as if the right words were written on the stone walls and not just the silent rock looking down at her. "I have these dreams, Ginger. Visions that become reality. I used to think it was normal because Will had them too. But then as we got older and we were warned about witchcraft and sorcery, told what happened to those who defied the laws of the guild, then..." Again, April was at a loss for words, but Ginger had understood.

"You know April, I truly believe that there are things that we cannot explain and that all alchemists have no explanation for. But instead of looking for an answer, they simply ignore these things. To be honest with you, I too have experienced and seen things that I wasn't sure I had only dreamed of. But the deeper we delve into the archive and unearth ancient knowledge, the more I begin to understand that the world is not simply black and white, as the guild teaches. Besides, we made a pact with each other, remember?" Ginger brushed a few strands of hair out of her friend's face and behind her ear so that Ginger could look April in the eye.

"We have decided to follow this path, wherever it may lead us. And if it leads us straight into the arms of witches and sorcery and therefore straight to hell, we will go through it together. We'll always be there for one other and help each other. You, Will, Jack and me. The four of us are an unbeatable team and with our clever heads and brains we will crack the riddle and find the meaning of everything whose question marks are currently making our heads spin. And as unnoticed as we have uncovered and deciphered everything, we will protect this knowledge well and hide it from others. What we are about to find, April, is freedom. And that's worth fighting for and kicking the arse of guys who are full of shit like Harris or Mr-whatever and teaching them some manners! The time when girls and women bowed their heads to a man, be it Jesus or a priest or the Pope himself, is definitely over! My goodness, we live in the 21st century! It's wonder enough that we've lived through it so far, don't you think?"

April looked at her friend in amazement and listened intently to her words.

"Why your change of heart, good Christian woman?" April asked playfully, but her eyes looked serious.

Ginger just shrugged her shoulders. "I don't know why this realisation came to me so easily. Seems like an angel appeared to me and gave me the heavenly message!" Ginger winked and April laughed softly. The two friends clasped hands under the blanket and as they gazed out into the snow and the night, April knew she needed to talk to her brother.

"And maybe, just maybe," Ginger added, staring at the falling snow, "I've been seeing dead people who are stuck in limbo, while I was feverish and pretty much out of it while I was sick."

"The song of death," April murmured knowingly, giving Ginger's hand another squeeze. The redhead nodded and as the two friends looked at each other, they understood what the card reader wanted to tell them. And just like that, the world shifted, and reality altered and April's heart beat faster and for the very first time in a long while, she felt excitement rush through her bones. And she thought of the story of the girls that had formed their very own coven, daring to defy the boundaries of alchemy and teachings of the church. Girls who must have been equally afraid as Ginger and April but also brave enough to venture into the unknown.

Chapter 9

A Touch of Destiny

"I'm restless. Things are calling me away.
My hair is being pulled by the stars again."
– Anais Nin, Fire

Although Will's wristwatch already showed seven o'clock in the morning, dark blue night surrounded the twins as they walked through the small cemetery in the early hours of morning. The mist hung thickly over the gravestones, which were covered in a thick layer of snow. Their tracks vanished among the graves as the twins lost themselves in the sight of the city. The lights of the city drew golden flecks in the glowing blue snow that adorned every gargoyle, statue and rooftop. There was nothing quite like this sight and in astonished silence April and Will marvelled at their beloved city, lost in their own thoughts. Wordlessly, Will held out his hand to April and just as silently, she let her hand slip into his. The many words and worries, fears and experiences of the last few days and weeks hung like a silk ribbon between them, undisturbed and full of understanding like ivy tendrils wrapped around the two sibling's hearts.

"I'm scared, Will," April said quietly, not taking her eyes off the snowy city. Will's grip on her hand tightened and he gently stroked April's knuckles with his thumb. Her gaze blurred as tears came to her eyes and wordlessly Will took April in his arms. Like a little kitten, April burrowed into her brother's shoulder and rested her cheek on his snowy coat against his chest.

"No matter what," Will whispered in April's ear, "no matter what happens, I'll always be by your side."

Will gently pushed his sister away, looked into her eyes, wiped the snowflakes from her cheeks and then kissed her on the temple.

"Nothing will happen to you, April."

"I healed him, Will! I watched Jack's skin heal! It closed over the wound before my eyes and..." April broke off, eyes closed, still seeing at all the blood, the scars, the mark. She had told Will about it. About how April had healed Jack. Without even knowing how she had done it.

"I don't see the harm in you healing one of your classmates, one of your *friends*, April."

"It happened so fast, Will. I... I just remember standing there, my hand over the wound, and I remember wishing it would go away, and then... it just...happened."

"May I ask why the wound was there in the first place?"

"I have no authority to talk about it," April said quietly, and the memory of the knife in Jack's skin made her shudder. Will watched his sister and saw in her eyes what they themselves had seen. He saw Jack's face pale and blank in front of him, the dim light of the washroom and the open wound on Jack's forearm. And it was only when April's hand let go of Will, breaking the physical contact again, that the images disappeared.

"I think," Will began slowly, shoving his hands into his coat pockets as they were freezing cold, "that this is no coincidence."

"What do you mean?"

Will sighed and started moving, April following him.

"I've always had those dreams, more vivid than others, the ones that came true. Some unimaginative, some meaningful, like yours." April nodded slowly, the snow crunching beneath her feet.

"I know," April said quietly, looking at her brother from the side. He had his eyes fixed on the ground, his brow furrowed, his whole posture radiating uncertainty, but he spoke with a clear and steady voice.

"But now it's no longer dreams that haunt me, but visions. I see... images of the future. And when I touch things, I see their history, I see the past in my mind's eye. How can that be?" April read despair in Will's gaze as he looked at her. The same fear and horror she felt in her very own heart.

"It seems to be the same for both of us," April realised and touched her brother on the arm. Another flood of images flashed through Will's mind, but this time he pushed them away and focused on his sister's face. He felt the warmth radiating from her, let his gaze slide over her cheeks, reddened by the cold, and to the snowflakes caught in her eyelashes. She was so beautiful.

"Do you think our parents know about this? That they know what we are?" Will asked into the silence and April just lifted her shoulders.

"Maybe. And even if they do, what could they have done? Run to the Council of Elders and tell them that their children might be witches?" Will twisted his mouth into a subtle smile and April did the same. And while the twins left the graveyard and the dead behind them, hand in hand, they decided to ask their parents about it during the winter break. Will knew he had to talk to Jack, just as April had done with Ginger. Will was well aware that everything that had happened in the past few weeks was not a coincidence, but an intricate pattern. An ornament that wound its way up from level to level, connecting and interweaving them all. Their threads of fate had been closely intertwined. Will could feel it in his bones that something was at work here, the scope and magnitude of which none of them had ever known. And this was just the beginning.

☽ ☆ ☾

The black car pulled up and her family's old chauffeur got out. His limbs were as long and thin as ever and his face as sallow and pale as the shreds of blown ash. April ran up to him with a smile and wrapped her arms around Vincent. He patted the dark hair of the young woman he had known and watched grow up since birth and then waved to Will. He stepped out of the monastery with Jack and all their luggage, one of April's suitcases in his left hand, and set it down next to the car. While Jack was introduced to Vincent and the luggage was safely stowed in the boot, April and Ginger were standing in the square, holding the other tightly in their arms, swaying gently from side to side. Other cars pulled up, other students got in and at some point, April finally sat in the back of the family car, Will and Jack opposite her, her head turned backwards, eyes searching through the rear window for Ginger's curly red head, while Vincent's eyes were locked on the rear mirror, looking around the forecourt for anyone or anything suspicious. He pulled a lever, the car locked itself from the inside and the engine started.

The drive to the Blackwell family home didn't take too long, but long enough for April to doze off, her head resting on her scarf, the cool windscreen close to her cheeks, lulled to sleep by the gentle rumble of the car. Jack and Will were silent for most of the journey, they both had a lot to think about. Will's thoughts were mostly with his sister and he was concentrating hard on untangling the threads in his head, while Jack thought about his home. The empty rooms where no one lived, the lifeless and cold marble stones, the fireplace in the library that had not been lit since his mother's death. Jack's eyes wandered incessantly over the unfamiliar landscape as the black car travelled mile after mile, leaving the Golden City behind and giving way to vast fields and forests. Here, too, the snow had covered nature and houses in thick white. Jack tried to imagine what it might look like in summer. Fields of flowers, green forests and the warm sun smiling down on everyone looking up. Had Will and April often played in the fields as children? Jack gave his friend a quick sideways glance, who looked at his sister, deep in thought. Jack could tell that something had changed in Will since he had been out with his sister the previous morning. He could see it in Will's gaze when he looked at Jack. Knowing, questioning, puzzled. Jack pulled the sleeve of his shirt over his wrist and then stared at the fabric of his jumper. If April had told Will? About the mark? And what would it matter if Will and April knew his secret? Weren't they a little like him?

"You can't trust anyone but yourself, Jack. Not even those who call themselves your friends. I've experienced it myself: when people prey on other people, there's no one who does not want to save themselves. Those who want to survive will do anything to do so, even if it means betraying other people for their own freedom." His mother's voice didn't stop whispering. Jack heard the fear in it, saw her hurrying from window to window as she drew the curtains.

"Quick, Jack! Hide in your room! Pull the covers over your head and pretend you're fast asleep. And if someone comes and wakes you up and you don't see my face, but the face of a stranger, say that you were fast asleep and have no idea what they're talking about! And if they ask questions, always say that you have no idea. Do you understand, Jack?"

Jack leaned back until he felt the headrest and closed his eyes for a moment.

Hush, Mama, he thought, digging his fingers into his forearm. The pain came immediately, sharp and unpleasant as the skin under the bandage opened up again. Jack imagined the blood oozing out of the wound and being soaked up by the gauze. It wouldn't bleed much, the jumper would remain untouched, the wound had healed too much for that. But he could still feel the pain.

"We're here!"

Will poked his friend in the side, startling him out of his half-sleep.

"Where are we?" came April's sleepy voice from the other side and Will smiled at her.

"Home!"

April pushed away the coat Will had put over her as a blanket and sat up. The car was just turning into the long driveway. The poplar trees on either side stood out darkly against the white of the snow and at the end of the avenue, an old house. Will smiled at Jack and even he was infected by the suddenly excited and happy mood. Vincent elegantly steered the car in front of the house and not a second later the front door was flung open.

Jindřiška Blackwell was standing in the doorway, her long dress and dark hair blowing in the wind and she was smiling. Before Will could reach for the car door, April had already pushed it open and ran towards her mother without her coat and let her take her in her arms. Will laughed and followed at a slower pace with Jack in tow, their coats draped over their arms.

"Will!"

His mother's arms pulled him close and for a few moments all he could feel was her warmth and the smell of her perfume. He let himself sink completely into the embrace and felt all the weight and fear fall away from him and dissolve like the snowflakes on his face.

"And you must be Jack," Will heard his mum say and released himself from the embrace.

"Jack Rosier," April added and smiled at Jack. He had been waiting a little way off, but now he stepped in front of Will's mum and held out his hand, which she immediately took.

"Pleased to meet you, Mrs Blackwell!"

"Please call me Jindřiška, after all, you'll be staying with us for a while, won't you? We're very pleased to have you here, Jack. I hope you'll feel at home! But now come on! Let's go inside before we can collect our frozen fingers in the snow!"

And with those words, she pushed her children and Jack towards the front door. Then she waved to Vincent, who had meanwhile unloaded the suitcases and brought them to the front of the house. Jack and Will grabbed them and helped Vincent carry their belongings into the house.

The smell of cinnamon, candles and fresh paint wafted towards Will as he stepped over the threshold. The wind whirled a few flakes inside, which immediately sank into the carpet and with a contented sigh, Will put down their luggage.

"There you are!" Will and April's father's voice sounded from down the corridor and Will peeked past his mum and sister. His dad poked his head out of the kitchen and waved at them.

"Dad!" April ran in shoes to her father and let him pull her into his arms. Will showed Jack where to put his boots and they followed April in their socks to the kitchen, where their mum was leaning against the doorframe. Will's father kissed his wife on the cheek as he walked past her to give his son a hug, then greeted Jack.

"You're later than we expected," Will's mum said, brushing her daughter's hair behind her ear.

"Too much snow," Will said and stepped up to the stove.

"Wash your hands first," his father said before Will could even raise his hand. April laughed, walked past her brother, washed her hands and then sprayed first her brother and then Jack with the water still on her fingertips, as she walked past and then lifted the lid off the pot first.

"You wicked creature," Will grinned at April, she only smiled.

"It smells really good," April said, beaming at her parents. Will let Jack past him to wash his hands and caught a brief glimpse of Jack looking at his sister, who was happily savouring the stew.

"Dinner will be ready in fifteen minutes," said Will's mum, nodding towards the hallway.

"April, why don't you show Jack where he's sleeping, and you Will can help me with the table?" The twins nodded in sync and April waved Jack along.

"And here's the bathroom!" said April, pushing open the door at the end of the corridor.

"Only Will and I use it, so you can put your stuff wherever you want." Jack nodded in reply and his gaze fell on April's face in the mirror, framed by bottles of creams, serums and perfume, her eyes scrutinising him through the reflective glass. She smiled briefly, turned round and switched off the light again. Jack followed her down the corridor.

"There's Will's room, but knowing him, it's certainly not tidy." With those words, April opened her brother's room and Jack peered past her. Mountains of books were piled up on every available surface. There were more things scattered on the floor, but Jack had the decency to not take a closer look and stepped back out into the corridor.

"My room," April said, pointing to the door next to it, which she also pushed open and switched on the light. "Tidy," she said with a smile and stepped inside. She put her bag down next to the wardrobe, hung her cardigan over the back of the chair at the desk and then had Jack carry her suitcase into the room, which he placed next to April's bag. And as he stood in the middle of the room and looked around, April realised that the sight of him in her room felt surprisingly familiar, completely against her expectations. It was as if Ginger stood next to her.

"You have a very nice room," Jack said softly, smiling slightly at April.

"Yes, you can see the forest from my room, while Will's room has a view of the garden. It's starting to get dark already, but with any luck we'll see some deer tomorrow in the late afternoon. I keep seeing them at the edge of the woods." They left April's room again and opened the last door on the floor.

"It's not very big, but the bed is all the more comfortable," said April and Jack stepped past her into the guest room. Completely enchanted, he let his gaze glide over the wallpapered walls, the white-painted wood and the bed. There was an empty shelf on one wall and a chair next to it.

"The wallpaper is similar to the one in my room," April said, not knowing what else to say. Jack nodded slowly.

"It's perfect," he said quietly and turned to April. She returned his smile and let her gaze glide over his figure. Her eyes lingered on his left forearm.

"How are you?" she then asked cautiously, and Jack tilted his head.

"What do you mean?"

April raised her hand slightly and pointed at his arm. Jack followed her movement and when he realised what April meant, he clenched his jaw. The smile disappeared from his face.

"Did you...cut...yourself again?" April's voice was so quiet that Jack could just make it out.

He didn't answer and when April lifted her eyes and looked Jack in the face, she saw that his gaze was fixed on her, his jaw muscles tense. He swallowed and April understood.

"I see, I'm sorry I asked that...wasn't very polite. I'll leave you alone and you can unpack. I'll call you when there's food." She spoke quickly and almost fumbled with her words, but before Jack could say anything, April had already left the room and he heard her go down the stairs. Jack sighed deeply and ran his hand over his face. Why did everything always have to be so complicated in his life?

The candles' glow was reflected in April's eyes as she laughed and talked about the past few weeks. Will had already finished eating and was turning his cup in his hand with a smile, his eyes resting on his sister. Jack only spoke when he was spoken to, otherwise he was content to immerse himself fully in the Blackwells' family life and soaked up every single moment. It seemed to him that instead of blood, warmth was now flowing through his veins, melting away a little of the cold that had resided deep in his bones for years. The meal had been really good; there were still a few potatoes in the casserole dish that had been stewing in the oven with herbs and Brussels sprouts. The bowl of bean salad and pot of stew were completely empty and when April fetched the apple pie from the kitchen, the smell of cinnamon spread throughout the room. The tea was sweet and warm and as Jack sat among the Blackwells, he felt tears gathering in the corners of his eyes, which he skilfully blinked away and no one else noticed.

"Have your parents been informed that you're with us?" Jindřiška asked Jack suddenly at some point. Jack raised his head and realised that the other three were also looking at him. He cleared his throat slightly.

"Well, my father doesn't care where I am as long as I turn up at home at the end of term."

"And your mother?"

Jack swallowed blankly.

"Jack's mother is dead, Mami," April said quietly, looking at Jack. He gave her a nod of thanks.

"I'm sorry to hear that," Jindřiška said and she put the cake fork aside. "For your loss and for asking."

"It's been years," Jack said with a pained expression, failing miserably at sounding unconcerned.

"Losing your mother at such a young age is a pain that stays with you for a long time," said Evan, the twin's father. Jack nodded slowly and avoided looking at anyone at the table. He wondered if Evan's mum was still alive, or if the twins' father had just said that to make Jack feel better.

When they had finished dinner, the whole family retired to the living room, which was also the library of the house. In the middle of the room was a fireplace with a fire burning, high windows and the walls were lined with metre-high shelves filled to the brim with books, some of which were even double rows and books pushed into the gaps. Jack immediately recognised that this room, along with the kitchen, was the heart of the house. A sofa and armchairs stood in front of the fireplace, blankets and cushions were piled up in a basket, which April and Will immediately pulled out and spread out on the floor. The parents sat down in the armchairs and April leant back against her father's legs. Will put the tray with the tea and cups on the table between the armchairs and told Jack to sit next to him on the sofa and took a chess set from one of the shelves. While Jack and Will played, the other three read their books, the twins' father reaching for his wife's hand and holding it in his, balancing the book on his knees, turning the pages with the other hand.

At some point, the parents said goodnight and reminded their children not to stay awake for too long. The twins nodded, April, lost in her book only mumbled a "good night", but didn't even raise her eyes. Will's queen hovered precariously over the chessboard and Jack used the moment to look over at April. The glow of the flames made her dark hair shimmer, and her eyes were hidden by her thick eyelashes.

Time passed, but Jack didn't feel for a second that it was running away from them. Here among the books and surrounded by the warmth of the house, Will at his side and April in front of him, time seemed to stand still. By now Jack and Will were also sitting on the floor, the chess game was almost finished, forgotten on the sofa, April had put a blanket over Jack's knees, her book lay half-closed on the floor next to her, a swan feather peeking out between the pages as a bookmark. They talked long and late into the night and the image of April leaning against the side of the armchair, her sparkling eyes, Will's laughing face, while the twins talked and talked and took Jack into their world, burned itself into his memory like a soot stain that couldn't be removed.

They talked about the church, the faith and the guild, about how easy it was to blend in with normal people as an alchemist, until their conversation moved on to spell marks in stone walls and lost paths in the catacombs. Will eventually lay down on the sofa. A glance at the clock on the mantelpiece confirmed to Jack that it was already very late. But even though it was three in the morning, Jack didn't feel tired. He was wide awake. April and Jack became silent when they both realised that Will had fallen asleep.

"I love watching him sleep," April said softly, smiling at the sight of her sleeping brother. "When he's asleep, he seems so carefree, so innocent. But when he's awake, a thousand thoughts plague him, and he always seems to be somewhere else. But right now, there's only peace on his face."

April looked at her brother pensively and then very carefully stroked a few of the brown strands from his forehead.

"About this afternoon..." Jack began cautiously after a moment of silence, but April interrupted him immediately.

"I'm sorry," she said, turning fully back to Jack. "I shouldn't have asked."

"No," Jack contradicted. "It's me who needs to apologise. We never talked about what happened. I left you alone with the whole situation, with...what you saw. I should never have allowed this to burden anyone and I left you with that knowledge without... I... I'm sorry. If I had been at our meeting place on time, if I hadn't forgotten, you wouldn't have come looking for me and never seen anything, never found out that you were..."

"A witch?"

Jack gave April a slightly pained look.

"What? Don't look at me like that," she said, turning her head towards the fire. The flames danced in her dark eyes. "I would have found out one way or another eventually," she continued. "I think I've known it somewhere inside me for a long time, I am just very good at lying to myself. I guess I knew it back when I first heard the voices and whispers of the witches in the catacombs."

"What witches in the catacombs?"

"Not so long ago, there was a group of girls at the school who had formed a witches' coven. A plague struck the convent, the teachers got to the bottom of it and found the girls. The council was informed and one night the guild knights came and took the girls away in a black carriage. No one ever saw or heard from them again. Rumour has it that the council had them executed and so they now haunt the monastery and the catacombs."

"And... you can hear them?" Jack asked cautiously and April nodded.

"Every time I enter the tunnels."

"Do Will and Ginger know about this?"

April's gaze travelled to Will's sleeping face. His features relaxed, his breathing deep and even.

"They know about the visions and dreams, but not about the witches. I didn't want to burden them with that knowledge," April replied quietly, then looked at Jack again.

"And why are you telling me?" His question lingered in the room while April's gaze travelled from his eyes to his arm. Jack also lowered his head and stared at the fabric of his sleeve.

"It's a devil's mark, isn't it?" April's voice was soft and gentle. Her eyes looked darkly into Jack's face and when he returned her gaze, he shuddered slightly.

"I told you because I know what you are. Because you know what I am," April said now without breaking eye contact. She didn't blink and Jack held his breath, unable to look away from the dark onyx pools her eyes had turned into. "I think you knew before I did, didn't you?"

"I wasn't sure," Jack said hoarsely, finally managing to tear himself away from her eyes.

Too long. He had looked at her for too long.

"You were born with the ability to smell out your own kind, didn't you know that?" His grandfather's words echoed in his mind. April's gaze still prickled on his skin.

"I suspected as much," Jack then added, ignoring the whispering in his head. "Witches can sense each other. I've been hiding and concealing what I am for so long, just like all the other witches out there." He nodded towards the window, where the black night turned the panes into mirrors. "It's not safe for us. Not here, nor anywhere else. The church and the guild are hunting us. Heavens, even all the sub-churches, sects and gnostic communities want us locked up. They hate us."

"But why?"

"Because witches are powerful." Jack's words weighed heavily in the room. April stared at her hands.

"And what about Will?" she then asked. "Is he a witch too? Like me? Like you?"

"Yes, but it's different when you're a male. Pure witchcraft, the ability to cast spells or perform any form of curse or ritual, is inherited through the female line in a family. Witchcraft in male witches, on the other hand, must be understood more as a kind of amplifier or catalyser. We male witches will never be able to wield the same power as you, but we can amplify or channel energies. That's why Will has such clear visions and clairvoyance. He channels your dreams."

April's eyes travelled over Jack's face. His face a bright spot in the dim light of the library.

"What about you? How do your powers manifest?" April now asked.

"I'm a seeker. I find things that others can't. I can read the energy currents and serpentines of the earth and therefore find places that remain invisible to others." *And I can smell out my own kind. Like some sort of animal.*

"Like the archive?"

"Yes."

"Does Will know about this?"

Jack smiled slightly now and shrugged.

"All Will has to do is touch me and look into my mind and he'd know all about me. But he'd never do that without my consent, so he doesn't know anything."

"Are you going to tell him?"

Jack returned April's gaze for a long moment until he answered her question.

"Eventually."

"Soon?"

"Maybe. That depends."

"On what?"

"On you, and how your powers will develop now that they've been awakened."

April frowned. "So, does that mean I can influence it?"

Jack tilted his head. "I'm afraid I'm no expert either, as any knowledge of witchcraft is forbidden knowledge. But I do know that witches have access to supernatural, otherworldly powers. That's why the church and everyone else hates us so much. The children of witches are of demonic origin. Driven by dark forces that twist and confuse our hearts, that give us clairvoyance and instincts normal humans do not possess. Seeing and knowing things before they happen, insight into knowledge that others have buried in the past. Witches are part of the dark matter of the cosmos and we hold more power in it than we think. And that's why the church is so afraid. Because we could end their reign over humankind and free the souls from the constant fear they preach."

They fell silent. April was lost in thought, trying to understand how her world had changed so much in just a few weeks, that she was now sitting on the floor in front of the fireplace, facing a young man who had recently been a stranger and with whom she was now talking about witchcraft, otherworldly powers and demons.

"Well, whatever," said April and stood up. Her legs were stiff from sitting for so long and she stretched. "As much as I appreciate our conversation here, I think we should go to bed. It seems that the details don't matter: according to the church, I will burn in purgatory for eternity and if what you say about everything else is true, we will be hunted for the rest of our lives. If I have to spend the next few years of my life on the run, it's better if I do it reasonably well rested." April grinned and Jack laughed softly. He had also gotten up and now helped April put a blanket over Will. They left the fire burning in the fireplace and as April quietly said goodbye to Jack by her bedroom door, she gave him one last, long look.

"How do you know all this stuff about witches and other...things?"

She had asked the question hesitantly, quietly, uncertainly.

"My mother," was Jack's simple answer and April nodded. She understood.

"I hope only half of what you've told me is true. Because if you're not lying, we're all in more danger than I thought," she added quietly and let her eyes wander over Jack's face. He lifted the corner of his mouth slightly, as if he were smiling, but instead he just nodded slightly and turned away.

As he closed the door to his room behind him, a suppressed sob found its way out of his chest.

"I wish you were here, Mama," Jack whispered softly, sinking back against the door onto the floor. He rested his head on his knees and stared into the darkness of the room, while the shadows continued whispering their secrets into his ears.

☽ ✫ ☾

The last few days of December blurred into a wonderful, swirling mess in April's memories. The days were filled with walks under snow-covered firs and pine trees, the lighting of hundreds of candles throughout the house, the Christmas Eve feast with her mother's family… April saw Jack's incredulous face when he beheld the variety of biscuits on the table and in her grandmother's kitchen, Will's laughter and conspiratorial winks. The annual walk to the small church in the parish, the village where April's grandparents lived. The midnight mass, the faces of the other people, the smell of cinnamon and vanilla. The walk in the cemetery on New Year's Eve, Will and April holding hands, placing a Christmas rose on each grave. Jack's figure leaning against a wall of the graveyard, watching the twins. Other mourners had scattered candles on graves and the ghostly lanterns made Jack look like a spectre in the darkness, having risen from the underworld whose gateway lay between the cemetery walls and bare graves, the jagged patterns of flames on his pale face, his eyes dark sockets trying to lure April out of the light and into the primordial darkness.

Late at night, when the twins' parents had retired and the three young adults were among themselves, they talked about the things none of them dared to say in broad daylight.

"Did your mother ever tell you that she belonged to some kind of witches' coven or something?" Will had asked Jack one evening, resting April's head in his lap and gently running his fingers through his sister's hair.

"Not directly, but she taught me a lot of things whenever we were alone."

"Like what?" Aprils had spoken softly, not hiding her undisguised curiosity.

"Did she ever talk to you about church and faith?" Will had asked further and Jack had nodded.

"Would you like to tell us a bit more about her? Your mother, I mean," April had asked quietly and sat up. Jack had nodded slowly, his eyes wandering to the flames in the fireplace, his gaze absent, and April imagined seeing in his eyes the little boy Jack had once been.

"My mother was brought up by nuns in a convent, alongside with her sister. She was taught by wise women who were in and out of the convent and who had an enormous amount of knowledge about herbs and ancient medicine. They were healers and some people would have thought they were saints, if they hadn't been so human. My mother once said that, compared to the nuns, the wise women had something primal and very animalistic about them.

"I once met one of these women when she visited my Mama in our Manor. I remember the evening very well. It was cold and pouring with rain. My Mama and I were home alone. We had made ourselves comfortable in front of the fireplace in the small lounge. My mother always read to me in the evening. She usually did this in my room, but as we had the house to ourselves, we read in the parlour that evening. It must have been around ten o'clock at night when we heard someone knocking at the door. My Mama got up immediately and told me to wait and stay put. I read fear and worry in her face, so I did as instructed and didn't move a muscle. It seemed like an eternity until my mother came back, not alone, but accompanied by an old woman. My Mama introduced her to me as her teacher. The old woman looked at me. She walked with a stick and her face was wrinkled. But when she turned her face at me, I looked into the face of a young woman and she winked at me merrily. I have never forgotten that face nor her. Like my mother, she was one of those people whose existence burns itself into your retina."

Jack's eyes had been fixed on the flames in the fireplace, seeing the images of the past as clearly as if he were leafing through the pages of a children's book, and with a subtle smile he had continued.

"With a snap of her fingers, the woman had conjured up a bunch of butterflies from her sleeves and I jumped for joy. My Mama laughed and then the ice was broken. I was allowed to stay up late that evening and listened to the conversations between the two women. I hardly understood anything they were saying, but I had rarely seen my Mama so happy and so I couldn't get enough of watching her. At some point, I fell asleep. When I woke up in the morning, I was lying in my bed. My mother was asleep next to me. When she woke up too, I asked her about the old woman and my Mama told me that she had left with the first light of dawn. She then told me not to tell anyone about the night-time visit, otherwise I would put the old woman and my mother in danger. We never spoke about the old lady's visit again, but since that night, my mother began to teach me certain things."

Will and April had peppered Jack with questions, some of which he had answered openly, others reluctantly. It was obvious how difficult it still was for him to talk about his mother, but Will and April knew that their lives depended on this knowledge and information. They never said it, but since that day when April had seen Jack's mark, they had all realised the danger they were in. Why April trusted Jack, she wasn't sure. Some nights, when she lay awake in her bed until the early hours of the morning and ran all the things they had talked about through her mind, the thought came to her, that Jack could also be lying. But maybe it was the fact that Will trusted Jack and April could always count on Will. Maybe it was the way Jack had looked at her over the graves on New Year's Eve. How the twins had sang an old song on the way home and Jack had sang along. But maybe it was just that Jack had become as familiar to April as Ginger. When April closed her eyes, she could see Jack's face clearly in front of her: the sharp cheekbones and jawline, his eyes that could look at her so piercingly and yet full of warmth at the same time. And whenever Jack looked at April like that, she thought she remembered something; a dream or a vision, something she couldn't quite put her finger on, buzzing beneath the surface like a stray moth in the twilight, a déja-vu picked out of ancient memories that were inextricably intertwined with the tendrils of hidden desires and a hunger that grew like ravenous flowers from April's chest.

Of course, there also came letters from Sergei, telling April how much he missed her and that he looked forward seeing her in Petersburg, and April could sense through all the words, that the young Ivanov truly had fallen in love with her. But she did not feel the same and wasn't sure she ever would. Dating Sergei was easy and felt like the warm summer breeze, running through fields full of flowers, and days spent frolicking around the meadow surrounding the dacha. Since the evening in the opera, they had gone out a couple of times, and April liked spending time with Sergei. She liked the way he held open doors, brought her flowers and was a true gentleman. She had liked going ice-skating with him or tasting ten different cakes in a café. He was kind, firm but also gentle. He was confident and had a good heart. April now understood, why all the other girls had been fawning over him all these years and she herself was not immune to his charm. But Sergei never awoke the same kind of desire she had wanted to give in that day in the church, when she had sat on that altar, Jack between her thighs, looking at her with those bright eyes while that dark power emanated from him, sucking April in, and she was helplessly drawn to it. Wanting more. More more *more*.

Ever since the day April's hands had healed the wound on Jack's arm, she had felt a pulsing in her veins that reminded her of the calm before a storm and longed for feeling that surge of power flooding her again, and the only sensation close to that, was whenever Jack looked at April with those hungry eyes.

Nothing Sergei could ever offer her.

Whenever April was unobserved, she stretched her hands out in front of her, closed her eyes and tried to feel that rush again. She imagined that the lights in her room went out under her hands or that a sheet of paper began to float. Nothing ever happened.

But the hunger for that feeling remained. It was as if a wolf had picked up the scent: April had smelled blood and she wanted more.

Chapter 10

Putrefactio

"How do I look away now that I have seen you?"
– Rachel Mennies, from 'April 18, 2017, 'The Naomi Letter'

"We need to talk," Will said, putting down his fork, as the Blackwells were enjoying their breakfast.

His mother lifted her brows. "Talk? About what? Did something happen?" She looked form her son, to her daughter, then her husband and to Will again. April folded her hands in her lap, looking at her brother, patiently, since it had been him who had decided that they wanted to talk about, well, everything, before they were departing for Petersburg the next day.

"When did the two of you plan on telling us what we are?" Will tried to keep his voice calm, his eyes had settled on the plate in front of him. Everyone was silent for a couple of breaths, then Jindřiška sighed, giving Evan a side glance, who nodded courtly.

"So, you have figured," Jindřiška murmured and let her gaze wander from her two children over to Jack, who as well was staring at his plate.

"Jack knows," Will said, before his mother could ask anything, as he saw her concerned look. "He's like us."

"Of course, he is," Jindřiška said quietly, taking the young Rosier in, but this time, her gaze more calculated. "Because witches can sense one another, right? We are drawn to each other and unknowingly we seek each other's company. Like calls to like. Which means, yes, Ginger is a witch too," Jindřiška said into April's direction, seeing the question written all over her face.

"I think it's better if we take this conversation to the library. Will, dear, would you be so kind and make some fresh tea?"

"I'll help you," Jack said immediately, rising from his chair.

Fifteen minutes later the Blackwell family and ⌐ack sat in their respective seats in the library, sipping on Black Tea, the scent of sliced lemon lingering in the air, while Aprils stared at the yellow pieces of fruit.

"Maybe it is best if you hear us out first," Jindřiška said, staring into the fireplace. Evan grabbed her hand and looked at her softly.

"I can do the talking if you want me to, my love," Evan said, but his wife shook her head.

"No, the story of my family is mine to tell and because the two of you are one of the brightest children I ever encountered," Jindřiška said towards April and Will, "I guess you've already done your research and figured out how this whole witch-craft thing works."

"We didn't figure it all out," April said gently, feeling how agitated her brother was, supressing his anger. A feeling April did not share with him, for she thought to understand why her mother had chosen not to tell the twins about their true nature.

"The main reason why we didn't tell you," Jindřiška began, taking another sip from her cup, which she then put back on the tray, "is the simple fact, that the more aware you are of something, the more it becomes visible. If the two of you had been aware of the powers sleeping inside of you, you would have tried to access it and thus you would have endangered yourself. And no, Will, I know you would have, I know you two well enough.

"As you may know, the power of witchcraft runs in the female line of a family, thus, although you, Will, possess certain kinds of powers, they are of a rather re-flective sort, much in difference to April's powers, which she can wield actively, once she masters them. Thus, it would also be only April who is able to pass it down to her children."

April made a choking noise, which drew out a snort from Will, knowing that his sister definitely wasn't planning on having children anytime soon. Even Jindřiška lifted the corners of her mouth but became serious again immediately afterwards.

"I know the two of you are angry with us, but believe me, when I tell you that we did what we thought would be the best for the two of you. Because of our work and…all our other dealings we are already a thorn in the side of the guild, and they have been watching our every move for years."

"What do you mean with other dealings?" April asked, tilting her head.

"We are part of a worldwide network of witches that have been in contact with one another for centuries now. That way we ensure that our kind is protected and no longer persecuted for what we are."

"So, they are still hunting witches?" Will murmured in disbelief, his gaze passing over Jack, who hadn't said a single word.

"Oh, yes, they are. And do you know what the guild does to witches?" Jindřiška replied.

"Bloodletting," Jack said, and the other four looked at him.

"What is *bloodletting*?" April asked into the silence.

"It is a… practice the guild performs on those they suspect to be witches or those who have been…proven to be witches. They believe that the power is in the blood, thus they drain them until the sentenced are hardly alive and during the bloodletting the suspects are being…interrogated."

"Tortured, to be precise," Jindřiška clarified with a husk in her voice, her eyes still lingering on Jack, who nodded.

"Yeah. They are tortured and because they have hardly any blood in their system, they are weak and powerless."

"And does it actually work?" Will asked with a strained voice, his gaze fixed on his knotted fingers.

"Not really," Jack answered, shifting uncomfortable, "but the witches who have survived the procedure are never again the same. The torture, the assault, the abuse…" Jack's voice broke. "My mother was never the same after that and she never regained her strength." April lifted her gaze, only to find Jack looking at her as well.

It wasn't the illness that killed her, but the environment she was in. It was poisoning her. Sucked all the life out of her over many years. So slowly and insidiously that by the time it was clear that she had been dying for years, it was too late...

April still heard Jack's voice, how he had spoken about his mother's death. Was this then what truly had happened? Had his mother been accused of witchcraft and then they had performed the bloodletting procedure on her?

She was never the same after that.

"I knew your face was familiar the moment you walked into that door," Jindřiška now said quietly to Jack, who averted his gaze from April to look at her mother.

"You knew her?"

"No, I knew *of* her and had seen her once at a gathering."

"Of the guild?"

"No, on Solstice. A gathering of witches. At that time, she still had her maiden name, Roşu. A beautiful name."

"A cursed name," Jack replied, and no one dared to reply anything.

"So, the guild hunts down witches and tortures them?" April asked, after she cleared her voice. She felt like crying.

"Yes," Jindřiška replied. "Do you now understand why I didn't want you two to know of your heritage? Your powers?"

"We agreed that we wanted that the two of you would grow up without the fear that someone meant you harm. We wanted you to have the most normal childhood and school experience as possible, knowing well enough that we ourselves do not adhere to the norm already, therefore we didn't want you two to suffer from our decisions," Evan added, and his wife nodded.

"And what about that network of yours?" Will asked then, grabbing his sister's hand absent minded.

"The network? Well, it is a union of all coven's we know of and who want to work with the others. The head of each coven is in close connection and constant correspondence with one another. We update and inform what's going on, what our enemies are planning, what the Vatican is planning, the various dealings of the guild across the globe…"

"Sounds like a mighty big thing," April murmured, and her mother nodded.

"It is and this is also one of the reasons why we kept you from it: to be part of such major political structures and being a part of that game should be a choice. This is why only the head of each coven is involved, for everyone else it's by choice."

"So, you're the head?" Will asked his mother, his mouth forming into a smile, but it was a kind one, which was answered by his mother with a soft laughter.

"No, I am one of those who chose to be part of it. And your father stands by my side, although he possesses no such thing as witch powers. But the network needs men like him, who support and protect us."

"We're sorry," April murmured, looking at her parents, slightly ashamed. "We didn't know you were involved in such big things and we didn't want to be mean and question your good intentions," she said, and Will nodded in agreement. Jindřiška stood up from her armchair and kneeled beside her daughter. She gently pulled her into an embrace and then pulled Will in as well.

"There is nothing to be sorry for, if anything it is us who are sorry for keeping so many things from you."

"It was your right to do so and probably also the smartest thing to do," Will admitted, earning a chuckle from his father.

"What now?" April asked, while she released herself from the embrace.

"Now? Now we are packing our bags because tomorrow we will leave for Petersburg, but tonight we shall attend a ritual not far from here. It is a gathering, similar to the one I spoke about before. Evan and I would have gone alone, but now… Well, it would be my pleasure if you all came along, since you all are witchborn," Jindřiška said, her gaze on Jack who answered with a smile, his eyes sparkling.

☽ ☆ ☾

They saw other cars parked at the edge of the forest, at least thirty, April counted. As instructed by her mother, April wore one of her long, black dresses and cloak, since it was awfully cold. Snow lay thick and glittering in the moonlight. April lifted her gaze up to the sky; it would be full moon in a couple of days. Excitement rushed through her bones as she waited for Will and Jack to get out of the car. Her mother and father already pulled the cloaks around them. Jindřiška wore a black dress like April, the men wore their usual clothing, also in dark colours.

"It's tradition to wear dark things during the darker months of the year," Jindřiška had answered April, after she had asked her mother why they weren't wearing white gowns or their traditional dresses. "You can wear your traditional costumes in spring, again," Jindřiška had added and handed April an old looking necklace. It had a fine silver chain and dark red stone pendant.

"Garnet," Jindřiška had said, when she saw the silent question in April's face, as she held the stone closer to her eyes.

"It's beautiful," April had murmured.

"And very powerful." Her mother had taken the necklace from April's finger and put it around her daughter's neck. "It shall protect you tonight from any evil spirits and forces that may try to enter your physical and astral body during the rite."

Now, standing in the freezing cold, blue moonlight making the snow sparkle, April held onto that stone. Although she was curious and very excited in prospect of experiencing something, she had never experienced before, she was equally afraid and anxious for it was exact this uncertainty that made everything so…unpredictable.

"You ready?" April heard Will say, as he stepped to her side. April nodded courtly, letting her gaze wander through the line of trees in front of them. She only saw thick, dark tree trunks and the snow on the forest floor. Darkness and light, an interplay of shadows, where moonlight met black branches. April felt Jack's presence before she could see him, or even look at him, as if he had emerged from the darkness of night itself. The shadows seemed to cling more tightly around him now, and April wondered what it was about him that even the shadows were drawn to him. Will took April's right hand and as she shifted her head, her eyes searching for Jack's, she held out her left hand. For a second they looked into each other's eyes. Jack understood April's silent plea and with a soft smile, he took her hand, intertwining his fingers with hers. April held her breath for a second from the rush of heat she felt surging through her body, a reaction to Jack's simple action of interlocking their fingers. It felt so intimate. April didn't look at him, but thus protected by her brother and Jack, she followed her parents as they began walking towards the treeline and then entered the forest.

They walked in complete silence and April had quickly lost track of time and the distance they walked.

"How much further do they want us to go?" Jack murmured at some point, speaking aloud what April was thinking. "We must have already walked a mile!"

"You think?" April whispered, not daring to speak any louder. She felt her brother's gaze on her, but she kept her eyes on the ground, as she didn't want to stumble over any stones, fallen branches, stumps or roots.

"Do you hear that?" Will said quietly, clenching April's hand a little more.

"What?" The three of them stilled, listening. April's parents kept walking, but then – she could hear it too: the distant sound of drums and voices.

"We must be close," April answered and exchanged a glance with her brother. Then she looked at Jack. "Have you ever been at such a…ritual?"

Jack tilted his head. "I have attended rituals and rites before, but none like this. None held by witches at least. This is also new to me." April didn't know whether that information comforted or unsettled her.

"What is the worst that could happen anyways?" Will asked into the silence, staring into the darkness ahead. Their parents had halted, after they had noticed that the three of them hesitated.

"I can think of many things that could go awfully wrong," April answered, and Jack snorted. "Well," he said tugging at April's hand and motioning the twins to continue walking, "at least, we're in this together."

Slowly, darkness gave way for a graveyard with tombs that seemed to be centuries old. April held her breath as she followed her parents. Red candles were lit and scattered all across the graves, tinting the night and silvery moonlight, as if someone had spattered red colour all over the scenery. Or blood. April shifted, turning her head in all directions. The drums were so near now, and she could already understand single words. But there was also that whisper in the air. The laughter in the wind she knew so well... Just before they were to round a corner, Jindřiška turned round facing the twins and Jack.

"What you are about to witness and experience," she said, with a quiet but serious voice, "you won't necessarily be able to understand and grasp with your mind. This is an experience for all senses and words will hardly be needed. Let yourself be pulled into the flow of things, don't fight it. Forget everything you have been taught about magic or witchcraft or alchemy, even. And don't forget: these people here are not your enemies. If anything, they shall take care of you, no matter if they know you or not. Just...be open, to receive, feel and experience whatever this night holds for you. Understood?" The three young apprentices nodded, not daring to object. If anything, it was too late now anyways.

"Then let's go," Jindřiška smiled, slid her hand into Evan's, gave her children a last smile, then they stepped around the tomb and their eyes beheld what they had heard from afar: a gigantic bonfire was lit in the middle of meadow. The earth trampled down by the many dancing and swaying bodies of women, boys and girls, men whose silhouettes seemed to melt into the flames. Tombs and black and bleak trees surrounded the area and the constant beat of the drum had lulled them into its rhythm within seconds. April felt herself being pulled to the right and she saw her parents taking off their cloaks and laying them on a gravestone. Someone took April's cloak from her shoulders as well and she felt Jack's hand slipping out of hers. She wanted to cry out, to not leave her alone, but her thoughts seemed to have been glued together.

"It's a sweet lullaby, isn't it?" A girl had appeared in front of April. She wore a black dress like April, her hair was loose and dry leaves were caught in it. On the crown of her head, she wore a wreath. Christmas roses and orchids, mistletoe, rosemary and thyme. The same girl lifted her hands and placed a wreath on April's hair.

"Now that you are crowned queen of the night as well, you shall come and dance with us!"

A blink of an eye later April was pulled into the round dance, she had looked at only seconds before. She felt the hands of other girls clasping hers, spinning her around, then handing her over to the next pair of hands. April felt as if someone had drugged her, as she found it more and more difficult to think straight or be fully aware of her surroundings.

"You have to let go," a soft female voice murmured into April's ear and she turned round to see the face of a woman. But there were so many of them. Beautiful faces, regal and full of life. Dilated pupils, sparkling eyes and soft lips. April felt a gnawing thought in the back of her mind: what did the others think, seeing her dance here with the other girls? What would her parents think of April, if she let go? Let loose? And what would Jack think, if he saw her giving into this pull of the drums? This delicious sensation she felt pulsating through her body as the music began to possess every cell of her? What would he think of her, unhinged? Out of control? He would probably be fucking turned on, April answered that question herself, as her mind conjured the image of him looking at her sitting on the altar, blood all around them. And what about Sergei? Sergei who thought so highly of her, who believed in her goodness and innocence, the way April had always wanted to appear to others. The way she had wanted to be, but never was. And then Jack had come along and had messed up everything for her. Was it his magical power that drew her in? Because they were alike? Or was it a simple chemical reaction in her brain that made her heart beat unreasonably fast? Or some depraved part of herself that she had never dared to admit was inside her? And what of Will? Will… April turned round but couldn't see her brother. Where was he? She listened into her heart, where usually she heard the faint echo of his, but right now all she could hear was her very own heart, beating in sync with the drums.

Let yourself be pulled into the flow of things, don't fight it. Her mother's voice echoed in her mind and April closed her eyes.

Maybe, just maybe she would give in. *Don't fight it.*

"Don't fight it, April," she whispered and opened her eyes again.

And then she stepped into the flickering shadows that danced around the bonfire and took the outstretched hand of a girl, that smiled at her – and let go.

She consisted only of music. Rhythm, heartbeat and fire. Blood rushed violently through her veins and her lungs ached. April had no idea how long she had been dancing in this feverish state, but she didn't seem to tire. Laughter filled her chest and the night had never been so beautiful. Giggling, April tore herself away from the dancers, stumbled into the shade of a tomb, her chest heaving, while ecstasy rushed through. Her body seemed to be aflame; there was no part of her that didn't seem to be filled with heat and April crushed with a hushed laughter into a wall. Thankful for the stability the stone gave her, she placed one hand on her chest, feeling her racing heart, which again elicited a giggle. And then there was suddenly Jack that stood in front of her. April wasn't sure what his eyes tried to tell her, all the while he asked if she was okay. April had forgotten about words, not knowing how to form them. Her lips only knew how to smile or… With a quick motion, April had grabbed Jacks shirt, pulling him towards her. His lips moved again, but the words made no sense to April. All she could do was smile. Her fingertips brushed Jack's collarbone and a shiver rushed through both their bodies. That was a language April understood.

Her hands trailed upwards, drawing the line of Jacks neck. God, April had never felt a more burning hunger for this man then right now. She wanted to feel his body pressing into hers, wanted to feel those arms around her waist, wanted those hands traveling up her thighs, skimming the soft skin, gently caressing her. She wanted his lips and those teeth on her throat. She wanted to rip open his skin and kiss his chest, the taste of blood in her mouth.

"April." Jack moaned softly into her ear, breathing hard, his chest heaving in front of April's face. With one hand he leaned against the wall behind her, as if he had to hold onto something, while his other hand had cupped April's face. She lifted her gaze from his chest up to his face, lifting herself up, now balancing on her tiptoes, her lips brushing his jaw. A growl escaped Jack's throat, but as April's lips searched for his, he turned his face away from her and buried it in her hair.

"April, stop it," April heard him murmuring into her ear, panting, his fingers now digging into her waist. The light pain brought April's attention to that area, noticing that their two bodies were flush against each other, and April giggled in delight as she realised how the two of them melted so perfectly into one another. April's fingers clawed into Jack's sleeve and with a soft moan she moved her hips to meet his middle. Fire burst through her as she heard Jack groan, but an instant later Jack had pinned her hands above her head, pressing her against the wall with his body and April could no longer move.

"Stop. This." Jack said quietly, staring into April's eyes. She blinked, not quite sure what he was saying. His fingers gently brushed over her lips, singeing her delicate skin where he touched it, and with that, Jack let go of her. He stepped back and all the hunger, all the desire, all that fire in his eyes – vanished. He looked at April with a cold expression and had April been in control of all her senses, she would have noticed the tremble in his body, telling her that his facial expression was nothing more but a mask, a simple, smooth lie to hide everything he did not want to see her.

"You don't want me?" April said, her voice heavy and her eyelids fluttered as she skimmed his face. Jack didn't answer and just stared at her. "Then do you want to watch me touch myself?" she said, and with a smile, she lifted the hem of her dress. A cool wind brushed over the skin of her ankles, her legs, her thighs – and Jack turned away abruptly.

And as he forced himself to walk away, the temptation that the devil himself must have sent to ruin Jack, he heard April's cackle and howling, and it continued to echo in his mind even as he walked straight into the dark woods and pressed his hands over his ears, not caring that he would miss the actual rite. Whatever this ritual dance had evoked in April, it made her feral and Jack was no longer sure that he was still in control of whatever kind of game they were playing with one another. If he stayed April would unleash what his mother had bound inside of him. Whatever those witches had done with her, whatever this fucking music did to her, it made her wild.

Jack stumbled into the woods until he was sure to be completely alone, then he unbuttoned his pants. It took less than a minute until he came hard and heaving, imagining himself deeply buried inside April, feeling all of her soft body wrapped around him, her breath on his neck and her soft moaning echoing through his mind.

☽ ☆ ☾

"How are you doing?" April's mother said, leaning at the doorframe to April's room, watching her daughter packing the last clothes. They would depart in about an hour and April hated when she wasn't sure what to pack. The throbbing headache that was surely a remnant from last night, wasn't helpful either.

"I am alright, I think," April answered truthfully and threw another cardigan into her suitcase. Jindřiška entered the room and closed the door behind her.

"About last night…" she began, looking at her daughter carefully. "How much do you remember what happened?" April bit her lower lip. She had known that someone would ask her that question and she had been thinking about an answer all morning.

"Not much," April said, feeling the lie on her lips like some bitter medicine.

"That's what I told your father as well, after he had accompanied me to a ritual for the first time," Jindřiška said thoughtfully, stepping to the window and looked outside. "And I advise you to give this answer if the others ask you, but between the two of us," Jindřiška turned and looked April straight into the eyes. "I know that you remember everything, because I do too."

"You do?" April's voice broke and she cleared her throat.

"Always. I remember everything. But the reason why you shouldn't tell the others is simple: they will never understand what it's like for us. What is like to lose control like this, to truly be free. That's why we need them; to protect us when we are in such a vulnerable state. Sure, being unbound by whatever holds us back in our day to day lives, grants us access to powers beyond our imagination, but it also leaves us unprotected. And here's another thing: that knowledge of what happened, what you saw, heard and felt, is yours to keep. Only you need to know what you're capable of and it is up to you to do with that knowledge as you see fit. And believe me, it's better if they think you don't remember, because in that state we're pretty unhinged, and if they knew that we are still aware of everything we say and do, even though we feel like we are being pushed and pulled by forces beyond our control, it is still us. It is who we are. And that's what scares them. Keep it to yourself, trust me."

April nodded, still looking at her mother, wondering where she had been during the ritual. After they had arrived on the site, she had lost her parents and only saw them again in the car, when Will had carried her through the woods and made sure she was tucked in safely. Jack had returned half an hour later. He had avoided looking at April, but she had stared at him, desire still pulsating through her body. Jack's hair had been a mess. Dry leaves and some mud sticked to it, his shirt only halfway tucked into his trousers and on his lips, she saw dried blood. Had she done this to him? April shuddered even now, thinking about what had happened. Sure, there had been forces at work, which April hadn't been able to control, but as her mother said: it had still been herself in that moment, just less…restrained, unbound and freed from all boundaries and conventions. And April wondered, if she would ever be able to look into the mirror again, now that she had seen who she truly was in the core of her being – what she actually was like. April wasn't sure if she should like it or be disgusted.

☽ ☆ ☾

April was sitting next to Jack in the back seat of the car that Sergei's family had sent them to Pulkovo Airport and was now taking the Blackwells to the Ivanovs' estate. The lights of the city flashed past the car window and April was glued to the windscreen taking everything in with wide eyes, which Jack acknowledged with a smile. Even though it wasn't April's first time in St Petersburg, the city never failed to completely captivate her. Fairytale-like, dark and mysterious, the stuff of which poems were woven, and dreams spun during the pink hour of dusk. April loved this city almost as much as she loved her hometown. Will stared out of the window too, lost in thought, thinking of the days ahead, which would be both lavishly festive and socially exhausting. Of the family, he disliked big celebrations the most, but the joy April felt during such occasions, and the sparkle in her eyes made up for all his aversions. And perhaps it would be less bad this year with Jack, who had also been invited by Sergei. The conversations and whispered confessions of the last few days, not to mention the witches' ritual the night before, occupied Will the most. There was so much that was still unclear and unresolved. Jack knew a lot, but not nearly enough for Will to know how to deal with the situation. Sure, they had talked to their parents and he knew now more about their dealings with the network and their relations with the guild and church, but it was not enough to protect his sister. Not after he had seen what powers were dormant in her bones, of which he had seen some unleashed the night before, as she made the wind and fire dance at her command.

The past few weeks had been a wake-up call and the twins had started to take a closer look for the first time in their lives: April and Will knew that their parents were among those frontier alchemists who dedicated themselves to research. Their theories and experiments skirted the edge of the impossible, always endeavouring to leave behind the areas they already knew and explore what lay beyond the horizon. In the past, Will had believed that their parents simply liked to push the boundaries and break new ground. Young alchemists who chose the path of in-depth study of alchemy by default eschewed a traditional, conventional life and lived it as they saw fit, either in the service of science and research, where they devoted themselves to the creation of healing potions and medicine, while others specialised in poisons and antidotes. Still others placed themselves in the service of a wealthy family, working there as teachers, counsellors or concocting specific potions for influential people, for reasons and purposes that were usually of political or economic in nature.

Will had always believed that although his parents were considered unconventional and somewhat radical in their thinking even in guild circles, as the Blackwells had never closed their minds to the possibility and awareness of witchcraft but had viewed it as an unknown variable in an equation, but with the newly acquired knowledge of the day before, Will's worldview had shifted, and he saw everything with new eyes. His mind turned over each event of his life, each sentence and piece of information their parents had provided them with, everything he had believed to be true, and what bothered Will most of all was the short-sightedness he and April had had about their lives and themselves. But maybe the Bible was right in some things, and there was a suitable time for everything, and maybe, just maybe, there was some kind of divine timing in all of this

It was as if the twins had spent their whole lives living and dreaming in a world that had seemed safe and natural to them, because there had never been any reason to question themselves or their reality. But with Jack's appearance and everything that had happened that school year, April and Will had been taken out of their twilight realm. His sister manifested powers that frightened her immensely. His own dreams and visions were terrifying and as much as the twins enjoyed the excitement of these new abilities, they feared the consequences that could befall them if they were discovered. April had never told Will, but he knew that Jack and his sister shared a secret that Will wasn't a part of. He had known it when he had touched his sister and read it in her eyes whenever she looked at Jack. Will had wondered if he was jealous, but all he felt was fear for his sister, which possessed him so much that he would get up in the middle of the night only to realise that April was still in her bed, breathing deeply and hopefully dreaming of a better world than the one the twins found themselves in. Whatever was written in the stars, if there was a God somewhere, Will would find a way to bend the Heavens if he needed to make sure nothing ever happened to April.

"What are you thinking about?"

Jack's voice brought Will out of his thoughts, back to reality, and he turned his gaze from the reflective windscreen to look at his friend, not without noticing in the reflection of the car window that Jack was slow to tear himself away from the sight of April and her smiling face.

"Nothing in particular," Will said evasively and knew that Jack saw through the lie, but left it at that, for which Will was grateful. There was much to talk about, especially after last night, but that would have to wait, until they were among themselves again, and Will doubted that would be possible at the estate of Sergei's family. Further, because Sergei now seemed to date his sister. Will shook his head in thought, still not getting over the fact that April had fallen in love with Sergei, when Will had been certain, that she had been speaking about Jack.

Less than fifteen minutes later, the Blackwells and Jack got out of the car in front of the large main portal of the family estate. The door opened and Sergei's mother, Viktoriya Ivanova, came running towards them in a thick shawl, followed a second later by Sergei and his younger brother Mikhail. They were all greeted warmly, hugged and kissed, the suitcases were carried into the house and even though it was already late, the Blackwells were served a small feast. There was a lively, colourful confusion of voices and laughter, tea was poured into cups, small cakes were pushed onto plates; Viktoriya gave April a fully laden plate with the words that sweet cakes were good for young women and that it was important that April ate a lot. She accepted the plate with a smile and forced her brother to eat half of it. Sergei, who had overheard everything, winked conspiratorially at April and put his finger to his lips. Jack had been completely taken over by Sergei's stepfather, Aleksei, who had heard that Jack had spent the last few years in Romania and who knew Jack's grandfather distantly. It was getting late and later and when April finally stretched out exhausted on the soft bed in one of the guest rooms, the swirling colours and impressions of the day swirled before her inner eye and with a smile she fell asleep.

April waded through a sea of blood that had flooded the floor of the entire church. Only a few candles lit the pillars, and the faces of the saints were contorted into mad grimaces. In the place of the holy mother, a gargoyle grinned down at April, its eyes twitching flames. At the front of the altar stood a throne of thorns and a man, shrouded in darkness, sat on it. The hood of his cloak completely covered his face. With each step, the blood slapped higher on April's legs, her dress was heavy and damp, and each step was more difficult than the last so that she sank to her knees in front of the throne, completely exhausted. Slowly, she raised her eyes to the figure on the throne. A bone-white hand emerged from one sleeve of the robe, holding up a golden, ornately decorated hand mirror.

"Look inside."

The dark voice echoed in April's ears and she tried to press her hands to it. No, she would not look in the mirror. She knew what she would see in the looking glass; someone she had avoided looking at all her life.

"Look!"

April shook her head. She wanted to open her mouth, to say something; to say that she didn't want to see, but suddenly she felt the iron grip of a hand on her chin, forcing April to look up. But instead of her own reflection, she saw the outline of the creature that had been hiding in her reflection for as long as April could remember; dark and hungry, a creature with human features, terrible eyes that threatened to devour everything. And the longer April looked at herself, the hand on her face now gentle and caressing, the more the familiar rage took possession of April's body. She trembled and her hands twitched. The hood on the man's head was pulled back and April saw in his eyes the same rage and hatred that ran through her own veins.

Chapter 11

Point of no return

"You are cold and flame. You are the crimson of amaryllis, the silver of moon-touched magnolias."
– Amy Lowell, from Opal

"How do I look?"

At the sound of April's voice, Jack turned round, and his eyes widened. In a flowing dress that seemed to float around her slender frame, April came down the last steps of the staircase to where they had all arranged to meet to walk to the ballroom together.

"Like a fairy," he said, which was the first thing that had come to his mind. It was true, in the countless layers of hibiscus-coloured chiffon, April did indeed look like a fairy, her dark eyes wide and staring unmercifully into Jack's soul. She frowned slightly and looked down at herself.

"Like a fairy? Oh no, it wasn't my aim to look like a fairy!"

"Why not, that's good! That way the people here won't suspect that you're actually a wicked witch!" Jack laughed lightly as he spoke, effortlessly catching April's wrist as she tried to punch him in the arm for his words and pulling her a little closer to him. Jack dared to lean in even further, his lips just inches from her ear, still wondering if she remembered anything of what had happened during the ritual.

"You look wonderful, April. Truly, you are beautiful."

April looked up into Jack's face. The mischievousness was gone, and in his eyes, she saw the strange interplay of warmth, seriousness, insecurity, affection and... pain. Jack's face was so close that April could feel his breath on her cheek.

"There you are!" April flinched as her brother stepped up next to her and put his hand on her shoulder.

"You look beautiful, my love," he then said, leaning over to April and kissing her on the cheek. Then he stepped back, looking around. "And where's your date?"

April chewed on her bottom lip, tasting the gloss she had put on so carefully only a couple of minutes earlier.

"He wanted to meet me inside," April answered.

Will snorted lightly. "Did he now?"

April punched him. "Don't be mean! He's my date, not my *boyfriend!*"

"I didn't know there was any difference," Jack murmured and earned a withering look from April.

"Well, if our beloved Sergei is waiting for his princess inside the ballroom, I suggest we better get going," Will chuckled. "Ready?"

April nodded, avoiding looking at Jack as much as possible, and then let the two young men accompany her to the hall.

The evening before Russian Christmas, the annual ball, fell on the first full moon of the year and was celebrated in great detail by the Ivanov family and hundreds of guests. The people were friends and relatives, many were members of the guild; others were artists or film directors, fashion designers, soloists from the state opera or gourmet chefs; the guests came from all over the world and travelled all the way to Petersburg from the largest metropolises to small Italian mountain villages, to celebrate the traditional Christmas together. When April, Will and Jack entered the room, they stood for a few moments, stunned: cascades of fairy lights and white roses were strung across the room; candle lit chandeliers, candelabras and crystal lamps mounted on the wall, made the walls glow with the most wonderful colour patterns and reflections; the women wore the most gorgeous dresses, everything sparkled and glittered, and April couldn't stop being amazed. Young men in their uniforms, tailor-made suits made of fine fabric, little girls with wreaths of flowers and pearl clasps and precious gemstones sparkled on their ears, wrists and collarbones, ribbons, flowers and pearls were woven into the hair of the young women and the whole scene had the supernatural glamour of snow glistening in the sun in a winter forest. The finest petals fell from the ceiling like snowflakes and

April could not make out where the flakes were coming from in all the play of colours and lights.

"There you are! I was wondering where you'd got to! April, you look so beautiful!" Sergei had stepped in front of them and smiled at the three of them with delight. Sergei held out his hand to April, which she took with a smile.

"Thank you," said April, nodding at Sergei. He could barely tear his gaze away from her, which both Will and Jack acknowledged with raised eyebrows and a slight clearing of Will's throat.

"Sorry," said Sergei, shaking his head with a laugh. "If you could excuse us for now?" Sergei said with a small bow towards Will and Jack, then led April to the side.

"Everything alright?" April asked a little worried, tilting her head in question. Sergei was still staring at her, but her voice seemed to wake him out of his trance.

"What? Oh yes, sure! I just…" He laughed nervously, then kissed April's hand. "You are so beautiful, you know. But I actually wanted to ask you something, before you meet everyone, and I introduce you to some of the people I want you to meet."

"And what could that be?" April asked, a smile tugging at the corners of her mouth.

"I was wondering, if it was alright with you, if I introduced you to my family and all the others as my girlfriend?"

April's brows shot up in surprise and a nagging feeling spread through her. Images flashed before her inner eyes; Jack with bleeding lips, standing in between tombs, his panting breath in her ear and his words that still echoed through her mind.

"April, stop it."

She swallowed hard and looked into Sergei's face. Then she forced a smile onto her lips. She would never admit that Jack's words had hurt her more than anything ever had. The rejection burned like acid in her stomach, but April was no longer a girl but a woman with desires and needs, and she would make sure that she would get what she wanted. And maybe, she would make Jack pay for taunting her, teasing and then refusing her. She would make him watch.

"Sure! We've been going out, so yeah, I guess that makes me your girlfriend, right?"

Sergei beamed. "Oh, I could kiss you!" He said, then pressed his hands on his mouth, slightly embarrassed.

"Maybe later tonight?" April offered, now laughing truthfully at the sight of the young man in front of her. Sergei lifted her hands, kissed them both and then, still smiling, he led her into the centre of the bustling ballroom.

While Sergei introduced her to various people and April made an effort to make decent small talk, her eyes kept wandering around the room until she spotted her parents in a corner, engrossed in a conversation with another couple who were about their age. April didn't know them, but thought they looked nice and decided to ask her mother about them later. Snippets of conversation in French, English, German and Russian reached April's ears from all sides. She listened for a while to two Ukrainian women, then to the words of an older gentleman who spoke in April's mother tongue with a strong French accent to a younger man, who later turned out to be Sergei's older brother.

When April met the first of her classmates and chatted with them for a while – she had lost Jack and Will in the crowd – Sergei reappeared, while April realised a little embarrassed, that she didn't noticed him gone, and asked her for the first dance, now that the orchestra had lined up and tuned the instruments. With a smile, April put her hand in Sergei's and allowed herself to be led onto the dance floor, joining the long line of women. There was silence for a few moments, the people in the hall turned towards the centre and April could see her brother and Jack on the other side of the hall, who had joined their parents. The music started and April let herself be gently carried away with each step by the orchestra's playing, far and wide out onto the dance floor; turn after turn, Sergei's hand around her waist, the dress swirling around her feet, the other dancers around her and April smiling contentedly.

"I didn't realise how much stamina you have for dancing!" said Sergei, trying to normalise his breathing as he led April off the dance floor.

"Oh, I have stamina for lots of things," April said with a laugh and winked. She loved to see Sergei flustered. He just shook his head with a chuckle and told her he would get them something to drink. With two full glasses in their hands, they made their way to the other side of the room, joining Will and a few other classmates who hadn't mingled with the dancers.

"Look at you, hello Rosier! Where have you been?" Andrei greeted Jack, who had just joined the small group. Jack nodded and raised the corners of his mouth half-heartedly, whereupon Will grinned into his glass, which was then taken from Jack's hand. Jack took a sip and handed his drink back to Will.

"Danced with one of the girls who all look pretty much the same," Jack then said, pointing unobtrusively with his head at a couple of young women who did indeed look quite similar.

"Oh, you mean the ambassadors' daughters," Sergei said, nodding in confirmation. "They really do all look the same," he murmured.

"Have you danced with any of them?" April asked her brother, who only raised his eyebrows.

"No, I'll leave that to Jack. The only one in this room I'd dance with would be you, love, but our good Sergei here hasn't let you out of his sight since the beginning of the evening!" Will twisted his mouth into a mischievous grin and savoured the slight blush that now adorned Sergei's cheeks.

"You could have just asked me," April replied to her brother, the sudden attention she was now receiving from everyone in the group making her very uncomfortable.

"I don't want to dance," her brother said quietly.

"Not your strong point?" Andrei asked with interest, but April shook her head.

"No, Will is an excellent dancer," she said, looking at her brother for a long time. "He just doesn't have the confidence in front of other people!"

"Oh, what's that I hear," murmured Kenna, who had been silent until now, leaning a little closer to Sergei and whispering conspiratorially. "I think there's some tension in the twins' paradise."

April narrowed her eyes, unhappy about how the conversation was going and not understanding what was going on with her brother. What had gotten into him? April knew he hated events like this, but usually he tried his best to not make it known to anyone and he just wouldn't stop picking on Sergei! She sighed silently.

"And all because of dancing," Ondine added and winked at April. She smiled half-heartedly and then tried to catch her brother's gaze again, but he stubbornly ignored her and stared at the other side of the hall without fixing his eyes on anything in particular. An awkward silence fell, which Jack managed to break by clearing his throat.

"Talking about dancing," Jack said, turning to April. "You owe me a dance, remember?"

April raised her eyebrows, certain that she had never said a single word to Jack about dancing. But when he gave a barely perceptible nod in Will's direction, April understood.

"I guess I do," she said and stepped forward. She put her glass down on one of the nearby tables and then took Jack's outstretched hand.

"Don't you need Sergei's permission?" Jack then asked, glancing at the young Ivanov, a smile tugging at his lips. "After all, he's your *boyfriend*."

Now everyone's attention was on Sergei, who looked slightly uncomfortably in April's direction and cleared his throat.

"April is not my property and can do whatever she wants. After all, she's a grown woman and can make her own decisions."

"Yeah, apparently," Will murmured with a hint of dislike in his voice. April felt a tightness in her chest and tears gathering in the corners of her eyes. What was wrong with Will?

"Hear, hear," Jack said, his eyes sliding over April's body, lingering for a moment on her lips. "Let's dance, then!" He pulled April unerringly towards the dance floor and she was more than happy to escape the conversation with the others.

She turned her head to look at her brother, but he was no longer standing with Sergei and seemed to have disappeared the moment she had turned her back on him. Jack noticed April's worry and unease and led her as far away from the others as possible. She felt Jack squeeze her hand lightly, bringing April's attention back to the actual moment. They stood on the dance floor, where Jack positioned her. Then he bowed slightly. Suddenly aware of her surroundings, April indicated a curtsy. Jack's hand slid down her arm and clasped her hand, with his other arm he gently gripped her waist and pulled her towards him. April held her breath for a moment and that well-known heat rushed through her body. Images from the ritual flashed through her mind and April bit her lower lip, to keep herself from sighing. She still saw Jack's face, shadows and red light, dancing across it, smelled the woods and ashes, while she bathed in that darkness that had promised April so many wonderful things, once she had stopped to fight it.

The orchestra started playing again. April raised her eyes and was now looking Jack straight in the face. He was so close to her that she could see the green colour running through his irises. She saw him once again in the confessional, his beautiful face and clear eyes. It had been almost dark around them then, but now the light of thousands of candles shone in a room full of people, and everyone in the room could see the two of them looking at each other, but in that moment, as Jack began to lead her across the dance floor, April forgot that too. One of his hands rested on her body, the other held hers. Lightly and wonderfully, Jack spun her around her own axis and everything in her periphery her began to blur. She didn't want to let go of all the feelings that had built up inside her throughout the evening; Will's brown eyes that had looked at her painfully, Sergei's blush and all her caution to act as normally as possible, not drawing any attention to her. To smile, to be kind, to be sweet. But with every turn, every light spinning around her, the swishing dresses of the dancers, and every breath Jack stole from her with every swing, April let herself fall into the glittering, colourful and ever-spinning kaleidoscope, her only focus Jack's eyes. For a moment, April closed her eyes and felt as if she was growing wings to carry her into the dark night sky. And perhaps she actually did; floating between dream and reality, caught in a maelstrom of time that spun around itself, becoming eternal. And when April opened her eyes, she saw that Jack was smiling. His eyes were gentle and full of affection. He had never looked at April like that before. Her heart beat faster.

His eyes had devoured her, yes, and she had looked at him with so much desire that it had burned her insides as well, but right now, this glance was so pure, so innocent, that it made April's head spin.

What would she find if she looked long enough into those eyes? Those beautiful, blue eyes; cold as the Northern sea and as wild as the Atlantic Ocean. Centred in this dance, this moment, anchored in time and space, her hand in his... Turn after turn, clothes rustling, violins singing; a soft sigh released from April's chest and the music faded.

For a moment longer than necessary, Jack held April in this moment they both didn't want to be over, but then Jack let go and took a step back. April swallowed.

"I'd like to ask you for another dance," Jack said, his voice husky, low but clear against the carpet of voices of the other guests, who had started chatting again, now that the music had stopped, but April heard only his words. Jack glanced to the side.

"But I think it would be better if we went in search of your brother."

The magical moment burst like a soap bubble and reality seeped back in. April nodded.

"Yeah, he didn't seem well at all before."

"Any idea why?" asked Jack, following April through the couples still standing around towards the exit of the hall.

"Not really, I know that he dislikes these kinds of events, with lots of people and all, but he seemed kind of annoyed with Sergei and..." April broke off, spotting her brother's figure out of the corner of her eye. Just then, Will pushed past two older ladies and slipped out onto one of the balconies, the doors of which had been covered with velvet curtains.

April stopped and Jack almost stumbled into her.

"What is it?" he asked, and April stared at the still-moving curtain. For a few tenacious seconds, April wasn't sure whether she should follow her brother out into the night or not. Nothing had happened between them, but the mood had changed, even Kenna had noticed. April licked her dry lips nervously.

"I think it's better if you talk to him alone," April said, looking pleadingly at Jack. Then she pointed her hand towards the balcony door and Jack followed her outstretched finger.

"He's gone outside?" Jack asked, frowning and taking a step towards the balcony door. "He probably wants to get himself killed by the fucking cold," he murmured quietly and shook his head. Then he looked at April, scrutinising her face.

"Are you sure you don't want to talk to him? We can also talk together..."

"No," April interrupted Jack and shook her head. Her face, which had been an open book of poetry during the dance, in which Jack wanted to read every page and taste every word a thousand times over on his lips, letting it burn into his memory, was now closed. Sealed. April's eyes were dark, cloudy waters again and her whole demeanour radiated something rejecting, so Jack gave in. Wordlessly, he turned round and followed Will into the winter night.

He was leaning against the balustrade of the balcony, his head bowed, his face barely visible in the darkness, when Jack stepped towards him. Will lifted his head when he heard footsteps, but when he realised it was Jack, Will's face relaxed again. Then he peered past Jack, his eyebrows furrowing.

"She's waiting inside," Jack said in response to Will's searching look.

Will's shoulders slumped.

"I didn't want to upset her," Will confessed quietly to his friend, who now also had his arms propped up on the icy stone and was gazing into the gloomy snowy landscape of the Ivanovs' garden.

"Perhaps you'd like to confide your thoughts to me or simply tell me what's on your mind?"

Will was silent for a while and Jack gave his friend as much time as he needed. Both their hands grew cold and Jack could no longer feel his feet as Will finally began to speak.

"There...are these moments when I just...can't take it anymore. So much... So much of our lives has been a lie, so much of what we've been told is so... wrong. So many people have been lying to us."

"Who are you talking about exactly?" Jack asked, feeling his throat tighten. *Please don't. Don't say that you found out about me.*

Had Will figured it out? Had he seen through Jack's half-truths?

"Well, the guild, the council of elders, our teachers and... even our parents!"

"But don't you think your parents were just trying to protect you, just as they said?"

Will snorted. "By letting me and April believe we were normal kids and not the spawn of hell?"

Jack's lips formed into a thin line and he frowned.

"I didn't... mean that," Will apologised, as he glanced sideways at his friend.

"Don't worry," Jack said, returning Will's gaze.

"It's just..." Will continued more quietly, standing up tall, his eyes on the sky, "that I *see* things I know are going to happen, and I'm so scared for April. I keep seeing her in front of me and... She's lying in a pool of blood that keeps spreading around her head and she's just lying there...motionless." Will clenched his fists over his eyes and shook his head, trying to banish the horrible images.

"When did this vision start appearing to you?" Jack asked quietly, concern now clearly written on his face.

"Months ago. The first night of the school year, during the new moon ritual," Will replied. Jack sucked in a sharp breath and Will looked at him questioningly.

"What is it?"

"I..." Jack didn't know how to continue the sentence and looked into the darkness for help, hoping that some creature of the night would take pity on him and swallow him up and drag him deep into the underworld so that he would be spared the answer.

"April once mentioned that she had some kind of vision that night, too," Jack said, generously omitting the fact that April had accused him at the time that Jack must have had something to do with it. "Or several visions, gruesome images, to be precise."

"She told me that too," Will said, wondering at the same moment what reason April had seen for telling Jack about her visions. Did Jack know more than he was letting on? Or did April trust him enough to tell him about her nightmares? She who was usually so distrustful of others besides him. But did it surprise him? After all, hadn't he been the one who had encouraged April to be friends with Jack and hadn't Will noticed that a lot had changed in the dynamic between his sister and his best friend since then? Will wasn't blind and knew how Jack looked at April when he thought he was unobserved. And Will knew April better than she knew herself, even if she would never admit it.

His sister liked Jack and was attracted to him, Will had sensed it in her memories when the twins had gone for a walk in the cemetery the day before the holiday, even though she put up a good show pretending to be in love with Sergei, dating him and all.

But all Will had to do was touch April and he knew exactly how to read her every emotion and felt it in himself. This ability had become better and better over the years and so it wasn't just feelings that Will could now pick up on, he could also see clear images of how things had happened. At first Will had resisted these visions, but April had encouraged him to allow the images. April and Will had believed that they only had these abilities because they were twins and were connected in a way that only twins could be. But the more time passed, and the more Will began to be able to use the same ability on other people, the more he realised that it had nothing to do with being twins and that there must be something else behind it. April and Will had never spoken to their parents about it, let alone Ginger or anyone else, but a lot had changed since Jack's appearance at school.

Will had changed, and April had changed too. They finally had talked to their parents, but it was a long shot from actually being able to understand what they were capable of and how their powers manifested themselves, now that they had been awakened. But hadn't Will always seen who April truly was? Hadn't he always been able to see deeper into her soul than anyone ever could? For as long as Will could remember, April had avoided looking in mirrors for the simple reason that the person she saw in there frightened her and had nothing to do with the person she was. But what if the two figures were one and the same person? Yes, their parents had tried to protect them from all this, and though April had agreed with their parents' decisions, didn't mean that Will had forgiven them for lying to them. Will sighed softly and looked out into the night again.

"What do you think your vision means?" Jack's voice sounded strained and Will turned his face towards him again.

"I hope I never have to find out," he then replied, shrugging his shoulders. "But I know I can't handle this on my own anymore. Not that I don't trust you or April or Ginger, but I think we're getting in over our heads and I'm afraid it's going to end badly if we don't do something now."

"And what do you want us to do? Tell the world that witches do exist and shouldn't be hunted down and treated like animals or toys?" There was mockery and cynicism in Jack's words and his face looked indifferent, but Will had quickly learnt to see behind that mask.

"It doesn't even matter what you want to call us, the fact is that we have abilities that others don't have and that we see things that come true."

"Remember, Will, only you see the future so clearly. For the rest of us, it's just a dark mirror of the present."

"Possibly, but in regards of April, we know that in addition to her dream abilities and insights, she also has the power to heal others. To heal you. And I'm not just talking about the wound on your arm that you never told me about, and no, that's not an accusation, I only know about it because I saw it in April's memories. And you know what I saw too?" Will looked at his friend expectantly, but Jack stubbornly looked out into the night. Whatever was coming now, he wouldn't be able to stop Will from saying it.

"What you thought inside you was forever irreparable, April can heal that too, Jack."

Will let the words sink in and watched the emotion on his friend's face.

Jack struggled with himself. He knew exactly what Will meant and had felt it himself when April's lips had touched the still healing skin, gently stroking the silvery scars and looking at him with those dark eyes and his blood on her mouth. A hint of red on her lower lips that Jack would have loved to kiss away.

"Jack? How do you feel about my sister?"

Jack's jaw tightened. "What do you mean?" he then asked, looking at Will. His voice trembled slightly.

"We both know exactly what I mean. After all, I'm not stupid and I know how you look at my sister," Will replied, tilting his head.

Jack didn't know what to say to that. At that moment, he felt completely defenceless. All his cards were face up on the table, forced by the unyielding gaze of the young Blackwell. The secret he had banished deep inside him to the others, where not even his shadows dared to go and only crawled out of their dungeons on the wildest nights of the new moon and spread like vermin in Jack's brain; nights in which Jack fought for self-control. Sometimes he would sneak out of the dormitory and wander the empty streets of the city, knowing that if he stayed in the room even a minute longer, he would wake Will and tell him everything. Then he would beg on his knees April for forgiveness, looking into her merciless eyes, waiting for her to deal him the deathblow and send him to the darkest pits of hell. And if he should one day find himself in that final realm, he would repent every day of his life, do penance for what he had done to his friends and what he still intended to do. But he was bound, could not break the vow he had made on his mother's deathbed. Jack could not go back without betraying her and sealing her eternal damnation.

"We're friends, that's all," Jack replied with a half-hearted shrug. Will's mouth twisted.

"Friends, my arse," he scoffed, "I saw you dancing earlier," Will said, shaking his head. "That was more than just friendship!" And as there was no further response from Jack, Will continued.

"I'm bringing this up not because I want to tell you to keep your hands off her, but that you should stop pretending and do something about it! Stop standing around passively waiting for hell to happen." Jack grimaced at Will's words but let him finish.

"Life doesn't wait for us, Jack! You don't know what tomorrow holds, but if you care about April, then...just fucking tell her!" A sudden heat took possession of Jack's body. The cold of the winter night was forgotten, and his hands were no longer trembling. Clenched into fists, he dug his fingernails deep into his palms.

"*Stop it,*" Jack said quietly. His voice was as cold and cutting as Will had ever heard it. He knew he had provoked Jack, deliberately.

Jack now looked Will straight in the eye.

"*Stop* saying that. It's not working. It just won't do." With those words, Jacks turned to leave. Will grabbed his arm and forced him to stop.

"Why not? Because of Sergei? To hell with that! They have been dating for two weeks, that's hardly worth anything!"

"You wouldn't understand," Jack managed to say.

"What if I did? I believe the craziest things!"

"This thing isn't crazy, it's just *repulsive!*"

The two friends looked at each other for a long time, neither willing to give in to their position.

"Let it go, Will," Jack said quietly, and all the tension left him. "The only thing that matters now is that you and your sister find out more about who you are. Maybe talk some more to your parents. That will clear things up for you and maybe shed some light on the darkness. As for me, my path in life was sealed when I was conceived. My path was predetermined long before I knew that one day I would come here. I have passed the point of no return a long time ago. And in this life, there is no room for someone like your sister, let alone you or Ginger. My life has an expiry date and every minute I spend with you is only one more stolen moment. But life isn't kind to thieves, Will! It's going to catch up with me and I'm going to lose all this again. And I know you know that. That's the only reason you're talking to me about your sister, because we both know she won't ever choose someone like me. And besides that, she has already someone and Sergei is a good man! A decent man. And there are more important things going on in her life right now, such as the fact that she has discovered what powers lay dormant inside her. I wouldn't want to take that away from her for anything in the world and I will be careful not to hurt her or you or Ginger. I can't ask more than this friendship from you; this alone is something stolen from someone else's life. So, I beg you, Will, as your friend, don't ask me again."

Will nodded slowly. He let go of Jack, whose arm fell to his side.

"I respect your decision, Jack. However, I want you to know that I am happy to give you my friendship. You deserve to have friends who value you and like you and want the best for you, and I want the best for you too. I want you to find peace within yourself one day and share it with someone else, because your heart is not made to walk blindly through the world. Your heart is made to love and live. And who knows, maybe one day you'll be able to understand my point of view."

"Thank you," Jack said quietly, and Will nodded to him. Without another word or a last look at the wolf moon above them, they left the balcony and the winter night behind them. And as they returned to the summer warmth of the hall and the Christmas feast, the moon cast its black shadows in a playful pattern through its blue light that fell from the sky to the earth on the dark stone and glistening white snow.

Chapter 12

Destillatio

"And I was helpless, tormented, and intoxicated
By the sweetness of your cruelty."
– Anna Akhmatova, from The Completed Poems of Anna Akhmatova;
Uncollected Poems and Fragments

Whatever Jack had said to Will about not wanting to draw April into the mess of his life, didn't keep him from watching her. Maybe it was deranged, a little masochistic and certainly unfair towards April, but whatever he had vowed to himself that night of the witches' dance and ritual, it took one glance in April's direction, and all his good intentions were forgotten. He had meant what he had said to Will and after Jack had seen what April was capable of, when he saw how she had commanded the night to follow her every flick of the wrist; winds howling, snow falling, and how all the other witches had gravitated towards her – he couldn't resist watching her. Jack was fairly sure, that April didn't remember any of what happened at the ritual, at least she behaved that way and Jack was more than just relieved, for it meant, that nothing had actually changed between them. They were still just friends, who occasionally were harmlessly flirting with one another. Nothing more.

The Blackwells were sitting in the salon adjoining their bedrooms in the East Wing of the Ivanov estate, enjoying their morning tea. The rest of the guests had been sleeping in various other rooms and those who weren't already leaving this morning, were expected again in the early afternoon, as their hosts had planned a sleigh ride through the countryside outside the city. It had been Viktoriya's hope, that her guests would be able to see the starry sky at night, with the moon glistening on the freshly fallen snow and then return for a midnight dinner at the mansion. The Blackwells and Jack sipped their tea and indulged in the food that had been brought up to them a while ago: boiled eggs and pickles, blinis, syrinki and cinnamon buns. But there were also honey glazed plums, peljmeni and vzvar. Jack's favourite were the gingerbread cookies, priyaniki, but as April leaned over to him, asking in a hushed voice, if he preferred these biscuits over the vanilokové rohlíčky of her grandmother, Jack pinky swore that there was nothing in the world that could beat her grandmother's baking skills and he would always prefer those vanilla biscuits. The smile on April's face that followed Jack's word, made his heart flutter and the world suddenly seemed so much brighter. Jack didn't hear Will laugh at them, for being so serious about biscuits, but Jack could feel a smile of his own settling on his face that seemed to be stuck there for the rest of the day.

"Can't sleep?" April's father sat on the sofa in front of the fireplace, a book balanced on his knees while sipping a cup of tea. Everyone else had gone to sleep already for it had been around three in the morning when all the guests retired to their rooms. It had been a wonderful afternoon and April had enjoyed the sleigh ride and midnight dinner. But no matter how tired she was, her thoughts kept her awake, mulling over so many things at the same time, that she had given up trying to fall asleep and had decided to get herself a cup of tea. She hadn't expected her dad to be awake still, but she was glad not being the only one who couldn't sleep and having some company this late at night.

"No," April sighed, got herself a cup of tea and settled in next to her dad. He put down his book and pulled his daughter into an embrace.

"What's keeping you up? The nightmares again?"

"No, no nightmares…just…thinking."

"I see." Evan kissed his daughter's hair and looked back into the flames. "You want to talk about it?"

"I don't know. I…" April sighed and leaned her head on her father's shoulder. "It has been just so much that happened in such a short amount of time."

"And you're feeling a little overwhelmed?"

"Yeah." April nodded.

"Well, that's normal, don't you think?"

"I guess."

"You had a good time at the ball?" April's dad then asked and looked at his daughter.

"Oh, yes, it was wonderful! I loved the decoration and the food and the dancing…"

Evan laughed.

"That sounds quite like you," he agreed, and April chuckled. Evan smiled as well, but then his face turned serious again.

"And what about the night of the ritual? How did that go for you?"

April shifted slightly.

"I don't remember much," she then answered, chewing her bottom lip. Her father laughed.

"Like mother, like daughter," he then said as he looked in April's confused face. "You mother tells me the same every single time. But do you want to know a little secret: I know she's lying. I know that she remembers everything that happens during those rituals!"

"What?" April breathed, looking at her father in astonishment.

"Yeah," Evan chuckled. "Your mother tells me she doesn't remember anything because she thinks if I knew the truth, I would no longer love her. But that's nonsense! You see, how could I love her less, if I have had the privilege to see all of her? I fell in love with her because of who she was at the time I met her. But then, I continued loving her, because I fell in love with every version of herself that she became throughout the years. A woman will change over time and you will meet many different versions of her. As her partner, you need to be open, to get to know each and every version of your woman and fall in love with every single one of them. And if you can manage that, you will live the most enriching life and will be rewarded in the most beautiful ways. Women love so deeply and it's heart-breaking to see just how often they aren't allowed to love someone with their full heart, for whatever reason. So, if there is any advice, I can give you, April, then to love with all you heart. Anything else will burn you out and leave you hollow and emptied."

"And what if I do love someone with all my heart but will be rejected?" April asked with a soft tremble in her voice and her father took her hands into his.

"Then you did all you could, and you can move on and heal. Life is too short to be half-lived and our time given is too precious to love half-heartedly."

"Okay," April sniffed and cuddled up to her dad. He kissed her temple and while he continued reading, April closed her eyes, tuning into the sound of his steady breathing, the soft rustling of book pages and fire crackling, lulling her into a deep, dreamless sleep.

☽ ☆ ☾

Many miles further west, Ginger sat on one of the wooden benches of the family church, where her father had held his sermons for many years every Sunday without fail. And Ginger had sat through all of them, keeping quiet, listening carefully, and memorising everything her father and community expected her to be. How she had to behave, what she wasn't allowed to do, what she was required to want in life, and all the other obligations she had as a girl. Ginger had kept quiet, listening on, but at the same time, she had always let her gaze wander over the gathered crowd, the flock of her father; her cousins, aunts and uncles; their nearest neighbours and some of the few servants the family still kept; the cook and her family, the chamber maidens, the driver and the butler. Ginger had grown up with them and they all knew her in and out, but it had only been Ginger's mother who had known about her wild heart. A heart that longed for the Highlands, the wind on her cheeks; feeling the cold earth beneath her bare feet, the smell of heather and rain yet to fall.

But now the church was empty and quiet, and it was only Ginger and her thoughts, because the dead that Ginger sometimes saw from the corner of the eye, did not like to come in here. They did not like the scent of the incense and they sure had a dislike for the bones of the Saint, that were stored in a box on the altar. No, the dead ones, that where stuck in limbo, either haunted those with whom they still had things to settle, or roamed the wide, blue coastline. Many of them lurked in the shadows of the lighthouse or the ruins of the fortress farther East. Ginger could not hear them but had always seen them. She had never known what she had actually been seeing, until recently when she had found answers in one of the books, they had taken from the underground archive and Ginger had finally understood, that she was neither delusional nor mentally ill. She was just *different*.

"You have been sitting here for hours," her mother's voice sounded from the entrance. "Aren't you cold?"

"No, I'm good," Ginger replied and waited until her mother had taken a seat beside her. She sighed as she did so, and Ginger scrutinised her mother worriedly. She hadn't been that well for months now, and the pains she felt in her joints and nerves did not go away. With the newly acquired knowledge, Ginger was fairly sure, that there would be some sort of witch's potion, that could cure her mother's ailment.

"Don't look at me like that, darling," her mother sighed and gently took Ginger's hand. "I shall be fine."

"Sure." Ginger tried to smile and was certain, she failed, for her mother knitted her brows and looked at her more closely.

"What in the Lord's name have you been doing here anyways?"

"Thinking," Ginger answered and looked again to the altar, behind which a simple cross was erected.

"Thinking about what exactly?"

"Everything, to be honest."

"And what does this ominous everything encompass?" Ginger's mother tilted her head slightly, still looking at her daughter.

"God. Our faith. The way this community lives together, my friends, my studies...well, everything."

"Why would you have to think so intensely about God and your faith? Do you experience a period of doubt? Has your faith been tested?"

Ginger laughed dryly, shaking her head.

No, her faith had not been tested. In fact, she had found that it had been nothing but lies. The bible had taught Ginger that she was born a sinner, that everyone who did not recognise God has their one and only Lord and praying to him in the name of his son, was ultimately destined for eternal damnation, that their soul would be lost forever. The bible had taught her that those who made use of witchcraft were demonic and had given into the whispers of the devil. The bible had taught Ginger that it was the man who was superior to the woman, that he was the head that thinks, and the woman the body. Ginger had been taught that if someone came her way, challenging her faith, telling her there was no God, it was only the devil in disguise, testing her, tempting her to give in to him, so that he could pull her over to the dark side, and that if she prayed, God would be there to guide her, that he would take her worries onto himself and that he would take care of her. That she should be sober and vigilant for the devil would still try to destroy her, and that she would be able to defy him in the power of the faith.

"I pray, every day," Ginger said quietly, her eyes fixed on the cross. "I call out to God. I search for an answer, anything, something… But there is only darkness."

"God has many ways in which he answers our prayers," Ginger's mother said softly, stroking the back of Ginger's hand.

"I no longer believe in that," Ginger said and pulled her hand from her mother's. "Because…one day the darkness reached out to me." Ginger heard her mother draw a sharp breath in and pressed one hand on her mouth, but Ginger continued talking. "And it was not the fallen angel, the Dark Lord, the devil himself I heard talking to me. No, it was the voices of my ancestors, the voice you, mother, lost, as well as my own. And they told me that truth is within us all and that our souls are immortal no matter what, and thus our actions do matter, because they shape our very past, present and future. Because time and space are actually the same, and we have power over that too. But they also told me that there is more to it than the eye sees and some of us are given the sight. And I believe you have it too, mother, you just shut your eyes for fear of what they might do to you, because you have seen and heard horrible things happening to those who dared to defy the teachings of the church. And I do not blame you for that. It is only now in this new century that women start reclaiming their power. And it's happening all around the world. In some countries these ancient practices never ceased to exist, because the church could not gain a foothold." Ginger sighed deeply and then turned to face her mother. She was pale, and her hands trembled, but Ginger felt only love when she looked at her. Love, pain and grief. She wished her mother would come with her and leave all of this behind. The confinement and the fear-mongering. The guilt-tripping and the abuse.

"I don't ask you to follow me on my path, although I wished you would come with me," Ginger then said gently, laying her hand on her mother's. "I simply ask you to let me go."

"I fear for your life, Ginger. And I love you too much…" Her mother's voice broke and a tear escaped one of her eyes.

"I know," Ginger murmured and wiped that tear from her mother's face. "But I will take care of myself, I promise you that. And I won't be alone. I have my friends. And one day a whole community, a sisterhood." Ginger smiled at the thought of it. Women and girls united, one family, taking care of one another, supporting each other, helping, growing and evolving together. Nurturing, full of love, kindness and truth. A sisterhood founded on love, understanding and honesty. No more lies. No more deception. No more abuse. Just truth, kindness and love. Women and girls had never sought out to fight each other. Women and girls did not want for war, for they would always be the ones that suffered the most in the end. Women and girls had the wisdom and love the world needed and would always find ways to communicate with one another and solve conflicts peacefully. Ginger dreamed of such a peaceful world, and she knew it was within humankind to create it. No God in heaven had the power to do so, and Ginger would certainly not abandon this life she was given on earth for the meagre possibility of an eternal life in the hereafter. There was no guarantee for a life after this one, not to mention a paradise, and Ginger had no influence or whatsoever over that. But she did have the power to create a good life *now*.

The church said humans were made in the image of God, in their moral, spiritual and intellectual nature, that humans had to seek to live like angels. To be good. Pure. Free from sin. But Ginger did not want to be like an angel: she wanted to live as a human and die as a human. Life was after all a human experience. And she would no longer let anyone tell her what that should look like.

No, from now on, Ginger would follow her own truth.

"Let me go, mother. Don't fear and let me go in love and peace. All I ask of you is your blessing."

"I thought you no longer believed in such things," Ginger's mother said, wiping away her tears.

"Well, blessings are not strictly biblical. In fact, their origins are in Germanic paganism and the very word means 'to mark with blood'."

"I am not marking you with blood! That's disgusting!" Her mother's eyes had widened. Ginger chuckled, before she turned serious again.

"I didn't ask you. I just ask you to give me your blessing, as a mother. So that I may have your divine protection."

"I am not divine, Ginger."

"Didn't you teach me that God is in each and everyone of us?" Ginger answered and smiled as her mother reached out to her, murmuring a prayer, and kissed Ginger's forehead. She hugged her child one last time, then rose from the wooden bench and slowly left the family church.

Ginger ran into the woods, laughing, screaming, singing. There was nothing holding her back anymore. With the last light of day Ginger had left the village, climbed the hills and then began to run. Night had taken over now, but Ginger could not stop. She felt as if the stars were pulling her farther and farther into the heart of the land, leaving behind all that she had ever known and was taught to believe. Now there was only her pounding, wild, wild heart, while she gulped in the air, not being able to fill her lungs enough with all this new and fresh air. She reached another peak of a hill and as she overlooked the dark lands below her, a laughter bubbled in her throat and with joy Ginger screamed.

"Who art thou in heaven, HOLLOW is thy name! *Fuck you*!" She laughed and howled. "Fuck you! Do you hear me? FUCK YOU!" And with that Ginger spun around and ran down the hills, screeching, her arms spread wide, imagining to be an eagle soaring over the highlands. The stars above her became streaks of light and the moon shone brightly on Ginger's path that led her deeper into the night. She squealed in joy, giggling and shouting.

"Stars and moon lead me into temptation! Let us get drunk on liquid night! Let me taste and feed on life, dive deep into this orgastic experience, so that I may greet death as my equal! For mine is the queendom, and the power and the glory, for ever and ever and EVER AND EVER!"

And as Ginger ran farther and farther, she let every cell of her body be filled up with freedom. Never again would she bow to any men, any church or doctrine. No. She was a free human being and forever she would be.

☽ ☆ ☾

A fortnight later Will, Ginger, April and Jack sat in the room in the attic, stacks of books around them trying to find the right translations for the symbols they had seen in the church, always comparing them with the pictures Jack had taken. He had developed them during winter break, while he had stayed with the Blackwells and April was still wondering what he had done with the picture he had taken from her. The only consolation she had was that she was certain he would never show it to anyone. How should he explain all the blood and the symbols and her sitting on the altar, like the sacrifice of a satanic ritual?

"I am not getting anywhere with this shit," Ginger breathed out and closed the book she was holding with a thud. She sighed and looked at the others. "I mean, I am learning a decent amount about blood rituals, blood magic, blood curses and what not, but there is nothing in these books that describes anything similar to what we have seen."

"Well, ours wasn't really a ritual, was it?" Will said, suppressing a yawn. "How are you two getting on with the translations?" He leaned over to April and Jack who had been working side by side, since they had been the ones who had taken it upon them to do the actual translation work.

"Could be better," Jack admitted and pointed towards the few lines they had deciphered. "Thus far all we have is five runes and their meanings; spirit, word or reason, providence, wisdom and power, and those are actually the five elemental or primordial forces that have been described in many different works such as *The Refutation of All Heresies* or the the *Exegetica* of Basilides."

"What on earth are you talking about?" Ginger interrupted him, staring at him in confusion.

"Gnostic teachings?" Jack offered as an answer and Ginger sneered.

"You mean those weirdos who believe God is both good and bad?"

"Yeah, exactly."

"So, you think we are dealing with some gnostical stuff here?"

Jack shook his head. "No, they just make usage of the same magical tools as all the others."

"Such as the pentagram," Will offered and the others fell quiet. "Did I say something wrong?"

"No," April murmured, got up and walked over to where the map lay on the floor. The very same Jack had pulled out of his coat weeks ago and had showed them the cross. "A pentagram has five corners and there are five primordial forces, right? Jack can you bring those photographs over here, please? There must be a connection!" Jack stood by her side moments later, laying the images next to the map, already knowing what April was getting at.

"Please tell me you are not planning on going to that church and drawing a fucking pentagram on the floor, light some candles or some other shit and invoke demons?" Ginger grumbled and looked at them with so much concern in her eyes that Jack chuckled.

"Maybe not demons," he offered, grinning at Ginger who had also crossed the room and stood now next to April, "but maybe some sort of portal."

"To the underworld?"

"Possibly."

"You really do mean what you said," Will said quietly, looking at his best friend. Jack shrugged and offered a smile.

"Does it surprise you?"

Will shook his head. "Not really, no."

The two young men looked at each other for a moment.

"What time is it?" April suddenly asked and peered at Jack's wristwatch.

"Quarter past eight, why?" He turned towards her.

"I got a date and I better get going." The other three looked at her in disbelief.

"Now?" Will asked, knitting his brows. April nodded as she made her way over to her bag and cloak.

"Yeah, why not? Sergei is my boyfriend, and he likes to spend time with me."

"We also like to spend time with you," Ginger offered, but her grin didn't really reach her eyes.

"I know and I am sorry for leaving early. I shall see you tomorrow then?"

"Tomorrow?" Ginger tilted her head. "Does that mean you are spending your night...with him?"

April sighed and looked at her friends. "It means that I am getting back late, that's all."

"Okay," Ginger nodded. "Be safe, I guess?"

"I always am. See you!" And with that April was gone. The other three looked at each other. Will was the first who spoke.

"Do you think that it will always be like this from now on?" He turned up his nose. "Do boyfriends have priority?"

"I don't know," Ginger answered, scowling at the papers in front of them, "I don't have one."

"But if you had one, how do you think things should be handled?" Will insisted, still staring at the door.

"I don't know, okay?" Ginger sighed and shook her head. Then she turned her head and looked at Jack.

"You're awfully quiet! Don't you have an opinion on this as well? After all, you're the one pining after her in silence!"

"What?" Jack paled and stared at the redhead.

Ginger grinned. "I knew it!" She laughed. "And here I was thinking you were okay with her dating Sergei!"

"I *am* okay with April dating whoever she wants! It is none of my business!"

"But if you said what you felt, it *could* be your business. Wouldn't you want that?"

Jack frowned. "I don't know why it should be any of *your* business, Ginger," he hissed.

"Wow, softly," Will interrupted them. "Let's get some things straight here: I am not a huge fan of my sister dating Sergei and that's not because I don't like him, but because I don't think they are a good match. Further, Jack has his reasons I believe, for not telling April why he stares at her like a lovesick fool and that's that. And no, I will not talk April out of this, but I will not encourage it either."

Jack and Ginger stared at each other in silence, after Will had finished talking.

"Maybe I should have encouraged you, Jack, to go out with her," Ginger then finally said.

"I wouldn't have listened anyways," Jack answered. "Besides, I still think he's a good man and April should be with someone good-hearted."

"So, *you* did encourage her, didn't you?" Will tilted his head, looking at his best friend more closely.

Jack shrugged. "She asked what she should do. And I told her that Sergei liked her and he's...decent, you know."

"And you're not decent?" Ginger asked, raising her brows, a grin tugging at her lips. Jack smirked.

"Unlike Sergei, I am up to know good." He winked and nodded towards the paper. "You guys want to continue working? We've got still an entrance to hell to find?" Will laughed and Ginger smiled now as well.

"I still don't know why you are so sure of finding a portal to hell," Ginger said. Jack answered with a smile.

"Because it is what I hope to find. If there is anything that can bring down the church and let us live in freedom as who we are, then it is hell let loose."

☽ ☆ ☾

Jack walked through the old part of the city, his backpack filled with new notebooks, gauze bandages and liquorice for Ginger. While he had been in the store, he had thought about what he could buy for April, knowing she liked strawberry dumplings the most, but only those made by her mother. And the longer he was staring at the various sweets, the gloomier he became, realising that there was nothing he could actually offer to her. Not in this case and not in life in general. No, he was a sorry excuse of a man who had massive problems, a horrible family and no future. If he pulled through with his plans, his days were counted. At the checkout, Jack's eyes fell on a bouquet of white roses and he remembered staring at April, her beautiful face framed by white blossoms, the thick and warm air of the greenhouse all around them.

He would buy her flowers, every single damn day. And as he left the store, he began imagining a different kind of life. A life in which he got to choose how he wanted his future to be. Of course, he would continue with his current businesses and side hustles, that had allowed him to make his own money, and he would inherit the family estate in Romania. With his father's death all his mother's possessions would also be his. In Jack opinion's that day could come rather sooner than later. April would probably prefer to live at his mother's dacha though, that belonged to Jack since her death, or they could buy a nice town house here in the city. But then again, April liked greenery all around her, for she loved to sit in the garden, read and paint outside. She had once confessed to Jack that she rather experimented with flowers and herbs instead of alchemical substances, such as sulphur, lead or mercury. Jack mused about planting a garden for her, where she could grow all the plants, she wanted to use for whatever. Of course, they would also have vegetables and maybe a cherry tree, but it would be Jack who would care for them. And each spring the blossoms would rain down on their little Garden of Eden, and in summer they would pick the cherries, red and ripe. He himself would continue his work in healing potions, and with April's healing powers, he was sure they would make a great team.

Will had been right that April had already begun healing him. She had galvanised Jack's heart, had brought it back to life, after he had buried it, for he no longer thought to have any use for it. It was a painful kind of healing, but then again, healing was always painful. But with her by his side it wouldn't hurt that much. And with each day, the memories of the years passed would be washed away too. With each season, beginning with the blooming of the spring blossoms, the long days of Indian summers and the withering roses in autumn, he would be able to let go. And each day he would try to find something to make April laugh. To see that gleam in her eyes. That sparkle. He would give his damn arm to see her laugh.

"I don't have it yet!" A familiar voice tore Jack out of his daydreams and within seconds he had ducked behind a low wall, glancing around the corner. In a narrow alley he saw Sergei, standing next to a hooded figure, with whom he was arguing, their voices hushed.

"We need it by the end of the week. Understood?"

"End of the week? That will do." Sergei nodded and the hooded figure turned to leave. Sergei stared after them, waiting. Waiting for what?

Jack straightened himself up and a heartbeat later Sergei turned round the corner.

"You know some interesting people, that's for sure," Jack said quietly. Sergei flinched, supressing a cry of surprise, looking at Jack in shock, paling.

"What are you doing here?" Sergei blurted.

"Running errands. So, what's the deal with mystery guy?" Jack answered and nodded towards the alley, in which the hooded figure had disappeared.

"Nothing important," Sergei said evasively, putting his hands in his pockets.

"As chance would have it, you are dating a friend of mine and since I care about her and I won't let anything harm her, it is of *great* importance to me."

Sergei sighed and ran a hand over his face. "It's…unresolved business my father left behind. That's all," her murmured.

"Debts?" Jack asked. Sergei nodded. "Mostly, yes."

"And what kind of crowd are you owing money to, exactly?"

Sergei winced. Jack understood. The *very* unpleasant people you could owe money to.

"Please don't tell, April!" Sergei said with a pleading look and laid a hand on Jack's arm. He stared at it.

"I won't," he then finally said. "But only as long as I am convinced, she's not in any danger."

"Thank you, man." The young Ivanov genuinely looked relieved. Poor guy. Jack did not plan on ratting him out, at least not now. Jack couldn't help it but feel relieved too, just because of very different reasons. Sergei was involved in dirty business too, just like Jack. It did not make him a better person, but at least Jack didn't feel as awful as before.

"If there is anything you need help with, let me know," Jack then offered, and pulled a cigarette out of his pocket, which he then lit.

"That's very kind of you, but…I hope I won't have to get back to it, if you know what you mean," Sergei said, staring at the cigarette. Jack inhaled deeply. He had quit smoking years ago, but these days… Jack rolled his head, vertebrae cracking. The pressure really began feeding on him and cutting himself was only a brief relief and ever since April had seen the wound, kissed the mark and his scars… Well, Jack didn't do it as often as before. He was afraid that reopening the wound would wash away the memory of how her lips had felt on his skin.

"Don't thank me for it. You're also headed back to the monastery?" Jack asked. Sergei nodded and thus they walked back together, talking about classes, about the current experiments they were working on, about holidays, Christmas, about everything, except April.

) ☆ (

Jack stood in the courtyard, watching the snow fall. He was smoking again. The clouds of air mingled with the greyish fume. There were many things he had to think about. Another letter from his grandfather had reached Jack this morning. His grandfather was becoming impatient and whenever that old man was impatient, he also became aggressive. And that was a fire Jack wasn't willing to play with. At least not yet.

The paper existed no more. He had burnt it before he had lit his cigarette, some of the ashes still graced the top of his boots. He shook them off and watched them fall into the slush. Disgusting.

He took another drag. Jack hadn't lied when he had told Sergei that April's safety mattered to him. In fact, it mattered to him a great deal more than it was convenient to him. His grandfather wanted to meet up, send someone who would talk shit to Jack, about how slow he was progressing with his mission, about how he didn't know how important this was, that they had been working for it all their lives. Jack snorted disdainfully. Those assholes had no idea what it meant to work for something all your life. They had no idea what it this mission *truly* meant, and they were fools. All of them. His grandfather included. They had no idea what they were messing with, and neither did the guild. Better for him.

Jack took another inhale and puffed the smoke into the icy air. Yes, April's protection mattered now the most. Especially since Sergei had gotten involved with the wrong people over which Jack had no control. Unlike the ones he was dealing with. No, better not to tempt fate. Jack would take care of it. April might have been a stranger when he had met her, but things had changed and Jack...cared. More than he wanted to admit. Apparently, he even failed concealing his feelings, for Ginger and Will had noticed. After that night of the ritual in the woods, when April had turned the tables and had revealed what truly lay beneath her politeness and those beautiful, dark eyes, Jack had vowed to himself to stay away from her.

And for a couple of weeks, he had done a good job. But last night during dinner, he had watched her kissing Sergei near the entrance of the refectory, and as she had spotted Jack, she deepened the kiss, her eyes burning into Jacks, staring at him with that damn sparkle in her eyes. A wicked smile had formed on her lips, after she ended the kiss, her gaze still on Jack's face, who had only raised an eyebrow. He had heard her laughter while she pulled Sergei with her around the corner, vanishing from Jack's sight. Oh, what a terrible, terrible, beautiful thing she was.

Musing over that scene, Jack took another drag, letting his eyes wander over the courtyard. He watched two lovers from afar, holding hands, and wandering in between the nearby graves and it wasn't until they got closer, that Jack realised that it was Will and April he was looking at. The twins were holding hands and seemed to be in a deep conversation, but then again, they weren't talking. Jack took one last drag, then snipped the rest of his cigarette on the ground, where it went out immediately. At this movement Will lifted his head and his face lit up as he recognised Jack. Will gently pulled his sister with him, as they made their way over. How come that the twins still looked like a young couple in love? Truly, twins were a mystery of the universe.

"I didn't know you smoked?" April said, once the twins stood next to Jack.

"Well, I haven't for a long time."

"What changed?" Will asked. Jack shrugged.

"It must be the season. Plus, it gives me a chance to excuse myself and go outside."

"There are healthier ways to get some fresh air," April scoffed, but Jack only smiled. Oh yes, he had wanted to stay away from her. But how could he, now that he had seen, who she truly was? When she had looked at him last night, challenging him, while she kissed the lips of another?

"Maybe I would quit for you," Jack said with a wink, ignoring Will's stare. Only because he had said he would stay away Jack hadn't meant, that he wouldn't continue flirting with her.

"As if," April murmured, then looked at her brother. "Shall we go inside? I am cold."

"Sure, my love," Will nodded and looked at Jack expectantly.

"Lead the way," he said and followed the twins back to the monastery.

☽ ☆ ☾

"What do you think is the reason why all these practices have survived in the east?" April asked as she skimmed through a journal, in which someone had written down the various divination practices, initiation rites and other, well, rituals.

"I guess it's because the witch hunt never really reached these regions," Ginger said, looking up from the book. It was getting cold in the attic, whenever the sun went down, and the heater they had brought up didn't work properly anymore. While they had gone up to the attic to continue their research after classes as they always did, Jack and Will had tried to repair the heater, while the girls flipped through journals and books.

"Is that so?" Will asked and Jack nodded.

"Yeah, that's why the guild hunts witches. The old traditions and rituals have merged with the teachings and practices of the Orthodox church. That's why people here are still Heathens while they go to church each week, praying to the Heavenly father, yet still believing in their saints, and worshipping them in the way they had worshipped the Old Gods."

"Crazy, isn't it?" Will said and smiled at his sister in disbelief. "I have never thought about it, but it makes a lot of sense. By the way," he turned to Ginger. "How's your mother? Did you hear anything from her? It must have been quite the scene when you made your big announcement that you'll leave your father's church!"

"Bet it was."

"Yeah, you never really told us about it," April said, tilting her head as she looked at her friend. When Ginger had returned to school, she had filled them in only briefly about what had happened. She sighed.

"Well, my mother is still writing to me, updating me on how everyone is and what she's been up to, but she keeps the letters quite formal and...dry."

"What about your father?" Cautiously, they looked at Ginger. She shrugged.

"Not much. When I told him, I would leave the church, he wanted to talk it out. After a couple of hours, he just shook his head and told me I should pack my bags and leave. He said that no daughter of his would ever become an apostate. But if I wished to be, I should just go and never come back."

The others fell completely silent.

"You haven't told us that before," April murmured, rose to her feet and hugged Ginger. The redhead pressed her face in April's hair, hiding the tears that had welled up while she was talking. April rocked her gently from side to side.

"He threw you out?" Will asked in disbelief and sighed deeply. "You know, you're always welcome to stay with us!"

"I know," Ginger muffled against April's hair. "And...thank you. I know that I don't talk often about what's going on, but I know I can count on you and that means the world to me."

"You are going to make me cry as well," April sniffed, tears already in her eyes. Ginger laughed and wiped her face. Jack handed her a clean handkerchief, and Ginger blew her nose.

"Thank you," she murmured into Jacks direction, who gave her a small smile. "I guess, I am just sad. I am not even angry, and that's what scares me the most," Ginger admitted as she had calmed down.

"That's because you see other people's point of view," Jack said. "It may not be of much help right now," he continued, "but we are all very proud of you." Will and April nodded. Ginger laughed, then sniffed.

"What? That I chose to be a heathen?"

"That you chose *yourself*," Jack corrected her and pointed into the round. "We all here are what the church calls demon-born and we all are enemies of the guild. What I am trying to say, is, that you are among your own kind and that you'll never be alone. There are many, many others out there just like us, and they all will be there for you, if you need them. Like calls to like. Those who are like you, will always find you. Trust me. Look at us, we're living proof!"

"Thank you," Ginger whispered and then let the other three hug her, making her forget for a couple of seconds that her family had cast her out and there was no going back now. They had passed the point of no return a long time ago. Long before that night of the Velvet Revolution.

Chapter 13

Storm in the Stars

"Thus, a stranger to heaven and earth, / I live and no longer sing,
It's as if you cut off my wandering soul / From both paradise and hell."
– Anna Akhmatova, from The Complete Poems of Anna Akhmatova;
Anno Domini MCMXXI

Ginger sniffed and wiped her face, angry that the tears were coming back so relentlessly. She had cried more then she liked to admit to herself. It was getting late and she knew she should go to dinner, but she just couldn't bring herself to do it. She wasn't hungry, and neither was she keen on showing her tear-stained face to her friends. Let alone all the others that were sitting at dinner in the refectory. The door to the music room was suddenly pushed opened, and Ginger lifted her head in surprise. No one ever came here after school hours.

"Sorry, I didn't know anyone was here!" Cynlaef stood in the doorway, looking straight at Ginger who sat on the floor, next to the old harpsichord. Ginger just stared at him and he – stared back.

"What?" she then grumbled, wiping her face again. "Never seen a girl cry?" Cynlaef bit his lips. Ginger squinted her eyes. "You want to stay there until the day after tomorrow or can you leave me the fuck alone?"

"You're crying," Cynlaef said, taking a step into the room. The door shut gently behind him.

"That's what I just told you." Ginger knitted her brows. She wanted to be angry. She wanted to shout at him. That he had dared to disturb her in her misery. But the crying had used up all the energy, dried her from all the fire in her veins.

"No one should be alone when they're crying," Cynlaef said softly and made his way over to Ginger. His steps were careful, each movement slow as if he did not want to scare her away, the way someone would approach a hurt deer.

Cautiously he looked at her, sitting down, a couple of inches between them, holding out a handkerchief.

"It's clean," he said quietly, and Ginger took it with a nod.

"I prefer to be alone when I cry," Ginger then said with a side glance.

"What about your friends?" Cynlaef asked. Ginger shook her head.

"They've got enough problems of their own, I don't want to bother them."

"I am sure they won't feel bothered, rather glad that they can be there for you," Cynlaef replied.

"Well, it wouldn't change anything would it? Because what could they actually do to help me? My problems would still be there, and they would only feel awful too," Ginger then said, staring at the soft fabric in her hands. The handkerchief was made of white linen, simple, no initials, no decoration, just a clean seam.

"They could comfort you," Cynlaef suggested and Ginger snorted.

"No," she then said, "I prefer to cry alone."

"Does that mean you want me to leave?" Cynlaef asked, looking at Ginger. "Because I'd prefer to stay with you. I do not feel well knowing you're here all alone, upset and in distress."

"It's not like I can force you to leave," Ginger murmured. She looked briefly at Cynlaef, who then smiled at her.

"I knew about the balls, by the way," he then said, and Ginger tilted her head in confusion.

"The balls?"

"Yeah, the thing about how Viking women would cut off the balls of their husband if he disrespected her? Sergei told me you two had talked about it!"

"Ah, yes," Ginger smiled weakly. "I remember." Then she looked at Cynlaef again. His blue eyes were still trained on her and Ginger took a moment to look at his face.

"Sergei told me you have Viking ancestry?" She then said, skimming his face for the features she believed every Viking descendent must have. Sure, there were those blue eyes, fox-like cheekbones and defined jawline. He was handsome in his very own way and Ginger imagined what he would look like with longer hair, bound together, braided and shorn at the sides.

"I do," Cynlaef said, smirking, then looking away.

"But Cynlaef isn't an Icelandic name, is it? Nor is it Norse? It sounds Anglo-Saxon."

"That's true!" Cynlaef looked at her in surprise. "How did you know?" Ginger shrugged.

"Well, we *are* of Viking descent, but my mum is just like every other mum and chose a name that she liked. Plus, it's a very rare name actually," Cynlaef said with a light grin and revealed a fine gab between his front teeth. He kinda looked cute. Ginger returned the smile.

"So, you're saying you're a rarity?"

Cynlaef laughed.

"No, I am pretty average," he then said, blushing slightly. Oh, that was beginning to be fun! Ginger already started to think about what she could say to make him blush more, when he spoke again, this time more serious.

"You want to talk about it? What's upsetting you?" He looked at her carefully. The smile on Ginger's face vanished and she sighed, looking away.

"You don't have to if you don't want, of course not. But I know from experience that it can help. A sorrow shared is a sorrow halved."

"There isn't much to tell," Ginger murmured, beginning to pick at the edges of the handkerchief. She really liked the feel of the fabric between her fingers. "I told my father that I would leave his church and church in general and he then, well, disowned me. Told me I am his daughter no longer."

"Ouch," Cynlaef murmured and Ginger could feel is worried gaze on her. "That is a very hurtful thing to say and to do. In fact, it's horrible!"

"Well, it feels horrible, if that's what you mean." Ginger laughed dryly, then she felt the tears welling up again. She blinked them away. "Who does that anyway?" she then said, her voice pressed, her hands shaking. "Disowning his own daughter because of something like that. Doesn't each person have the right to believe in whatever they want?"

"I couldn't agree more," Cynlaef said. "I mean, for example, I myself do not believe in Jesus, the holy spirit or a heavenly father. I believe in fate. And the gods. You see, my mother only sent me here because this is the best school there is for alchemical studies, but I'm what Sergei likes to call a *pagan*. But..." Cynlaef smiled again. "He does so lovingly. After all, Sergei is one of my greatest friends. And he respects me as much as I respect him."

Ginger smiled again. She thought about how Sergei had asked her if April had a boyfriend. His reluctance and how visible it had been that he had such a massive crush on her friend. Would he still be so in love with Ginger's friend, if Sergei knew that April was a witch?

"Faith should not divide anyone," Ginger said softly. "If anything, it should bring us together! And for that we do not even have to believe in the same thing. For some it may be God, for others the Ancient Mother and for some..." She looked at Cynlaef again, and his blue, blue, blue eyes. "...fate."

"Very true." At her words Cynlaef had touched his chest, and Ginger's eyes locked on it, seeing that there was something under his shirt. Cynlaef followed her gaze and laughed lightly. A little embarrassed, he pulled out a necklace, revealing Thor's hammer on a string of leather.

"Oh, so you're one of *those* guys," Ginger chuckled now.

"I fear, I am." Cynlaef laughed.

"May I touch it?" Ginger then asked, her fingers prickling with the need to touch the talisman. What was that hammer made of?

"Sure!" Cynlaef took the necklace from his neck and handed it over to Ginger. Carefully, she took it, and her fingers traced the cool metal. Brass. Cool and kind of heavy, but Ginger liked to hold it in her hand.

"It's beautiful," Ginger murmured and then gave it back to Cynlaef.

"You should keep it," he said, folding her hands over it. Ginger raised her eyes, looking directly into his face. His hands were still clasped around Ginger's and the moment he realised and let go, Ginger wished he would not. His touch had been warm, reassuring and...comforting.

"And replace the cross that I just got rid of with a hammer?" She said jokingly, but then added with a serious tone, "I could not take it. It's important to you and..."

"You're important to me too," Cynlaef interrupted her. He blinked as if he had just realised what he had said and blushed. "I mean..." His voice trailed off, and Ginger kept staring at him. Cynlaef sighed, ruffled his hair and looked at her quickly.

"This might not be the best moment, but since I am already half-way there..." he murmured, then straightened himself slightly. "I have meant to ask you out since forever but never really dared to," Cynlaef confessed, now looking directly into Ginger's face. He had such blue, blue, blue eyes.

"You can do it now, if you want?" she offered, and smiled as she saw the surprise in his eyes, making them shine even brighter.

"Well, then...What about next weekend? Would you have time to go out with me? I mean, only if you want to go out with me, of course."

"I think I do." Ginger smiled and closed her hands tightly around the brass. The god she was taught to love and fear, had not answered any of her prayers, but maybe there had been others watching over her, weaving and knotting fate with their own divine hands, pulling the strings of life.

☽ ☆ ☾

The usual lilac blush covered the February skies. This was always the time of the year when April began to long for summer. Sure, she loved the darker months of the year and revelled in what those seasons brought; warm blankets and cups of tea, all the wonderful baked goods, snow and late nights reading in the library at home by the fireplace. Autumn and winter held their charms and there was so much beauty to be found in the storms, the harsh winds and bleak lands. Black trees, like skeletons stretching their arms into the sky, freezing winds and December's crimson sunsets. But winter had its way of gnawing at the bones, biting into the flesh and making the heart feel so heavy.

April wandered through the courtyard, lost in thoughts. Weekends weren't special days at the monastery but enjoyed by everyone: the apprentices were free to go wherever they wanted in the city, and many did just that. Weekends were the time when couples usually went on dates or students ran their errands. April had spent the last ones with Sergei, letting him take her out, going for walks, ice-skating and drinking hot chocolate in her favourite cafés. This weekend though, April hadn't felt like going out; she felt the well-known melancholy creeping up her spine and settling in her head and April had learned that long and solitary walks usually did help. She had been out for hours, taking her time, walking around the school's garden, peeking into the greenhouses, smelling flowers and daydreaming of long summer days; fresh berries cooking in a pot on the stove, the taste of sweet cherries, freshly baked bread with cream cheese and homemade jam. Running through the fields, spending hours on the swing in the backyard or hanging out at the nearby playground; helping her grandparents in the garden, harvesting all the fruit, baking for hours and hours in the kitchen and putting all the treasures in the freezer, alongside the extra berries and fruit for future mouth-watering delicacies. With each thought about summer and every core memory that she recalled, the warmth spread through her body and she found herself almost smiling, when she turned round the corner, her gaze falling onto Jack. He sat on one of the garden walls at the far end of the yard. On the other side of the wall, was one of the alleys of the city, where also common people passed by. April wasn't sure if they knew what kind of school they actually were, but then again, did she really care?

Jack had spotted her from afar and lifted his hands. Slowly, she made her way over to him.

"I thought you wanted to quit smoking?" April said as a greeting and watched Jack puffing out smoke, cigarette in his hands and his lips forming into a mocking smile.

"You don't like it?" He said, shifting his weight.

"Not much," April answered, crossing her arms and looked up to him, where he was still sitting on the wall. Jack flicked away the cigarette and jumped off the wall. He coughed. April raised her eyebrows.

"See, it makes you sick! Besides, you didn't have to get down for me," she said, tilting her heads towards the wall.

"As much as I do enjoy seeing you looking up at me from beneath, I don't like talking down on women. But that sight of yours, does leave room for the imagination," Jack said, grinning and took a step closer to April. His eyes travelled over her face, then down to her waist and up again. The late afternoon sun reflected the golden sparks in his eyes, and it was one of those moments when April was no longer sure what colour they had. His grin faded and instead he looked at her pensively, as if he wasn't quite sure about... Well, about what? Dear Lord, she hated when he looked at her like this! It made her blood boil and flattened her breath. It switched off the logical thinking part of her brain, making her lose control. Just like that night in the woods. But was she truly out of control, or did she finally gain it?

"Maybe," April answered, her voice soft, "I would enjoy it too." Her heart pounded. Did she say too much? Leaned too far out of the window? Jack smirked, taking another step towards April, edging her to the wall.

"Yeah, maybe, but I believe in worshipping and serving the woman first." His voice sent shivers down April's spine and she was glad when she felt the cool stone of the wall beneath her palms, having something to hold onto, because she was sure as hell that at some point her knees would give in, if Jack kept looking at her like that. Oh, she hated how weak he made her feel. How bold she was when he teased her. How embarrassed and courageous his words made her. He was a fucking paradox. He made her come alive and woke up that deep, feral desire and it pained her to know, that no matter how much she tried, it would never feel like this with Sergei.

"I think you did it on purpose," April blurted out.

"Did what?" Jack took another step towards her.

"Making me go out with Sergei so you can play these games," she answered, palms pressing into the wall. Something flickered in Jack's eyes and a mischievous gleam settled over them.

"I have been playing games from the beginning," he murmured, and April suddenly was no longer sure what he was talking about, but then he continued talking, leaning in closer, stealing away the air she needed to breathe. "But it makes it more fun that way, doesn't it?" He smirked and lifted his hands. Ever so gently, he brushed a loose strand of her dark hair behind her ear, his fingers touching her skin, lingering at the nape, far too long to be casual.

"And why's that?" April breathed, clenching her hands. Oh, she could feel her knees give in. Jack smiled and leaned in even closer, his lips brushing the shell of her ear and she could feel the air of his breath snaking down her skin setting her on fire. He had never gone this far. Not like this. The last time it had been her, who had pulled him in, the rush and heat of the music in her veins. She still remembered how it had felt like, their bodies flushed against each other, could still hear Jack's soft moan and growl. Did he truly not desire her? He had refused her, yes, but right now...? Her eyes flicked up to his face and as she saw her own hunger reflected in his, she knew, they both had been playing games. The question was simply, who would be the first one to give in.

"Because it turns you on." Jacks voice vibrated through April's body, his words making her remember where she was. "Tell me," he coaxed softly, "does it turn you on knowing that anyone could see us right here? That one of Sergei's friends or he himself could see me touching you like this? Two friends, hidden in the shadows of the walls..."

"If that's your idea of friendship, then it's a pretty messed up one, considering Ginger or my brother," April panted, feeling Jacks hand slide around her waist.

"You knew from the beginning that we could never be friends, April," Jack answered, his other hand touching her chin and lifting it up so that he could look into her eyes. "Friends is the label we have given ourselves so that we could keep some distance between us and that's a good thing."

"Why? Because you don't think about me like that? Is that why you refused me in the woods?" April narrowed her eyes. She saw surprise flicker through Jack's eyes, realising that until now he must have thought that she didn't remember much of that night of the ritual, since it was what she had told him and her brother the day after.

"Oh, precious, since that night in the confessional, I haven't thought about you in any other way but this." His fingers graced her neck again, sliding down, tracing her collarbone. April could feel all of her body react to these simple touches and she had to bite hard on her lip not to let any sound escape her mouth. Jack registered that with another wicked smile.

"You haunt my dreams and every waking moment, April. There is no day that passes that I do not wish to make you mine and do all the sinful things to you, that I cannot stop thinking about. And though I am a selfish bastard, I cannot risk being selfish with you. I want to protect you from anything and anyone that could do you harm, and that includes myself. I promised it to you, remember? That I won't let it hurt you if I can."

"So, you're just a hypocrite? About…everything you feel for me?" April felt that her hands were trembling again. She hated feeling weak like this.

"No, I would not lie to you about this. But I warn you: do not tempt me. You're playing with things you cannot control. Things that are even out of my control."

"And what if I do not want control?" April said, laying her hands onto his chest. "What if I want you?" she whispered.

"Then hell shall open up and devour me, before I devour you," Jack responded, a soft tremble in his voice.

"You're just a coward, that's what," April replied and this time it was her leaning closer towards him.

"I warned you," he murmured, his eyes fixed on her lips.

"I heard you the first time," April whispered, staring at his lips. "Now kiss me."

A branched snapped some distance away, and Jack stepped away instantly, turning round to see who was coming down the orchard.

"Oh, hey, what are you two doing here?" Sergei appeared moments later between the trees, his cheeks red from the cold, his hands buried deep in the pockets of his coat.

"Smoking," Jack answered and gave him a wry grin. To her surprise, April saw that Jack had lit a cigarette in his hands, standing one arm's length away from her. How had he managed to light a cigarette within a second without her noticing? She had probably been too occupied, trying to bring her emotions under control, knowing someone would round the corner every moment. She was still trembling ever so slightly, but not from fear but the awakened desire that still rushed through her. She crossed her legs hoping it would stop the throbbing between her thighs.

"I didn't know you smoked!" Sergei now said, looking at April.

"Yeah, well, gave us a chance to catch up on some things, since you have been keeping our dear April pretty busy with all those dates of yours," Jack answered, taking a drag. He smiled, looking at his fingers, then let his gaze wander over April, taking in her flushed cheeks, her crossed legs, and the spot of blood on her lips where she had bit herself a little too hard. "We're lab partners, so we needed to clear up some things, plan ahead, you know. But don't worry, you can have her back, she's all yours." Jack winked at April.

"I belong to no one," she hissed.

"Of course not, princess," Jack chuckled, threw his cigarette on the ground, and stubbed it out. "See you around!" He nodded into Sergei's direction, not even looking at April as he made his way out of the orchard. *There is no day that passes that I do not wish to make you mine*, echoed Jack's voice in April's head and she bit down on her lip even harder. She hated him, that was for sure.

"So…" Sergei stepped next to April, taking her hand and kissed her on her abused lip. "You want to go for a walk?"

"No." April shook her head. The heat between her legs had become overbearing and all she wanted was that Jack finished what he had started. With an impatient tug, April dragged Sergei into a nearby garden shed, where they kept all the orchard nets and baskets for harvesting, ignoring his silent protest.

That night, April laid in her bed, unsatisfied, her body trembling with the ache of wanting to be touched. Sergei's hands had not nearly been enough and April wanted Jacks lips between her thighs and his tongue licking up the mess he had made there. She wanted to feel him everywhere until she forgot how to spell her own name.

☽ ☆ ☾

April refused to look at Jack all throughout the next day. During morning classes April listened to Ginger's whispering, as she told her everything about her first date with Cynlaef, and April couldn't stop smiling. It had been such a long time since Ginger had seemed so happy. There was this sparkle in her eyes whenever she said Cynlaef's name and a light blush lingered on her cheeks the entire time. It was like watching a rose coming into bloom and April hugged her best friend tightly, whispering into her ear, how glad she was. After lunch they had lab work and April made sure she was sitting as far away from Jack as possible. What bothered her the most, was that there was nothing in Jack's behaviour that revealed anything about yesterday's encounter in the gardens. He was polite as usual, asked the same heretical questions in class as always, worked efficiently by her brother's side as usual, and offered April and Ginger to clean their workspaces like always. April wanted to scream.

Sure, she had a boyfriend but if Jack wanted to continue playing these games…why not. And though society may not have approved of such behaviour in women, she had never neglected herself her wants and needs. And what she wanted right now, was Jack. But not like this. Not when he was acting like this. Not when he had the upper hand in this game. April was pretty pissed at the end of the day, though she tried to hide her discontent while she was working with Will, Ginger and Jack on their research.

"Do you think since this seems to be some kind of blood ritual," Will asked after a while, supressing a yawn, "that there will always be some sort of blood sacrifice needed?"

"I guess," Jack said, not looking up from his books.

"That sounds a little too simple to me," Ginger interrupted them and pointed on the page she was currently reading. "Blood sacrifices are very specific! Like, depending on the kind of ritual you are doing, specific animals or materials are required."

"But it did work out just fine, didn't it?" April asked, looking straight passed Jack, her eyes fixed on Ginger's red hair.

"Yeah, but what if that chalice on the altar stood there exactly because it is part of the sacrifice?"

"I mean, we could go and try it out?" Will interjected. "Say, let's take some other bowl and use someone else's blood."

"And tempering with something we hardly know anything about?" Ginger scrunched her nose.

"I'm with Ginger," Jack said quietly. "It is dangerous to play around with these kinds of things."

"Yet it was *you* who suggested to play around with this dangerous thing in the first place," April now said, looking straight into Jacks eyes. He lifted an eyebrow.

"I never forced you to do anything," he answered, narrowing his eyes.

Will and Ginger exchanged quick glances, sensing the arising argument.

"We all agreed that we were doing this together," Ginger said carefully, eyes darting between Jack and April who were still staring at each other.

"True," April said, a smile curling at her lips. "Then why don't we just go down to the church and cut open Jacks skin for a change? I am sure he won't have much of a problem with that, since he made me do it last time and seems to have experience with these kinds of things!"

April knew she had gone too far, and she regretted her words the same moment she saw hurt, actual hurt flicker in Jack's eyes. It was there for a brief second, then it was gone, and cool blue waters hid what lay beneath the surface.

"No one's going to cut open anything," Will interrupted, closing his book with a thud. "We will continue with the research as planned and translate the symbols. That way we can make sure that we know what we are dealing with and will be able to plan accordingly. Agreed?" Silence. April and Jack were still staring at each other, until Ginger let out a groan.

"Come on you two, can be please just move pass this? Whatever it is that you're angry about each other, can't you just kiss and makeup?"

Jack's and April's heads snapped to her and Ginger held up her hands defiantly.

"Sorry, no kissing then," she murmured and shook her head. "My bad."

"I think it's better if we called it a day," Jack murmured, getting on his feet.

"Alright," Will agreed and the girl's nodded. In silence they put away the books and then descended the stairs. They heard others making their way to the common rooms, while others were still at dinner, the sounds echoing through the halls and corridors. As they reached the bottom of the stairs and stood in the corridor that led to the cloister, Will's voice made them stop.

"Since we didn't get much work done tonight because of the two of you," he looked at April and Jack, "I suggest you go for a walk and talk it out. Because it sucks for Ginger and me having to be around you two, not even knowing the reason why you're fighting, and I am tired of this!" He gestured between them. "You need to clear things up. You either talk it out or have some make-up sex, I bloody don't care!"

"Will!" Jack and April hissed at him outraged, while Ginger only giggled.

"That's *not* funny!" April snapped at her friend, which made her laugh only more. Jack had gone pale.

Will had crossed his arms, unimpressed. "What are you two waiting for?" he asked, gesturing towards the portal. "I am damn serious! Go! Now!"

April stared at her brother angrily, then turned on her heels and walked out into the night. She didn't care if Jack was following her, just knew, that she had to get away, otherwise she would slap someone. Preferably Jack.

After a while her breathing calmed and that was when she heard footsteps behind her. She turned and saw that Jack was following her, keeping a healthy distance between them, so that she could not punch his goddamn face. April didn't know how long they had been walking, just that her hands were freezing, and her anger slowly turned into regret, remembering what she had said to Jack. She would never forget how hurt he had looked at her. It had been an awful thing to say, knowing that Jack cut himself. April stopped walking.

"Jesus Christ!" Jack said, walking nearly into her. She turned round. Jack looked at her in surprise, his face not revealing anything else. It was a white, cold surface, a beautiful marble prince, that looked at April with those clear blue eyes.

"I am sorry," she said straightforward, watching Jacks eyes widening ever so slightly. "I shouldn't have said what I have said. It was…a horrible thing to say. I didn't mean it."

"You were angry," Jack answered, tilting his head. "And you *did* mean it," he added. April sucked in her bottom lip and looked away.

"I did," she confessed quietly and was surprised when she heard Jack chuckling.

"At least you're being honest," he said. "Besides, I couldn't be angry with you, even if I wanted to." He sighed and walked pass April, and she followed him.

They walked on in silence for a while. They had once again found their way back to the orchard and with a shiver April recalled the things that had happened here the day before. They reached the same spot near the wall, but now it was almost completely dark around them and it was hard for April to make out Jack's face. Maybe it was the darkness that gave her the courage or the desperation of having to say *anything* to break the silence.

"Can I ask you something?" At April's question, Jack turned his face towards her and nodded slowly. She took a deep breath. "Why did you start cutting yourself? Why…are you hurting yourself?"

Jack sighed silently, knowing April would ask that question one day.

"To be honest…" Jack turned, leaning with one shoulder against the wall, arms folded so that April could look into his face, "I've never been able to accept it. To accept *what* I am." He brushed over his sleeve beneath which April knew was his mark. "My Mama was an insecure, secretive woman, she lived in constant fear and anxiety. At least, she was that way ever since I was born. She taught me the basics of living with it. In particular, that no one was ever allowed to find out what I was and that I should never let anyone see the mark. She always told me that she would protect me from all the evil in the world, but most of the time it felt like I was protecting *her* from everything. The mark... Just looking at it brings out so much anger, disgust and hatred in me. I kept trying to cut it out... and yet I never could."

April inched closer so that she could see Jack's face more clearly. She read so much pain and despair in his eyes and would have liked to take him into her arms and comfort him, but she didn't dare bridge the seemingly insurmountable distance between them and touch him. Not after what had happened yesterday. When Jack continued talking, his words were little more than a whisper.

"Having the mark is incredibly dangerous, but it's the last thing I have left of my mother. And I can't let her go."

"I think it's always wrong to cut off a part of yourself, no matter what," April said carefully.

"You're probably right," Jack replied quietly and looked up at the sky. The dark trees loomed out of the night like barren ghosts. There was still some snow, but the rain had washed most of it away or melted it. They were both lost in thought, April thinking back to the night she and Jack had argued with Harris, while Jack thought about his mother and home. *Home* was probably the wrong word; *temporary residence* was a better word. The Blackwells' house was a home. Or the Ivanovs' estate. But Rosier Manor was a house as cold as the white marble from which it had been built. Sculptures frozen into eternal stasis, leaning over banisters and balustrades, suspiciously eyeing every person who passed beneath their wings. Whenever he thought of his family, the Manor or his mother, he felt an irrepressible desire to plunge a knife deep into his arm and whitewash any other pain and paint the walls of his inner torture chambers with new colour. The knowledge of what he had been sent here to do, because he could do what no one else could, what he felt compelled to do...

But the real tormentors in his mind were not the voices of his grandfather or father, no. His tormentor stood beside him, gazing into the black night of the new moon, her skin peeling out of the darkness like moonlight. A dark fairy of the night, the stuff of every nightmare, lifting him into unearthly realms, where flowers grew from his chest in full ecstasy, white and deadly, wrapping around his neck, strangling and sucking all the air from his body and in between this young woman's lips. Dark blood and the heavenly glow around her; she would be his angel of death and deliver the final blow between his ribs the day she would learn the truth. And she would, Jack was under no illusions. And it would be him, who would tell her the truth. That was the least she deserved. But until then, he no longer wanted to deprive himself of April and her magic, wanted to immerse himself in the nightshade and stumble drunkenly through the darkness. All he had to do was reach out his hand. She was so close.

And then she looked at him. April's dark eyes bore into his, and he felt his pulse quicken, his breath quiver. Mist hung hazily between them; an inseparable chasm separating his world from hers, and between them the black water and veils of the here and there-before.

She was so close and still looking at him.

"You think they know?" April's voice tore him from his thoughts.

"Know what?" Jack asked hoarsely, still not taking his eyes form her.

"Ginger and Will. That we…"

"That we what?"

April bit her lips and Jack lifted his hands to touch them. He caressed the abused flesh, knowing he would taste blood if he kissed her.

"That we…" April couldn't bring herself to finish the sentence, Jack's fingers still gracing her lips. She shivered.

"Are you cold?" he asked, stepping closer. April sucked in breath. He couldn't do this again. She wouldn't let him seduce her with all his lovely words, only to leave her even hungrier and unsatisfied.

"No," she answered and took a step back from him. Jack registered it with a raised eyebrow.

"I think they both know," Jack then quietly answered April's unfinished question, the air now heavy between them. Like a sleepwalker April stumbled away from him, trying to find some common sense in her. They needed to talk it out. She needed clarity. Or he could also just kiss her, touch her and give in to her silent plea. She stumbled again, but her hands brushed the bark of a tree and gratefully she leaned against it. Jack stood directly in front of her seconds later

"What do you want, Jack?" April asked, swallowing hard.

"I told you what I wanted," he answered. "But I also told you the reasons why I cannot."

"And yet you keep playing with me like this? You cannot touch me like this, if you want me to believe what you're saying about keeping distance between us. This is not what distance looks like!" With that, April lifted her hand and touched Jack's face. He could feel that her hands trembled and saw her chest heaving.

"I don't want to corrupt you," Jack said, savouring her touch. With a flutter he closed his eyes, only to open them again, when he heard a soft gasp escaping April's lips, as he touched her waist. "You look so innocent and pure," he murmured, taking her face in between his hands. "So beautiful, so untainted."

"I am more depraved than you think I am," she said, her voice husk. She didn't even know she could sound like this.

"You sure about that?" Jack's breath brushed over her collarbone and the top of her cleavage, as he bent down and kissed her neck ever so softly. "I think I am very much aware of how depraved you are," he murmured against her skin. "I saw you looking at me when you kissed that poor Ivanov boy. You are no good. All I did was making you see who you truly are by making you go out with him."

"And did it work?" April whispered, almost breathless. Her breasts tightened and felt the wetness collecting between her legs.

"Oh, precious," Jack murmured, licking the soft skin of her neck. "Of course, it did. Because you were made to be mine," Jack said and then he kissed her.

April felt her body dissolving into all directions. And although she was completely bereft of any air, she knew that all she had ever needed, were those lips pressed onto hers, sucking out all air from her lungs. And every time their lips met again and again the fire burned its mark onto her sensitive skin. She tasted blood, not sure if it was his or hers, but who the fuck cared. Jack licked her lip, sucking it between his teeth and bit her. April moaned and let her teeth travel over his bottom lips, her tongue licking up the blood, tasting it in his mouth – and finally April tore herself away. Jack's growl sent shivers down her spine, but April pressed her hands firmly against his chest, her eyes capturing his gaze.

"What?"

"This…is *wrong*, isn't it?" April panted, all of her aching to taste him one more time. More. She needed more. More of him. More more *more*.

Jack raised an eyebrow, while he cupped her face with such tenderness, that April feared she would start to cry. This man was too much for her poor nerves.

Because you were made to be mine.

"Wrong?" He echoed her words, then pressing his lips against her neck, his tongue drawing a line up to her ear. "Then maybe you want to go back to your pure-blooded Russian prince, letting him tell you what a *good girl* you are, when we both know that you're not."

"You're mean," she said and gasped when Jack wrapped both his arms around her waist, pulling her so close that there was not an inch between them.

"And you're a cruel, beautiful thing," he coaxed gently, and nibbled at her bottom lip. "Nothing was ever as easy as falling in love with you," he murmured against her lips and then looked into her eyes.

"You…you're in love with me?" April's voice trailed off, barely audible, a hush carried away by the winds.

"Yes, April," Jack whispered and kissed her again, this time even softer and slow. "Yes, I am in love with you."

April breathed in, feeling the warmth spread all through her body and sighed, his touch was pure bliss, resurrecting her from whatever grave she had lain in, until he had come and had lifted her up to the heavens. She felt Jacks hands exploring her body, trailing up and down her sides, sliding into her coat, pulling her even closer, caressing her hips, her waist and his tongue on her neck, on her lips –

sucking and licking it, consuming her – and April just gave in. She let herself fall, and each kiss transformed the air around them into liquid night. Trembling, her hands clenched the dark fabric of Jacks coat, roamed further, feeling the seam of his shirt and April longed to feel his skin beneath it. Jack licked her lips and as if on command April moaned. She felt him smiling against her mouth and it was then when she finally understood, why the angels had descended from heaven, tempted by the devil to give into the desire, give into this rush; madness it may have been, but the more oxygen Jack stole from her lips and she was drowning in the taste and scent of him, the more she was willing to see, just how far she could fall. April felt a storm in the stars erupting around them – descending into hell was easy, thus had spoken Vergil. And this time, April would not even have to find a hidden portal beneath a Catholic church – she only had to give in.

Jack buried his hands deeply in April's hair, gently pulling her head back, while she tilted her neck to give him better access. With a soft hum Jack's lips graced her sensitive skin and while he was so close, April stood on her tippytoes and took the chance and pressed a kiss onto his neck as well. With amusement in his eyes Jack looked at her, smiling and gently stroked her cheek. Just as Jack opened his mouth to say something – he heard a whisper. He lifted his eyes, listening to the murmuring voices coming from between the trees, his senses stretched to the limit.

"Do you hear that?" April whispered.

"Yes, I do."

"That's *them*," April murmured, looking at Jack with wide eyes. "They're the witches I told you about!"

And the moment April uttered the words, Jack saw them among the trees: shimmering, misty figures, long hair tousled as if tangled in an invisible current. Clothes blown away by a wind from another world and their faces... Jack stared at the creatures, felt the icy cold emanating from them and creeping along the ground towards them, felt his hands begin to tremble and he swallowed hard. Gone was the heat and the warmth that the electricity and fire between them had flushed his body. There was only cold winter air now. The same coldness that had resided in his bones for ages. April's eyes were fixed on Jack's face and just as she was about to turn and look at what had captivated Jack's gaze, he grabbed her by the shoulders, turned her face towards him, away from the ghosts, pressing her head to his chest.

"Don't look," he whispered, almost choking on his own words, he spoke so hastily. "If you look at them, they will try to gain access into your mind. Your witch powers are like a bridge they can use to nest in you, and with souls that have never completed the transition to the realm of the dead, you never know which side they're on, and whether they're hostile or not!"

April stood stock-still, as he cradled her head, and she breathed in the scent of his chest. She thought she could feel his heartbeat – frantic, loud and hard. She lifted her eyes, staring at his face, her gaze resting on his lips. Cracked from the cold, bit open, skin torn by her very own teeth. There was still some blood oozing from them, and again April felt an unbending force burrow from the depths of her core and reach for the surface. April could let it out, let it take over, let it do whatever it wanted. She felt the hunger for more. Kissing Jack had woken something in her and it wanted to be freed. In her veins April felt the thunder of a storm brewing, the pulling sensation of rain, and in her chest a wild pounding heart that no longer beat in the body of a human being. April opened her mouth, Jack's eyes still wide, and then – sudden, freezing cold.

Jack slid his hand over April's eyes and kissed her again. There was desperation in this kiss, fear and... She felt something clashing against that pulsating, vibrant energy that had begun to uncoil itself within her, and April knew instinctively, that she was feeling him. It was Jack's magic, his powers that had intertwined themselves with hers. And as the world around April went dark and the warmth of Jack's hand spread through her eyelids and throughout her body, April felt as if she was stepping into a flaming inferno.

The gates of hell seemed to have opened all around her and hissing flames shot out of the ground. Gusts of wind coursed through the fire and tore at April, causing her to stumble, but she was caught by arms. Jack stood in front of her, holding her form, staring at her. He lifted his gaze, let his eyes wander, and now April saw that the most misshapen creatures were crawling towards her from all directions;

winged monsters, angels with tattered wings; the dead, half-dead and half-putre-fied, the smell of decay, of blood and innards – and then the shrilling scream of the maw from which the hellfire had burst. And there in the distance, the burning silhouette of a church. The crackling of fire, and the acrid smell of sulphur filled the air, and all those noises; shrieks, screams, gasps and howls of terror, cries of agony – as if in pain, as if… April's hands clawed at Jacks arm, feeling herself hurting him, and then – blood dripping out of Jack's eyes.

"April…" he whispered and a second later his body disintegrated into a swarm of a thousand moths. April screamed. Black blood was now oozing out of the ground, pouring out beneath April's feet, and she screamed and screamed, as the blood rose higher and higher within seconds; the hot flames began to scorch her skin, as Jack's lips had burned hers, moments before and icy cold crept further through April's body, eating through her chest and closing in around her heart. Cold claws dug into April's core – and she blacked out.

"April! God*damn* it, wake up!"

Someone was shaking her. April felt her head swinging back and forth, part of a body that didn't seem to be her own. Someone shook her again and with a gasp, like a drowning woman breaking the surface of the water, April opened her eyes.

Above her she saw blackness, then the outlines of branches. She was in Jack's arms on the ground of the orchard, the image of moths eating his eyes still before her, and at the same time there was Jack's face, whole and intact, as beautiful as always, only his gaze, distorted by fear, a blemish – a crack in a Michelangelo paint-ing, the shadowy face behind the lines of a poem by Edgar Allen Poe.

"April?" Jack's voice trembled, his hand stroking her cold cheek. Slowly, April sat up and Jack supported her with both arms.

"What…happened?" April's voice was raspy and scratchy in her throat, as if she had been screaming for hours.

"I don't really know myself," Jack confessed quietly, supporting April's back with one hand and brushing damp earth from her hair with the other.

"When I..." Jack broke off and shook his head. "The spirits of the witches came at us and I covered your eyes and then we were suddenly somewhere else. I could see thousands of...beings, dead and other...creatures around us and there..." Once again, he couldn't find the words to continue, his hand resting in April's hair. She remained silent. April tried to remember more clearly, but the images vanished as soon as she thought about them. Only the icy cold remained.

"I can't remember exactly," Jack confessed, as if he had read her thoughts.

"Me neither," mumbled April. A leaden tiredness came over her unexpectedly and without wanting to or being able to control it, she slumped against Jack. She closed her eyes, leaning her head against Jack's chest, the fabric of his coat scratching her cheek. She was so infinitely tired. Without exchanging another word, Jack put his arms around April, kissed her forehead, then lifted her up and carried her out of the dark orchard.

April had already fallen into a doze, when Jack turned round and nodded to the figures, who were barely distinguishable from the black tree trunks in their dark cloaks, and they began to retreat into the dark night, becoming invisible again. Only the bare trees, the whispering of the night and the memory of a terrifying spectacle remained.

Chapter 14

Coagulatio

*"For now, we see through a glass darkly, but then face to face.
If it is face to face, there must two be looking."*
– Margaret Atwood, Alias Grace

Jack sat hunched over his notebook in the defective girls' bathroom, where he always holed up when he wanted to make sure no one disturbed him. It was the middle of the night and everyone was sleeping, except him. But how could he, after what he had witnessed just hours before? When April's and his magic had collided, and they had opened what Jack suspected to be a slip between dimensions? And though everything he had seen was the perfect image of the hell as described in the bible, it could not be hell itself, that would have been too easy. Right? It *could* not be, that the two of them had managed what his grandfather and the Order of Lucifer had been trying for years, and which was also the very reason Jack had been sent to Prague. It was simply too easy. Jack had gone over their notes over and over and over again.

Facilis descensus averni. The descent into hell is easy.

What if Vergil had been right in the end? Maybe Jack had overlooked something in his research, jumping to conclusions without having all the facts.

April's magic, that darkness she hid so well from others, but was not able to hide from him, was like an answer to an equation he had never been able to solve. An echo in the eternal abyss; an answer to all his desperate screams whenever the darkness consumed him more and more. Jack wasn't sure what it was within April that called out to him. Whatever force kept the primum mobile in motion, which had been there long before the magnum opus of alchemy had begun, was the same force that was spinning their hearts. A simple, alchemical reaction that had made Jack fall in love against his will yet so predestined by fate, for it was April herself that was part of that infernal equation, without her even knowing so. She was not only the loophole Jack's grandfather believed her to be, to lift the curse, but she was also the one whose blood opened the gates to hell, for she was the descendent of those whose blood had sealed the entrance in the first place. And it was through Jack that they had managed to do so: they truly were a match made in hell. The demons that had sown his mother's body during his conception had done their job well.

Just like him, April was just a pawn in the game others had been playing for a very long time, and he hated himself even more, for realising this only now. Jack groaned and buried his face in his hands.

A couple of days earlier he had thought to be still in control of everything; to be able to master the game others had set up to trap him. He had found all the backdoors and had managed to pull the strings so that things were going his way. What had changed?

Jack could see April's face even when he closed his eyes. It was always there. It was her, who had turned the tables, not in his favour and against his will yet... Had it not been him, who had given in? He remembered how she had looked at him, his angel of death; her dark eyes boring into him, staring deep into his soul and unleashing each and every desire, one more sinful than the other. He had felt the falling, the moment he had told himself *fuck it.* and had kissed her. He had been weak and tempted, he had messed it up all by himself. Maybe he deserved it, for all the lies and half-truths he had told her.

Jack laughed drily, and to his surprise he felt something wet on his cheeks. Astonished he looked at his hands and as he licked the liquid sticking to his finger, realising that he was crying. He felt the tears burning hot on his cold cheek. He hadn't cried since his mother's death. That day he had learned to truth about his birth; the truth of his conception and the crimes they had committed against his mother. He had watched the life flowing out of her body and when she could barely speak anymore, she ordered Jack to open the window. Of course, he got up, stood on the stool and pushed open the skylight, the only small window in the attic, where his mother had spent her last weeks. And as he had turned round, a tired smile on his face, he saw the light fading from her eyes and he swore that *something* broke free from her body, spiralled through the room and then had vanished through the window and into the golden light of the afternoon. Jack had cried for many, many hours but when he stood in the family's chapel, his mother washed and clothed on a stretcher, there were no more tears left. Jack remembered hearing the bell chime five times and moments later his father's footsteps as he walked into the chapel.

"I'm taking the night express back to Bucharest," Jack had said quietly, as his father had stopped a couple of paces behind him.

"The funeral is not for another two days," his father had answered. "Don't you want to be there when they bury your mother so that she can rest in peace?"

"Why would I want to do that, if she could haunt you for the rest of your days?" Jack had replied, turning to face his father. "After what you all have done to her, it seems to me a rather fitting end, don't you think?" And with that Jack had left the chapel, not looking back, not even to catch a last glimpse of his mother. He had bid his farewells and he had made his promise to her: he would avenge her and when he had brought down the guild, the order and the church, she would find her well-deserved peace. And now, Jack had messed it all up. Simply because he had fallen in love with the girl he was supposed to deliver to the order, because she was the only one who had the power to do what they wanted. When his grandfather had ordered Jack back from Romania and assigned him his mission, Jack had asked why he was the one who had been chosen, since he was one of the youngest members and this had seemed to be far too important. His grandfather had handed him a photograph in a simple silver frame.

"Who is she?" Jack had asked, staring at the old black and white picture of a beautiful young woman. Dark hair and big eyes, deep as the black waters of the infernal river Lethe.

"Her name was Agatha King and this here…" His grandfather had pulled out another picture, of a girl, well, young woman, who looked pretty much the same, but the photograph was in colours and clearly rather new. "Is April Blackwell. They are Doppelgangers. Fascinating, isn't it? April is the youngest off-spring of the Blackwell family, who has been a thorn in the paw of the guild for a while now. Unfortunately, the Blackwells do not seem to be aware of it. Or if so, they do not move accordingly." Jack had continued staring at the photographs, the resemblance of the two women was too uncanny.

"Why do you have their photographs?" Jack had asked, eyeing a stack of papers, handwritten notes, letters and…more photographs. The order had clearly been stalking the girl, for there were many pictures of her; the kind paparazzies made, when spying on celebrities. There were pictures of her with a young man, walking hand in hand, grocery shopping, or with another girl with red hair. There were pictures of her with other men of various ages, but all of them good-looking and well dressed, in front of hotels or bars. Or just her alone; standing in an alleyway, a graveyard or at a bus station.

"Agatha or Miss Blackwell? Well, it seems that they are related and thus, also related to you, Jack."

"Really? If you don't mind me asking, but why is this of any interest to you or important for my task? I doubt you are gathering information on her just because she's my relative."

"You're a smart boy and you're right: she is of interest to the whole family and the Order of Lucifer as well. You may be aware of what kind of person Agatha King was. She murdered dozens of alchemists in cold blood, she was crazy, mad, a lunatic. And as you may know, she was not very fond of your father either and even less so, after he exposed her as a witch. Apparently, her dislike went so far, that she cursed the whole Rosier family. But nature has its ways of balancing things out, providing let's say, loopholes. And it is my hope that April Blackwell is said loophole."

"How can she be a loophole for a curse that doesn't affect her?"

"Because she carries Agatha King's ghost within her. Somewhere inside of her, Agatha King lives on and thus, the curse can be broken by April Blackwell, because she is her Doppelganger. Do me a favour Jack, besides what I am already sending you to the city for, keep an eye on Miss Blackwell and let me know if she shows any signs of powers. And if she does, I expect you to deliver her to me."

Jack had squinted at the pictures, not sure if he liked what he had been told to do. Finding another entrance to hell, after the rumours around the Faust house had proven themselves to be false, was one thing. But spying on a girl, a woman, and then delivering her to the order without her consent, was…wrong.

"Powers? What do you mean by that?" Jack had asked, feeling the mark pulsing under his sleeve.

"You know very well, what I mean, boy. Witch powers. You know, unlike your father, I do not condemn them, on the contrary: witches derive their powers through and from the Dark Lord. They are demon-born, creatures of hell and thus of great value to me."

"And how am I to recognise those kinds of powers?"

"You can smell them," his grandfather had answered, his eyes fixed coldly on him. Jack remembered the cold shiver that had run through his entire body and how black his grandfather's eyes had been in that moment. "You were born with the ability to smell out your own kind, didn't you know that?"

Jack had never been more afraid in his life than in that moment. He had kept his secret so well hidden, the truth of his nature, knowing what kind of man his grandfather was, for his mother had told Jack everything about how the church excommunicated his grandfather's order and how they had renamed themselves in the name of the fallen angel, Lucifer, the Dark Lord, whom they then began to serve instead. Jack had always know what his grandfather was capable of. The horror he could inflict on people. Jack hated his father, but in comparison to the old man, was Alexandru Rosier a meek shadow. Even after their fall from grace, which had hit Jack's father the worst, since he had been a knight of the guild for many years, Jack had always known how to deal with him. Sure, he was a fanatic and still worshipped the so-called true God in secret, but he was never someone Jack considered to be an actual danger.

And now that Jack found himself face to face with the possibility, that hell was a place closer than they had thought and it was a simple alchemical reaction; magic, archaic, as old as time, and not an ancient blood ritual, Jack wasn't sure what would happen. It depended all on April. If she was willing, if she could see beyond the lies, then maybe... Maybe it was too late already, for Jack had seen the figures lingering in the orchard, waiting to take her, for they knew what she was. Jack knew that it was a matter of hours, now that the order had been informed, but maybe, it was enough time still. He straightened himself.

Although his plans had failed, he could still choose another path. If April helped him, he could do what the old prophecy promised: that the demon-born would bring down the Holy Church. And wasn't Jack himself an even worse abomination in the eye of God then any witch could ever be? Whatever bargain his mother a stroke with the demons during that horrible night of his conception, they had been awakened by April's magic and Jack wondered if it had been the demon parts within him all along, that have lusted after her. Knowing that if he led her into temptation and she would sin by giving in, that all of him could finally break free and unleash a hailstorm of destruction. And as Jack rose to his feet, he toyed with the idea that maybe his plans had not failed, but simply...changed. That it was only now that his demonic powers had stirred, after those parts of himself had finally tasted what they had longed for – their equal, born from the same darkness – that he could now actually fulfil his nature's true desires and make them pay for what they had done. And maybe, along the way, April would find it in herself to forgive him, for what he had done, when he had sold her soul with no more than three words.

And forgive us our trespasses, as we forgive those who trespass against us.

☽ ☆ ☾

When April woke up, the clock on her bedside table showed three o'clock in the morning. She sat up with slight difficulty, still drowsy. The dormitory was completely dark, all the other girls were soundly asleep. April realised that she was still fully dressed. An unpleasant taste in her mouth drove April into the washroom. She fumbled for the light switch and at the same moment as the neon tube began to spit its light, April closed her eyes. Through the closed eyelids, she could see the light flicker, then switch on completely. April felt her way to one of the washbasins and ran cold water. First, she rinsed her mouth, then she washed her face. The icy wetness startled April out of her doze and she opened her eyes. Her gaze fell on her hands, fingernails full of dirt, and with a furrowed brow, April began to scrub her hands. The water from her face ran down her neck and April shuddered. Involuntarily she raised her eyes, and after many years, she looked into the mirror. Her eyes stared back darkly, wide open with dark circles, hungry, knowing. April instinctively closed them again. She knew why she never looked at herself, because what she saw, said more than April would have liked.

And then she heard the whispering again.

April knew that the spirits of the witches were here in the washroom with her, even before they made the lamp flicker. The cold crept up April's legs and goose bumps spread all over her body.

"What do you want?" she whispered barely audibly.

"We've come to warn you."

"Warn me of what?"

"Someone's coming to catch you."

"Someone evil."

April's heart skipped a beat.

"Who are they?"

"Hunters. They wear the skulls of animals…"

"…to conceal their faces."

"To hunt more easily."

"For witches do not fear them."

"Many witches like them."

"But they feed on them. They capture the witches…"

"What are they doing here?" April asked and giving the answer herself. "Do they know about me? About us?"

"Yes."

"They know there are witches here..."

A cold shiver ran down her spine.

"How do those hunters know about us?"

The wispy voices laughed. Evil. Unpleasant. April felt an icy breeze on her arms. She clutched the sink tighter, keeping her eyes vehemently closed.

"Someone told them..."

"Someone told on you..."

"Who?"

Another laugh.

"Stupid, little girl. Stupid, blind girl..."

Hot anger flared up in April. She wheeled round, striking blindly into the void, and a hiss sounded. Then it was completely silent again and the cold disappeared. With her back to the mirror, April carefully opened her eyes. Slowly, peering through the slits – but she was alone again. The neon light burned on her retina and April switched the light off. She remained at the door for a few moments, looking into the silent dormitory. The steady breathing of the other girls, one murmuring in her sleep, someone turning over.

So peaceful. So blissful. So... innocent.

Who had betrayed her?

"Jack!" April sat down next to him on the bench and stuffed her bag under the desk. Having gone back to sleep after the scene in the washroom with the dead girls' ghosts, April had slept through breakfast and gone straight to the classroom where they had half-class lessons this morning. Ginger and Will were a few rooms away, so Jack was the first one April could warn.

"April! How are you? We were so worried! Ginger said you were still asleep and didn't want to wake you up and..."

"It doesn't matter," April interrupted him in a lowered voice and looked at him meaningfully. Jack raised his eyebrows questioningly. The door opened and Madame Tarkovsky entered the room. April quickly leant over to Jack. "We have to be damn careful," she whispered. Just as she took a breath to continue, Madame Tarkovsky tapped her cane on the table and the last people in the room fell silent.

"Later," April murmured quietly, and Jack nodded.

"Well, good morning everyone, I hope you've all prepared for today's lesson! As announced before the winter holidays and agreed with Mr Zagajewski, today marks the start of our short lecture series. You've been divided into groups to review the material you've learnt so far."

Jack and April exchanged a quick glance with each other. They were in a group of four with Ivaylo and Ren. Fortunately, it wasn't their turn to present for another two weeks, because Jack and April were very behind with their part of the work. But there had simply been enough other things that had somehow always been more important. Jack raised his eyebrows and April nodded. Yes, they would definitely sit down together after classes today and catch up, which meant that their research lesson with Ginger and Will would be cancelled.

"Then I'll ask group one to come to the front, that would be Sergei Ivanov and Juniper Robinson in this half-class with their lecture on the first stage *Calcinatio*."

April turned her head to Sergei and followed him with her gaze as he stepped in front of the class and handed Juniper a few cards with key words. Then he returned April's gaze and smiled slightly. April did the same. Jack frowned. Ginger and Will were now giving more or less the same lecture at the same time in their half-class and there was nothing Jack would have liked better at that moment than to see Will and Ginger standing there at the front instead of Sergei. Poor boy, he had no idea how Jack had made April moan last night, even though it was Sergei who called her his girlfriend... After that gruesome episode in the orchard, Jack hadn't had the chance to talk to April. He had planned on telling her everything this morning, therefore he didn't care too much about clearing up things about their relationship and Sergei, since he had no idea, how April would react, when he told her, well...*everything*.

"If I could have your attention," Sergei said in a self-assured voice and nodded to his lab partner, who then began her lecture.

At break time, April pulled Jack out of the classroom and into a corner a little further away from the others. As the school didn't have a bell, the breaks took place at the teacher's discretion and so only Jack and April's half-class lounged around in the cross corridor while all the other half-classes were still sitting in their respective lessons. She could hear Sergei and Juniper talking to Madame Tarkovsky about their presentation, as their teacher gave them their feedback.

"So, what's going on?" Jack asked, trying to read April's face. Ever since she had sat down next to him, her expression had been tense, and even more withdrawn than usual. Her eyes flitted to the other students and then back to Jack.

"Listen to me carefully: we're in danger!"

"What? How...?"

"Let me finish!"

"Sorry."

April exhaled shakily. She was uneasy.

"This morning, around three o'clock when I woke up, I went to the washroom and the spirits of the witches where there and they spoke to me. Don't worry," she added quickly when she saw Jack's face, "nothing happened to me, I'm fine. They just wanted to talk to me."

"And what did they say?" Jack knitted his brows, worry gnawing at him.

"They said there were witch hunters in the forest." April's voice was barely more than a whisper now and Jack had to lean closer to hear her.

"Apparently someone here at the school got suspicious and probably informed the council. And they've sent some people and they are apparently looking for us."

Jack didn't look so convinced. "And you're quite sure about that?"

"If I say so myself!"

"I only ask because it was the spirits of those witches who told you. Yesterday in the orchard, there..." Jack broke off and let his gaze wander over April's face.

"What?"

Jack shrugged his shoulders. "I'm just saying that the witches didn't seem very *friendly* yesterday."

"They're dead. And were betrayed. I'd be anything *but* friendly myself!"

"Possibly. Still... Even if we could trust them, what if it's not us, but the hunters are looking for someone else?"

"And if not? What if someone has actually found out about us? I don't even want to think about it!" Jack sighed deeply.

"All I'm saying is, that we can't know for sure."

"No, but what is certain is that we have to be extremely careful!"

"Guess we'll have to put our research on hold for a while."

April nodded. Her gaze slid to the other end of the corridor, where Juniper was laughing out loud and Ondine was grimacing. How nice it would be to be able to live as easily and carefree as the others.

"About yesterday..." Jack began cautiously, leaning against the stone wall. His gaze had been fixed on April the whole time, her lips pressed together and her eyes looking wearily out into the world. Now they were focused on him again.

"What do you remember?"

April blushed instantly and broke their gaze. Jack coughed, concealing his chuckle. Oh, she looked glorious with that blush on her cheeks.

"I didn't mean the... I meant...after we... You know..." He didn't dare to look at her, knowing if he would, he would slam her against the wall and kiss her into oblivion. He would lift her skirt and touch her where he longed to feel just how wet he could make her. He wanted to make her moan, mark her neck with his teeth and show Sergei and all the other guys that she belonged to him. That she was his.

You were made to be mine.

April didn't dare to look at him either. But when she finally mustered to talk, she sighed lightly and leaned against the wall next to Jack.

"Less than I'd like," April then said, her gaze lost between the arches of the cloister. "I remember this place we were suddenly in, or that only I was in and only I saw, I don't know. There was…a chasm and fire all around. A church that was on fire and…there was blood everywhere." April closed her eyes and felt like she was drowning in the sea of red again. She shook herself slightly.

"I saw the same thing," Jack said quietly, and April looked at him in surprise.

"You did?"

"Yes."

"And what do you think we saw?"

Jack swayed his head. "I'm not sure," he said, running his hand over his mouth. "I've been thinking about it all night and the only explanation or theory I have is this." Jack turned so that he was now only touching the wall with his shoulder and could look at April fully. He ignored the throbbing in his pants but couldn't help his eyes looking at her lips. He just had to look at her and became hard within an instant.

"What if, when I covered your eyes and…kissed you, you somehow channelled your power through me, thus your powers were magnified, since male witches are like catalysators, and we opened a gate or passageway to some sort of dimension," Jack said and crossed his arms. He wanted to fuck her so badly, but this was more important. Unfortunately. He guessed he had run out of luck a long time ago.

Jack cleared his throat and continued talking.

"What if the combination of my magic and yours have opened up some kind of otherworld, an elsewhere made of… fire and blood?" He looked at April uncertainly and with a wry grin. Even to his ears, his theory sounded abstruse.

"A hell," April said slowly.

"Hell is a place, and I have a much stronger feeling that what we saw wasn't really a place, but a kind of borderland, a periphery, an…in-between, so to say. For hell must be more tangible, don't you think?" April tilted her head in thought, biting her lower lip, then looked back at Jack. She let her eyes wander over his beautiful face, his cheekbones, his lips, taking in the slight arch, his pale skin and the dark circles around his eyes – he truly must have been awake all night long.

"If there is a hell, there must also be a heaven, right?" April's eyes lingered on Jack's face – thoughtful, searching, enigmatic, almost dreamy – and then on his lips. Jack averted his gaze, not sure if he was willing to drown in those eyes of hers again. Not when he was so fucking hard for her. He needed to keep his wits together. This conversation was not over, and the worst was yet to come.

"I don't believe in heaven," he said raspy.

"Then how do you know for certain that there is a hell?" April replied.

"Because others have been there before us."

"And what if they were just dreaming it?"

"Then I wish this life was just a dream too and I could simply wake up and…" He broke off.

"And?"

"Doesn't matter." Jack sighed deeply, his eyes on the ground. "In any case, there is no heaven and no God, because if there were, and if he *truly* were omnipotent and good, he would be able to put an end to all suffering." Jack's hands trembled at the thought of the figures among the trees, the familiar cloaks and animal skulls on their heads. Jack looked at April, at her beautiful, beautiful face, the puzzled expression in her eyes, and he laughed dryly. His beautiful angel of death.

"God or devil, this life has made me what I am, and I wish… I wish I could end it. Just…"

"Jack, what's wrong?" April stepped towards him, her voice insistent, confused, not knowing where this outburst was coming from. But Jack backed away from her.

"You don't want to get too close to me, April. For all we know, it's my fault you're suffering. That you're having these visions and yesterday almost… I thought they were going to take you with them." Jack only whispered the last words. "When we were standing among the trees, I was so scared for you, April."

Jack couldn't resist and lifted his hand. He stroked April's cheek with his fingertips, not caring if anyone could see them. Especially not Sergei. And for a brief, terrible moment, he wanted to call him over and tell him what it was like to kiss April. Ask him if she also moaned loudly into his mouth and pressed her breasts against his chest and if she shuddered beneath his touch as well and... *No.*

Jack took a deep breath. He needed to pull himself together. He needed to tell April the truth.

"When I carried you to your room," Jack continued, his finger still grazing April's soft skin, "Ginger and Will were so upset and scared, and I realised there was no going back. Somehow, I always thought there must be a loophole somewhere. A solution I hadn't thought of before, an ace up my sleeve... But the truth is, that we chose our fate a long time ago. Maybe even before this life." Jack lowered his hand again. He turned his head towards the garden in the centre of the cloister and at the same moment it began to snow.

As if through a fog, Jack heard the excited and joyful shouts of the others in their class as they pointed out the snow to each other and began to rave about their last Christmas. In his memories, Christmas was full of April's face, dancing under falling petals, and the light of a thousand candles reflecting the glittering of her dress as he spun her through the ballroom.

"Remember how I said I wouldn't let what you sensed in me do you any harm?" asked Jack, and April nodded slowly. Her mind was still reeling, and she could still feel Jack's touch burning on her skin. And just looking at him made it so hard to concentrate on what he was saying, when all she wanted to do was to push him into the wall and suck at those beautiful lips.

"I don't think I can keep my promise," Jack whispered. "I think, April, I'm a terrible person. But maybe, if you listen to me, letting me explain then... If you knew about...everything, then maybe you...could forgive me. I want you to know the truth."

"Jack..." April said, grabbing his hand. "You're scaring me, what the hell are you talking about?"

"There's no going back, that's for sure and certain," he muttered, more to himself, staring at April's hand holding his. He slowly lifted his eyes again and looked into those hauntingly beautiful eyes; those seas of onyx in which he wanted to drown himself. "But if I have to spend the rest of my life apologising, making up for what I've done wrong, and you still look at me like *that*," Jack continued unperturbed, brushing a strand of April's hair behind her ear and kissed the back of her hand, which was still holding his. "Then I shall believe in a heaven. But until then…"

April would never learn what Jack would do, because at the same moment five figures appeared at the end of the corridor. They all wore the long cloaks of the guild, their hoods up, long swords at their sides and silver mask with golden ornaments on their faces.

"Guild knights," April breathed, completely frozen, and Jack turned round too. April's hand almost crushed Jack's, and the two of them looked motionless at the knights walking straight towards them through the corridor. The world seemed to slow down.

"April Blackwell?" A harsh voice came from under one of the hoods and against all her instincts, April stepped forward, letting go of Jack's hand.

She wouldn't let on. She wouldn't be afraid.

I am not afraid. I am not afraid. I am not afraid. I am not afraid of you.

"That's me," she said, her voice more confident than April felt. Her heart pounded in her ears and she forced herself to breathe. The knight on the far left held up a roll of paper which he had pulled out from the sleeve of his cloak, while another reached for April's wrists and clasped heavy iron chains around them.

"April Blackwell, by order of the Guild and the Holy Church of Rome, you are arrested on charges of sorcery and witchcraft!"

Epilogue

Demon-born

"The wind of swans was blowing,
The sky deep blue in blood."
– Anna Akhmatova, from The Complete Poems of Anna Akhmatova;
Anno Domini MCMXXI

It was warm in the greenhouse. Far too warm. But Jack was frozen to the bone. Outside it had been dark for a long time and in the refectory the young alchemists of the monastery school were sitting at supper, their voices hushed and silent; they had stared at Jack like a leper as he came down the stairs. But he hadn't thought for a second about going to dinner. Minutes before, he had thrown up in the washroom. The bad feeling still lingered. Here, among the fallen flowers of the plants above him, the floor of the greenhouse pleasantly cool, he could breathe again. Slowly, counting to five, in, then out again.

He could still see Will's face, the shock and horror, eyes glued on his sister. And poor Ginger... And it was all Jack's fault. Because he had waited too long. Because he didn't stick to the plan. Because he had changed his mind. Because he fell in love with the woman he was meant to seduce only. The woman whose true nature he wanted to discover and once he finally did, he didn't do what the order had expected.

No, he had given into the temptation, and instead of handing her over, so that she would be protected from the guild, he had done the selfish thing – and had kept her to himself. That beautiful woman, delicate like a petal, born to die.

The flowers filled the greenhouse with their heavy and moist scent. Lilies and roses. Hyacinths and honeysuckle. Jack reached for a blossom, white and brown, crushed. Just as he felt. He turned his head. All around him-rotting leaves and flowers, the saplings – far above his head. Out of reach.

Renewed waves of nausea shook his body. Jack pressed his hand over his mouth – and kept breathing.

He could hang himself. In the church. It would send a message to the guild. Mock the church. Put a spoke in his grandfather's wheel. Yes, to fly once, under the wings of the painted angels, and crush – his neck and spine breaking. He would deserve it.

Demons were not allowed to love angels and Jack had pushed his angel into the abyss, had torn off her wings. He had dragged April into the darkness, and had made her his equal, for demons had once been angels too.

Because you were made to be mine.

Jack saw the blood before him, as it flowed through the nave of the church, the images of his nightmares bleeding into reality, washing the floor of the greenhouse red. Or had they been April's dreams all along, that he had seen before his mind's eye? In his hand he crushed the blossom of a fire lily.

All around him was rot. And he – the cause of the decay.

ALCHEMY

I know that you watched me sleep,
Yesterday, when I closed my eyes,
When I breathed, calm and deep
As my chest gently rose, gently fell,
Your own breathing changed,
That's how I could tell.

I know that you watched me sleep,
Yesterday, when being drunk on liquid night,
When I was thinking about the words
You had whispered into my ears,
I don't want to be loved or liked,
I just want to be yours.

I know that you watched me sleep,
Yesterday, when hope lit up your eyes,
When I recalled your trembling hands
As they flood us both with alchemy
But now I sleep and now you know,
As you watch and sit, and on your knee,
A volume of Edgar Allan Poe.

ACKNOWLEDGEMENTS

Since I am rewriting this for the thousandth times – I shall keep it simple:

To my most wonderful mother, for all the love and support you've given me all my life. Thank you for always believing in me and encouraging me to pursuit my creative dreams. I love you more than I could ever put into words.

To my beloved sisters, the most amazing partners in crime, smart-asses and witches. I could not imagine who I would be without you and am proud to be sharing our creatives adventures with one another – wherever our paths will lead us from here.

To my darling friends, for always being by my side while I was becoming who I am, not shying away from my darkness, weirdness and other curiosities. I hold our endless conversations, letters and time spent together with so much love in my heart. It is through you, that I found that my stories and written words have meaning and impact.

I guess I also need to thank all the artists, authors and creatives that have inspired and influenced my work all throughout my life. Who would I be without their glorious stories? Their paintings, photographs, films, dance productions, musicals and compositions?

Last but not least, I want to thank myself. I know, this journey hasn't been easy and has begun many, many years ago when writing was the only thing that helped me to deal with reality, but back then I would have never imagined that one day I would be writing these words – but here we are.

I am proud of myself. For all my work, dedication, willpower, passion and hope.

I am proud of myself for having pulled through with it despite all the shit I have dealt with and still am.

Because in the end, I still believe: *la vie est belle.*

KEEP IN TOUCH

Instagram:
@jael_jarmila
@_princessmacabre

☽ ☆ ☾

Alchemical Hearts – Hollow is Thy Name Copyright © 2024
by Jael Jarmila Livas

All rights reserved. All contents of this book, except the quotes at the beginning of each chapter and book, are protected by copyright. Unless expressly stated otherwise, copyright is held by Jael Jarmila Livas.

Publisher: BoD • Books on Demand GmbH, In de Tarpen 42,
22848 Norderstedt
Print: Libri Plureos GmbH, Friedensallee 273, 22763 Hamburg
ISBN: 978-3-7597-9344-7